BEAUTY AND THE BROODING BILLIONAIRE

DONNA ALWARD

FOR THE TWINS' SAKE

MELISSA SENATE

MILLS & BOON

First Published in Great Britain 2020
by Mills & Boon, an imprint of HarperCollinsPublishers,
1 London Bridge Street, London, SE1 9GF

Beauty and the Brooding Billionaire © 2020 Donna Alward
For the Twins' Sake © 2020 Melissa Senate

ISBN: 978-0-263-27867-5

0220

MIX
Paper from
responsible sources
FSC™ C007454

This book is produced from independently certified FSC™ paper to ensure responsible forest management.

For more information visit: www.harpercollins.co.uk/green

Printed and bound in Spain
by CPI, Barcelona

BEAUTY AND THE BROODING BILLIONAIRE

DONNA ALWARD

CHAPTER ONE

JESS TOOK ONE look at the lighthouse and knew that the search had been worth it. After weeks of wandering, and months before that of her pencils hovering over her sketch pad, the battered white-and-red lighthouse on Nova Scotia's east coast stood firm against the brisk, briny wind.

In some regards she wondered if the lonely structure *was* her. Tall, a bit battered from the winds of life, but still standing.

Her agent was after her to do another show. "Your last one was such a success," Jack had insisted. "An original Jessica Blundon commands top dollar right now."

"You can't rush the muse," she'd replied, deliberately keeping her voice light. "I don't paint to order."

She hadn't been painting at all. Not since Ana's death. Her mentor. Her best friend. The older sister she'd never had. Losing Ana had devastated her and killed her creativity. Her life had suddenly become colorless and empty. No significant other. No children. No best friend.

She'd isolated herself far too much. So after a good year of grieving and moping, she'd decided to stop hiding away and go in search of what her life was going to look like. The best place to start, she figured, was finding her passion to paint again.

And while she didn't "paint to order," she did do this as

her career. Like most creatives, it was impossible to separate what she did from who she was.

The biggest shock had been that when she was finally ready to put brush to canvas, she couldn't. The block had been real and infuriating, until about six months ago, when she'd finally started sketching.

And traveling. She'd left behind the waters of the Great Lakes—Chicago—and gone west, to Seattle first, then San Francisco and down the coast to San Diego. The Pacific had been beautiful, but it wasn't what she was looking for. She was searching for that feeling, right in her solar plexus, that told her when something was just *right*. The Gulf of Mexico hadn't been it, either, though she'd adored her time in New Orleans and along the panhandle. She'd come closer to finding "it" the farther north she'd gone; past the barrier islands in the Carolinas, to the beaches of New Jersey and then the rugged coastline of Maine. On a whim she'd jumped on the CAT ferry in Bar Harbor and headed to Canada. She'd sketched lonely beaches, colorful coastal houses, gray rocks made black by the ocean waves. Trees budding in the mild spring weather. All lovely. But nothing that had felt inspiring. Nothing that created the burn to create.

Her sketchbook was full of drawings, but the lighthouse before her? It was that punch-to-the-gut feeling, and she relished the trickle of excitement running through her veins. "This is it, Ana," she murmured. "It's time."

The brisk wind off the ocean tossed her hair around her face and bit through the light cotton shirt she wore. May was definitely not Nova Scotia's warmest month, even though the sun shone brightly and warmed a spot between her shoulder blades. She needed to get a different vantage point. The angle here was too sharp. But the lighthouse stood on a bluff jutting out toward the sea, and the only path to it seemed to be from the property before her. And the gate that baldly pronounced Private Property—Do Not Enter.

"Private property," she grumbled, peering over the metal barrier. She couldn't see the house from here, and the drive led to the left while the lighthouse was off to the right and then south. Lips set, she swung her bag over her shoulder and put her foot on the bottom railing of the gate.

"Not electric." She grinned and then nimbly hoisted herself over the metal railings and landed on the other side.

It didn't take long for her to get a glimpse of the house. It was an imposing but beautiful structure, with gray siding and stonework and what would be marvelous gardens in another month or so. Fledgling hostas, their leaves still tightly furled, and a variety of tulips and hyacinths kept the beds from looking sad and naked. Jess expected that there were other perennials beneath the surface waiting for the summer warmth to wake them. The house had a fantastic panoramic view of the Atlantic coastline, and a sloped lawn led to what appeared to be low cliffs. She wondered if there was a beach below. And she'd like to look, but first she wanted to skirt the property and get to the isolated lighthouse, so she could take some pictures and perhaps make a sketch or two.

The ground was hard and rocky beneath her feet as she set off to the lonely tower. She'd made a friend at the nearby resort, and Tori had told her about the hidden gem, suggesting its semi-neglected state might add to its allure. She hadn't been wrong. The weather-beaten clapboards on the outside were in sad need of fresh paint, and as Jess got closer, she realized that the gray wood was worn surprisingly smooth from wind and salt. There was rust on the hinges of the door, and she wondered if the thing would even open or what she might find inside if it did. Dirt? Mice? Other creatures? She looked way up to the top, where the beacon lay, silent and still. Did it still work?

The lighthouse was full of character and secret stories. Her favorite kind of subject.

After her cursory examination, she pulled out her camera and started taking shots. Different angles, distances, close-ups, and with the Atlantic in the background. The ocean was restless today, and she loved the whitecaps that showed in her viewfinder, and the odd spray from waves that crashed on the rocks below.

After she took the photos, she thought she might like to get a few of the house, too. It was more modern and certainly very grand, but still with that lonely brave-the-elements esthetic that she loved. She swung around toward the property and came face-to-face with a pair of angry eyes. The man they belonged to gave her a real start.

"You're trespassing," he said, his voice sharp and condemning.

He looked like a hermit. It was hard to tell his age, because his hair was shaggy and his beard was in dire need of trimming, but she guessed maybe forty, or a little older. The brown shirt was wrinkled and slightly too big for his lean frame, and he wore faded jeans and worn boots. All in all, he was a little bit intimidating. Not just his looks, but the expression on his face. He was angry, and he wasn't bothering to hide it.

Somehow, though, she found him rather compelling. Rugged and mysterious, and beneath the scruff his looks were quite appealing. She rather thought she'd like to sketch him. And while he was intimidating, he didn't seem…dangerous. Just grouchy.

"I was only on the property for a few minutes. I stayed right along the edge until I got to the lighthouse."

"The lighthouse *is* on my property. I'm assuming you saw the sign, and chose to ignore it."

She didn't have an answer to that, because it was true. Except she hadn't realized that the lighthouse was on his private property. Weren't they usually parkland or municipal or something? How many people owned their very own lighthouse?

She put on her most contrite face. Despite his abrasive manner, it appeared she was in the wrong here, not him. If she wanted to have access to this perfect aspect, she needed to appeal to his...friendly side? If he had one.

"I'm really sorry. I truly didn't realize the lighthouse was part of your property. I'm an artist, you see. I'd heard about it from someone at the Sandpiper Resort, and they assured me it was worth checking out. I wouldn't have trespassed if I had realized I wasn't just, well, cutting across your lot."

He crossed his arms.

Now she was getting annoyed. Had she done anything so very awful that meant he had to be so...disagreeable?

She tried again. "I'm Jessica Blundon." She held out her hand and smiled.

He didn't shake it. Instead, his dark eyes assessed her from top to bottom, making her feel...lacking. One of his eyebrows lifted slightly, a question mark. She held his gaze, refusing to cower. If his goal was to intimidate her, he was failing. Despite his horrible manners, she did not feel the least bit threatened. This dog's bark was worse than his bite, she figured. There was something in his gaze that she responded to. He wanted to be left alone. It wasn't long ago she'd felt the same, so she merely lowered her hand and wondered what was hidden behind the beard and longish hair and grumpy exterior.

"Well, Miss Blundon, you're on private property. I'll

ask you to delete those photos off your camera and go back to where you came from."

Her mouth dropped open. He was actually going to get her to delete her pictures? She closed her mouth and frowned. "Is that really necessary? I mean, it's not like the lighthouse is some giant secret."

"It's my lighthouse, on my property, and I don't want you to have pictures of it." He reached into his pocket and took out a cell phone. "You can delete them or I can make a phone call and have the cops out here."

Now he was being utterly unreasonable, and any curiosity or sympathy she'd felt fled. "I could walk away and take my pictures with me. Unless you're planning to personally restrain me."

She lifted her chin, met his gaze. Something flared there, and nerves skittered along her spine. Not of fear. But of awareness. Mr. Hermit was enigmatic, and no matter how much he tried to hide behind his ragged appearance, he was actually quite attractive. There was something familiar about him, too, that she couldn't quite place.

His gaze dropped to her lips, then back up again to her eyes, and for the first time, his mouth curved in a slight smile. "Good luck," he replied. "I know your name and I know you're at the Sandpiper. Not too hard to tell the RCMP where to look."

He'd call the Mounties. He'd really do it, over a few stupid pictures. She lifted her camera and glared at him. "Fine. I'll delete the damned pictures." Her heart broke a little bit just saying it. She needed them. The first true inspiration she'd had in two years...darn it. She held his gaze and got the sense he wasn't bluffing.

"You could just give me the memory card."

"I don't think so. It wasn't blank when I got here. I'll

delete the ones I took just now but that's all. And you're being a jerk."

He shrugged. "I've been called worse."

Jessica switched to view mode and with growing frustration started deleting all the beautiful pictures she'd already taken, all the while calling him worse in her mind. He was being completely unreasonable. She toyed with the idea of keeping one or two, trying to hide them from him, but then figured why bother. When she looked up, he held out his hand.

"Oh, for Pete's sake," she muttered, taking the strap off her neck and putting the camera in his hands.

He scrolled through, appeared to be satisfied, and handed it back.

"Thank you. You can leave now."

Her cheeks flared at being so readily dismissed. She shoved the camera into her tote, fuming. He hadn't even offered his name when she'd introduced herself.

She met his gaze. "For the record, you didn't have to be so rude."

Then she swept by him. She was only a few feet away when she thought she heard him say, "Yes, I did." But when she looked over her shoulder, he was standing with his back to her, looking out to sea.

She hurried on, but when she got to a curve in the property, she turned back. He was still standing in the same spot, looking angry and lonely and lost.

She reached for her camera and took one hurried shot, then scurried back to the gate.

Bran sensed when she was completely gone, and let out a low breath.

Solitude. All he wanted was solitude. For people to leave him alone. The months of pretending in New York had taken their toll. He'd lost himself in his grief, only pulled out occasionally by his best friends, Cole and Jeremy. There'd even been times when he'd smiled and laughed. But then he'd gone home to the reminders of the life he'd once had, the one he'd been on the cusp of having, and he'd fallen apart. Every. Single. Time.

When he'd started to self-medicate with alcohol, he'd known he had to make a change. At first it had been just beer, and in the words of his grandmother, "it's not alcoholism if it's beer." He'd used that for a long time to justify his overindulgence. But when he'd graduated to Scotch, and then whatever alcohol was available, he'd known he was in trouble. He needed to sell the brownstone and get away from the constant reminders. Get his act together.

Jennie would be so angry to know that he'd resorted to alcohol to cope. And so he'd thrown out all the booze, because Jennie's memory deserved better.

The house in Nova Scotia was damned near perfect. Sometimes Jeremy and his new wife were close by, providing him with the odd company to keep him from transitioning from eccentric to downright crazy. No one knew him here, or if they did recognize his name, they didn't make a big time about it. He had groceries delivered to the house. Couriers delivered anything he could buy online...there wasn't much shopping nearby anyway. He spent hours staring out at the sea, trying to make sense of everything. Wondering how to stop caring.

Wondering if he'd ever be able to write again.

The one downside was the stupid lighthouse. In the beginning, it had been an incentive to buy. It was interesting and unusual, and he'd liked the idea of owning it. What he hadn't counted on was the foot traffic, skirting his prop-

erty and solitude with cameras and picnic blankets and…
He shuddered. At least once a week he found a condom on
the ground. It wasn't so much the idea of it being the site
for romantic trysts. He could appreciate a romantic atmosphere. But heck, would it be too much to ask for people
to pick up after themselves?

Today he'd seen the reddish-blond head, and he'd had
enough. The moment she'd pulled out her camera and
started taking photos, he was ready to put on his boots.
But when she turned to take a picture of the house? That
was the clincher. He valued his privacy far too much. So
far reporters hadn't found him, as they had in New York.
But it was only a matter of time. She didn't seem like a
journalist or a paparazzo, but he couldn't be sure.

He watched a gull buffeted by the wind and sighed. She
was right; he'd been a jerk about it. And part of that was
because she'd been trespassing, and the other part was because he'd immediately realized how pretty she was. Early
thirties, he'd guess, with blue eyes that had golden-green
stripes through the irises, making them a most unusual
color that deepened when she got angry, as she'd been
with him when he'd demanded she delete her pictures. A
dusting of freckles dotted her nose, pale, but enough that
it made her look younger than she was. But there were
shadows there, too. And the fact that he'd been curious at
all set him on edge.

He started back to the house, turning over the encounter in his mind. Jessica Blundon, she'd said. The name
sounded vaguely familiar, but he wasn't sure why. Maybe
she was a reporter.

Once inside, he went to his "den," a round-shaped room
on the bottom floor of the house with windows all the way
around. There was a fireplace there for when it was cold

or damp, as it had often been during the end of the winter when he'd moved in. A huge bookcase was near the door, the shelves jammed with a mixture of keepers, books on writing and stories he had yet to read. The furniture was heavy and well-cushioned, perfect for curling up with a book. He picked up his laptop and hit the power button, then started an internet search.

It wasn't difficult to find her. The first hit was her website, and the second was for a gallery in Chicago. Her site had her picture on a press page, but also a catalog of her paintings. He wiped a hand over his face. She was good. Really good. The gallery page brought up a press release from a showing she'd done…nearly two years ago. He flipped back to her site. It didn't appear to have been updated recently.

Had she not been painting all this time? Or had she been secluded away, working on something new?

Something sharp slid through him, and he recognized it as envy. He wasn't sure he'd ever feel whole enough to write again, and his agent had got him an indefinite extension of his contract, with his publisher saying he could turn in a manuscript when he wanted. Hell, at this point his publisher had more faith in him than he did in himself. The only thing keeping him from paying back the advance and killing the deal was that he was in his thirties. What else was he going to do with his life? At least with the open contract, there was something left ahead for him. More than just picking away at his trust fund, and existing.

And here *she* was, with her messy hair and bright eyes and pink cheeks, living life and standing up to the ogre.

Because that was surely what he'd become, and he hated himself for it.

But he was certain he didn't deserve any better.

He lowered the cover of the laptop and set it aside, then picked up his coffee and took a cold sip.

He'd stopped drinking. But nothing else had changed. And that scared him to death.

Jessica looked around the gardens of Jeremy and Tori's house and let out a happy sigh. The property didn't have the wild restlessness of the one with the lighthouse, but the scent of the ocean was strong and the burgeoning perennials added bursts of color. Tori had invited her to dinner, and now they sat outside, listening to the ocean and having tea. Tori held her three-week-old baby in her arms, the tiny bundle making small noises as she slept. Jessica held back the spurt of jealousy. She'd had a chance at a husband and family once, and had blown it. She'd been all of twenty-four and had wanted to travel and paint and not settle down yet.

He hadn't waited. Broken heart number one.

Now she was in her thirties with no relationship on the radar. She'd started to accept that a partner and family was not in the cards for her. It seemed that everyone important in her life always picked up and left in one way or another, and after a while a heart got tired of taking all the risks and never reaping the rewards.

It didn't stop her from getting wistful and broody around Tori's newborn, though. And when Tori asked if she'd hold the baby while she popped inside for a light blanket, Jessica had no choice but to say yes.

Little Rose was a porcelain doll, with pale skin and thick lashes and a dusting of soft, brown hair. Her little lips sucked in and out as she slept, and she smelled like baby lotion. Jess cradled her close, looking down at her face and marveling at the feel of the warm weight in the crook of her arm. She did like babies. A lot.

When Tori came back, Jess held out her hand for the blanket, unwilling to give the baby up just yet. "She's comfortable here and it'll give you a break."

"You mean I'll get to drink my tea while it's hot?"

Jess chuckled. "Exactly." She tucked the crocheted blanket around the baby and leaned back in the chair. "Thank you again for asking me to dinner. The food at the inn is lovely, but a home-cooked meal was very welcome."

"It wasn't anything fancy."

They'd had salad, grilled chicken and some sort of barley and vegetable side dish that had been delicious. Jeremy was now inside, catching up on some work while they enjoyed the spring evening.

"It was delicious. Besides, I was hungry. Someone made me angry today, and I went for a run on the beach after to burn off some steam."

Tori leaned forward. "Angry? Who? Not one of the staff, I hope."

Tori had resigned her position at the Sandpiper Resort, but she was still close with the staff and popped in on occasion to help with events or answer any questions the new assistant manager had. That was how Tori and Jess had met, and they'd ended up chatting and then sharing lunch on the resort patio.

"No, not staff. You know the lighthouse you told me about? I went to see it. Get some pictures…it's gorgeous, just like you said. I got that tingly feeling I haven't had in a really long time. And then the owner showed up. Man, he was a jerk."

She expected Tori to express her own form of outrage, but instead her eyes danced. "So you met Bran."

"You know him? Like, personally?"

"He's Jeremy's friend."

Jess lifted an eyebrow. "You might have warned me.

What an ogre. Hard to imagine him being friendly to anyone."

Yet even as she said it she recalled the flash of vulnerability in his eyes. And while his hair was in major need of a haircut, it had been thick and wavy, a rich brown tossed by the sea breeze. Roguish.

"Bran's been through a lot. He just moved here in February, too. The house is lovely, isn't it?"

"I didn't get to see much of anything. I took some pictures of the lighthouse, and then he stomped out and growled at me and made me delete all the photos I'd taken."

Tori frowned. "He's usually not quite that grumpy."

"He was downright rude." She sighed. "That lighthouse was it. I got the rush I get when I'm particularly inspired. If I could have kept one photo, I could have at least started a sketch."

Except she did have one photo. The one she'd taken of "Bran," now that she knew his name. Facing the ocean. She'd looked at it after her run, and had felt his loneliness.

Something else jiggled in her memory. "You said his name was Bran?"

"Short for Branson." Tori leaned forward. "Do you want me to take her now?" She held out her hands for the baby.

"She's asleep and fine here as long as you're okay with it."

"Are you kidding? When she's sleeping I get to relax." She sat back in her chair. "I just don't want to take advantage."

Jessica turned the name over and over in her mind. Branson. The dark hair, the eyes...

"Branson Black," she said, her voice a bit breathy. "That's him, isn't it? The author?"

Tori frowned. "He keeps a very low profile here. No one in town really knows who he is."

"Of course. It'd be like having Stephen King as your neighbor."

Tori laughed. "Not quite. He's not that famous."

Jess tucked the blanket closer around the baby. "He's pretty famous. And he hasn't published anything since—"

She halted. She remembered the story now. Since his wife and infant son had died in a car crash.

It all came together now. His isolation. Desolation. Growling to keep people away. He was buried in grief, a feeling she could relate to oh, so well. A pit opened in her stomach, a reminder of the dark days she'd had after Ana's death. And a well of sympathy, too. How devastated he must be.

She met Tori's gaze and sighed. "It was in the news."

Tori nodded. "I don't want to betray a confidence, you understand. But yes, he's been struggling with his grief."

"And values his privacy. I understand now." And her frustration melted away, replaced by sympathy.

"Do you?" Tori's eyes were sharp. "Because he's one of the best men I know. He's one of the reasons Jeremy and I are together."

Jess stared into the flickering fire. "A few years ago I lost my mentor and…well, the best friend a person could have. I'm just now starting to paint again. So yes, I get it. Grief can destroy the deepest and best parts of us if we're not careful."

Silence fell over the patio for a few minutes. Then Tori spoke up. "I'm sorry about your friend. And I agree with you. Which was why I sent you over there in the first place."

Jess's head snapped up. "You did?"

Tori nodded. "He needs someone to stir him up a bit. Looks like you did."

Jess wasn't too sure of that. But her heart gave a twist,

thinking of what he'd lost, what he was suffering and how alone he must feel. Because she'd been there. And she'd come out the other side.

He hadn't. And that made her sorry indeed.

CHAPTER TWO

BRAN HAD BEEN up for a walk at dawn, made himself breakfast, had thrown in a load of laundry and was now left with most of the day stretching before him. Each day he had the same ritual. Walk, eat, some sort of menial chore. Check email. Anything to procrastinate so he wouldn't spend hours staring at an empty document. He got through those daily rituals just fine, but the moment he opened up a new file on his laptop, he froze.

He wrote mysteries, and right now, anything dealing with a murder and victims was too much. Even though Jennie and Owen had been in a highway accident and not victims of violence, he just couldn't deal with the idea of dead bodies. The grief was too much. His memory was too vivid.

Instead, he went upstairs and out on the balcony. The fresh air bit at his cheeks, carrying the tang of the ocean as the sky spread blue and wide above him. The lighthouse stood sentinel at the corner of the property, and he shoved his hands in his jeans pockets, thinking of yesterday and the woman who'd shown up uninvited.

She was right. He'd been a jerk. Right now he didn't know how to be anything else. But he was slightly sorry for it. Maybe would be more sorry if she'd been hurt by his gruffness. Instead, she'd been annoyed, and her eyes had sparked with it. It was hard to be sorry for that. She had beautiful eyes, annoyed or not.

He'd been standing there for twenty minutes when a movement caught his eye, just off the shore. He frowned. Was that a boat? He squinted; the sun glinted off the water in blinding flashes, but yes, there was definitely a boat out there, maybe a few hundred yards off the coastline. Certainly no farther. The sea was still rough, and he watched the boat bob and rock, at the mercy of the waves.

Foolish person. The boat couldn't be more than maybe fifteen, sixteen feet. On a calm day, and with a skilled pilot, a boat like that could fare pretty well in open water. He'd certainly gone fishing in his and had no trouble at all. But today wasn't calm. The surf had been high since the storm earlier in the week, and whoever was at the wheel wasn't looking very competent, either. He frowned, and turned to get his binoculars from downstairs. When he returned, the boat was closer to shore, and still bobbing as it drifted.

He lifted the binoculars, focused in, and cursed.

What in hell was she doing? Foolish woman! Out there in a boat, camera around her neck, trying to take stupid pictures! Had he not made his point? He ran his hand through his hair and lifted the binoculars once more. A rolling wave hit the boat sideways, throwing her off balance. She fell, and his heart froze for a few moments as she disappeared from view. Had she hit her head? Was she okay? He held his breath until he saw her struggling to stand again. She turned the craft into the waves, and he hoped to God that she was going to give it some gas and get out of there. But she didn't. She wanted her pictures too badly. As she lifted her camera again, another heavy wave crested and knocked her to the side, while water splashed over boat and woman. If she wasn't careful, she'd be knocked overboard. Or worse…she'd be swept in toward the jagged rocks at the point. The lighthouse was there for a reason, after all.

Another wave swamped the boat and panic settled in his gut. He took off the binoculars and raced down the stairs, out the front door, and to the natural steps leading to his beach and the private dock. It took only a few moments for him to throw on a life vest and start the engine of the boat that was only slightly bigger than hers. He drew away from the dock and opened the throttle as he made his way toward her, his heart pounding as the boat lifted and bottomed out with each rolling wave. If she wasn't swept overboard, she was going to hit the rocks, and neither outcome was particularly appealing. The water was freezing, and while he was confident in his piloting skills, he wasn't so sure about his rescue ones. The only option was to get her out of there.

He got close enough to see that Jessica's delicate pale skin was even paler, her eyes wide with fear. Her jaw tightened as she saw that he was behind the wheel, and she waved him off. "I've got this!" she called. "Go away!"

His fear disintegrated and anger took its place. "Are you kidding me?" He pulled as close as he dared without danger of them crashing together. "You're either going to fall overboard or run into those rocks! Do what I tell you."

Her face flattened. "No man is going to tell me to—"

He swore, and loudly, and Jessica's mouth clamped shut in surprise. "I'm going to tow you back," he shouted. "No arguments. Now shut up and let me help."

When she didn't argue, he figured she'd either finally seen common sense or was too scared to do otherwise. It took several minutes for them to secure her boat to his, with the ominous cliffs of the point coming ever closer. Bran gritted his teeth and pushed the throttle forward, taking up the slack between the two boats as the motor labored to take them both into the oncoming waves and away from shore. Jessica, to his relief, had finally done what he'd told her and was sitting obediently in the captain's seat. The chop smoothed out as they got closer to the tiny cove sheltering his beach, and once they got close to the dock, he stopped, put down his anchor and pulled Jessica's boat close enough he could board. She stood, avoiding his gaze, and stepped away from the wheel.

He stepped in just as a wave sent her off balance and crashing into him.

She was damp from spray, and yet warm and soft as he caught her in his arms and their bodies meshed together awkwardly. Bran put his hands on her upper arms to steady her and push her away. But the damage was done. Her gaze caught his and her cheeks—already rosy from the wind and water—reddened. His gaze dropped to her full, pink lips and his irritation grew. It was bad enough she was a thorn in his side…it was too much that she was also adorable. She bit down on her lip, and he nearly groaned. Adorable wasn't quite the right word. Infuriating and… sexy, dammit.

He pushed his way around her. After disconnecting the towrope, he guided her little boat into his dock and secured it. He left her on the wooden platform and, ignoring the freezing temperatures, dove into the water. Perhaps it would help cool his temper, which was still raging.

The icy shock definitely cleared his mind. He wasted no time climbing the little ladder into his craft, then started the engine and guided it in to the dock. Soaked and shivering, he jumped out and glared at Jessica, who was standing on the dock, looking quite chastised and embarrassingly repentant.

He would not let that get to him. He would not. He focused on tying the knot and not on her frightened face and big eyes.

"Get your things and come to the house," he ordered, and he didn't wait to see if she followed or not. She would if she had any sort of sense at all.

But he didn't check; he heard her feet scrambling up the stone steps behind him. He hurried to the house and stripped off his shirt the moment he got in the door. Within five minutes he'd dumped his wet clothes in the tub and had on warm, dry jeans. He was walking toward the front door with his sweatshirt in his hand when he stopped short.

She'd come inside, just into the foyer, and stood staring at him and his bare chest. Her cheeks blossomed an awkward shade of pink, and she bit down on her lip as he shoved his arms in the sleeves and pulled the shirt over his head. But something strange threaded through him at her silent acknowledgment of...what? Attraction? Awareness? What a ridiculous thought.

He opened the door and guided her outside again, then put a set of keys in her hand. "Where did you get the boat?"

She cleared her throat, and the awkwardness dissipated as they were back on topic. "Cummins's, about a mile from the resort."

He knew the location. "Take my car and drive there. I'll take the boat back. Then I'll drop you at the resort and that's that."

"Branson, I..."

His gaze snapped to her. "How do you know who I am?"

She didn't answer, and he held back a sigh of frustration. It had to have been Tori or Jeremy. "It doesn't matter. Take the car."

He stalked off to the dock again. Damn woman was nothing but trouble.

It took thirty minutes to get to Cummins's boat rentals, and Jessica was already there, her backpack slung over one shoulder. Bran held on to his anger as he turned the boat over to John Cummins, then followed Jessica back to where she'd parked his car. He got in the driver's side and immediately hit his knees on the steering wheel; she'd moved the seat forward. Held back another curse word as he adjusted it, and turned onto the road leading back to the Sandpiper.

He never spoke to her once.

She never spoke to him, either.

The drive was short, and he dropped her in front of reception. Then, and only then, did she speak.

"Thank you," she said quietly, and backed away from the door, as if afraid to say more.

He didn't answer. She shut the door, and he put the car in gear and steered back onto the main road.

But a hundred yards up the road, he pulled over to the side and gulped for air as the shakes finally set in.

The shakes had held on for a long time, part of an anxiety attack that had been utterly debilitating. When he'd been good to drive again, he'd eased his way home, parked the car and had stood at his front door for ten solid minutes, knowing he should go inside, unsure of what he wanted to do when he was in there. The urge for Scotch was strong, so it was just as well he didn't have any. He didn't want to be alone, but the idea of having company was repulsive. The adrenaline in his body told him to pace; the idea of lying down on his long sofa and avoiding everything held similar attraction.

She could have died. Died! For being utterly foolish.

It was just a damned lighthouse. There were dozens along the coast. She could pick another one.

If he'd let her keep her pictures yesterday, this never

would have happened. And if she'd been hurt, or worse, today, that would have been his fault.

Like he didn't already have enough guilt. It was bad enough he had Jennie and Owen on his conscience. The last thing he wanted was to add to the tally of people he'd failed.

In the end he went inside and sat on the sofa, staring at the unlit fireplace. It didn't take a genius to figure out that his fear and anger were all tied up in Jennie and Owen, and how he hadn't been able to save them. Or how his selfishness was responsible for them being on the road in the first place. Jennie hated driving from their place in Connecticut into the city, but he'd been too busy to drive home to see them.

All his life he'd promised himself he'd be different from his father, who had always been too busy working to spend time with his wife and son. He'd promised himself he'd be there, and present, and cherish every moment so his kid would never feel alone or unloved. And he'd failed spectacularly.

Since he was too busy to go home, Jennie had been going to surprise him with a midweek visit while he was doing promo for his latest book.

And they'd never made it.

Jessica probably hated him. He certainly wasn't overly keen on her at the moment. But she was alive, and he'd take that as a win.

And hopefully that would be the last he'd see of her. Surely, after today, she'd learned her lesson.

Jessica felt like a complete and utter fool.

An online course and a few fun rides on the lake years ago, and she'd considered herself suitably experienced to be piloting a boat on rough waters. To Cummins's credit, he hadn't been keen on renting her the boat, but she'd assured him it was a short trip and she'd be fine. And she had been, at first. Until she got near the point at Bran's place.

She'd wanted to get the pictures and get gone. But the waves had been bigger than she'd expected, and more than once she'd hung over the side and retched. The crosscurrent had made everything more difficult, and one particular roll had knocked her down, her shoulder ramming against the fiberglass side.

It still hurt, but not as much as her pride.

She looked at the bruise forming on her shoulder and sighed, then gently put her arms in a soft sweater and pulled it over her head. The moment she'd seen Branson coming toward her, she'd been relieved and then embarrassed all at once. She didn't need rescuing, for Pete's sake. She'd never needed rescuing. She was very good at picking up when things went wrong and starting over. She'd done it when her adoptive parents had divorced. When her mom had died. When she'd lost jobs in the days before she could make a living with her art. After her horrible breakup. Even Ana hadn't rescued her...not really. She'd just appeared, ready to be a friend, a confidant, a professional mentor. She had made Jessica's life richer, but she hadn't saved it.

Today Jessica felt as if Branson Black had literally saved her life. She'd been reckless—not unlike her. But she'd got in over her head, and he'd come to her rescue. He hadn't been pleased about it, either. He hadn't even grunted when she said thank you when he dropped her off.

Twice now she'd got off on the wrong foot with him. Instead of sneaking photos from the water and never having to deal with him again, she'd made it more obvious than ever that she was a pain in his neck.

And for that, she needed to apologize.

She had no idea how to do that, but she'd come up with something. And kill him with kindness if she had to.

Room service sounded like a perfect idea, so she ordered and then took the memory card from her camera and popped it into her laptop. When she opened up the directory and brought up the first picture, she sighed. It was out of focus, but not too bad. But there were only two or three that were even close to being useful. Then the lens got wet and every single picture was blurred and smudged.

All of that for nothing. She'd only accomplished making him hate her even more. Tomorrow she would apologize. And then she'd find another lighthouse. Or something else that sparked her creativity and gave her the burn to create again. In the meantime she'd keep working, because nothing helped get the muse back in business like being ready for her.

CHAPTER THREE

BRAN WAS DRINKING coffee on his deck when he saw someone coming through the stand of trees toward his driveway. He shifted over to the side so he'd be less conspicuous. Maybe it was Tori, or Jeremy, though they usually called first. It took only ten seconds for him to realize it was Jessica. Again? Frustration burned with the coffee in his mouth. Hadn't she caused enough trouble? What the heck was it about his lighthouse that was so intriguing, anyway?

But instead of turning toward the lighthouse, she headed straight for his front door.

Something twisted in his gut. He watched as she drew closer, carrying a paper sack in her arms, her sunshiny hair glinting in the morning sun. There was something so pure about her, so bright and light. He waited out of sight for her to go to the door; heard the knock echo both below him and through the house.

He should answer. Yesterday he'd been so angry and hopped up on adrenaline and fear that he hadn't said anything to her other than snapping at her to take his car to the boat rental. Both their encounters had been antagonistic, but last night, as he'd sat in the twilight, he'd realized that yesterday's foolish actions could have been avoided if he'd been nicer at the start and let her keep her photos.

Because he felt that responsibility, he was trying not to

be too angry with her. Letting go of his anger left room for other feelings, though. Ones he truly wasn't ready for nor desired. At the very least, discomfort at the sheer amount of time she was in his thoughts at all.

She knocked again. He should go down. And yet the idea of company, of small talk...what would he say? It was different when it was Jeremy or Cole or even Tori. And when he was out in public and didn't have to actually have conversations of any consequence. It was a hello and thank you to the cashier at the market. A thank you to the lady at the post office. What would they say...especially after yesterday?

In the end, he hesitated long enough that she abandoned the door and started back down the drive, only without the paper bag.

Whatever she'd brought with her, she'd left for him. An olive branch? And he was up here like a coward. While he wasn't feeling social, he didn't like that idea. There was nothing to be afraid of. At least today, no one was in any danger.

He stepped to the railing. "Miss Blundon."

She turned around and looked up, shading her eyes with her hand. "Oh! You're up there!"

Did she have to sound so delighted by the discovery? Surely seeing him wasn't exactly a pleasure. Not after the way he'd treated her.

"If you'll wait a few moments, I'll be right down."

"Of course." She smiled at him, a bright reward in his otherwise bleak day.

The whole way down the stairs he wondered what he was doing. He'd moved here to get away from people. To... work through his feelings without any burden of expectation. And now he was going to open the door to a red-headed sprite with eyes that snapped and a bright smile. As if yesterday had never even happened.

He'd say thank you for whatever was in the bag and send her on her way.

When he reached the door, she'd retrieved the bag and held it in her arms again, and met him with the same bright smile.

"Good morning!" she said, holding out the bag. "A peace offering for getting off on the wrong foot. Feet. Whatever. Twice."

Her babbling shouldn't have been charming. He instinctively reached for the bag, then regretted it because it meant automatic acceptance. He couched it in the crook of his arm, aimed a level stare at her and said, "Peace offering, or repentance for yesterday's shenanigans?"

Her eyes crinkled at the corners when she laughed, making her look adorable. "Both." She lifted an eyebrow, just a little. "But yes, peace offering. Because you were also mean, Branson Black."

He chuckled, the sound unfamiliar to him, and he fought to take it back but it was too late. Her grin widened.

"Mean?"

"Yes," she asserted firmly. "Mean. So I brought you some things to maybe help with that."

He looked in the bag. He could see a bottle of wine, a few packages of snacks, a pound of coffee and a mug. "What's all this?"

With a pleased expression, she said, "I figured you're either stressed and need a drink, are grouchy from hunger, or undercaffeinated." She hesitated, then added, "Yesterday notwithstanding. That was terrible judgment on my part, and I'm sorry."

He was charmed. He couldn't help it. Particularly because she was blunt and right. He had been mean. And yesterday she had shown terrible judgment.

"You're still after my lighthouse."

She sobered. "There are no strings attached to this gift. I didn't listen to you, and yesterday I acted impulsively. I could have been in danger, and you went to great trouble to make sure I was okay. This really is just a thank you."

He didn't want to like her, but he did. She was so upfront. And she didn't tiptoe around him, like anyone else who knew who he really was. He stepped back and opened the door wider, a silent invitation. He didn't always have to be rude. And she'd apologized, which he appreciated.

Truthfully, his ogre status was getting hard to maintain. It wasn't his normal way. It was just his way of punishing himself.

She stepped inside and halted in the foyer. "Now that's something. I didn't have a chance to tell you yesterday, but this—" she swept her arm out wide "—this makes a statement."

A table sat in the middle of the open space, while the hardwood staircase wound around it, forming a column that went to the top of the house. A skylight there beamed sunlight into the entry, a natural spotlight on the flower arrangement on the pedestal table.

"It does give some wow factor," Bran admitted.

"It sure does. This is a gorgeous place. Airy and roomy."

"Since you've only been three feet inside the foyer, would you like the twenty-five-cent tour?"

Did he really just say that?

"Sure. I promise to keep my camera in my tote bag this time."

He looked over, and her face held an impish expression that made his lips twitch. "Ha ha. Come on. I'll put this in the kitchen first."

He led her through the expansive downstairs. The kitchen was spacious and modern, and while he'd furnished one of the large living rooms, he'd left the other, the one closer to the den, unfurnished. She made appropriate sounds of approval at his den, and then they went upstairs, where she gave a cursory glance at the bedrooms and then sighed at the ensuite bath, which had a stunning view of the water. "Oh, man," she murmured, stepping inside. "A Jacuzzi tub with an ocean view. All you'd need is a book and a glass of wine and you'd be in heaven."

He was treated to a vision of what that might look like; her pale skin surrounded by bubbles and damp tendrils of hair down her neck…a long, wet leg and flushed cheeks from the heat of the bath. He tried, unsuccessfully, to shake the image from his mind. A better idea would be to get her out of his house. Or at least out of the upstairs.

She turned to him then and put a hand on his arm. "I have a confession to make. I figured out who you were after my first visit here. Now I kind of understand why you were so angry. I know I violated your privacy. I really did just come to say that I'm sorry. For everything, Mr. Black."

He hated being called Mr. Black. It reminded him of his father, who had insisted on it from nearly everyone. The only person he'd ever heard call him Peter was his mother. And it had always been Peter, and never Pete. "Branson," he replied, taken aback by her honest little speech. "And I was rude. You're right. I didn't have to be such an ass."

She laughed. "Thanks for the tour, but I should probably get going."

She slid by him, trailing a scent of something that reminded him of lily of the valley.

It really had been a peace offering, then. She hadn't pressed her case about the lighthouse. Hadn't asked him a thing about his books or his family…and what happened was no secret. It had been all over the internet and made it to several print publications. The one good thing about being an author was that his face was less recognizable than other celebrities. Clearly it hadn't escaped her notice, though.

Then again, she was somewhat of a celebrity herself, at least in the art world. Or so it would seem.

"Miss Blundon?"

She turned around and smiled. "If I have to call you Branson, you have to call me Jess."

"Jess." It suited her. "About yesterday… I own part of the blame. If I hadn't been such a jerk, you wouldn't have had to rent a boat. What I'm saying is…if you want to take some pics of the lighthouse, that would be okay."

The way her face lit up made him glad he'd said it. Her eyes sparkled, and her smile was wide and free and full of joy. How long had it been since he'd felt such an unfettered, positive emotion?

Not even at Jeremy and Tori's wedding had he felt so light. Their wedding had been a happy, wonderful occasion, but bittersweet for Bran. He'd been remembering his own wedding day years earlier.

But this was simpler. Granting a small favor, really, and it felt good.

"Really? I'd love that! Would it be possible to do a few sketches while I'm here?"

How could he say no now? Suddenly he realized he'd put himself in an awkward position. He'd thought a few pictures wouldn't hurt. But he wasn't sure he wanted her hanging around.

Her smile faded, and she put a hand on his arm. "I'm sorry. If it's too much, just say so."

The warmth of her hand seeped into his skin. Her fingers were strong, elegant and slim, like a pianist's, and unadorned with any rings or nail polish. Was he enjoying the contact a little too much?

"A few sketches would be okay," he answered, then cleared his throat. "I won't jump down your throat if I see you at the lighthouse, okay?"

She squeezed his arm. "You mean I have permission to access it?"

He had no idea why he was going along with this, other than the fact that he knew he'd been horribly grouchy the day before, and he didn't like that about himself. "Yes, that's what I mean."

Her gaze softened. "Thank you," she said quietly. "I've had such a hard time lately, and this is the first place that's really fired up my creativity. It means more than you know."

He could relate. He hadn't written a word in nearly two years. But he merely nodded as she turned away and started down the stairs. He followed closely behind, not too closely, though. And wondered at the strange feeling settling in the middle of his chest. It was pleasure mixed with anxiety, an odd combination of enjoying the contact while feeling like it was a foreign sensation.

Had he been hiding away too long?

He walked her to the door, feeling more unsure of himself with each step. When they reached the threshold, she opened the door and stepped outside, then turned around to face him.

"I know this probably sounds presumptuous and odd, but do you think we could be friends?"

He chuckled dryly. "That is not what I expected you to say."

She shrugged. "Just to clear the air, I read the news. I'm very sorry for your loss, and I understand that it takes time to recover from something like that. I lost someone very special to me around the same time."

He swallowed around the lump that had suddenly appeared in his throat. "Thank you."

"And I just started painting again. So just so you know, giving me access to the lighthouse actually means a lot. There were times I thought I'd never feel that passion again, but here I am." She spread her arms wide.

She didn't say that he'd get there too. Didn't give assurances that all he needed was time. Simply said that it meant a lot to her. He appreciated that more than she could know. He'd just about had it with the well-meaning but empty platitudes.

"You're welcome," he replied, his voice rough.

There was a pause while he searched for the right way to say goodbye. She shifted her weight to her other hip and then smiled again. "Okay, so I'd better go. Have a good day, Branson."

"You too. And thank you for the peace offering." He attempted to smile back and saw her eyes widen. Wow. Did he really smile so rarely that it came as a complete surprise?

"Okay...bye, then." She took a step backward, then gave a little wave before turning away from him and heading across the lawn toward the bluff and the red-and-white sentinel standing guard.

He shut the door, then went to his den. The broad expanse of windows gave him a perfect view, and he watched as she picked her way over rocks and bumps, her footsteps sure and light. She pulled out her camera and started snapping, and after a while put it away and pulled out a sketch pad. A half smile on his face, he shook his head as she picked a large rock for a seat, plopped herself on it and started to draw.

Then he sat down and opened his laptop. Stared at the screen for a few minutes, then opened his browser.

He wasn't quite ready. But for the first time since losing Jennie and Owen, he felt that someday he might be.

Jess hadn't planned to stay at the Sandpiper so long, and when Tori offered up her boathouse as an alternative place to stay, Jess snapped it up immediately. The building was adorable, with a warm and welcoming red door, tons of natural light, the coziest of galley kitchens and a single bedroom. The bunk beds inside had a small double on the bottom and a single on the top, so she put her clothes in the tiny dresser and made herself comfortable on the mattress with the cheery comforter sporting nautical designs in navy, red and white.

According to Tori, she and Jeremy had considered making it a vacation rental. But they were waiting to do that since Tori's time was taken up with being a brand-new mom. Jess stared up at the bottom of the bunk above her and let out a happy sigh. She'd take this over a hotel room any day.

After a twenty-minute nap, she got up and went to the kitchen to make a cup of tea. While it was steeping, she looked around the tiny living room and examined the light sources. Sketching wasn't a big deal. If she wanted to paint, she had different requirements for light and space. A few adjustments and she'd moved some of the furniture, pushing it closer to the wall. The wicker rocking chair found a new home on the sweet white-railed porch, and she wondered if Tori would be amenable to taking out the coffee table altogether. Then it would be just about right.

But she wasn't ready to start painting yet. Today she'd started some preliminary sketches that she liked but wasn't crazy over. Carrying her tea, sketch pad and pencils, she went to the porch and sat in the afternoon sun, sipping and contemplating. She turned the page over and started something different. Just the very edge of the lighthouse intruded on the right-hand side of the paper; and then, just to the left of center, she started moving her pencil, beginning an outline of a man, hands in his pockets, staring out to sea.

There was something captivating about him. She wanted to say that it wasn't because of his celebrity, but now that she knew, it kind of was. She'd read one or two of his books…figured he'd released something like ten now, maybe a dozen. Mysteries and procedurals, where she couldn't wait to turn another page and was afraid to at the same time. She admired a brain like that, so willing to wander into the darkness and face it unflinchingly, and with such detail. Now, having met him, and knowing he was grieving, she had another impression. In all his books, there was still a thread of hope through them. The bad guy always got what was coming to him. The main characters always came through with a happy ending.

He didn't get his happy ending, though. She knew how that felt. Broken hearts, crushed dreams. Jess had never quite had the family she'd always wanted. And as she made sweep after sweep on her pad, she saw the outline of a broken man coming through.

She didn't notice the time until the sun went behind the trees, dimming her light. She'd been working for hours, and she tilted her neck, working out a creak. With a sigh she picked up her phone and checked her messages. There was one from Tori, inviting her up for drinks later. She checked the time…inviting her for drinks in twenty minutes, to be exact. She'd worked throughout the late afternoon and what normally would have been dinner. She went inside, closing the red door behind her, and opened the fridge. She wasn't about to have drinks on an empty stomach, so she took out a container of hummus and nibbled on some crackers and veggies. Her hair was tucked in a bun and held there with a pencil, but she didn't really care. It was Tori and Jeremy, and they seemed like the most laid back people she'd ever met. On went her flat sandals, a quick smooth over her flowy skirt, and she was off along the gravel path to the main house.

Branson's car was in the driveway and she hesitated, wondering if Tori had asked him to join them. They'd made peace yesterday, but she wasn't sure she was ready for couples drinks and a social call where he was concerned. She nearly turned back when Tori's voice called her name. She couldn't turn around now and pretend she hadn't heard. Her careless hair and slightly wrinkled skirt would have to do. And she could fake her way through small talk, couldn't she?

"Hi!" she called out, skirting the house and heading to the backyard patio. Clearly this was where the action was in the Fisher house. She shivered; it was only May, and she hadn't thought to bring a sweater.

"Hi yourself," Tori offered. "I'm out here grabbing Rose's blanket. I left it out earlier. Come on inside."

Grateful to be going inside for the visit, Jess let out a breath and held the door as Tori went in, her arms full of baby and blanket. Jeremy was at the island pouring drinks. "Hey, Jess," he said. "Glad you could come up."

"Jess?"

She turned around abruptly. Bran was there, at the end of the hall, staring at her. Oh, Lord. He hadn't known she was invited. Her face heated and then together they stared at Tori, whose eyebrows lifted in an expression of innocence.

"What? Jess is staying in our boathouse so she can

paint. And you haven't been over in a week. What's the big deal?"

Bran leveled his gaze on her. "Because you set it up, Miss Innocent."

Great. He had no desire to be there with her. And she wasn't exactly comfortable, but she wouldn't have put it precisely that way. Then again, her initial encounters with Branson had demonstrated his usual manner was blunt.

Jess stared at both of them, then over at Jeremy, who cracked open a can of tonic water. "Don't look at me," he said, pouring the fizzy liquid into a glass.

Tori kept the innocent look on her face. "What? You guys can be civil, right? Lord, it's not like I set you up on a blind date or something."

Except it felt like it. Jeremy pressed a glass of merlot into her hands with a murmur of, "Humor her." The glass of tonic and lime went to Tori. "Bran?" he asked. "What are you having?"

"That tonic will be fine. I'm driving, after all."

Huh. That was surprising. She admired his zero tolerance attitude. "I'm lucky I just have to walk down the path," she said, trying to lighten the awkward atmosphere. "The boathouse is perfect, Tori. I was wondering though if there's somewhere I could put the coffee table? The living room is perfect for me to work."

"Of course!" Tori sat on the sofa and Jess sat beside her, and they immediately started chatting about the boathouse, the decorations and Jess's future plans for it. It was a good distraction from glancing at Bran the whole time, who was still looking rather hermit-like, but with a pressed shirt and his hair tucked behind his ears. The first time they'd met, she'd thought him to be in his forties, but now she thought it was probably younger. Midthirties, maybe. She tried to imagine him with a man bun and nearly laughed out loud. That wasn't for Bran.

He was too… She frowned. *Too much* was all she could seem to come up with. Jeremy said something and Bran chuckled, a low, rough vibration that reached in and ignited something in her belly. Oh, no. This was not a good thing. He was far easier to dismiss as a grouchy old ogre. She didn't actually want to like him. Or feel the stirrings of, if not attraction, curiosity. She was after his lighthouse. Nothing more. Even if she had started to sketch him earlier today.

Jeremy got up and refilled her wineglass and she settled back down into the sofa, relaxing more. She had friends, of course she did. But over the last few days she had thought back to those relationships. Some were lifers. Some had been relationships of utility, for a time only and then moving on or drifting apart. Some had been intense and brief, leaving her an empty vessel at the end. She listened to Jeremy and Branson and heard that rusty laugh again… They had been friends since they were boys. Jeremy drew her and Tori into the conversation with tales from Merrick Hall, the prep school he and Bran had attended together. Before long they were laughing, and Jessica was wondering about the third best friend, Cole, who sounded like the instigator of the bunch. How wonderful it must be to have friends like that. Like she'd been with Ana. There were times she just missed her so much.

She was just lifting her glass to take a sip when Bran's gaze reached over and held hers. Unlike their other meetings, this time his eyes were warm and hypnotizing, his lips holding the tiniest bit of humor, slightly hidden by his beard. Her body responded; there was something untamed about him that drew her in. Which sounded silly, of course.

He was anything but uncivilized. Perhaps it was just his restless energy. Whatever it was, she couldn't look away.

Tori appeared with some crudités and crackers, and Jess averted her eyes and instead focused on fixing a cracker with soft cheese and red pepper jelly. It was delicious, and since she'd missed having a real meal at dinnertime, a welcome addition to her stomach after two glasses of wine. When baby Rose woke and needed attending, Jess felt it was time to make her excuses and head home. Tori would be wanting to settle the baby and get some rest.

Bran seemed to agree, because he stood and collected glasses from the coffee table. "Thanks for having me over," he said, taking them to the kitchen.

"It's good for the hermit to come out of his cave once in a while."

Jess couldn't help it. She snorted as she carried dirty plates to the sink. Tori grinned and Jeremy gave Bran a slap on the back.

"Hey, I get out." Bran aimed a sharp look at Jess, a teasing glint in his eye. "I mean two days ago is a prime example."

"Branson," she said firmly, wishing he wouldn't tell this story. But Tori and Jeremy were staring at them both, and Branson smiled. She really wished he wouldn't do that. His smile was devastating.

"What happened?" Jeremy took the bait.

Jess attempted a preemptive strike. "Branson gave me a lift to the resort from the boat rental place, that's all." She pinned Bran with a "please don't do it" glare.

"What were you doing at the boat rental place?"

"I'd rented a boat."

"But what was Bran doing there?"

He lifted his eyebrows and grinned again. "Come on, Jessica. It's a good story."

"It's embarrassing."

"Hey, you laughed at the story about my underwear earlier. Fair's fair."

He was right. She'd giggled at the antics of the boys at boarding school, while sympathizing with the children they'd been, finding love and acceptance among strangers rather than at home. She was going to say he'd been thirteen at the time, but she also knew Tori was not going to let them leave without him spilling the beans. She sighed and capitulated. "Fine."

She shouldn't have worried. It became crystal clear that Bran was a born storyteller. Tori rocked Rose in her arms and Jeremy stopped putting dishes in the dishwasher as Bran told the tale with suspense in all the right spots, a dash of humor here and there, and without making her sound utterly stupid. Even she was caught up in it, and she was the subject! He finished with, "So I gave her the car and I took the boat back to Cummins's, and then dropped her off at the resort."

Tori shook her head. "What an adventure!"

Jess folded her hands. "Well, all's well that ends well. Rather than see me risk my own neck again, Branson let me take some pictures of the lighthouse, so I don't anticipate any new nautical mishaps for a good long while."

"You brought me food. What was I going to say?"

She laughed. "You could have kicked me off your property like you did the first day. Or ignore me altogether."

"Ignoring you would only have made you do something crazier."

She suddenly realized that Jeremy and Tori were watching them with amused expressions. "And on that note, I think it's time I headed to the boathouse. Thank you both for inviting me up."

"Don't be silly. We're friends now. You can stay in the

boathouse as long as you need. You can be our vacation rental trial run. And the door is always open. It's nice having you around."

"I'd better head out too," Bran said. "New parents need their sleep."

He said it easily, but Jess caught a glimpse of something on his face, a tension around his mouth that hadn't been there before. He and Jeremy were best friends. It had to be a painful reminder to see his friend happily married with a new baby, when Bran had had those things and lost them.

"I'll be in touch about the property for Cole," Jeremy said, oblivious to Bran's expression. "You can help me with that if you like. Something new just came on the market that might be perfect."

"Sounds good," Bran said.

He followed Jess to the front door, and they waved goodbye to their hosts. She expected him to head to his car while she took the path to the boathouse, but he fell into step beside her.

"What are you doing?"

"Walking you home."

She sighed. "It's not necessary. I'm not in danger of capsizing on my way to the boathouse."

"No, but you also didn't turn a light on."

Darn, he was right. The boathouse loomed in the darkness, and she could make out the form of the porch, but she hadn't turned on the outside light.

"The light attracts bugs," she explained.

He chuckled. She wished he would stop doing that. It made her insides all warm and tingly.

Their feet made soft crunching noises on the graveled path. Jess could hear the sound of the ocean shushing against the sand, and somewhere nearby, in a tall tree, an owl hooted. She sighed, loving the solitude and peace of this place. "That's a great horned owl," she said softly. "Who cooks for you?"

"What?"

"Listen to his call. *Who cooks for you?*"

The owl hooted again, and Bran murmured, "Well, I'll be damned."

She smiled in the darkness. It took only another few moments and they were at the porch of the boathouse. "I didn't lock the door," she said, "so I don't need to see the lock. Thank you for walking me, though."

"You're welcome."

"Branson?"

It sounded odd, using his first name, but after yesterday's rescue, it hardly seemed necessary to call him Mr. Black.

"Yes?"

His voice was husky in the dark. She held in a sigh.

"You are a wonderful storyteller. I was so afraid you were going to throw me under the bus in there. But you didn't. You made it sound like some great adventure. Even I was waiting to hear what happened next, and I was there."

"Thanks."

She put her hand on his arm. It was firm and warm beneath her fingers. "What I'm trying to say is…don't give up."

Silence fell between them for a few moments, and Jess found herself looking into his dark gaze. The shadows only lent to the intimacy of the moment, and briefly she wondered if he were going to kiss her.

But then the moment seemed to pass, and she took her hand off his arm. She'd said enough, and hopefully had given him something to think about. "Good night," she whispered, then went inside and shut the door.

CHAPTER FOUR

FOR THREE DAYS Branson watched as Jessica sketched at the lighthouse. After the first day, he left the gate open so she wouldn't have to walk so far. He'd spent his time doing some research. Not for a book, but on the lighthouse he now owned. He wanted to know more about the history of it, and so he'd dug into Google, visited the local library and accessed the provincial archives. The lighthouse was over a century old, made defunct after World War II, and most importantly, he'd found a book from the seventies with ghost stories and local lore at the library that he found most intriguing. His lighthouse had a history, with enough mystery to have his mind turning a plot over and over in his mind.

"You are a wonderful storyteller," she'd said. The compliment had taken him by surprise. He wasn't even sure why he'd felt compelled to recount the incident at all; maybe to prove to Jeremy that he wasn't the hermit everyone said he was. Maybe because he'd missed it. Or maybe just because he'd enjoyed the evening so much, and seeing the gleam in Jessica's eyes.

Her eyes were rather extraordinary.

He took his glass of iced water upstairs and went out on the balcony. He could see the point so clearly here, and Jess had started bringing a folding chair rather than perching on a rock to do her sketching. He'd been watching her for a few hours now, wondering if she'd put sunscreen on her fair skin; the spring sun was still capable of delivering a sunburn even though the temperatures were cool, particularly near the water. After a while he wondered if she'd eaten anything all day. He certainly hadn't seen her put her work aside to break for lunch. Did she get a crick in her neck sitting like that, as he did when he sat at his computer too long?

And why was he standing here thinking of all these questions?

It was going on two when he emerged from the house carrying a plastic bag in lieu of any sort of picnic basket. The wind buffeted his shirt and the chill reached inside him, even as the sun warmed the top of his head. Jessica didn't hear him approach until he was a handful of steps away from her, then she looked up and a smile lit her face. It had been an unconscious response, he realized, and the idea that she'd been glad to see him sent a spiral of warmth through his body.

It was only some lunch. Nothing major. He didn't need to feel…guilty. They were friends. Maybe not even friends. More like *friendly*.

"Hi," she greeted, putting down her pencil. "What brings you out here?"

He lifted his hand. "Food. I don't think you've eaten, and the last thing I need is you fainting and falling off a cliff and me having to rescue you again."

She laughed, that light, easy sound he'd enjoyed the other night, too. He even smiled a little in response.

"I promise I would not faint. Or fall off a cliff. I'm made of tough stuff. But I am hungry. What time is it?"

"Nearly two."

"Oh, my." She stretched her neck, first lifting her face

to the sky, then leaning it toward her right shoulder. "I had no idea."

Bran lifted the bag. "It's not much, but I thought you could use a bite."

"That's very kind of you."

He handed her the bag and then moved away, turning to face the house again.

"Aren't you going to join me?"

He shouldn't want to. That he did—very much—was exactly why he shouldn't. He turned back to face her and hesitated, long enough for her to nod at the flat rock nearby. "There's room for both of us there, and I'll share."

A part of him said, *What would it hurt?* while a second part reminded him that Jennie and Owen would never again have picnics on a cliff on a spring day.

Jessica got up from her seat and tucked her sketch pad and pencils away in her bag, then grabbed the lunch bag and went to his side. "You have that hermit look on your face again. What is it?"

"I shouldn't be here."

"Why?"

She asked the simplest and hardest questions.

Then she reached down and took his hand. "Is it because it feels too much like living again?"

He pulled his hand away. "Stop it. Stop trying to get into my head."

She didn't get upset. Didn't get mad or sad or indignant. That might have been easier. Instead, she just looked at him, her face open and honest and dammit, compassionate. "I'm sorry." Her voice was quiet and sincere. "You have to get through this on your own time. Thank you for the lunch. It's very thoughtful."

He started walking back to the house. Got about fifty feet and turned back, his stomach churning. She was sitting on the rock, peering inside the bag and looking lonely. He'd snapped at her when she hadn't deserved it. "Yes," he called out, and she lifted her head. "Yes, because of that."

Jessica nodded, then shifted over and patted the rock beside her. "The invitation is still open, and I'll mind my own business."

He doubted that. And the odd thing about it was that he wasn't sure he wanted her to. There were so many feelings bubbling inside him, feelings he hadn't been able to share with his family, or even with Jeremy and Cole. He could just imagine the looks on their faces if he shared his deepest thoughts. Those thoughts were pretty dark. But how long could he hold them inside?

Slowly, he made his way back to her and sat on the rock, resting his elbows on his knees. "Here," she said, taking half the chicken sandwich he'd made and handing it to him. "Eat half. There's too much in here for me anyway."

He took the sandwich and took a bite. She did the same, and after she chewed and swallowed, she lifted her face to the sun again, drinking it in. He stared at the column of her neck and had trouble swallowing his bite of sandwich.

When she lowered her chin, he took another bite and moved his focus to the sea spread out before them. True to her word, she didn't say anything. Just ate the lunch he'd prepared—the sandwich, some sliced apples and a couple of cookies he'd had in the pantry—and drank the water bottle full of lemonade he'd put inside.

She took a drink and then offered it to him. He accepted, took a long pull of the sweet and tart liquid, and then handed it back.

"Your lemonade is very good." She smiled as she offered the compliment, and then bit into a chocolate chip cookie.

"Thanks."

She grinned. "After your stories last night, I kind of thought you might have servants to help with things like picnic packing."

Bran angled her a sideways glance, and realized she was attempting to lighten the mood by teasing him. "Oh, my parents still do. The perks of an affluent childhood—never having to lift a finger."

"Or have the satisfaction of accomplishment?"

His lips dropped open in surprise. "Yes, I suppose." He pondered for a moment. "I guess that's the difference between entitlement and actual achievement, isn't it?"

"There's something rewarding about self-sufficiency."

Jess's lips set in a line as she said it. He wanted to ask her what she meant, but was afraid of either of them prying too deeply into past issues. Instead, he turned to the topic at hand, and gestured toward her bag with her sketching materials.

"Your drawings are coming along okay?"

She nodded. "I'm having so much fun. It's a combination of things, I think. The location is simply amazing. But I also think I finally got to a place mentally where I am ready to create again. It feels like the magic happens from both things coming together at the same time. Just the sketching is giving me so much joy."

He hesitated for a long moment, then said, "Do you ever feel guilty for being happy?" He couldn't look at her, but he felt her gaze on him. Nerves churned in his belly just asking the question. Not that he was happy. He wasn't. But could he go through his whole life like this? Did he want to?

"You mean do I feel guilty moving on after grieving someone so close to me?"

He nodded, unable to speak. It seemed they were going to get into the difficult subjects anyway.

"Not now. But I did for a long time. I felt as if I didn't deserve to be happy. That I somehow owed it to Ana to be miserable. And so I was." After a pause she added, "It's a hell of a way to live. I did the same after my mother died, though it was different. My parents divorced when I was ten. I guess I just… I don't know. Didn't feel as emotionally safe with my family as I did with my best friend. She'd never given me a reason to doubt. Besides, I think we grieve different people in different ways."

Another few moments of silence, and then she spoke again. "And I didn't lose my spouse and my child. I can't know what you're going through, Branson. I just know that someday you should be happy again, and not feel as if you're betraying them by moving on."

Tears stung the back of his eyes. She had spoken in a plain manner, with truth and gentleness, and said words that not even his best friends could manage. They tried to bring him back to the world of the living, but they didn't talk about the grief. It was painful relief to be able to do so.

"It's been two years. Owen would have been three now. We might have had more children. And I can't remember…" He swallowed heavily, fighting tears. "I can't remember the exact sound of his voice when he said *Dada*. Why can't I remember that?"

He didn't realize he was actually crying until Jessica put the bag aside and shuffled over, putting her arms around him. Then he noticed the wetness in his beard and on his cheeks. He was mortified to be falling apart in front of her, but he was helpless to stop it.

"It's okay," she said, rubbing his back. "Every single thing you feel and say is okay. There is no one way to grieve and no timetable."

He sniffed and rubbed his hands over his face. "I'm so

sorry. A week ago I was yelling at you and now I'm bawling all over you."

"Don't apologize. I get it. It's probably easier with someone you don't know." Her hand still made circles on his back, and it felt warm and reassuring. He'd been so touch starved. He should move away, but he wasn't ready to yet. She rested the crest of her cheek on his shoulder for a moment. "When Ana died, it was like all the light went out of everything. She was my rock and my best friend. She'd seen me through creative slumps and successes. Through relationships that came and went…she was my person. When I lost her, I lost my anchor and my compass all at once. But eventually I realized that she would be so angry with me for not living.

"It wasn't like flipping a switch, you know? It wasn't like I decided to live again and just started doing it. I had to take baby steps. I stumbled a lot. I pushed through when joy was just not showing up. But happiness is a little like creative inspiration. Sometimes we can't sit around and wait for it to show up. Sometimes we need to go looking for it. Or at least put ourselves out there so we can grab pieces of it when it rushes by."

"I don't know how to do that."

"You will. Something will snag in your brain, and you'll feel the urge to write it down. Or little snippets will come to you, and you'll write a bit and hate it, maybe, but little by little it'll happen. And when it does, you mustn't feel guilty about it."

"Is that how it's been for you?"

She nodded against his shoulder. "At first I started little random sketches. Then I thought I'd travel around and try to get back in the groove again. This past week, here? I finally feel energized and excited to work on something. And I know Ana would want me to."

"What happened to her?"

Jessica paused, then sighed, a sorrowful sound that made him want to hug her back. "She had cancer. One day she was fine. The next day she had stage four pancreatic cancer. In less than three months she was gone."

He could hear the grief in her voice, and he reached over and put his hand over hers. "I'm sorry."

"Thank you."

They sat, comfortable with quiet, for a few minutes. Then Jessica leaned away, taking her arms from around him, letting out a sigh. "It really is beautiful here. So wild and untamed."

Gulls swooped overhead, and Bran let the sun soak into his skin as the dull roar of the ocean on the rocks below filled his ears. "It can be lonely," he admitted. "And comforting at the same time."

"I get that," she agreed. She looked over at him. "You okay now?"

He nodded. "I am. Sorry I got all emotional."

"You don't have to apologize to me," she replied. Then she smiled. "Though I do think this qualifies us as actual friends now."

His gaze dropped to her lips. He shouldn't be thinking it, but he wasn't sure she was the kind of woman he could ever be just friends with. It was probably good she was just here for a short time.

"Friends," he echoed. "You're sure?"

"You brought me lunch. We shared stuff. Pretty sure that makes us friends." She leaned back onto her arms. He smiled as he looked over at her. She was so artless. Now she was sunning herself like a lizard on a rock. He did like her. Very much.

"Well, then," he answered, and adopted a similar posture. They sat for several minutes, until the sun went under a cloud and the wind took on a chilly bite. "I should probably pack up for the day," Jessica said on a sigh. "I'm going to lose the best light."

"How much longer are you staying on the South Shore?"

She shrugged. "I don't know. A month? Two? Tori and Jeremy have said I can rent the boathouse for as long as I need. I'm going to start painting soon."

There was a hesitation in her voice that told him maybe she wasn't quite ready yet, but he wasn't going to call her on it. As she said, it took baby steps. If she was finding joy, he was happy for her.

And maybe one day he'd find joy, too.

Jessica pressed the cell phone to her ear and let out a sigh. "I know, Jack. I know. It's been a long time. But I don't want this to be rushed. For God's sake, I haven't even started the actual paintings."

His voice was sharp and clear. "Sure, but you're excited. I can tell. And we can set up a showing now for fall. I just need the commitment from you."

She pinched the top of her nose with two fingers. "That's too fast. The fact that I'm even working again is a blessing. I don't want to add the pressure of a show when I might only get one decent painting from this summer. I'm sorry Jack, but the answer's no."

He softened his voice. "Hey, I know you're scared. Coming back is hard. The world just needs more Jessica Blundon art. You're going to be back in Chicago by the fall, right?"

"I was planning on it. I can stay here for a few months, but I do have to go home sometime."

"Then let me do some asking around. We might be able to work something really innovative without booking an actual show. An exclusive, a handful of paintings maybe.

Tie it in with something else. Just say you'll stay open to possibilities."

She laughed a little. "I always stay open to possibilities. And you are too coercive for your own good, Jack."

"Which is why I'm your best agent." Affection and teasing came over the line, and she relaxed a bit. "I don't want to stifle your creativity with pressure, but I also don't want you to miss out on opportunities. I'll be in touch."

"All right."

"Love you, kiddo."

Her eyes stung a little from the easy declaration. "I love you too, Jack. Thanks for not bailing on me."

"Never. Chat soon."

She hung up the call and sighed. The idea of having a showing in the autumn was exciting, but she was sure she wouldn't be ready. While she was ready to work, and even enthusiastic, there was no guarantee that every single work would be ready to show. For now she wanted to create and just revel in the process again. Feel the brush in her hand, the pressure of the bristles on canvas like a beautiful, private language only she could understand. The colors and the smell of paint and turpentine, acrid and as much a scent of home to her as bread baking or apple pie. The scrape of the palette knife. The process was the essence of who she was. She didn't care about shows or accolades. Right now feeling like herself again was all she wanted to focus on.

The rest would come. In time.

She was late getting to the lighthouse because of Jack's call, and the wind was particularly brutal, whipping her hair out of its braid and lifting the corners of her sketch pad. She clipped them down and tried to ignore the gusts that slapped at her, instead focusing on the door of the lighthouse. It was beautifully scarred, the rusty hinges crooked but strong enough that the door didn't droop. It looked as if it hadn't been used in ages, maybe decades, and the battered boards seemed almost like a fingerprint of what time had wrought.

At the foot of the door, just to the side, was a small clump of daisies, stubbornly blooming against the elements and in the rocky soil. Jessica dashed her pencil across the paper, capturing their proud, resilient heads. She smiled, and wrote along the bottom right corner, *Marguerite*. It was the French word for *daisy*, and it felt right.

"Good afternoon."

She jumped, grateful that her soft pencil hadn't been against paper. Bran stood just beside her and behind, his hands in his pockets. "Sorry," he said. "I didn't mean to scare you."

"It's so windy I didn't hear you." She rolled her shoulders. "I've been admiring the daisies. Pretty stubborn to be blooming amid all this salt and rock."

He looked over her shoulder at her sketch. "You like the door."

"It has character. And secrets."

To her surprise, a smile spread across his face. "Are you interested in finding out what some of those secrets are?"

"What do you mean?"

He took a key from his pocket. It was big and old, and she wondered if it would still work. "It works," he said, as if reading her mind. "I had the building inspected before I closed the purchase. The structure is old, but it's sturdy."

Excitement bloomed in her chest. "Of course I want to see inside!" She gave him some side-eye. "Unless it's overrun with mice. In which case I'm not too keen."

"Fair enough. And I haven't been inside either, by the way. First sign of rodents, we're out."

She stood up and tucked her sketch pad away. "Are you kidding? You haven't gone in, not once? You've been here since…"

"February," he supplied. "And it is damned cold here in February. Now though… I'm curious. I thought you might be, too."

"I am. I've never been inside an actual lighthouse before."

This one was small compared to many, but she was interested to see what surprises and treasures were inside. Bran went to the door and fiddled for a while, jiggling the key in the lock. "I wonder if the salt rusted the lock?" he mused, but then the key seemed to find home and turned over with a solid click.

The hinges creaked as he pushed the door open.

She followed behind, stepping into the hollow-sounding space that closed out the sound of the wind. The bottom of the lighthouse was simply a large, single room. An old army cot was against one wall, with a wool blanket heavy with dust covering the mattress. There was a table and chairs there, too, and an oil lantern—empty—sitting on the table. A space jutted out from the otherwise square base of the lighthouse, and a wood stove was in the corner, the flue vented out through the top of the addition. When Bran went to examine it, she stopped him. "Don't," she said quickly. "I promise I'm not usually a wimp, but I have visions of that stove either being full of mice or that birds have made a nest in there."

He chuckled and stepped back. "I'll explore that on my own, then."

"Thank you." She shuddered. She hated mice, and she also hated the thought of a bird flying out of the iron stove and getting trapped in the room.

"It's pretty plain, isn't it?"

She wandered over to the army cot, pushed up against the wall. What a lonely spot. "Was there ever a lighthouse keeper?"

He nodded. "The lighthouse was made defunct in the late forties, after the war. But before that there was. And one before him. Back to 1893, when the lighthouse was built. There was a house, too, but it burned in the twenties, apparently."

She was intrigued. The light in the room was dark and gloomy, thanks to a lack of windows. A sparse amount of sunshine traveled down to the bottom level from a singular window above, along the staircase that led to the actual lamp. She went to the staircase and looked over at him. "I'm lighter. I'll go first and make sure it's sound."

"Please be careful."

She smiled in reply and turned her attention to the rough steps leading to the top. The spiral staircase was narrow, but solid, and Jessica held on to the handrail as she climbed up…and up…and up, Branson's footsteps close behind. She reached a trapdoor at the top, and with a little help from Branson, released the closure and pushed it open.

Light poured in, brash and cheery, along with a gust of cool air. Apparently the windows at the top were not airtight, and the wind gusted around the structure, whistling eerily through the cracks.

Jessica had never been a big fan of heights, but she couldn't deny the view was spectacular. She could see for miles—up and down the coast, and also inland, to where the main road cut through the trees and clearings where other houses were built. None of them were as grand as Bran's.

"Wow," Branson said, standing close behind her. There wasn't much room in the top, and she could feel the warmth of his body near her back. "It's tiny. But look at the size of the lamp."

She looked. "I can't even see a bulb or anything. Is there one?"

"I think it's so old it might have been a lantern. And all these lenses. Cool, right?"

It was cool. It was one of the neatest things she'd ever seen. And the lenses…so many angles and slivers of light and texture. She wished she'd brought her camera. Wondered if Bran would let her come in here again. She thought about the challenge of painting simply *light*. Tingles ran down her arms and she turned to him. "I need to paint this. Look. It's all glass and angles and light and can you imagine what it would look like on canvas?"

His gaze locked with hers, and the power of it slammed into her. They were utterly alone, at the top of an abandoned lighthouse, and the intimacy of the moment was too strong to be ignored. His gaze dropped to her lips briefly, and a slow burn ignited low in her pelvis…attraction. Desire. She tried to push it away. She had no business being attracted to him, especially after their rather personal conversation earlier in the week. He certainly wasn't in any headspace to return any attraction.

"Do you want to go outside?" His voice was rough as he backed away and moved toward a small door leading to the 360-degree platform.

She inhaled a deep breath and accepted the distraction gratefully. "Yes, but I don't trust that railing."

"Me either. It's probably rotted. Stay close to the building."

She followed him out, watched as he gingerly stepped on the platform. Despite its age, the wood seemed mostly sound. She stayed close to the wall, buffeted by the wind until they reached the other side of the lighthouse, which was sheltered and afforded a view that went miles down the coast. The water sparkled so brightly it hurt her eyes, but her chest filled with the fresh, salty air, and she felt a freedom she hadn't felt in a long, long time.

She turned and saw Bran watching her, and she smiled, feeling a connection with him that was new. He smiled back, surprising her, and stepped closer. Her heart hammered at his nearness. A pair of gulls screeched, their cries swallowed by a gust of wind.

"Bran," she murmured.

His gaze tangled with hers, dark, complicated. She shouldn't want him to be nearer. Should suggest they go back inside. Should say she was cold or something…but the truth was she wasn't cold and she didn't want to go back inside and she wanted to sink her hands into his rich mane of hair and feel his beard against the soft skin of her face. Oh, Lord. They had just said they were friends. Now she wasn't so sure.

And she'd called him by a shortened version of his name. Not Branson, but Bran. It seemed too intimate and yet suited him perfectly.

"Jess," he answered, also shortening her name, and all the delicious tension ratcheted up a notch.

He lifted his hand, cupped the back of her head and drew her close. She had barely caught her breath when he dropped his mouth to hers, and she wasn't sure she could still feel her feet.

His lips were full and soft, and his tongue tasted of coffee as it swept inside her mouth. Oh, the man could kiss. Her toes were practically curling in her sneakers as his wide hands drew her up and held her against him even as she melted. Instinctively she reached out and grabbed his shoulders, holding on, fingers gripping his shirt. He shifted, letting her down a little, his hand dropping to the hollow of her back, and she did what she'd wanted to do for days. She slipped her hands into the thick mass of his hair, luxuriating in the soft fullness, the untamed wildness of it.

He groaned. She shifted her weight and…

Her foot went through a board.

She cried out, losing her balance. Branson tore his mouth from hers and pulled her firmly into his arms, his face full of alarm. "Not as sturdy as we thought," he said, backing up a few steps away from the weak spot. Jessica hadn't even had time to be afraid. One moment she'd been kissing him; the next she'd been yanked against his body while his face paled.

She looked over the railing. It was a long, long way down. Dizzying, even. If both her feet had gone through… she would have fallen straight down to the rocky ground below.

"Let's get back inside," he said firmly, leading her back the way they'd come, opening the door and practically shoving her inside. Once he'd secured the door again, he let out a breath. "Okay. That was unexpected."

She didn't know if he meant the near accident or the kiss, and she wasn't about to ask him. Both events had her feeling off balance and speechless.

"I'm fine, really," she assured him, startled by his still-pale face while her heart pounded from the adrenaline. "It was just one foot."

"We shouldn't have gone out there at all. Shouldn't have…" His stormy eyes caught hers. "I shouldn't have kissed you. I'm sorry. I don't know what came over me."

Her feelings were momentarily hurt. He was apologizing for kissing her, as if she hadn't been there, just as involved as he. He wasn't solely responsible. She lifted her chin. "Are you sorry because you regret it or sorry because my foot went through the wood? Just asking if I should take this personally or not."

His lips fell open as he stared. "Take this personally? Jess, you could have fallen. A fall like that would have killed you."

His face was so tortured right now that her heart squeezed. Considering his past, of course this was upsetting. But she stepped a bit closer, enough that she could put her hand on his forearm. "What I'm asking is if this is about the danger or if you think kissing me was a mistake."

He didn't answer. She watched as he swallowed, his throat bobbing with the effort as she slid her hand to his wrist and twined her fingers with his.

"Kissing me isn't wrong, Bran," she said softly. "It's just a kiss. I liked it."

His thumb rubbed over hers. She was sure he didn't realize he was doing it, but it did strange things to her insides. "You shouldn't say things like that."

"Why? We're adults. Kissing is...kissing." She tried a flirty smile, unsure of how it really looked, figuring she probably appeared awkward. But she was trying. She wanted to keep this light. And she wanted to kiss him again. There was nothing wrong with that, was there?

So she eased herself even closer and lifted her other hand to his face. His eyes closed as her thumb rubbed over the crest of his cheekbone, a soft caress to a man who appeared to need it desperately. She wondered how long it had been since he'd been touched. If there'd been anyone since his wife's death...considering how he hid himself away, she somehow doubted it. Was what just happened the first physical intimacy he'd had in two years?

"Branson," she whispered, and his eyes opened. "Please kiss me again. Please."

There was a pause where she didn't think he was going to, and then he dipped his head and touched his lips to hers.

It was different from the kiss outside, which had been windswept and turbulent and unexpected. This was gentle, deliberate, decimating. Jess leaned into him as he folded her into an embrace, and kissed her with a thoroughness that left her breathless and wanting more.

But more was too much, at least for today. So she contented herself with the kiss, the nuances of it, the way he delved deeply and then retreated to nibble at the corner of her mouth, stealing her breath. The way his broad hand curled around the tender skin of her neck, where her pulse drummed heavily. How his body was solid and warm and unrelenting in all the right places, while his lips were soft and persuasive.

She was the one to break away finally, a bit overwhelmed by her own feelings and desires. If it were up to her, they'd christen the lighthouse right here and now, or perhaps dash over the rocky knoll to the house and find their way to his bed. Those desires were natural and exciting, but it was different with Bran. He wasn't the type to sleep with a woman impulsively, or to simply slake a thirst. Not after what he'd been through. So she stepped away, bit down on her lower lip, hoping to memorize his taste, and took a deep, yet shaky, breath.

"You're some kisser," she said, trying a smile. "Please don't apologize for that."

He turned away and faced the windows, looking out over the ocean, and cleared his throat. She smiled a little to herself as she recognized the moment for what it was. She wasn't the only one aroused from that kiss. Secretly, she was glad that stopping was difficult for him, too.

"You're not so bad yourself," he replied, his voice rough. "But—"

"Don't say but," she interrupted. "Let's just leave it as a very nice moment between two very nice people, with no regrets or expectations."

He turned his head to look at her. "Is that possible?"

"I think so. Besides, you're not ready. I'm not stupid, Bran."

He nodded. "We should go back down. The afternoon's getting on."

He opened the trapdoor, and Jess started down the stairs. They were plunged into darkness again as he shut the door, blocking out the light. The small window partway up gave them a sliver of grayness to navigate by, and then they reached the bottom. Branson opened the door and Jess stepped outside into the blustery wind, while he followed and locked the door behind him.

She shouldered her bag and gathered up her gear. Without asking or offering, Bran carried her folding chair and one of her bags to her car, which sat at the end of the lane—she still didn't park at the house. Didn't feel it would be right.

They were nearly to her car when she let out a breath and said what had been on her mind for the last ten minutes. "Bran?"

"Yeah?"

"You weren't thinking of…her, were you? Your wife? When we were kissing?"

And then she held her breath. She could understand him not being ready. Could understand if she was the first sexual contact he'd had since losing Jennie. But she did not want to be a stand-in. Bran didn't have much of a poker face. She peered up at him, hoping she could tell if he were lying.

He didn't look at her, but faced straight ahead. "No," he said firmly. "No, I was not thinking of her when I kissed you."

She should have been relieved. But the underlying anger in his voice killed whatever joy she might have felt.

Because maybe he hadn't been thinking of his dead wife. But he wasn't happy about it, either. And that left her exactly nowhere.

CHAPTER FIVE

BRAN DIDN'T GO to the lighthouse anymore. He had no problem with Jessica setting up there, and he sometimes caught glimpses of her, but he didn't watch from the balcony or take her food or ask if she'd like to go inside.

He'd kissed her, for God's sake.

He poured himself another coffee and wandered through the kitchen, aimless. He'd wanted to be a hermit, to go somewhere isolated and alone to work things out in his head. And it had been fine for a few months. He'd popped into Jeremy's on occasion, and Tori made sure he wasn't too solitary. He hadn't come to any conclusions, but at least he'd been able to stop pretending that he was okay. He didn't have to go through the motions for anyone. And if he wanted to fall apart, he was free to do so without being watched by friends, colleagues and even the press.

Now he was getting a bit of cabin fever. Maybe it was the June weather. The days were warmer and things were really starting to grow. Tulips and daffodils had come and gone in his perennial beds, and the hostas were showing their broad, striped leaves. Now other perennials he couldn't name were sprouting in his flower beds, along with weeds. There was some kind of leafy plant growing in a clump behind the house that he had no idea what to do with.

He could garden, he supposed. Just because he never had didn't mean he couldn't.

But not today. Today was bleak and rainy, a gloomy cover of cloud hanging over the coast while rain soaked into his green lawn. He looked at the lighthouse and wished the light was there, flashing into the distance. Instead, it just looked cold and neglected.

There was the section of platform where Jessica's foot had gone through, scaring him to death.

The railing that wasn't safe, either. How easily she could have lost her balance and gone through it. His heart seized just thinking about the possibility.

The hand holding his coffee paused halfway to his lips as a scene flashed into his head.

A scene. With characters, and danger and a question only his writer's brain could answer. *Did she fall or was she pushed?*

Excitement zipped through his veins. He took his coffee and headed straight for the den and his laptop. This time when he booted up, he didn't bother opening email or his browser. He went right to his word processing program and started typing.

When he looked up later, two hours had passed, his coffee was cold, his brain was mush and he was equal parts relieved and scared.

He could still write.

He could maybe move on.

And he was still carrying guilt with him. Only this time he didn't want to feel guilty for doing something that used to be as natural to him as breathing.

After saving the document, he heated his coffee in the microwave, looked at the time and grabbed a muffin from a plastic container on the kitchen counter. He'd missed lunch but he didn't care. He'd written. Maybe not a lot, but it was a start. And he was standing in his kitchen with two-hour-old coffee, a just-okay blueberry muffin and no one to share his excitement with.

He could call Jeremy, but Jeremy worried too much and would tell Tori, who would ask too many questions in her quest to be helpful. Besides, he wasn't sure either of them would truly get it. He thought about Cole, who totally understood loss and moving on, but who was a workaholic who scheduled his recreation time like part of his to-do list. Bran wasn't close with his own family, and the last people he wanted to talk to about making this kind of a step were his in-laws. They loved him. He loved them. But their relationship was so painful now, tinged with grief and regret. They hadn't spoken since he'd moved into the house.

He picked up his phone and sent a text instead. It said simply:

I wrote today!

There was no immediate answer, so he finished his muffin, pondering more about the kernels of the story he'd begun. Right now he had only a scene. He wasn't even sure who the villain was, or the story question. There was no outline, no solid plot. But there was something. There was a victim and a suspicious death, and that was definitely something to a mystery writer.

His phone vibrated on the countertop, making a loud noise in the silence. He picked it up and saw it was Jess, replying to his text.

That's wonderful! Happy for you!

And she truly was. He knew because she understood.

His thumbs paused as he tried to come up with a suitable response.

It is because of you. I have a dead body at the bottom of the lighthouse. Not sure if she was pushed or if she fell. All because you scared the heck out of me last week.

The phone vibrated in his hand.

I'm trying not to be alarmed by any of that. Seriously, congrats on catching a glimpse of your muse. Give her time to come back to you slowly. Accept what she offers you. Soon you will be good friends again.

His heart warmed. She had such a way of putting things, of seeing the good side, of offering hope. And that was something he hadn't expected to have for a very long time.

Still, she was right about one thing the other day. Writing a scene was one thing. Moving forward on a personal level was something he was not ready for. Her question had rocked him to the soles of his feet. No, he hadn't been thinking of Jennie when he'd kissed Jess. And that had hurt him deeply. He didn't ever want to forget the woman he'd loved. The mother of his child.

He didn't want to fall in love again, either. If he'd learned anything, it was that life was precious and nothing was guaranteed. He'd loved Jennie, loved their son with all his heart. He'd promised to do better for them than his father had done for him. And then he'd done the exact same thing: he'd put work ahead of his family. And the consequences were devastating. He never wanted to go through that again.

Which brought his thoughts around full circle to Jess. He liked her. A lot. And there was no denying he was attracted to her. That kiss the other day had awakened something in him that had been dormant for too long. It was a good thing that she was just here for the summer. Someone passing through his life, not sticking around. There was a little bit of safety in that, after all. The confusing thing was how to proceed. Should they be friends? Could they be friends without being physical? Could they be physical without falling in love? Because the last thing he wanted to do was set up unreasonable expectations.

Bran figured he was probably overthinking, so he pushed the thoughts aside and went out to the lighthouse instead. He walked around the perimeter, examined the ground around the base, looked up at the platform high above. Brow furrowed, he took the key and went inside, then lugged the single mattress up the stairs, trying to ignore the dust and probably mold that had settled into it. Once outside, he gingerly felt his way to the railing, making sure not to get too close. And then he tipped the damp and heavy mattress over the edge, seeing where it fell.

A person would be heavier, but the placement at the bottom was what he was after.

He went inside, shut the trapdoor and timed how long it took him to get back outside and to where the "body" lay. Satisfied, he dragged the mattress back inside and left it on the floor in a puff of dust.

It really was a shame that it was in such disrepair. Had the previous owners not cared? The house was three thousand square feet of elegance and had been lovingly cared for. The lighthouse, full of history, was a derelict.

Maybe he could be the one to restore it.

Energized, he trotted back to the house. First, he wanted more words. There were some adjustments that needed to be made in the scenes he'd just written. And after that, he'd start researching restoration.

He didn't need to think about Jessica Blundon at all. He just needed something to keep him occupied, and this was perfect.

Jess spent one more week sketching at the lighthouse, but Bran never came out anymore. She didn't even see him on his balcony, or in his gardens. It was as if he was deliberately avoiding her ever since they'd shared that kiss. Or kisses, rather. There'd been two. One impulsive. The other not. He wasn't pleased about either.

Now she had started painting, and while she missed sitting out in the sunshine, she was enjoying her time in her makeshift studio with the familiar smells and tools around her. Her loft in Chicago was bigger, but this suited her just fine. She had only to take a few steps to make a cup of tea or something to eat. The ocean was outside her door. And while she didn't want to overstay her welcome, Jeremy and Tori had become friends and she saw them often. Baby Rose was growing each day, and Tori was starting to look slightly more rested as she got more sleep. Jeremy doted on her in a way that was so sweet it made Jess's heart hurt.

She'd never had a love like that. She'd loved, sure. But each time that particular blossom had bloomed, it had ended up wilting, too, until there was nothing left but to move on. She tried not to overthink it. Ana had always said that there was no one good enough. That no one understood what it meant to be a creative. Or they were jealous of her talent. Compliments all, but lonely just the same. And each time a relationship ended, a little bit of hope for a family of her own died, too.

But she could live a fulfilled life just the same. It was all about being happy with what you had, rather than spending too much time wishing. Wishing just led to disappointment.

Right now she was working on her first painting, starting small, working from the sketch she'd made of the door and the daisies beside it. She wanted to do a whole series here, not just of the lighthouse but of the whole experience of being on the South Shore.

But she missed Bran. She'd be lying to herself to deny it.

A week passed. The end of June approached and she worked long hours, taking time only for walks and meals. She spoke to her agent and negotiated with Tori to stay at the boathouse until the end of August. Then she, her sketches and paintings would head back to Chicago. She could finish there in her own studio.

Finally, on a Friday night, Tori asked her up to the house for dinner. Jess pressed her phone to her ear and asked the tough question. "Is Branson going to be there?"

"No," Tori replied. "He's gone to Halifax for something. It's just us. And I'm not even cooking. Jeremy is stopping for fish and chips on the way home."

Her stomach growled. That sounded so good… "Okay, then. Let me clean up and I'll be there. What should I bring?"

Tori laughed. "Yourself?"

"How about wine? Or can you have any?"

"I can sneak a glass. I've got enough milk expressed to feed Rose. That would be lovely."

So Jessica washed up, changed into a simple floral maxi dress, twisted her hair into a messy topknot and grabbed not only a bottle of pinot grigio but a basket of early-season strawberries. They'd make a simple dessert after their takeout meal.

When she arrived at the house, Tori was outside in the backyard, putting plates on the patio table while Rose kicked and played in a playpen covered with a fine mosquito net. "Are the bugs bad?" Jess asked, handing over the wine.

"No. I'm just overly cautious, I think, and hate the thought of an itchy bite on Rose's delicate skin. To be honest, I just love eating dinner outside. Unless it's raining, we eat out here nearly every night."

"You guys are the cutest."

Tori beamed. "Do you think? Wait'll I tell Jeremy. 'Cutest' isn't something he's used to being called."

They went into the kitchen briefly and Tori put the wine in the fridge to chill, then put the berries on a shelf. "You know, six months ago I was living in a tiny little house and working at the Sandpiper. It's hard to believe this is my life now. I'm so lucky. I'm so *happy*."

They went back outside, sitting in the shade next to Rose's playpen. "How did you and Jeremy meet, then? He's from New York, right?"

"Connecticut originally." She reached inside the netting and handed Rose a ring with keys on it. The baby shook her fist and the keys rattled, making her even more excited. "He came here on business last summer and stayed at the Sandpiper. Two weeks later he was gone." She met Jess's gaze. "When he came back at the end of November, he discovered I was pregnant."

"Oh, wow." Jess sat back in her chair. "So you got married?"

Tori laughed. "If only it were that simple. But we did in the end. After we fell in love with each other. And now here we are. We're going to split time between here and New York. Jeremy's actually looking for a place for us on Long Island. He'll commute in to work. And he has a flat right by Central Park."

Three residences and all of them pricey. "I didn't realize he was so rich."

"Neither did I. He and Bran and Cole are all loaded. I call them the Billionaire Babies."

Jessica coughed. "Did you say Billionaire Babies?"

Tori nodded. "You didn't know?"

"I knew Branson was successful, but a billionaire?"

Rose started to fuss so Tori took her out of the playpen and sat her on her lap. She straightened her little dress as she chatted. "Oh, most of his money is family money. To be honest, I don't think their childhoods were great. Lots of money, not much love and high expectations."

A billionaire. A freaking billionaire. And yet he was living proof that money was no guarantee of happiness. He'd lost the people most important to him. No money could protect him from that. The conversation they'd had during their picnic came back to her. She'd teased him about servants... but she'd only been teasing. He'd been serious. Of course he'd had servants. Hot embarrassment slid into her cheeks.

"Does it change things?" Tori asked.

"What do you mean?"

Tori rubbed Rose's back and a little burp came out, making them laugh. Tori cuddled her close but then leveled her gaze on Jess. "Knowing he's rich. Does it change how you feel about him?"

Jess frowned. "Why would it? I couldn't care less about his bank balance. Besides, I barely know him."

Tori was quiet for a long moment, and Jess felt her cheeks warm. "Are you sure?" Tori asked.

"Sure about not caring about his money, or sure about barely knowing him?"

"About not knowing him," Tori said. "I believe you about the money. To be honest, I found it a little intimidating at first."

Jess sighed. She did, too. She did just fine on her own, and was successful in her own right. But she wasn't megarich. "It doesn't matter either way. He's still grieving for his wife and son. Even if I were interested, he's not."

"So nothing's happened? Nothing at all?"

Tori sounded so hopeful. And Jess had never been one to kiss and tell, but she hadn't really had a girlfriend since Ana. She missed having someone to confide in, and Tori knew Bran better than most. Would it hurt to get someone else's perspective? Was she overthinking all of this or getting it wrong? Because she certainly hadn't been able to get him off her mind.

"We kissed," she admitted, the heat in her cheeks now a burning flame. "But just one time, really. He hasn't spoken to me since."

Tori leaned forward, her eyes flashing. "Oh, that's wonderful news!"

Jess laughed in spite of herself. "How do you reckon? I mean, we're not speaking." Besides the text about writing again, she thought to herself. But that didn't really count.

"Bran wasn't even leaving the house. Jeremy was so worried. The fact that he kissed you? Major progress." Suddenly her face fell. "Oh, I'm sorry, Jessica. I didn't take into account how you were feeling about it. Are you doing okay?"

She sighed. "Yeah, I'm okay. I mean…it was pretty great. But I could tell he was mad at himself after, you know? So it didn't really end well."

"Well, something happened to him to light a fire beneath his butt. He told Jeremy he was going to Halifax for a few days to look into restoration of the lighthouse. He said it's in rough shape, and he wants to fix it up."

Jess sat up straighter. "Are you kidding?"

"Not at all."

Jess was gutted. The lighthouse was beautiful as it was, strong and scarred. Granted, the platform at the top could use repairs, and it was dirty inside, but restoration? For what purpose? It would be covering up all its character. It would be as if he were erasing anything that smacked of the two of them together. And that stung. Even if it didn't go anywhere, she could take a nice memory away from that afternoon. She certainly didn't feel the need to paint over it.

In fact, the whole encounter had enhanced her approach to the paintings. Imbued her with a new emotion that would only be beneficial.

She was still stewing when Jeremy came through the house to the backyard through the house, carrying a huge paper bag in his hands. "Someone call for dinner?"

The smell of fries and fish filled the air, and Jess's stomach rumbled again. She was hungry, and what Bran did with the lighthouse was his business, wasn't it? She had absolutely no say. She had her sketches. Branson Black could do whatever he liked. And now she knew he had the money to do it. Despite the big house and beautiful car, she'd had no inkling he was so wealthy. He wasn't flashy about it. She'd give him that much.

Jeremy laid out the meal, and Jessica went inside to get the wine and the corkscrew that Tori had put on the island. When she went back outside, Jeremy was holding Rose and Tori was filling her plate with food. It was so perfectly domestic. She wondered if Bran had experienced these moments with his wife and baby. Surely he had. And she could understand how a person might not come back from a loss like that.

She was sympathetic. But it didn't mean she was willing to be…disposable.

Pasting on a smile, she took a takeout container and emptied it onto her plate. It certainly smelled delicious. Jeremy put Rose in her playpen again and worked on opening the wine. She'd stumbled onto the sticking point that had been nagging at her ever since that day at the lighthouse.

He'd treated her as if she was disposable. And maybe he
was angry at himself. But there was no question she'd felt
cast aside, and that hurt. After going through most of her
life feeling invisible, being seen and discarded hurt even
more than not being noticed at all. This was why she didn't
put herself out there anymore. It just wasn't worth it.

But she wasn't going to let it ruin her evening, so she
shook some vinegar on her fish, picked up her fork and
dug in. It was perfectly flaky, the tartar sauce creamy and
flavorful, and there was a plastic dish of coleslaw for them
to share. The conversation turned to other things, namely
Jeremy's search for a property for the third in their trio,
Cole, who wanted something he could use as a corporate
retreat. So far not much had turned up on Jeremy's radar.

When the meal was over, Jess carried the dirty dishes
back to the kitchen and returned to the table with the carton of freshly washed berries. As the evening cooled, they
talked and Jess had another glass of wine while Tori gave
Rose a prepared bottle.

Jess was barely over thirty, but the family scene had
her biological clock ticking madly tonight. When Rose
was finished eating, she took her from Tori's arms to give
her a break and to get baby snuggles. She hadn't thought
about wanting children a whole lot, but spending time with
Rose these past weeks had made her wonder. She smelled
so good; like milk and baby lotion and fresh cotton. The
fact that the baby settled so easily into her arms made her
feel motherly and strangely competent. It took no time at
all before Rose's little lashes were resting on her cheeks
and her lips opened slightly, slack in slumber.

She was such a sweet little thing. And for the first time
in years, Jessica let herself really yearn for what she didn't
have. What she might never have. And she held on tight.

CHAPTER SIX

THE SUN WAS setting and Jeremy had just lit the citronella torches when the slamming of a car door echoed through the still evening air. Jess frowned and looked over her shoulder, but couldn't see anything. A few moments later, Tori met her gaze and nodded. *Bran*, she mouthed, and Jess swallowed tightly. She was still thinking about the kiss, and thinking about him restoring the lighthouse. She bit down on her lip. She couldn't escape the notion that he was fixing it because he wanted to essentially cover up what had happened between them. A fresh coat of paint and some new lumber would erase a lot, wouldn't it?

"Good evening, Bran," Tori said softly. "Come on in and have a seat. You want a drink?"

"Naw, I'm good for now." He came into the circle and nodded at Jess, his gaze settling on her and the baby in her arms. "Jessica. I didn't know you'd be here."

Or else he wouldn't have come. She summoned her pride. "Likewise."

He hesitated, but then sat. "Sorry. I didn't mean that the way it sounded."

Her cheeks heated and she let out a breath. "It's okay. No biggie."

Jeremy jumped into the middle of the awkwardness.

"So, Bran. What brings you by? How was the trip to Halifax?"

"Good." Bran smiled, and it transformed his face. Jess realized she'd hardly ever seen him smile, and that when he did she forgot just about everything in her head. His face completely changed, relaxing and opening more, while his soft lips curved beneath his beard.

The beard that had tickled her chin and neck not long ago. She pushed the thought away.

"You're really going to change the lighthouse?" Jess asked, trying hard to keep censure out of her voice. She had no claim to it. Her creative "tingles" held no weight when it came to what he chose to do with the lighthouse It didn't mean she had to be happy about it.

He nodded. "Yeah. It's in pretty rough shape. I honestly think it's been neglected for decades. First we're going to make it safe. Then we'll worry about cosmetics."

"You don't think all the changes will erase its character?"

"If I leave it as it is, it'll rot away. I don't want it to disappear."

"Not to mention how it might work against resale value," Jeremy pointed out, lifting his glass as he sat in a padded chair. "Sometimes selling points become liabilities real fast."

Jess's gaze met Bran's. "You're thinking of selling already?"

When he shook his head, she was relieved, though she couldn't say why. Her life wasn't here, and there was nothing really between them anyway. Why should she care if he stayed or not?

"No," he answered firmly. "I don't plan on selling for a while. Even if I go back to New York eventually, this is a great place to retreat to, you know?"

"What made you decide to take on the lighthouse, anyway?" Tori asked.

"A discovery that the platform and railing at the top aren't safe." He didn't look at her this time, but his smile had vanished. "Half the boards are rotted. The lamp is fine and won't be used again anyway, but I've got someone coming out to have a look at the foundation and make sure that structurally we're sound. It's been neglected. It's a beautiful piece of history that's mostly been abandoned. At least maybe I can be a better steward to it."

She wanted to be angry or at the very least annoyed that he was going to paint over the battle scars the building had sustained over the years. There were stories there. Stories he should appreciate as a writer. But it was hard to argue with wanting to take care of something and cherish it.

"I think I got used to its weathered look," she said quietly.

Now he looked at her, his gaze inscrutable. "I know. But it's about safety. The last thing I want is for someone to get hurt."

She couldn't look away. He said it while looking directly in her eyes. And the moment on the platform spun out in her mind—the wind, the moment her foot went through the rotten board and the instant freezing fear, and the feel of his strong body against hers as he held her tight.

He might be able to walk away from their kisses that day without any problem, but she couldn't.

She was smart enough to realize that she was falling for Branson Black, the most unavailable man she'd ever met.

Dammit.

Rose squirmed a bit in her arms, and she finally broke eye contact. "Shh…" She adjusted the weight of the baby in an effort to keep her settled, but Tori got up and came to retrieve Rose. "Her naps in the early evening are getting shorter. Which is a blessing for me. Now she'll stay up until about eleven, and sleep through until five. It feels like absolute heaven."

Jess's arms felt cold and empty without the baby, a thought she didn't want to delve too far into. Instead, she smiled and got to her feet. "I really should go anyway. I'm up early these days to work. But thank you once again for dinner. I'm going to have to have you down to the boat-house for a meal soon."

"That would be lovely!" Tori snuggled a fussy Rose against her shoulder.

Of course Jess didn't quite know where she was going to seat everyone, now that the main floor space was tran-sitioned into a studio. But no matter. They'd figure it out. Maybe it would turn into a picnic on the beach.

Bran stood as well. "I'll walk you home," he said.

Jeremy laughed. "Sure, bro. It's like a hundred yards to the boathouse. You're not fooling anyone."

Jess blushed and Bran stared at his friend. "Shut up, Jer," he said mildly. But Jeremy merely chuckled and didn't say anything more. Jess was cluing into the fact that Bran was a still-waters-run-deep kind of guy, and that when he spoke, people generally listened. It was a trait that could be frustrating but that she admired, too.

This time when they reached the boathouse she invited him in. "Why don't you come in for a bit? It's still early."

He stepped inside and took off his shoes, leaving them on the tiny mat by the door.

"You know, I've never been in here," he mused, peek-ing ahead. "It's tiny but kind of cozy."

"I think it's somewhere between six and seven hundred square feet. Single bedroom, bathroom, living room, small kitchen. But as a getaway, it's sweet." She led him through to the living room and smiled as his eyes widened. Her easel was set up, and a small covered table held brushes, paint, palette knives and an apron that was smattered with a rainbow of colors. To her it was the most comforting sight in the world. To him, it must look like chaos.

"Wine? I have white and red. I might have a beer in here somewhere."

"None for me. I'll take water if you have it."

She looked at him closely. Realized she'd never actually seen him have a drink other than lemonade or coffee, which he seemed to drink constantly. "I have sparkling."

"That'd be great."

She went to the fridge for the bottle and poured some into a glass with ice, then handed it to him. "Do you mind if I do?" she asked, motioning toward the half-empty bottle of red on the counter.

"Of course not." He smiled at her. "So this is your studio."

"For now. It's a lot smaller than my place in Chicago, but it suits my needs better than I ever expected."

She poured some wine into a glass and turned to him. "I was only going to stay a week or two, you know. Move on like I've been doing for months. And then Tori offered me this place…and it's been wonderful. The peace and quiet. The cute towns and scenery. I understand why you chose it to…" She paused, feeling suddenly awkward. "Well, to regroup, I suppose. Or recharge. I know it's working for me."

"Yeah." He hesitated a moment, then said, "Are you upset about me restoring the lighthouse? I know you've used it as inspiration."

Jess took a sip of her wine. "I was at first. For a few reasons that were nothing but selfish. But what you said about being a steward is right. And so is safety. I'm so sorry I scared you that day."

"It wasn't your fault."

She gestured to the front door. "Do you want to sit outside? There's more room."

"Sure."

The little porch gave a glimpse of the water, and as evening settled around them, they sat in the Adirondack chairs and let the soft sound of the waves soak in. He sipped his water; she savored the wine and let out a happy sigh. The sky turned shades of lilac, peach and pink, a natural palette that filled Jess's soul with comfort.

"It's beautiful tonight."

"Yeah. There's something about the ocean that just calms me and energizes me at the same time."

He let out a long sigh. "It soothes. The sea just is. It crashes and rolls, it waves and breaks and chases the sand. Twice a day it moves in, then retreats, leaving treasures behind. When our world is small and filled with worries, the ocean is endless and constant."

She shouldn't have been surprised at his being poetic; he was a writer after all. But the description touched her just the same. "Is your world small and filled with worries, Bran?" She'd held her breath as he spoke, but now let it out slowly.

"Not as much as it used to be. The sea has worked its magic on me, too."

"I'm glad."

"And so have you."

Her breath stopped. "Me?"

He looked over at her, his eyes black in the growing twilight. "Yes, you. I'm sorry for the way I acted that day." She didn't need to ask which day he meant. "I was feeling guilty, and mad at myself, and I took it out on you. You did nothing wrong, Jess."

She held his gaze. "Neither did you, Bran. You just weren't ready for it. But it wasn't wrong." She reached for his hand. "I might be overstepping here, so please don't be angry when I say very bluntly that you are not married to her anymore."

His throat bobbed as he swallowed, then he squeezed her fingers. "I know. But I'm in that spot where I feel as if moving on means I'm forgetting her."

"You'll never forget her. Allowing yourself to have a life and move on doesn't mean forgetting."

"In my head I know that. But that day, I reacted. I reacted when I kissed you and I reacted when I put you in your car to leave. It was wrong and I owe you an apology."

"Accepted. And I'm thrilled you're writing again."

She thought he would pull his hand away, but he kept his fingers twined with hers and she tried not to think too much about it.

"Me, too. It's slow going, but it's a start. I haven't said anything to anyone else, though. I don't want to set up expectations."

"Not even your agent?"

"Not yet. I want to have a solid start before I talk to him about it. It's early days. But one of the reasons I went to Halifax was to visit the archives and do a little digging."

"And did you find out anything interesting?"

"Lots. Like rumors of U-boats off the coast in the forties. The presence of spies during the war. It's feeding my muse, and she's been hungry a long time."

"Looks like this place is kind of key for both of us. Two lost souls, huh?"

"I'm not feeling so lost right now."

His dark gaze had her insides fluttering again, so she got up and held out her hand. "Can I get you a refill?"

Slowly, ever so slowly, he pushed himself up from the chair. He was so tall, and in the dark, with his beard and hair, he looked intimidating and dangerous. But not truly dangerous...more enigmatic and sexy.

"I can get it."

He took the glass and went inside while Jessica let out a long, slow breath. She was not immune to him in any way. She'd been prepared to be angry with him about the restoration. To let it be the thing that kept him at arm's length. Instead, he'd stated his reasons and the distance evaporated. Every time she set up some sort of block, he knocked it down with ease.

She was here only for the summer. He was not for her. And she seemed to lack the willpower to push him away.

He returned with a full glass and instead of sitting, went to the railing and looked out over the sloping lawn and shrubs to the beach below. "You wanna walk?" he asked.

A moonlight walk on the beach? Could she possibly say no?

"That would be lovely," she whispered.

He drank his water and put the glass down on the arm of the wooden chair, and then held out his hand. She took it, hoping he couldn't tell that hers was shaking. What a ninny she was, trembling over holding hands at her age. It wasn't like she hadn't ever been in love and he was some sort of first. He was just...different.

Like now, with his hair blowing back from his face in the ocean breeze. He'd left his sandals inside her door and his feet were bare as they approached the silky white sand. She tugged on his hand to stop him for a moment while she slipped off her Vans and let her toes sink in, the sand still warm from the day's sun.

He still had her hand. She swallowed tightly and kept her fingers tangled with his. Admitting that she'd been lonely was hard. She considered herself strong and self-reliant. She always had been, with a good dose of obstinacy thrown in for good measure. But she'd needed this, she realized. Even more so since she lost her best friend. She needed contact and intimacy. Clearly Branson Black was not Mr. Right. But he was doing a pretty good job being Mr. Right Now.

"I never imagined soft white sand like this up here," she said, her steps lazy and squishy in the thick sand. "I always imagined it farther south. In the clear waters of the Caribbean. But this is amazing."

He was quiet for a few moments, then lifted his chin and drew in a deep breath of sea air. "I met Jennie in Nova Scotia. Not here. On the other side of the province. I decided to take a road trip and drove north through Maine, took the ferry from New Brunswick to Digby, and ended up on the Fundy coast. She was working the summer doing marine research. My plans to travel to Prince Edward Island and Cape Breton just disappeared. Once I met her, that was it."

"She was from here?"

"No, she was on some university grant summer research program with Boston University. I was still living in Connecticut. For nine months we drove back and forth and saw each other on weekends. And once she graduated I asked her to marry me."

"You were young."

He nodded. Breakers swept over the sand, brushing their feet, and Jess mulled over the fact that he was telling her about his wife while they were holding hands. Still, she wasn't going to interrupt. She was curious, and she got the feeling this was not something he talked about often.

"We were, though she was younger than me. We ended up with a two-year engagement and pulled out all the stops for the wedding." He looked over at her. "I would have been happy with the courthouse, but if you knew Jennie..." His smile was sad. "I wanted to give her everything she desired. And I could, so I did."

"She was lucky to have you, Bran." Jess squeezed his hand as they kept taking lazy steps up the beach.

"Was she? Because I got caught up in myself and didn't cherish her enough. I have regrets, Jessica. More than you know."

She stopped and pulled on his hand, making him stop too as she looked up into his face. "I think whenever someone dies, we all have regrets of some sort. You loved her. Maybe you weren't perfect, but you loved her. That's so clear to see in the way you talk about her."

"I did." He sighed. "Jennie was my home. The warm, loving space I didn't have as a child. And I blew it. I was angry about the accident for a long time, and then the sadness threatened to pull me under. Now I'm wanting to start living again, and it feels so strange to be doing it without her. Without our baby, too. God, he was the sweetest thing." His voice thickened and he cleared his throat. "I hope you never have to go through anything like that in your life. I wouldn't wish it on my worst enemy."

He turned and they started walking again, while Jess's thoughts were in turmoil. She'd had her share of loss; not just Ana but of her adopted mother, too. Her dad was still around but had remarried, and they weren't that close. And while her life growing up had been okay, she'd always wondered about her birth parents. She knew nothing about them.

"I was adopted when I was two. I don't have memories of before, but I know that CPS stepped in and removed me from my home when I was a year old. After my parents divorced I stayed with my mom. And then she died several years ago. I was nearly engaged once, but he didn't want to wait for me. So I guess we all have something. You're holding on to regrets. I think I'm just used to the people I love not sticking around."

"Damn. I'm sorry. I mean, I'm not particularly close with my family. My dad is a workaholic and a bit… I don't know, cold. And my mom is okay, but we've never been a tight family. Still, I know they're there."

"And they sent you off to boarding school."

"Yeah, but you know what? I met my best friends in the world. It ended up being the best thing that could have happened. Cole and Jeremy became my family."

She smiled a little. "You certainly seem to have good memories."

"The best." He sighed. "You know, my life's been a bit charmed. Yeah, I lost Jennie and Owen, but we loved each other. I'm blessed to have had that, I guess."

They'd stopped again, and she turned to face him and put her arms around his middle, wrapping him in a hug. What a bittersweet blessing, to have found perfection and to lose it so young.

"Hey," he said softly, and his wide, warm hand came to rest on the middle of her back.

She sniffled. "Sorry. I just thought you needed a hug. Or that I needed to give you one."

"It's okay. You can hug me."

And his other arm came around her and hugged her back.

Bran drank in the scent of her hair, something soft and floral that mixed with the salty tang of the sea. She was so warm, and so very, very generous. What she'd said about her childhood was surprising. He'd imagined her having this warm and picture-perfect family, completely well-adjusted and loving. But she'd had her share of heartbreak, too, and yet she still found a way to be…open.

It took a certain strength to be able to do that. And something special to make him respond to it, after months of numbness.

Jennie would have liked her. It should feel odd to have such a thought, but somehow it wasn't. Jennie had had that sweetness wrapped in strength, too.

It felt so good to be held.

He pulled her closer against him, let his hand glide over her back, touching warm skin. God, so good, the touch of another human being. She responded, slipping her hands beneath the hem of his T-shirt, and he could feel the gentle marking of her fingernails on his back. He groaned with pleasure, moving his hand down her ribs, his thumb grazing the tender skin between breast and waist through the soft material.

"Bran," she whispered, and his body came alive.

He lowered his head and nuzzled at her ear, pleased when goose bumps erupted on her skin. She tilted her head, and he touched his lips to the soft skin of her neck, up to her jawline, over to her lips, which were slack and waiting for him. The kiss was a wild and wonderful thing, full of passion and acknowledgment of their attraction. She stood up on tiptoe and wrapped her arms around his neck; he lifted her up off her toes and held her flush against his body as he plundered her mouth. Her hands sank into his hair and his pulse leaped. If he wasn't careful, he was going to lay her down on the sand right here and now. At Jeremy's house. He understood now why his lighthouse was the perfect spot for a tryst. A little ocean, some moonlight, add a lot of desire and things had a way of happening.

Her chest heaved with her breathing, and he placed his hand over her heart. He was shocked to discover she wasn't wearing a bra as her small, firm breast pressed against his hand.

His control was on shaky ground.

So he lifted her up in his arms, cradling her close, and started walking toward the water.

He was nearly to his knees when Jessica figured out what he was doing. She pushed against him and started to laugh and protest at the same time. "Bran! No! You are not going to throw me in the water!"

He grinned. "Throw? No. But we need to cool off, and there's only one way I can think of to do that."

She struggling against him some more, but suddenly she was laughing too, and the sound filled his heart with something that felt…joyful. Water splashed up over his knees as the waves rolled in. It was cold; there was definitely going to be some temperature shock. But nature's equivalent of a cold shower was in both their best interests right now.

"Bran!" she exclaimed, as a wave rose up and touched her bottom, making her arch against him.

He laughed, the sound rumbling in his chest before erupting into the evening air. His shorts were wet now, and another step had them in up to his waist. "Ready?" he asked.

"No!" She squealed and twisted in his arms, laughing the whole time. "You are not going to drop me into the ocean. You are not—"

He took one more step, then let her go with a splash. And then he dove under, hoping to cool his jets.

When he surfaced about ten feet away, Jessica had come up and was still spluttering and wiping her hair away from her face. She looked so indignant that he burst out laughing. The look she turned on him was positively venomous, and then she started toward him. When she was five, maybe six feet away, she started splashing him, the water hitting him in the face and he had to stop laughing to keep from getting a mouthful. Instead he turned, stepped toward her and yanked her close, where she couldn't splash anymore.

"You. Are. Incorrigible." She was still laughing but said the last word on a sigh. He kept his arm around her and she kicked up from the bottom, pointing her toes up through the surface. "I can't believe you did that."

"Me either." He let her go, and they bobbed around in the water for a few minutes. His cargo shorts were heavy and his T-shirt uncomfortable, and his legs were already starting to go numb from the cold. Still, he found it hard to be sorry. It had been so long since he'd done anything impulsive or…or fun. Kissing Jessica and then taking a plunge in the Atlantic had been both.

Her dress billowed around her, moving with the waves as she ran her fingers through her hair, which was far darker now that it was wet. It made her skin glow in the moonlight, and her eyes shone at him. Quick as anything, she ducked under the water, the tips of her toes giving a little splash like a mermaid. When she surfaced, she was several feet away, standing hip deep in the water.

The fabric of her dress clung to her skin, highlighting every curve and point, and his mouth went dry. Perhaps a dunking in the sea hadn't been the best plan after all.

Sex would be a mistake. For both of them. Wouldn't it?

To distract himself, he swam out until he started to get tired, and then turned to come back. Jess was treading water a few hundred yards away, as if waiting for him. He swam in, and then they went to shore together. The exertion had helped expend some of his restless energy, and when they got to the shore, they hurried out of the water and onto the beach.

"Come up to the boathouse and towel off. You must be freezing."

No more than she was.

The slow, meandering walk of earlier was replaced by quick steps in the sand, and a shorter angle to the path leading away from the beach. Jessica stopped and grabbed her shoes, and when she stood he noticed her lips were blue from cold. He was shivering, too. The days had been summerlike, but the nights were still chilly and being soaking wet made it even worse. In the space of a few minutes, they were at the boathouse. He stood on the mat while she disappeared into the bathroom and returned with two big, fluffy towels.

She scrubbed her hair and rubbed it over her arms and legs. He did the same. And wished her dress wasn't quite so see-through. It wasn't helping his resolve to keep things nonsexual.

"You're freezing," she said, looking up at him. "Let me put your things in the dryer."

"I don't exactly have anything to change into."

Suggestion swirled around them, but Jessica was the one to break the moment. "I have a blanket. I know it's not optimal, but you can't go home like that. Unless you want to go to Jeremy's and ask for a change of clothes."

He lifted an eyebrow. "No, thanks. He'll ask too many questions."

"Well, then. Hang on."

She disappeared into the bathroom and came out again with another towel and a soft blanket. She handed him the towel first. "You can put this on like a skirt, to cover your...sensitive bits." Her cheeks flushed. "And then wrap the blanket around you."

He grabbed at the hem of his T-shirt and swept it over his head, though it stuck to his shoulders as he pulled it off. He dropped it on the floor with the first towel, and when he saw her owlish expression at his bare chest he paused with his fingers on the button of his shorts.

Her cheeks were ruddy now and she turned away. "I'll just go change and then put my stuff in with yours."

A laugh built in his chest as he took off his shorts and secured the towel away from his…what had she called them? Sensitive bits. The blanket was large enough that he wrapped it around himself like a cape. When she emerged from the bedroom, she gathered up his wet clothes and scuttled off to the laundry room. He heard a few beeps and then the low hum of the dryer.

When she came back out, she stopped in the kitchen and put water in her kettle. She'd changed into yoga pants and a soft sweatshirt with paint stains on it. Her hair was starting to dry a little, with bits of natural curl framing her face. He felt like an idiot standing there in a towel and blanket, but what the hell. Nothing about their relationship so far had been ordinary or exactly comfortable.

She looked over at him and laughed. "You look silly."

"I feel silly."

"How about that drink now? I have some Scotch. It might warm you up."

He met her gaze. "I don't drink anymore."

Her face changed. First there was surprise, followed swiftly by embarrassment. Then a growing realization and acceptance. She'd been at his house. To Jeremy's for drinks, but he'd never partaken in anything alcoholic. He didn't make a big deal of it, but he could see her putting the pieces together.

In her blunt fashion, she met his gaze and asked, "Are you an alcoholic?"

CHAPTER SEVEN

BRAN SHRUGGED AS he considered her question. "I don't know. I mean, I don't know if there's an actual criteria I would meet or anything. What I do know is that I was self-medicating to deal with my grief, and I stopped." He hesitated, then decided to be completely honest. "Jennie would be pretty angry with me if she knew I'd turned to alcohol as a coping mechanism."

"What took its place?"

"Getting out of New York. Long walks on the beach. And there were times it was really hard. But I don't keep any in my house, and it makes it easier."

Her lips dropped open and an expression of dismay darkened her face. "Oh, Bran. I gave you a bottle of wine that first day for stress. I'm so sorry."

He waved it away, and nearly dropped the blanket. "Don't be. You didn't know. I've still got it. You're welcome to it sometime when you're visiting."

Her blue eyes touched his. "Will I be visiting?"

It was hard to draw breath. This was the moment where they were maybe becoming a thing. Maybe not sex. Maybe not ever sex. But agreeing to spend time together rather than finding ways not to or chalking it up to coincidence. He nodded slightly. "If you want to."

Her voice was soft. "I'd like that."

He was in danger of moving closer to her again, what with her soft voice and big eyes. "Can we sit down somewhere? I'm feeling kind of ridiculous here."

"Of course!" Her eyes sparkled as she looked at him. "If you can make it around the drop cloth, there's a decent sofa."

He took a look at her current painting as he went by. It was the lighthouse, a full rendering of it, with the soft colors of a sunrise taking shape behind. She was so talented. Even partially completed, the painting seemed to breathe, have a life of its own. "This is beautiful, Jess."

She turned and smiled, then gestured toward the sofa. "Thank you. I'm playing with some colors with that one, and so far I'm liking it."

They sat on the sofa, the plush cushions soft and comfortable. Jess tucked her feet up underneath herself, relaxed in the corner of the sofa. It was a bit more difficult for him to find a comfortable spot, what with the towel and the blanket. When he finally got situated, she was grinning broadly.

"Don't make fun of me," he said, but his voice held a trace of humor.

"Hey, you were the one who decided to go for the swim, not me."

A sigh escaped his lips. "Only because we were getting too close to…"

His words trailed off. To what? Making a mistake? Making love? Both phrases made his chest tighten. He opted for humor. "To getting naked on Jeremy's beach."

She coughed and laughed at the same time. "Oh, can you imagine if they'd seen…"

He met her gaze evenly. "That dip was my equivalent of a cold shower. I like you, Jess. We have chemistry." She made a sound that was the equivalent of "yeah, we sure do." He held the blanket tightly in his fingers. "I'm not sure sex is in our best interests right now."

She nodded. He wished he didn't notice how full her lips were when they were open just that little bit. Or how her eyes glowed, the little tiny striations of gold and green in the blue making him think of the water at the edge of the lake at Merrick. Or even how her chest rose and fell anytime things heated up between them. Even now, just talking about it and not touching. He was so attuned to her.

Her throat bobbed as she swallowed. "Because of Jennie."

"Yeah. It wouldn't be fair to you."

"Tell me about her, Bran."

He broke eye contact and looked away. Across the room was a matching love seat and one of the pillows was out of place.

But she edged over closer to him and put her hand on his blanket-covered knee. "You need to talk about her. There's no judgment here, Bran. Just talk. Tell me what she was like. Tell me why it's so hard." She squeezed his knee. "I can put on some coffee if you want."

He debated. It was strange thinking about telling the woman you'd almost had sex with about your dead wife. And yet not so strange thinking about telling Jess. Besides, if she knew everything, maybe this horrible, wonderful attraction between them would be nonexistent, and he wouldn't have to worry about making a mistake.

"I don't need coffee," he murmured, resting his hands on his knees. The hem of the towel cut into his pelvis, but he didn't care.

He'd already told her about how he and Jennie had met. But the last year of their marriage…everything had changed.

"The year or so before they died was really different for

us," he began. "Owen had been born, and Jennie was such an amazing mother. Like Tori, you know? Loving and caring and tired and fun. She'd spend hours counting his toes and making him laugh. Or just sitting in a rocking chair with him while he slept, wanting to hold on to those first baby days forever." Emotion rose in a wave and he fought it back, not wanting his voice to crack as they spoke.

"Does seeing Tori make it worse for you?" she asked softly.

"Sometimes. It just hurts, seeing Rose grow and knowing that one day soon she'll start having the milestones that Owen never had. But it's not their fault, and he's my best friend. I can't stay away, you know? That's not fair."

She nodded and put her hand on his back, rubbing reassuringly, just like she'd done that day of their picnic on the rock. "But it still hurts."

"Yeah." He took a deep breath. "My career had really taken off by then. My eighth book had just released, and it was a big deal. It hit the lists in its first week, and there was a bunch of appearances set up." He frowned. "I let it go to my head a little bit. I had to be here, there. Signing books. Doing interviews. I'd gone to our apartment in the city for a few weeks to tackle it all, planning to go home on the weekend in between. But another opportunity came up and I was so tired that I stayed in the city." He tried not to think about the argument he'd had with Jennie about not going home that weekend. She'd been 100 percent right about how he was losing sight of his family.

"The next week Jennie decided to surprise me by driving up from Connecticut. We'd fought about me not being home, and we didn't fight often so it felt so very wrong and off. I had no idea what she was planning until I got the call from the police." His chest cramped so much it nearly made him lose his breath. "I was listed as next of kin, our address the one in New Haven. By the time they reached me, the accident had been cleared and their bodies at the hospital."

His voice finally broke. "I can still see them there, Jess. She was cut up bad. But Owen…he looked like he'd just gone off to sleep. God, I pray he was sleeping and never felt anything. I hope it was all so fast that neither of them suffered or knew what was happening." The well of emotion threatened to strangle him. "They shouldn't have been on the road that night. And they wouldn't have been, if I'd been less full of myself and had gone home as we planned. All she wanted was for us to spend time together as a family, and I was too damned important and busy."

Jess's hand was still rubbing his back. "You blame yourself."

"Of course I do!" he snapped, then let out a breath. "She was my wife. He was my son. The two most important people in the world to me, and I let them down so badly. It should have been me."

"You don't feel you deserve to live."

"No! Yes. I don't know." He shifted away from her hand. "That's the thing, Jess. For a long time, I didn't want to live. And now I do, and I'm left wondering if that makes me a horrible person."

Jess was quiet for a long moment. She finally let out a long breath and angled her body toward him. "When Ana got sick, I was so damned angry. But I didn't cause her cancer. You didn't cause that accident. It was an accident, and they happen."

"But she wouldn't have been on the road at all if I had just gone home like she'd asked."

"And maybe you would have had an accident going home. Would you want Jennie to feel like if she just hadn't asked you to come home that you'd still be alive?"

"Of course not."

"She made a choice, Bran. She could have waited until the weekend. She could have taken a different route, left at a different time. Ana might not have had cancer. What I'm saying is…to think any of this is actually within our control is so flawed. But we look for explanations and blame so we have somewhere to put our grief."

She sniffled and Bran realized she was crying. He wasn't, not this time, but she was, and seeing the wetness on her cheeks and the redness of her eyes nearly undid him. She was so beautiful, inside and out. And he was so very unworthy.

He pulled her close. "You loved her very much."

"More than anyone ever in my life, I think. Even the guy I thought I was going to marry."

"Were you *in* love with her?"

She lifted her head sharply, looked into his eyes. "Oh… no. Not that way."

He chuckled and his arm tightened around her. "Are you surprised I asked?"

"A little. Would it matter to you?"

He shook his head and lifted his shoulders in a shrug. "Why would it? It takes all kinds of love to make the world go round. I never assume anything."

She pushed away and turned on the sofa, sitting with her legs crossed, but she still held his hand. "You know, I didn't expect you to surprise me more than you already have tonight, but you just did." A sweet smile touched her lips. "And every time you surprise me, I like you a little bit more."

She shouldn't like him. It made things harder. And yet he found himself rubbing his thumb over her wrist in a comforting gesture. He could still see the trails tears had made on her cheeks. "I'm sorry you lost her," he said quietly. "She sounds like a wonderful woman."

"She was. And I'm sorry you lost Jennie and Owen. But we're alive, Bran. You and me. Alive and we have lives to live. You can't punish yourself forever. I can't be sad forever."

"Jess…"

"And I feel most alive when I'm with you."

If she kept it up with that soft voice and her big eyes, he was going to have to go for another dip in the sea. He should look away. But he couldn't. Her gaze held him prisoner, his breath shortened as the moment drew out. He was still holding her hand; meanwhile the towel and blanket were feeling rather constrictive.

"I'm not relationship material, Jess. You need to know that. I have nothing to offer someone in that way."

Had she somehow moved closer? "I don't recall asking for a relationship. Or any sort of promises," she whispered. "I don't want them, Bran. I'm here for a matter of weeks, and then I'm going back to my life." She lifted her other hand and cupped his jaw. "Besides, I'm trying this thing where I live in the moment."

In this moment he knew exactly what he wanted. But she asked him first.

"Stay with me," she murmured.

He swallowed around a lump in his throat, his heart pounding with what he was sure were equal measures of arousal and fear.

But he didn't have time to think. Jess shifted and slid one leg over him, so that she was straddling him and he was having serious doubts about the reliability of the towel. She kissed him softly, on the crests of his cheeks, the corners of his eyes, the spot just above his lower lip, until he could hardly breathe. In less than a moment he lifted his arms, sending the blanket cape falling to the side as he wrapped her in a tight embrace. And then they kissed, long, slow, deep, until his brain was swimming with nothing but the feel of her, the scent of her skin, soft and salty from the sea.

When the sofa grew uncomfortable, Jess slid off his lap and held out her hand. He knew what she was asking. Knew it might be a mistake. But he also knew he had never wanted something so badly. This feeling alive thing was addictive, and he needed another hit. There was one thing standing in his way, though. And it was something he'd never risk.

"Jess, I'm not prepared."

Her cheeks pinkened delightfully, but she shook her head. "It's okay. I've been on the pill for years."

He put his hand in hers and stood, his towel falling away.

Jess tried not to stare, but Bran was standing naked in her living room. Tall and lean, with a small scar on his lower right abdomen, and a soft dusting of hair from his chest down to his navel. She wanted this. But the fierceness with which she wanted him was unfamiliar, and gave her a moment's pause.

Then she met his gaze and he lifted a single eyebrow. She tugged on his hand, leading him past her easel and canvas to the small bedroom and the bottom bunk.

"There's not a lot of head room," she whispered, catching her breath when he came up behind her and his body grazed hers.

"I'm not planning on standing up." His voice was low and seductive, warm at her ear. "Unless you want to."

Oh, my.

Jess took a deep breath and pulled off her hoodie. She

still wasn't wearing a bra, and the night air made goose bumps rise on her skin. Wordlessly she shimmied out of her yoga pants, and once she was naked, Bran reached out and pulled her close.

She was afraid. Not of him. But of being overwhelmed.

But he took his time, kissing her, touching her with light strokes, lighting her on fire and making her melt at the same time. His skin was warm on hers, and she marveled at the intimacy of the feeling, skin on skin. When her knees grew weak and he laid her down on the mattress, his eyes found hers in the dim moonlight cast through the window. "Okay?" he asked.

Tears pricked her eyes and she blinked them away. He was so considerate. So gentle. So…everything.

"More than okay," she assured him.

His gaze held hers, his eyes widening for a moment as they came together, key into lock. Jess felt a pang in her heart, the bittersweet knowledge that she'd fallen for a man she couldn't have, or could have but only for a little while.

But living in the moment meant embracing the moment, and she was determined to do that. So she reached up and looped her hand around his neck, pulling him down for a kiss. If she couldn't have Branson as her love, she could at least have him for her lover. And when their breathing finally slowed and the sweat dried from their skin, she had no regrets.

Jess shifted beneath the blanket, trying not to wake Bran. The sun was barely up, and the light in the bedroom was watery and dim. But it was enough that she could make out his features completely. The bit of hair that was in a tangle on the pillow. His lips, open slightly as he slept, and the way he linked his fingers together over his belly. She liked that the most, as it seemed like a cute little quirk individual to him. He was a back sleeper. She was usually a sprawler, but sprawling was impossible in a bed this size and shared with a man of his build.

They were both naked under the covers. His clothes were still in the dryer, and she was on the inside of the bed, closest to the wall, and hadn't gotten up to pull something on after…

After.

Her chest cramped, in both delicious memory and delightful anticipation. He'd been a thorough, attentive lover. There'd been a moment where something threatened to overwhelm her, and maybe him, too. Their eyes had met and their smiles faded. In that moment sex had become more than just sex. It had become his first time since Jennie. She was sure of that. And for her…

It had been connection. Bone-deep, in-the-blood connection with another human being. For all her live-in-the-moment Zen-ness, deep connections, trust…those were rare occurrences. It was why losing Ana had hurt so badly.

People didn't tend to stay in her life. But this time there was no danger of that. She was going into this with the knowledge and understanding that in a matter of weeks, they'd both be moving on. No surprises, no being blindsided, no one hurt. Bran let out a sigh and something soft and sentimental wound through her at the sound. A smile touched her lips. This summer would be one of healing, for both of them if they were lucky. And they'd be able to look back on this as the summer they made their way back to the living, with fond memories.

Bran stirred and shifted to his side, then his eyes slowly opened. She met his gaze evenly, the smile still on her lips. "Good morning," she whispered.

"Good morning." His cheeks colored a little and she loved that he was blushing right now, just a hint of pink above his beard.

"You okay?" Mornings-after could be awkward. Things were different in the light of day. Last night they'd been swept up in each other, but now...now they had to navigate the dynamic.

He nodded slightly, then shifted his arm and said, "Come here."

She shifted over and curled in next to his side. His skin was soft and warm, and the smattering of hair on his chest tickled her breasts.

His arm tightened around her. "I'm okay. You?"

She nodded, her cheek rubbing against his shoulder. "Me, too. I was afraid it might be...awkward."

He chuckled, a low sound that moved his chest and made her smile. "It is, a little. I'm very out of practice with mornings-after. But..." He moved his head so that he was looking down at her, and she tilted up her chin. "We've been fairly gentle with each other so far. I figure if we can keep doing that, we're okay."

"Except, you know, when you kicked me off your property."

A smile lit his face. "Yeah, except then. And when I saved you with my boat. I didn't say you weren't a pain in my ass."

She laughed, then they grew quiet again. She was thinking about how their friendship had evolved when her stomach growled loudly in the silence.

"Someone is hungry."

"I have eggs and sourdough bread. Maybe even some bacon. You want breakfast?"

"I would. But it means not sneaking away before Jeremy has a chance to see my car."

She pushed away and rested on her elbows so she could see him better. "That would bother you, huh."

"Him knowing? Not that, exactly. It's more the questions to follow." He lifted an eyebrow. "I hate when people want me to explain myself."

"I have an answer for that."

"Do tell."

She grinned. "Practice saying this phrase—*It's none of your business.*"

Bran's face straightened into a serious expression. "It's none of your business."

"Nope. Not convinced. Try again."

This time it was accompanied by an angled eyebrow. "It's none of your business."

"Better. Let's practice some more. Hey, Bran, how's the new novel coming?"

He grinned. "It's none of your business."

"What's it about? Come on, you can tell me that."

Firmer this time: "It's none of your business."

"Good! And wow. You spent the night with Jess. Are you sure that was a good thing?"

He rolled slightly and placed a kiss on her naked shoulder. "Oh, I'm very sure it was a good thing," he replied, his voice husky.

"Tsk-tsk. That's not the right answer."

"Yes, it is," he murmured, running his fingers through her hair. "But it's none of Jeremy's business, or Tori's either." He kissed her, long and slow, and then slid out from beneath the covers and left the bedroom, presumably heading toward the dryer and his clothes.

Her body was still humming from the power of that kiss, though. He was very, very good at it.

She slipped out from beneath the sheets and pulled on underwear and last night's yoga pants and top. She'd shower later, before she had to make the trip to Halifax to pick up more supplies.

Branson was in the kitchen, already boiling water for making coffee in her French press, his shorts and T-shirt wrinkled from being in the dryer overnight, but looking entirely scrumptious. She let him work his magic—clearly he knew his way around coffee—and dug out eggs, and bacon she bought at the farmer's market. She put the latter to fry in a cast iron pan, then set to work slicing sourdough bread for toast.

The scent of bacon and coffee filled the air and she smiled up at Bran, who'd found her mugs and had poured her a cup of coffee. It was nice having him here, though it played havoc with her heart a little. She was not sticking around. It wouldn't be good to get used to this kind of domestic scene, would it?

Bran took over toasting the bread while Jess drained the bacon and then cracked eggs into the pan. "How do you like your eggs? Over? Yolks hard or soft?"

"Over and just set."

Just like she preferred hers.

Soon they were seated at her tiny table, with bacon, eggs, and pots of butter and jam between them for the toast. "Delicious," Bran said, chewing on a strip of bacon.

"Big breakfast is one of my favorites," she admitted. "Sometimes I even like having breakfast for dinner."

He laughed. "Me, too. Only with pancakes."

"Mmm… Or waffles."

She spread raspberry jam on her toast and took a bite. "So. What's on your agenda for today?"

He shrugged. "Changing my clothes. Going over some of the stuff from yesterday, with the restoration and stuff. You?"

"Actually, I think I'm the one heading to Halifax today.

I want to visit a shop there for more supplies. I've only been there once since arriving. To be honest, I could stand a little city life for a day. As much as I love all this nature, I miss people sometimes. The vitality of it."

Bran was quiet for a moment, took a sip of his coffee, then looked her in the eye. "What if I went with you? We could make a day of it. You could pick up your supplies, and we could go for dinner someplace nice downtown."

"Like a date?"

Again, he shrugged. "If you want to call it that. We could just call it hanging out."

It did sound lovely. A couple of hours drive on a beautiful summer day, an errand or two, and then a fine dinner... She hadn't done that in a long time. Especially with company. She'd spent the last several months traveling alone, and she'd enjoyed it, but she couldn't deny it was a lonely existence.

"You're welcome to come along."

"Do you want me to drive, or take yours?" He lifted an eyebrow. "If we take mine, you can have some wine with dinner. I'm happy to be your designated driver."

It was a generous offer, but she already felt a little odd, considering he wasn't drinking at all. "I don't need wine," she said, popping the last crust of toast into her mouth.

"You say that, but the place I have in mind has a very good wine list. And it doesn't bother me, Jess. Truly."

She took his plate and stacked it on her own. "Then I accept. It sounds like a very nice day, and since my cooking is plain at best, a dinner out sounds lovely."

"Perfect." He pushed away from the table and then checked his watch. "It's nearly eight. Jeremy will have noticed my car by now. Time to answer the inevitable questions, and head home for a shower. What time should I pick you up?"

She pondered for a moment. "Eleven? It would give me a couple of hours to work before we go."

"Sounds perfect."

She took the dishes to the sink, and when she turned back again, there was an odd moment where they stood and stared at each other.

"Okay. So the awkward exit is a thing," he said, then took a step forward and kissed her on the cheek. "Thanks for last night," he murmured, his lips close to her ear. "I'll see you in a few hours."

She nodded, feeling a little breathless.

And then he was gone.

Jess stared at the door for ten seconds, then shook herself into action. First, work. Then, a shower.

And then, the rest of the day with a man who could never really be hers.

CHAPTER EIGHT

Bran returned at just past eleven o'clock. He'd left without encountering Jeremy, nor was there any questioning text message from either him or Tori. They either hadn't noticed his car, or they were minding their own business. If he were a betting man, he'd say they had slept in and missed his exit. Because Jeremy wouldn't hesitate to put in his two cents.

This time, instead of parking in the main driveway, he pulled in next to Jess's car. She came outside and shut the door behind her, and his breath caught a little.

He wasn't supposed to be feeling this way. Not now. Maybe not ever. And yet he wasn't going to cancel their plans. It was just a summer thing. He wasn't going to fall in love, so that wasn't an issue. And they were both clear on that, weren't they? She was leaving to go back to Chicago. Why shouldn't they combat some of their loneliness with each other?

Jess wore a pretty little dress with a light blue background and tiny pink flowers, with cute little blue sandals on her feet. She looked as fresh and pretty as a spring morning, with her sunny hair shining and grazing the tips of her shoulders in soft waves. A bag was slung over her shoulder, a pastel-colored tapestry kind of thing that suited her completely. "Have you been waiting?" she asked, descending the two steps to the graveled walk.

"Only for a few minutes. You look very nice." He moved to the passenger side to open her door. Lord, she smelled delicious, too. Like sweet peas softened by hints of vanilla.

"Thanks." She smiled up at him. "No paint-stained jeans and tees for me today. If we're going to dinner, I wanted to dress up a little."

She looked him up and down too, as he held open the door. "You also look very nice."

He needed a haircut, but there hadn't been time. But he'd trimmed his beard and put aside jeans and tees for dress pants and a button-down shirt in off-white.

"Well, let's hit the road," he suggested, and watched the long length of her leg as she slid into the car and he shut the door behind her.

They drove to Halifax in just under two hours. The highway traffic was light, and they only hit one small section of construction. Bran used the car's GPS to navigate his way to the art supply store Jess had picked, and went inside with her as she browsed and made her purchases. They stowed everything in his trunk, and then he suggested a walk in the popular public gardens.

The sun was bright, and there was a light breeze as they made their way to the entrance. "It's a beautiful day," she said, letting out a happy sigh. "This was such a good idea, Bran."

"The gardens will be packed, but I hear they're beautiful. If you like flowers."

She patted her bag. "I'll make a confession. I brought a small sketch pad with me."

He laughed. Laughing was so easy with her, particularly when she looked up at him with a twinkle in her eye. "Of course you did."

"Don't tell me you don't always have a notebook with you."

He angled a wry look in her direction. "Of course I don't." Then after a moment, he added, "I voice record on my phone."

But he wasn't interested in dictating now. He just wanted to spend the afternoon with her, in the early summer sun, and live in the moment.

It was miles better than living in the past.

The garden was heavy with tourists and what appeared to be a couple of bus tour groups. As they entered the ornate iron gates, a strange amphibious vehicle approached the intersection, loaded with tourists and a guide narrating local history. They sent up a strange cry of "ribbit-ribbit" as they passed, and then Bran chuckled. "The Harbor Hopper," he said, nudging her and pointing. "Want to go? From the look of it, it's one of those land and sea tour things."

"Oh, my," she replied, laughing as the vehicle pulled away, the guide changing topic. "I'm not sure I'm dressed for that."

"I'm sure you wouldn't fall in." He took her hand in his. "But if you did, I'm a strong swimmer."

"One ocean rescue is enough for me." She pushed up her sunglasses. "Oh, Bran. You were right, this is gorgeous."

They wandered along the paths, meandering slowly around all the different flower beds, examining species of tree and shrub and bloom. Couples posed for pictures and selfies on a small stone bridge, and Jess kindly offered to snap photos of a couple on their honeymoon. The smell was absolutely heavenly: fresh-cut grass and the heavy, sweet scent of lilacs; rhododendrons in various shades of purple, the size of cars, were in full, showy bloom, and the annual flower beds offered bright rainbows of colors. They ambled in the shade and stopped for Jess to take out her pencils and sketch a laburnum tree, the yellow chains of flowers reminding Bran of a sunshine-hued wisteria.

They stopped again and sat on a bench near the pond. A middle-aged man fed the ducks on the bank, and Bran was happy to sit and watch as Jess worked away, her pencil strokes brisk and confident. A tiny replica of the *Titanic* floated on the water, and Bran considered telling Jess the city's connection to the disaster, only he didn't want to interrupt her.

She was in another world when she sketched. Her focus was razor sharp, and nothing escaped her notice as her gaze darted between subject and paper.

He was happy to people watch. He leaned back on the bench, crossed an ankle over his knee, and watched the dynamics between parents and children, old and young, couples on dates and those who seemed to have been together for a long time. They were the ones who didn't have to hold hands to show intimacy; it was in their relaxed body language and the easy way they touched each other in passing, speaking of a comfort and devotion that pricked at Bran's capricious contentment. Strangers wandered together, name tags stuck to their shirts from some sort of guided tour. They were smiling and polite as they talked to each other, pointing out blossoms and reading the species signs dotted throughout the garden.

A father and son left the pathway nearby, the boy holding his dad's hand as they picked their way over the grass toward a handful of ducks near the water's edge. "Dada, ducks!" the boy exclaimed. Bran guessed he was maybe three. He swallowed thickly. Owen would be about the same age now, if he were alive. Would he have liked ducks? Held Bran's hand, maybe in Central Park on Saturdays?

Watching the two of them play by the water, the way

the father patiently kept the boy from the edge, or pointed out all the different colored feathers from each species, warmed his heart. The ache was bittersweet; he was sure he would never quite get over losing his child. But it hurt less today.

Jess looked over at him, put her hand on his knee. "They're sweet, aren't they?"

He nodded, unable to tear his eyes away. "He's a good dad."

"You can have it again someday, you know," she offered gently. "When you're ready."

Bran tore himself away from the father and son scene and met her gaze. "No," he said quietly. "I can't. I can't go through that again. But I'm getting to a place where I'm okay with it."

"Then maybe you'll get to a place where you'll consider it again, too. You never know."

But he shook his head. "No," he repeated. "I know. I had my shot at a family, and I won't chance going through this hell again."

The pink in her cheeks deepened. "I'm sorry," she murmured. "I didn't mean to press."

"You didn't. It's just…there's not much I'm sure of. But that's one thing I am. And I've made my peace with it."

The father and son had moved on, skirting the pond. And Bran got up from the bench, ready to move on, as well.

Jess shoved her sketch pad into her bag and hurried to catch up with Bran, who was starting down the path toward the middle of the gardens. She hadn't meant to upset him, but clearly she had. She should have known better than to bring up fatherhood. It was still too raw for him. At the same time, she'd never been more sure that their relationship was destined for a dead end. He really didn't want a family again, and she did. Being with him, and being around the Fishers had shown her that she did want children of her own. And a partner to share life with. And yet something held her back from saying the words out loud. She could tell Bran all about life not giving guarantees, but she also understood why a person wouldn't want to set themselves up for potential heartbreak.

After all, she'd been doing it for years.

And still there was Bran to consider. It would be easier to end things right now. Probably smarter, too. But she didn't want to. Not yet.

"Hey, wait up," she called, trotting to catch up to him. When she did, she took a deep breath and matched her steps to his. "You gonna be okay?"

He nodded. "Yeah. I'm okay."

"I overstepped, Bran. I really am sorry."

He reached down for her hand, a reassuring gesture that touched her heart. "I know you are. And don't worry about pressing me. It's good for me. It helps, even when it makes me grumpy."

Forgiven, she kept her hand in his as they made their way to the large gazebo that was the centerpiece of the gardens. People milled around, and there was a line at a small building to their left, which appeared to house public bathrooms and a small café, complete with ice cream. The large patio area was full of people enjoying the sweet, cold treat. "You want some?" Bran asked.

"Do you?" She wasn't really hungry, even though they hadn't had lunch. The big breakfast had been super filling, but could she really pass up ice cream in the park?

"A small one? It looks delicious."

They detoured into the building and waited in line for the hand-paddled treat. When they got to the front of the line, she chose blueberries and cream for her flavor.

Bran went for a more sedate maple walnut, and then they emerged out into the bright sunshine again.

"Let's find a place to sit," he suggested. "Someplace with shade. I don't want to be responsible for you getting a sunburn."

She was sure the sun had already left a bit of a burn on her shoulders. Her pale complexion meant she burned easily, and she hadn't thought to bring sunscreen today. "How about up there?" She pointed to the top end of the garden, where there was an open area bordered by benches and leafy trees. There was even a chess table adding character to the area.

"Perfect."

Her ice cream was starting to melt by the time they got to the benches, and they picked one that was shaded and would remain so as the sun shifted. For several minutes they ate in comfortable silence. Despite the earlier tension, Jess couldn't remember the last time she'd been so comfortable with someone. They didn't need to talk. Didn't need to fill up the space with empty words that meant nothing. She finished her ice cream, and he finished his, and he took their garbage to a nearby trash can. When he came back, he put his arm along the back of the bench, and she relaxed against him, her head resting in the curve of his shoulder.

"People watching," he said softly. "I love people watching."

"Ana and I used to make up stories about people," she offered, a smile touching her lips. "Like that woman there." She nodded toward a woman several yards away, sitting on an identical bench and reading. "What's her story, do you think?"

Bran tapped a finger to his lips. "She's waiting for

someone, but he's late. He's always late, so she brings a book so she doesn't look as if she's waiting."

"Well, that's sad. Why does she have to be waiting for a man, anyway?" She lifted her eyebrows. "I think she's single. Maybe she's just broken up with someone because she wants to be put first. So she's putting herself first and spending an afternoon exactly how she wants—in the gardens in the sunshine and with a good book."

"The heroine of her own life."

"You bet." She grinned up at him. "Do you always go for the sad and tragic?"

"Waiting for someone isn't exactly tragic."

"I don't know. Waiting for someone who is chronically late and doesn't care enough to show up on time… I mean, if someone loves you, they should be impatient. Like they can't wait for that moment when they see you again. A thirst that needs to be quenched."

He laughed and squeezed her shoulder a little. "Are you sure you're not a writer?"

"I'm an observer," she answered. "Okay, tell me another one."

He looked around for a moment, then nodded. "That old gentleman there." The man in question was walking slowly along the path with the aid of a cane. A cap shielded his eyes, and he wore a long-sleeved shirt and pants even though the day was hot. "He comes here every day to walk. He used to come here with his wife, but she's no longer with him. But it doesn't matter to him. He's not sad. He walks and he remembers, and he's thankful for the years they had together. And when he gets home to his little apartment, he tells her picture about everything he saw. Because she's still with him."

She loved the wistful picture he drew with words. "You're a romantic, Branson Black. Don't deny it."

He shrugged. "I suppose I can be. When I'm not murdering people and creating horrible villains."

"Everyone has a little darkness inside them. It's all about the choices."

He was quiet for a few moments.

"I saw the darkness for a while, Jess. I'm not gonna lie."

"I know, sweetheart. I know."

"It's not so dark lately, though. I have you to thank for that."

Her heart warmed, and a tingly sensation wound its way from her chest down to her belly. Sometimes she wished she didn't have this visceral reaction to him, and other times she reveled in it. Today he'd made it clear that he wasn't interested in anything serious, wasn't looking to have more children or a family. Where did that leave her? She wanted those things. Maybe not right this minute, but eventually. Hoping for him to change was a sure path to disappointment. This summer—these few weeks—were all they would have together. She wanted to cherish them, but to do so she had to remind herself that she could not fall in love with him, and she had to live in the moment.

Could she do that? Because if she couldn't, she should walk away right now.

She looked up at him. He'd closed his eyes and lifted his face to the sun that filtered through the leafy canopy.

As if he could sense her gaze, he said, "You should sketch. You know you want to."

She did, so she leaned forward and retrieved her sketch pad. But it wasn't flowers or trees or strangers that she drew. It was him, and the angle of his jaw, the crisp edges of his lips, his soft eyelashes, and the way his unruly hair touched his shoulders when his head was tipped back.

She wasn't in love, but she wouldn't lie and say her heart wasn't involved. Of course it was. Her pencil moved quickly across the paper, then she reached for another with a softer lead. She wanted to capture the unguarded moment as best she could before he opened his eyes and caught her.

The sketch was rough but there was something in it she liked. It wasn't perfect, but the sweeping strokes captured an urgency and energy that surprised her.

Bran opened his eyes, squinting and looking at her. She turned the page over and smiled up at him, hoping he hadn't seen the sketch. She wanted it just for her.

She wanted to have something to remember him by when their time together was over.

As, of course, it would be.

CHAPTER NINE

HE TOOK HER to dinner at a seafood restaurant in the city's downtown core. While she went for a seafood pasta, he ordered steak and an appetizer of mussels in a garlic cream sauce. Best of all was the history of the place, which had its beginnings as a school, then as a mortuary, particularly during the time of the *Titanic* sinking and a massive explosion that had leveled the north end during the First World War. Jess listened raptly as Bran told her what he knew of the place, and then grinned when he said it was haunted.

"Do you really believe in that stuff?" she asked, taking a sip of the fine semi-dry white she'd ordered.

"Of course I do. Don't you?"

She shrugged. "I don't know. I mean, I think it's possible. I just haven't experienced anything that would, you know, make me really believe."

After a moment of hesitation, she looked up at him. "Have you ever, you know, seen a ghost?"

He furrowed his brow and picked at his potato for a few moments. "No? I mean, not actually seen a ghost. But I've felt things that I can't really explain."

She held her breath as she asked, "You mean Jennie?"

He sighed and met her gaze, his eyes sad. "You know, at times I kind of wish Jennie would show up. I'd like to see her again. And then as soon as I think that, I realize that if she did, it'd scare me to death. I don't know what I'd do. Or say."

And make it harder to let go, Jess thought, but she kept the words locked inside.

They changed the subject and chatted over the magnificent dinner, and even though Jess was stuffed, she agreed to share a serving of lemon tart. It was after eight when they finished and made their way back to his car. It would be ten before they reached home, and just dark, as the days were long. Jess was determined now not to return to the maudlin subject of his wife; it had dampened the mood earlier and while she had no problem being an ear for his thoughts, twice during the day she'd felt as if there was a third person on their date. It seemed Bran was determined, too, because he'd reverted back to his easy manner as he opened the car door for her, and closed it solicitously before getting in on the driver's side. Once behind the wheel, he hesitated, then reached for her hand.

"Thank you for allowing me to tag along today. It was nice, don't you think?"

Yes, it had been nice. Despite the conversation getting heavy at times. She'd enjoyed his company, but something had been missing. So nice was a perfectly adequate word.

"What's wrong?" he asked quietly. He hadn't yet started the car, and the silence around them was heavy.

She shifted in her seat and looked over at him. "Did things get weird today? Are you having regrets?"

His eyes warmed. "No, I'm not. I'm sorry if I got moody. It's just that…well, for a long time, that moodiness was a constant. Lately not so much." He squeezed her fingers. "Lately I've found myself enjoying things. I forget to be sad. So when those moments creep in, I'm not ready for them." He smiled a little. "I think it's a good thing, really. Forgetting to be sad. Maybe someday I actually won't be sad at all."

She squeezed his hand back. "Thank you for telling me," she said softly. "I wondered if I'd done something wrong."

"No, nothing," he assured her, and then leaned over the seat and kissed her gently. "You are lovely and sweet and strong." He kissed her again, and she melted a little, leaning into the soft and seductive contact. "You're just what I need, Jess."

Her heart slammed against her ribs as she opened her mouth and led him to a deeper kiss. Desire darkened the sweetness of it, like rich chocolate over marshmallow. He let go of her hand and threaded his fingers through her hair, and she moaned against his lips as his strong fingers massaged the back of her head.

He pulled away, a little reluctantly, she thought, and stared down at her. "We're in a car in broad daylight," he said, his voice a bit rough. "Put a pin in this until we get home?"

"It's a long drive," she said.

"We could spend the night in the city. Drive back in the morning."

The suggestion came as such a surprise she was temporarily dumbstruck. Finally she managed a weak, "Bran…"

"Order room service for breakfast."

Never in her life had she ever rented a hotel room for sex. And yet the two-hour drive seemed interminably long, and the idea of spending the night in a hotel was exciting. His gaze held hers and the tension in the car leaped. "Bran," she said, trying for a low note of caution. Instead that single syllable—his name—came out with a breathy sort of yearning. "I think… I want to…"

Oh, dear.

He turned the car on and pulled out of the spot, navigating a few streets until he reached the hotel she'd noticed earlier, across from the gardens. He parked in the underground garage, and without looking at her, got out and came around to open her door.

She grabbed her tote bag while a rush of feelings swept through her body. Excitement. Arousal, for sure. Anxiety. Were they rushing things? Was this really a smart idea?

"Relax," he whispered, taking her hand as they made their way into the hotel and to the front desk. Within moments he'd secured them a room and was guiding her to the elevator.

As they waited for the elevator, Bran took her hand. Jess swallowed against a nervous lump in her throat. Were they really doing this? Last night had been one thing. They'd been in her place, talking and snuggling after a make-out session on the beach. It had seemed…a logical progression of events. This was different. The bell dinged and the doors opened, and Bran guided her inside. She let out a long slow breath and asked herself a sudden question.

What would Ana do?

Jess bit down on her lip. Ana wasn't here. But Ana had lived life until the last moment, and she'd undoubtedly tell Jess to grab what happiness she could while it lasted. Jess chanced a look over at Bran, and he looked back at her, unsmiling, his dark eyes gleaming. None of the intensity in the car had been lost, and she got a thrill seeing the desire in his eyes.

No one was guaranteed another day. Look at Ana. Look at Jennie. You had to grab each day and its precious, fleeting moments.

The doors opened and they stepped out, then hesitated while Bran scanned the plate on the wall with arrows to room numbers.

They were off again, down the hall, stopping in front

of a door, waiting while he let them in and shut the door behind them.

Jess had a glimpse of a king-sized bed covered in white and gold linens, and matching draperies on either side of an elegant desk. It was more luxurious than even Bran's room at his house, but the moment after the door shut, the sheer opulence of the room was forgotten. Bran's mouth was on hers, his hands were on her waist and she was swept entirely away into a sea of sensation.

CHAPTER TEN

BRAN WOKE WITH light streaming through the window. He checked the clock beside the bed: five forty. The days were incredibly long at this time of year. Last night, before they'd fallen asleep, sated, it had still been daylight. He'd slept straight through, dreamless. He regretted that he hadn't awakened in the night, simply to make the hours last longer.

Jess was breathing slow and deep beside him, her face turned toward him, her hair strewn on the white linen of the pillowcase. She was so beautiful, with her sunrise-colored hair and delicate lips. An unfamiliar tenderness washed over him. The sex was fantastic, but it was more than that. They were friends.

He wondered if that friendship would be ruined now that they'd slept together. Certainly, after the summer, their relationship would be over. And yet he'd miss her. She understood him in a way that was so…well, easy.

Yes, he was going to miss her.

She shifted and rolled to her right side, so that her back was to him. It was early to wake her, so instead he slid closer, gently putting his arm over her waist and snuggling in, spoon-style. He closed his eyes and drank in the scent of her hair and the light musk of her skin. For two years he'd slept alone. The last two nights he'd had Jess with him, and it would be too easy to get used to her there. Spending time with her was one thing. Having fun was fine. But he wouldn't use her as a tonic for his loneliness, and he wouldn't get too used to her.

Last night had been impulsive and exciting, but they couldn't make a habit of this, could they?

But reality was hours away, and he wanted to absorb every moment he could. So he closed his eyes and imprinted the moment on his memory, until she woke up.

He didn't mean to fall back asleep, but when he opened his eyes again, Jess was facing him with a soft smile on her face.

"Good morning."

"Hi," he answered. Her foot slid along his calf, just a light caress, but it instantly brought his body to attention. "Sleep well?"

"Too well," she laughed. "I think I got more than a full eight hours. I don't remember the last time that happened."

He wiggled his eyebrows, and she laughed again. Maybe keeping it light was the way to go.

"I think we wore each other out."

She blushed, and he loved it.

A piece of hair had fallen over her cheek, and he reached out and tucked it back behind her ear. "So, what do you think? Room service?"

"Why not?"

"What do you like?"

This time she wiggled her eyebrows, and he laughed. Lord, she was such a ray of sunshine. "Everything," she answered.

His brain took a direct trip back to last night, and his body wasn't far behind. But while they'd been a bit crazed and frantic, he didn't want to assume this morning would be a continuation. As much as he would like it to be. He pushed the thoughts aside as best he could and rolled to the night table, where he grabbed the folder containing the in-room dining guide. A few minutes later he'd ordered a veritable feast, due to be delivered in thirty minutes.

She sat up, the sheets tucked under her arms, covering her breasts. "So…uh…want to shower before breakfast?"

He swallowed tightly. "Together?"

There was that blush again. The air of innocence around her was enchanting. She didn't need to ask again; they made their way to the luxurious bathroom and spent five minutes cleaning up and fifteen finding mind-blowing pleasure. After they'd caught their breath and dried with the fluffy towels, they dressed in the hotel-provided robes and waited for their meal.

When it came, he watched as she loaded her plate with French toast and fruit and bacon, then drizzled on enough maple syrup that it puddled under everything. He liked her so much. Liked just about everything about her. But as they shared a laugh over her love of the syrup, he realized something important.

He didn't love her. Or at least, he wasn't in love with her. It came as a huge relief. He didn't want to love again. And they were having fun, weren't they? A summer fling.

He bit into his omelet and frowned. Jeremy and Tori had a summer fling and look at them now. But that wouldn't happen to him. Jess was on the pill, and so there wouldn't be a surprise baby popping up. Even so, perhaps he'd be wise to stop at a pharmacy and grab some condoms just in case. There was no harm in doubling up, was there?

"You okay, Bran?" Jess's light voice interrupted his thoughts. "You look like you disappeared for a moment."

"I'm perfect," he replied, feeling on surer ground now. "This is delicious. And so are you."

She blushed and he grinned. "What?" she asked, tilting her head a bit in that adorable way she had.

"You blush a lot, and I like it."

The pink color deepened. "I blush at everything, so there."

"Mmm-hmm." He stood and leaned over the table to get a taste of her maple-sweet lips. "I still like it."

After breakfast they dressed in their clothes from the day before, and Bran dropped the key at the desk before they made their way to the parking garage. In no time, they were back on the highway and headed home. Bran's heart felt lighter than it had in years, and he tapped his fingers on the steering wheel in time to the music playing through the speakers. Jess told him about her agent wanting to set up a showing in the fall, and how much she was enjoying painting again. Truthfully, Bran couldn't wait to get home and open his laptop. He wasn't going to push, but he felt the urge to write, and he wanted to strike while the iron was hot. He'd always been a disciplined writer, working consistently but also riding a wave of inspiration when it hit.

It seemed no time at all that they arrived at Jeremy's, and he parked behind her car at the boathouse. He helped her take in her packages from the art store, and then hesitated on the threshold. "So, I'll see you soon?"

She nodded. "You know where I am." Her smile was sweet. "I'll be here, painting."

"Good." He reached out and pulled her close again, kissing her lightly. "I had a really great time," he murmured against her mouth.

"Me, too."

He left her standing there on the porch, and found himself whistling as he slid behind the wheel of his car and backed out of the lane, heading home once more.

* * *

Jess changed out of her dress and into more comfortable clothes—denim capris and a T-shirt—then organized her new supplies and studied the painting she had been working on for a week. She was happy with how it was progressing, and she spent an hour and a half working on it, trying to focus. But something wasn't quite right.

She stepped back and thought for a moment, and then, to her surprise, she rushed forward and removed the canvas from the easel and replaced it with a fresh one.

Something else was calling to her right now. She pulled out the photo of the first day, and then the sketch she'd done, and knew she had to paint it. The one with Bran looking out to sea.

For a moment she rolled her eyes and let out a sigh. Two nights with a man and suddenly he was her subject? And yet, she'd been drawn to that moment time and again over the last few weeks. The loneliness telegraphed in his body language, in the gray sea beyond him and the weary lighthouse. A thread of excitement wound through her as she started the process of turning canvas to art. She forgot the time, forgot to eat, forgot everything but the work until there was a knock on her door.

She checked her watch, shocked to discover it was almost four in the afternoon. She removed her apron as she made her way to the door, and opened it to find Tori on the other side, a frown immediately replaced by a relieved smile as she saw Jess in the doorway.

"Oh, good, you're all right!" Tori slipped into the boathouse, leaving Jess feeling off balance. She'd been so swept up in work that the interruption had her head trying to catch up.

"All right?" she parroted, following Tori into the main room.

"I stopped by yesterday and you didn't answer."

"Oh, is that all?" Jess laughed a little. "I went into Halifax for supplies."

Tori's brow wrinkled. "You did? But your car was here. And I texted, too. Gosh, I hope I got the right number."

Jess felt the heat creep up her neck. She hadn't even checked her phone since yesterday afternoon. She'd been utterly preoccupied—first with Bran and then with work.

"How did you get to Halifax?" Tori asked, and the heat reached Jess's ears.

"Oh, um, Branson had some things to do so we went together. No biggie." She smiled widely. "And it saved me from having to navigate the city. Bran's much more familiar."

Tori's face sobered. "You and Bran, huh?"

Oh, Lordy. She had such a horrible poker face. "Yeah, well, we get along okay now." A memory slid into her brain, of his face in the shower this morning, and she struggled to breathe. "At least he doesn't hate me anymore."

"Oh," Tori said, "no danger of that. He walked you home the other night."

"It's no big deal," Jess replied. And hoped beyond hope that Tori hadn't seen his car yesterday morning.

"Well, I'm hoping Jeremy and I didn't make a mistake." She rested her hand on the countertop. "We kind of pushed you two together, you know? Bran needed someone to shake him up a bit. But…" She peered into Jess's face. "It's more than shaking up, isn't it?"

Jess had to make light of this. She really didn't want Tori to butt in, or start asking more detailed questions. For one, she didn't know how she'd answer. The last two nights had been amazing, but they'd also shaken her more than she wanted to admit.

"I promise you have nothing to feel badly about. I like

Bran, he likes me, and sometimes we spend time together without fighting." Indeed. "Really, Tori, it's no big deal."

"So you're just enjoying each other's company?"

Jess let out a relieved breath. "Yes, that's exactly it."

Tori tapped her finger on her lips. "Hmm. Okay. I'm going to shut up now because I don't want to pry too deeply. I just…well, we love Bran, and I like you a lot, Jess. Jeremy and I don't want to see either of you hurt."

The words were heartfelt, so Jess relaxed a little and motioned toward the tiny table and chairs. "Listen, sit down for a bit and let me get you a drink."

Tori did sit, and as Jess went to the fridge, she called out, "So where's Rose this afternoon?"

"Sleeping. Jeremy's home and working in his office, with the baby monitor next to him." Jess turned around and saw Tori smiling. "I love her to bits, but going somewhere, even for thirty minutes, without a baby and the requisite gear is so nice."

"You didn't venture far," Jess teased. "Soda water okay? I have some flavored stuff. Lemon lime or grapefruit."

"Ooh, grapefruit, please," Tori replied. Jess retrieved two cans, opened them and poured them over ice before returning to the table. She sat across from Tori and tried to relax, though she was still feeling odd about the whole thing. She wasn't accountable to anyone, but the night away was still more of a secret than anything, for the simple reason that she wanted to avoid questions.

"You started a new painting," Tori said, staring at the white canvas. "What's this one?"

"Actually, it's from a photo I took the first day. Bran was looking out over the point, and he seemed so lost and lonely. The image hasn't left me alone, so I figure it's time to get started on it."

Tori's voice was soft. "You really care for him, don't

you? Oh, Jess. I'm afraid we really did goof. I don't want to see you fall for him, only to get hurt."

The consideration was genuine, and Jess patted Tori's hand. "It's fine. We like each other but neither of us is after anything serious. We've talked about it, Tori, so truly, don't worry. I'm going to paint to my heart's content, and at the end of the summer I'm going to head back home to my life. Besides, Bran is not in a relationship place. He's still too hung up on his wife."

"I never knew her. Jeremy says she was lovely, though, and that they were very happy."

"Hard to compete with that." She took a sip of her soda water. "Not that I want to. Still, we enjoy spending time together. That's all there is."

And the sex, she thought, but didn't say. She and Tori had become friends but weren't quite close enough to be confidants of that sort.

"So you aren't falling in love with him?"

"Of course not."

Jess said the words with confidence, but she knew deep down it wasn't strictly true. No matter how often she repeated the words to herself—summer romance, short-term fling—she couldn't erase the sight of Bran while they were making love, the intense expression on his face as he gazed into her eyes as if no one else existed. He was an extraordinary man, smart and sexy and deep, sometimes grouchy and other times sweet, and a man who knew how to love a woman with all his heart. Of course she was falling for him. Her head was in the clouds, and there was going to be an awful thud at the end. The difference was this time she wasn't going to be blindsided. She saw it coming and could prepare.

And yet, she looked at Tori and said, "Men like Bran

don't come along often. I'd be a fool not to spend whatever time I can with him. Even knowing the outcome."

Tori nodded and looked down in her glass, and looked up again, her eyes bright as if she might cry. "I felt the same way about Jeremy." Her voice was soft and dreamy. "And I was fine after he left, mostly. Until he came back. You're right, though. Bran isn't ready for anything serious. As long as you know that, and you're having fun… more power to you."

"I appreciate you caring, Tori, I do. But I've got this."

"Of course you do. You're a strong woman. I think that's why Bran likes you. None of those men are the kind who like pushovers."

"I think that's a compliment."

Tori laughed. "The best kind. Now, I'd better get back up to the house. I truly am glad you're okay. I was worried you'd got sick or something."

"I'm absolutely fine," she replied. "But thank you for caring." At least Tori hadn't realized that Jess hadn't returned home until this morning. The conversation had been personal enough without that information being out in the open.

After Tori left, Jess made an early dinner since she'd missed lunch. She checked her email on her phone; no texts from Bran. That was okay. After the past forty-eight hours, maybe he needed time to process everything. She certainly did.

Because she was falling for him, no question. But he didn't need to know that. And neither did Tori.

CHAPTER ELEVEN

BRAN LOOKED UP from his laptop and squinted. Ever since his return from Halifax, he'd either been embroiled in research, or working on the opening chapters of the new book. It had felt wonderful working again. The words weren't quite flowing, but they were there, ready for him to pluck out of his brain and put them on the page. Now the story had a basic outline, he had pages full of notes and his master document had the better part of two full chapters written.

Not long now, and he'd call his agent and tell him the good news. Maybe send him some pages. But right now, the light was dimming and he'd been working the better part of sixteen hours.

He checked the date on the bottom right corner of the screen. Was that correct? Had he been back from Halifax for three days already? And he hadn't heard from Jess. Not once. Nor had he texted.

He hit the save button and slumped back in his chair. He wasn't sure what to do about Jess, really. To say he wanted her was an understatement. Having sex again had been amazing…she was a good lover, sweet and generous and passionate. Their nights together had been wonderful, but he'd stayed quiet for two reasons. One, he'd gotten the bug to write and he wanted to catch the words while they were there, no longer out of reach. And two, it would be very easy to get wrapped up in her. Spending a few days regaining his equilibrium seemed like a good idea, especially after their dash to the hotel. That wasn't his usual style. There was a "can't keep my hands off her" edge to his feelings, and it was strange.

She was different from Jennie, and he was so glad. He still hadn't forgotten the way she'd asked if he'd been thinking of his wife when he'd kissed her. He wasn't into looking for a substitute. That wouldn't be fair to Jess, or to him.

But she hadn't called him, either. And that made him wonder if she was having second thoughts.

It wasn't something he wanted to talk about over the phone, so he closed his laptop, changed his shirt and drove over to the boathouse.

The porch light was off, but light poured from the windows onto the stone path leading to her door. It was nine at night; was she up working this late? Perhaps she'd been painting just as much as he'd been writing.

Then the sound of laughter filtered out through the open window, and he hesitated. She had company?

Maybe he should do this another time.

He hesitated for a full ten seconds, then he heard Tori's laugh and Jeremy's low voice, and then another round of laughter. Something unfamiliar swept over him, and he realized it was loneliness. Not the welcome, self-imposed kind he'd reveled in for the last few years, but the kind that longed to be a part of something warm and fun. Before he could change his mind, he stepped up onto the porch and knocked on the door.

Jess answered, her face alight with laughter as she stood with the door open. "Well, hello, stranger."

"Hi," he said quietly, a little off balance by how happy

he was to see her face. It had been what, three days? And he'd missed her terribly.

"Come in. Jer and Tori are here. And little Rose is asleep."

In that much noise? He wasn't sure how it was possible. Owen had always awakened at anything over normal speaking level.

He stepped inside and took off his sandals, padding to the kitchen in his bare feet. Jeremy and Tori were sitting at the round table, with cards in their hands.

"We're playing cribbage," Jess explained. "Tori taught us how. Jeremy is about to get skunked."

He had never played the game in his life, and stared at the oddly shaped board with different colored pegs in various spots. "Oh."

"We're almost done this game," Tori said, taking a sip of what appeared to be sparkling water. "Come on in and watch the carnage."

"There's sparkling water and ginger ale in the fridge. Help yourself, Bran. And chips on the counter."

The small gathering was very different from social occasions he'd gone to as a member of the Black family. No one ever helped themselves, or sat as an odd man out during a game of cards while munching on chips straight from the bag. Instead, it reminded him of days spent at Merrick, playing poker with the guys, drinking contraband beer and pooling snacks.

He'd loved those days. Missed them.

So he helped himself to a ginger ale and grabbed the bag of chips and pulled up a fourth chair to watch. Tori deftly dealt five cards to each player and put one on the table, though he wasn't sure what it was for. Then each of them studied their cards and removed one from their hand, adding it to one on the table.

"All right. Jess, your go."

Branson didn't ask questions, just watched as they took turns laying cards and occasionally moved their pegs on the board. Jess's brow wrinkled each time she considered her play, and he thought she looked adorable. Jeremy sat back in his chair in an indolent posture, very reminiscent of his body language in school. And Tori sat straight and kept an easy expression on her face. He bet she'd be good at poker.

When all the cards had been played, they counted points in some weird format that had something to do with fifteens and runs. Jess had a dozen points, putting her within a few of Tori. There was laughter when Jeremy had four points, keeping him short of the line that had an S beside it. And Tori moved only six. Apparently the four extra cards were hers, too, but to Jess and Jeremy's glee, contained no points.

"One more hand," Jess said, "and this time the crib is mine."

He grabbed a handful of chips and watched.

Jeremy laid a seven after Jess, which gave him two points, putting him one shy of the skunk line. Another round he announced "thirty-one for two" and it put him over, which caused a victorious whoop. "What happens if he doesn't cross?" Bran asked.

"You lose double," Tori replied, grinning. "You just snuck over, Jer."

They continued. Jess played a card and gave a yelp of triumph as she moved three points, so close to Tori and ever closer to the final hole on the board.

At that moment the sound of a baby crying interrupted the game. Jess frowned. "Darn, I'm sorry. I think I woke her."

"It's all right. She'll be fine until we finish this hand."

But Bran looked at Tori and noticed that her relaxed

face now had the shadow of tension around her eyes. Tori played a card, and then it was Jess's turn; Rose's crying got louder.

"We can pause the game," Jeremy said. "It's no big deal."

Bran tamped down the apprehension building in his chest and stood. "You guys finish. You're nearly done. I'll go get her."

He walked to the bedroom with heavy steps, totally unsure of himself but knowing he needed to do this sometime. Rose was two months old and he had yet to hold her, even though Jeremy and Tori had named him her godfather. The cries reminded him of a little lamb, bleating with distress. After taking a deep breath, he stepped into the room, went to the bed and scooped her up from the pillow barrier that Tori had set up, even though Rose was nowhere near old enough to roll over yet.

The moment he cradled her against his chest, her cries changed to whimpers. She was so tiny and warm, and he could hear her sucking on her fist as he tucked the light blanket close around her. She smelled like baby lotion and the combination of milk and diapers, and the familiarity of it snuck in and pierced his heart. But there was more than pain there now. There was emptiness but also something more, something warm and glowing that crept in around the corners. Memories that were bitter but also sweet. Her soft, downy head nuzzled into his neck and his throat closed with emotion, tears stinging the backs of his eyes.

"Hello, Rosie. I'm your godfather." He kept his voice low and soothing, and he rocked back and forth a bit as he used to with Owen when he'd been fussy. The cranky noises eased into something that was half-slurp and half-coo, and he closed his eyes and rested his cheek against her.

"You want your mama, huh? Let's go find her."

He reentered the kitchen, and the room suddenly quieted at the sight of him with the baby in his arms. Cards were forgotten in hands as Jeremy's eyes widened and Tori…ah, damn, Tori gave an emotional sniff, and he found his own emotions raw and hovering right at the surface.

Then Jess was there, getting up from her chair and pasting on a smile. "Oh, there's my girl! Look at her all sleepy and snuggly." She went to Bran and didn't take Rose from him, but put her hand on the baby's back. "Tori, do you want me to change her?"

Jess's interference seemed to jolt the others into action, and Tori put down her cards. "Oh, sure, that'd be great! I can get a bottle ready while you do that. Thanks, Jess."

"It's okay. I know where your bag is."

She retrieved a diaper and wipes from the diaper bag in the kitchen, and then motioned for him to follow. He did, following her into the bedroom, where she put down a soft flannel blanket and then took Rose from his arms.

"Unless you want to do the honors?" she asked.

"I, uh…"

She looked up at him, a blinking Rose in her arms. "Baby steps?"

He nodded, unable to say anything more. But he watched as she deftly undid Rose's soft pajamas, changed her diaper and dressed her again, talking softly to the baby the whole time.

"You're very good with her," he observed, his emotions once again riding very close to the surface.

"I like babies." She picked up Rose and set her on her arm. "Isn't that right, sweetie?" And then she met Bran's eyes. "I'd like to have my own someday. But that option hasn't really presented itself. And I'm not at the point where I'm prepared to take things into my own hands."

"You'd like a family, then."

She nodded. "I would. Figuring out how that would fit into my life is another story."

With Rose tidied and dressed, there was no reason to linger, and Jess headed back to the kitchen. But Bran hesitated a moment.

She wanted a family. Babies of her own. If he'd ever thought that this could work between them at all, the idea just died a quick death. He never wanted to do that again. No matter how sweet Rose was. Or how adorable Jess's children would be, with their sunrise hair and blue-green eyes, and a healthy dose of freckles.

Back in the kitchen, he watched while Jess, Jeremy and Tori played out their final hand. Jeremy was over the skunk line, and Jess gave Tori a run for her money, but Tori won by three small points. Rose was in Tori's arms, the bottle braced up so she could eat, and Jeremy pegged the last points for his wife.

"Well," Tori said, sitting back. "That was fun. You're a fast learner, Jess."

"You're a good teacher. Another drink? Anyone want more snacks?"

"We should probably be going," Jeremy said, looking at Bran briefly.

Bran wanted to say that there was no need, that he hadn't come for a specific reason, but the truth was, he had. To test the waters, so to speak. Hoping that Jess's silence wasn't her being angry at him. That she'd been just as busy as he had.

"Yes, and once Rose is fed, she'll go back to sleep. If I can put her in her crib for the night, I might get some good sleep, too."

"Or, you know. Pay attention to your husband."

"Or that." Her grin was teasing but their gazes held, and Bran knew that look. They were so in love. Despite having a baby, they were still in the stage of not getting enough of each other.

He looked at Jess, whose cheeks had gone pink as she picked up dirty glasses from the table.

A few minutes later, Tori and Jeremy said their good-byes and the house was quiet again. Bran cleared his throat. "I'm sorry I interrupted tonight. I should have called first."

Jess put the glasses in the small dishwasher and shrugged. "It's fine. We were just playing some cards. Tori hasn't gotten out a lot since Rose was born, and doesn't want to leave her with a sitter yet. I think Jeremy was getting a little worried."

She closed the dishwasher and turned to face him. "Was Jennie like that? How old was Owen before you got a sitter?"

He frowned and turned away. "Don't ask me things like that."

But she stepped forward. "Was tonight the first time you held Rose?"

"Jess. Stop." His voice was firm. "I didn't come over to talk about babies, okay? I just… I realized that it's been three days and I didn't call, and I was feeling like a heel about it."

She stopped and stared at him, angling her head a bit as if trying to puzzle him out. "I didn't call you, either."

"Why?"

She looked over at her small living room and then back at him. "To be honest, I needed some time to think. And I've been painting. A lot."

He let out a breath and some of the tension tightening his body. "I've been writing, too."

"I guess our trip was inspiring." Her eyes lit with a bit of the fire he loved, and he was transported back to the hotel room. The way she looked, tasted, sounded.

"So…"

"So I'm not the kind of woman who has to be called hours after being dropped off. I'm not that insecure, Bran. And we both agreed this is not…a real relationship. We want different things. Besides, I have no claim on you or your time. I told myself I was just going to enjoy what time we had."

Her words should have made him feel better, as they essentially let him off the hook. But somehow they didn't, and he couldn't pinpoint why.

"Had," he said quietly. "Past tense?"

"That's up to you." She moved forward. "It got to be too much for you, didn't it?"

"I don't know." He paused and ran his hand through his hair. "It's just a lot. I'm dealing with a lot. You're the first woman I've been with since Jennie. And yeah, tonight was the first time I've held Rose. I'm moving back into the world of the living, but it's hard. I'm not sure I have it in me to navigate…nuance. With a relationship."

She nodded as if she understood completely, but how could she?

"Would it help if we set ground rules?"

He gestured to the small table and chairs. "Can we sit to discuss this? I feel weird standing here, as if we're facing off."

She obliged him by taking a seat, but angled her chair so that their knees bumped slightly. It helped that she was touching him, actually. Like an anchor to keep him grounded, when he could very easily be overwhelmed.

He could still smell the scent of baby, and his brain remembered a past life he couldn't access anymore. And never would again.

If anything, the past month had taught him that he could move forward without them.

"We both agreed this is a summer thing. That I'll be

going back to Chicago and my own life, and you'll be here or wherever else you call home." She folded her hands in her lap. "And since we really do like each other, I think we also agree that there might be a little bit of fear that we'll get too attached to each other."

"Like?" He lifted an eyebrow.

She smiled gently. "Okay, more than like. I care about you, Bran, and I think you care about me. And neither of us wants to get hurt, or be responsible for hurting the other person."

"True."

"So, ground rules. I'll go first. No more overnights."

He blinked. He'd thought she was going to say no sex, but she'd said no staying over. He nodded, thinking of how the intimacy of waking up together made things so much more complicated. "Agreed." Then he added a condition of his own. "No declarations."

"Declarations?"

Bran wasn't sure how to word this one. "I mean, we care about each other. But we both agree that this isn't going to turn into love. I'm not ready for that and like you said, we want different things. So no declarations of love."

"Absolutely. No danger there."

It made him pause for a moment, how quickly she'd said "no danger there." Again, he knew he should be relieved, so why was there this nagging feeling that something was off?

He pushed the feeling aside and ticked off another one on his fingers. "Space to create, and no getting upset when either of us is unavailable because we're working."

She grinned at him. "That's an easy one."

"Maybe. But not for a lot of people. Not everyone gets it."

"Canceling plans is fine, but the courtesy of a call is nonnegotiable. That's just being polite."

"Deal. Or at least… I'll try. I've been known to lose track of time. Anything else?"

She studied him for a long moment. "We agree that we can add to the ground rules as needed if and when things come up we didn't think of tonight."

It was odd, setting rules for something as simple as a casual relationship, but Bran also knew that setting the rules now meant their relationship would stay casual, which was what he wanted. What they both wanted.

He let out a sigh. "Does this feel weird to you?"

And then she laughed, that light, musical sound that he enjoyed so very much, and he smiled, too. The awkwardness and tension of the evening fell away, and she leaned forward, putting her hand over his. "Of course it does. But we both feel the need to protect ourselves, and Bran, I needed to be honest. The only way this is going to work is if we're honest with each other."

Something undefinable flickered behind her eyes, and he briefly wondered what it was, but then she got up from her chair and went to stand in front of him. "And now," she whispered, "will you please kiss me? Because I've been dying for you to for over an hour."

CHAPTER TWELVE

SETTING GROUND RULES seemed to be working. Jess was an early bird, so she was up early each morning, sketching and painting, and usually touched base with Bran when she broke for lunch. Some days they'd venture into the nearby town for errands; sometimes she drove to his house and they spent the day on the beach below his low cliffs, dipping into the ocean and soaking in the sun.

They made love on a blanket in the sand, and in his enormous bed. One evening there was a thunderstorm and the power went out, and so they gathered all the candles he had and put them around the bedroom, making love to the sound of the rain.

She loved his house. Even though it was big, it wasn't cold. No expense had been spared, and sometimes they cooked dinner together in his vast kitchen, which was much better equipped than the boathouse. One afternoon he wrote in his den, and she pulled a book out of his bookcases and read. And because that first day she'd mentioned the Jacuzzi, she arrived one evening to find a bath drawn and a glass of wine waiting from the bottle she'd gifted him, so she could soak and watch the ocean through the windows. It had felt incredibly extravagant and surreal. Even more surreal when he'd held her towel when she got out…

But she didn't stay over, and he didn't stay at the boathouse, either.

It should have been absolutely perfect.

Bran and Jeremy's friend Cole came to town and stayed at Bran's, which put a bit of a kink into their social plans. And yet Jess thought it lovely when she saw the two of them together. Cole was tall and fair, with a magnetic personality and an energy that was contagious—something that had a positive effect on Bran. He smiled more and laughed often, and Jess got a glimpse of the man he used to be. She already thought him pretty amazing. But this…it was different. For a little while, it seemed as if the weight of the world was off his shoulders, particularly when he, Cole and Jeremy were all together. She remembered what he'd said—that they were family.

Today they were all going to an island offshore to look at property. The whole island, in fact, with the exception of ten acres that was owned by someone else. Cole was considering buying it and turning the mansion into a corporate retreat that he could use for business. Jess tried not to be awestruck when she realized that she was accompanying three billionaires on a shopping spree worth what they were calling a steal—nearly seven million dollars.

The five of them were making a day of it, or at least the better part of a day. Tori's mother was coming to stay with the baby, and it was Tori's first day away from Rose for more than an hour. As she and Bran met the others at the wharf, Jess could tell that Tori was both excited to be going along, and anxious about leaving Rose. She put an arm around Tori's shoulders and gave her a squeeze. "It'll be all right, Mama," she said with a smile. "Grandmas need a chance to spoil babies anyway."

Tori smiled back. "I know. It's just first time nerves. I've got to do it sometime."

Cole had rented a boat for his stay, a fast and luxurious Boston Whaler docked at a nearby marina. The island itself wasn't far outside the bay, but it was only accessible by boat or, Cole explained, by the helipad on-site. Tori looked at Jess and shook her head. Neither of them was used to such luxury, and Jess grinned up at Bran as he sat beside her. "Helipad, huh? Does Cole have his own helicopter?"

Bran shook his head. "Naw. He just charters when he needs to."

Jess's and Bran's definition of *need* seemed to vary, but today she didn't care. Today she was free and ready for fun. How often did one get to visit a private island, anyway?

Cole piloted the boat, and it wasn't long before they were at the island. Instead of docking right away, Cole took them all the way around. Jess got a glimpse of an enormous house with well-trimmed grounds sloping toward the water; the west side had more of a rocky shoreline but the east side had a beautiful sandy beach, similar to the one at Jeremy's, and what looked to be white, soft sand like that by the Sandpiper Resort. The dock was at the southern tip of the island. An ancient fishing boat was already docked, as well as a smaller craft.

Jeremy got off first, and held out his hand to help Tori and then Jess, with Bran and Cole following. "The other Realtor will be at the house. But there should be a golf cart up there—" he pointed to a garage-type structure at the top of the path "—that we can use to get to the main house."

Jess followed the direction of his finger and noticed not only the garage, but a large house behind it. "That's not the main house, is it?"

He shook his head. "Nope. There's about ten acres that's owned by another party. The house is hers. The rest of the island, about eighty acres or so, is what's for sale."

Interesting. Jess hung back and waited for Bran, and

together they walked side by side behind the others. "Your friend is seriously going to buy his own island," she said incredulously.

Bran nodded. "Looks like it. He's right. It's a steal. Besides, Cole's changed a lot in the last year. He tries not to show it, but he has."

"How so?"

"He took over his father's businesses when he was only twenty-three. He's accumulated more since, and I've never seen anyone work so hard or play so hard. It caught up with him and while he won't come right out and say so, I think he hit some burnout. He stepped away for a few months."

"He's okay now?" She looked up ahead. Cole was talking energetically with Jeremy and Tori, his hands gesturing wildly. It was impossible to imagine him slowing down, let alone grinding to a full stop.

Bran nodded. "I think so. But this place…it's different. He doesn't want it to simply acquire something new and shiny. He wants to use it to help executives and companies. Corporate retreats. Team building events. That sort of thing. It's not very Cole, but people change when life kicks them in the ass."

"Like it changed you."

"Cole and I grew up in the same world. We wanted for nothing, but that came with heavy expectations. My parents never wanted for me to be a writer. It was a waste of my time, they said. For a kid who supposedly had every privilege, it felt very much like I was in a cage. Until I got to Merrick and found Cole and Jer. So when my life went sideways, it wasn't all my money or status that got me through it. It was those two."

He looked over at her. "You've been kicked, as well. But you know, quite often we're better people for it."

She wondered at that, really. She knew he'd do anything

to turn back the clock and redo that night two years ago. But if he also liked the changes that had happened this summer, that was something huge. "Are you happy, Bran?"

They stopped for a moment and he faced her. "I'm happier than I've been in a very long time, and it's unexpected. I have you to thank for that."

He leaned down and placed a gentle kiss on her lips. She was stunned; while it was no big secret that she and Bran were spending time together, for him to make such a gesture while they were with his friends felt huge.

"Come on," he said. "We need to catch up or we'll miss our ride."

They climbed on the golf cart, squeezing three of them on the bench seat in the back, and Jeremy drove them past the farmhouse and down a long lane, clear to the other side of the island. The land vacillated between green forests and meadows with waving grass and wildflowers, wild and untamed. But before long the landscape turned into landscaped lawns and gardens, and a grand house appeared.

Cole turned around from the front of the cart and grinned. "Twelve thousand square feet. A dozen bedrooms, eight bathrooms, a kitchen that's a chef's dream and hopefully a room I can convert into a boardroom-type meeting room. What do you think?"

Jess grinned. "It's ginormous!" It was more the size of a hotel than a house.

Cole laughed. "I don't do things halfway. Didn't Bran tell you that?"

She nodded, still grinning. "He did."

The Realtor was waiting for them, and Jess and Bran once again brought up the rear as they were taken on a tour of the house. Jess had never been in anything like it, and was absolutely dazzled. There were indeed twelve bedrooms, each beautifully appointed with gleaming wood furniture and expensive linens. The bathrooms had marble counters and gold fixtures; three had Jacuzzi tubs and there was a sauna downstairs, next to the fully equipped exercise room. A theater room with a large projector screen and theater seating made Jess's eyes goggle.

Back upstairs, the Realtor showed them the addition on the back that held an indoor heated pool. The kitchen was huge, with double stainless-steel refrigerators and a large range with spider burners as well as double wall ovens. There was a small dining area, and then a large adjoining room with a table for at least twelve. To go with the bedrooms, Jess supposed.

One of the large rooms off the foyer could be turned into the meeting room Cole wanted. The other had a conversation pit, and a grand piano in front of tall, gleaming windows.

It was easy to see that Cole was in love with the place, and he and Jeremy kept their heads together, discussing details. Tori took out her phone and called home to check on Rose, and Bran caught Jess's eye and pointed outside. "Come on," he said quietly. "Let's explore outside."

"I'd like that."

The sun was bright and cheery as they stepped out of the grand house. "Oh, it's amazing," she said, "but too big for me."

"I know. But for what he's intending to do with it? It's perfect."

"Probably." She peered up at him. "I think for me it's... not really a home. It doesn't have that homey kind of feeling about it."

Bran studied her for a moment. "Do you feel that way about my house?"

She took his hand, and they started to walk across the plush lawn. "Not really. Yours is different. With yours, it *can* be cozy and welcoming and have that vibe. The possibility is there. I don't know how else to explain it."

"What would it take for it to be that way?"

The answer came to her mind so quickly it left her speechless. *Children*, she thought. *Family. Love.*

She couldn't say those things, so she simply answered, "Healing."

He tugged on her fingers and turned her toward him. "I'm trying."

Her heart squeezed at the honest confession. "I know. And you're doing just fine." She slid closer, wrapping her arms around him and nestling close to his strong, wide chest. "And along the way, you've been healing me, too. For what it's worth, I've loved every moment in your house, from the first time I walked in and saw you with your shirt off."

His arms cinched tightly around her, pulling her close as he laughed. His breath was warm on her hair as they hugged, his body tall and strong and the kind a woman could lean on when she wanted. The brisk wind off the ocean buffeted their bodies, but they stood firm against it, holding on to each other, the moment touching Jess's heart more than any of their more intimate moments. He pulled back a bit and cupped her face in his hands, his smile replaced with a look of wonder. "You've changed everything," he said roughly, and brought his lips down on hers for a kiss.

It was a hell of a time for her to realize she'd broken the ground rules. She'd gone ahead and fallen in love with him. But she wouldn't say it. Not and ruin what they had, when it was so fleeting to begin with.

Bran tried not to think about that kiss as he strolled along the beach with Jess. She stopped now and then to pick up shells, and took off her shoes to dip her toes in the cool water, the light breakers ruffling over her feet before creeping up on the sand and then retreating again. Her hair had come out of its bun and whipped around in the stiff breeze, and her laugh carried to him, making his heart hurt and yearn for things he couldn't have.

He'd seen her feelings on her face even if she hadn't said the words. She had turned away and laughed, running for the beach, but the distraction didn't quite work. He'd seen it, the way her lips fell open the slightest bit with words unsaid and the soft vulnerability and surprise in her eyes. He didn't want to say goodbye to her, not yet. The summer was just coming into its own. There was a good six weeks they could have together if they didn't let emotions get in the way. So thank God she hadn't said what had been written all over her face.

A gull cried overhead, circling above them. He could just pretend it had never happened, that's all. No declarations of love. That was the rule. And despite his suspicions, she hadn't broken it.

Cole, Jeremy and Tori joined them briefly, then as a group they left the beach and made their way back to the golf cart for the return trip to the dock. Bran remained quiet as Cole admitted that he was putting in an offer, and talked excitedly about his plans.

Back on the mainland, Jeremy offered Jess a drive home since they were going to the same place anyway, and that meant Cole and Bran drove back to his house together. Bran was quiet on the way back, until they were nearly at his house. Cole broke from his monologue about the island property and frowned at Bran.

"You know, I wasn't expecting you to have fallen in love this summer."

Bran's head swiveled so fast he nearly put the car in the

ditch. "What? I'm not in love. Don't be ridiculous." He chuckled tightly, as if to show how ludicrous of an idea it was, and focused on the road.

But Cole's expression was grim as he continued to stare at Bran. Bran kept glancing over, until Cole finally said, "Dude, it was written all over your face today. You light up when she's around."

"Lighting up is not love, dumbass. It's enjoying someone's company."

"You know, I'd be tempted to say, 'if you say so,' but I'm not, because this is serious, Bran. I want to be happy for you. But I'm not sure you're ready, and she seems like a great person. She doesn't deserve to be hurt."

Bran's temper flared. "If you think Jess and I haven't talked about it, you're wrong. Both of us have our eyes wide open."

And then he thought of the way she'd looked at him today, and his heart stuttered.

They turned onto his lane and made their way into the garage. The doors echoed in the silence, and Bran opened the door from the garage to the house.

Maybe Cole would let the matter drop.

"Hey, listen. Jeremy and I have been talking about it, too. We're both concerned for you. He said your car has been there overnight. And that you guys went to the city and spent the night earlier this month."

Heat rushed through Bran's chest as irritation flared again. "That is no one's business but ours."

"You're right."

"And it's just sex."

Cole started laughing, putting his hand on the island in the kitchen to brace himself. "Oh," he said, catching his breath. "Bran, you're a horrible liar. I've known you for most of your life. You don't do casual sex. You don't get with a woman without your heart being involved. Brother, you are lying to yourself."

Bran opened his mouth to speak, but Cole held up a hand. "Hey, don't get me wrong. Losing Jennie and Owen was such a horrible, horrible thing, and you deserve to move on and be happy again. I just… I find myself feeling protective of you. I don't want you to get hurt."

Those last words took the heat out of Bran's anger. Cole was a workaholic and he played hard—when he made time for it. But of the three of them, he was the most protective. Like the big brother of the group. As much as no one wanted to admit it, Cole was the glue that bound them together.

And Cole was always there for them…even when he wasn't taking care of himself.

Bran let out a breath. "I can't love her, Cole. There's no danger of that. But I care about her a lot. She's fun and full of life, and she doesn't let me get away with anything. I'm actually writing again, which is a total surprise and a massive relief. But she lives in Chicago. I live here and in New York. We both agreed that this is a temporary thing where we just enjoy each other for the time we have. Because life is short."

Cole went to the fridge and took out two cans of soda. He handed one to Bran and then snapped the top on his own and leaned against the counter. "Okay," he said quietly, "okay. Maybe that's true. But Bran, it's okay if you fall in love with her. You know that, right? I'm worried about you, but it's not *wrong*."

A pit opened up in Bran's stomach as he looked at his friend. How could he make Cole understand when he was finding it hard to understand himself? He wasn't even sure he was capable of being in love. And the look on Jess's face today scared him to death. Not so much because she loved him but because he couldn't feel that way in return.

"I can't, Cole." His voice was low and rough. "My heart won't let me. Maybe it would be easier if I could. Right now I'm trying to look at all the positives. I'm not hurting so much. I'm getting out, I'm writing again. Anything more is a lot to ask for."

"Yet up until she showed up in your life, you weren't doing any of those things. Doesn't that say something to you?"

Bran let out a sigh of resignation. "Yeah," he said, looking past Cole and out at the backyard. "It tells me she deserves someone who can give her a lot more than I can."

And in that moment, he knew he had to stop what was between them.

CHAPTER THIRTEEN

JESS POURED HERSELF some orange juice and tried to decide if she wanted yogurt and berries this morning or something a little more comforting, like toast with butter and jam. She was feeling rather out of sorts after yesterday. The trip to the island had been fun and she'd enjoyed it, but she wasn't so sure about her latest revelation.

She didn't want to be in love with Bran. Up until yesterday, she'd been able to logic her way out of it. But then there was that moment. The moment he'd kissed her, however, something had shifted. Something profound and deep and joyful and sad and terrifying all wrapped up in one ball of emotion.

She loved him, and she wasn't sure if she should break it off now for the sake of self-preservation, or if she should give herself these final weeks as a gift, no matter the end result.

She really wished Ana was here to give her advice and ask her the right questions. Tori was a good friend. Jess had other friends in Chicago. But none like Ana.

A wave of grief threatened to swamp her, so instead she reached for her pillbox, which contained her vitamins and birth control. She stared at the little plastic strip with surprise. How was it that she was on her two sugar pills? It meant she'd get her period anytime. She went to her bedroom to get the next month's supply out of the drawer and put it in the little sleeve. So much had changed since her last cycle. It had literally been only a little over a month since she'd met Bran. Her whole world had been turned upside down.

She was just eating her yogurt when her phone buzzed. It was a text from Bran, explaining that Cole was in town for only a few more days and they were going to spend some time together, but he'd be in touch by the weekend. That was that, then. She'd have time to think and make some decisions before seeing him again.

And in the meantime, she'd paint. There was nothing that helped her work through her problems like putting her heart on canvas.

By Saturday Jess was starting to panic.

She was three days into her new pack of pills and she hadn't had a period at all. Granted, being on the pill made them lighter, but usually on her second sugar pill she started, like clockwork. She laid in bed, staring at the bunk above her, trying not to freak out over the fact that she might be pregnant. Because she'd replayed every detail of her nights with Bran, and had discovered that the morning after their hotel stay she hadn't taken her pill at all. She'd missed it completely. It shouldn't make a difference, but it could. They'd had room service, and she'd come home and had been so distracted that she was sure she'd missed her pill and her vitamins.

She couldn't be pregnant. Oh, Lord, what a mess that would be. She wanted children but not this way. Not with a man who didn't want any. Not on her own with no support. She didn't know how to be a mother.

She threw off the covers. Okay, so that might be putting the cart a long way before the horse. She really couldn't do anything until she took a test. Maybe she just missed for whatever reason. And if it was positive, then she'd figure things out. One step at a time.

The drive to the pharmacy didn't take that long, and Jess figured there was no point in waiting and putting off something that wouldn't change the outcome. So she took one of the tests out of the box and into the bathroom she went. Then she came out and made coffee while waiting the three minutes suggested.

When she went back in and looked at the stick, she let out a huge breath.

Negative.

Her hand shook as she dropped the test in the trash can and sat on top of the toilet for a moment, trying to make sense of her feelings. There was relief, of course, because this was so not the right time and even though she was in love with him, Bran wasn't the right man no matter how much she might want him to be. But there was also disappointment. She thought of all the times she'd held Rose, snuggled her close, and how she longed for her own family. Those feelings were there, too. At least the result had clarified much of her thoughts. She and Bran wanted different things. They were just fooling themselves with ground rules and flings and whatever else. He was a good man. They might even be good for each other. But that didn't mean they had a future.

She was just fixing her coffee when there was a knock on the door and then it opened, as she'd left it unlocked as she usually did during the day. Bran came through the door, a small smile on his face, and a paper bag in his hand. "I went to the bakery," he said, holding up the bag. "And got chocolate croissants."

She wasn't ready for this conversation, so she smiled

back and kept it light. "I just made coffee. I'll get you some."

"Sounds good. How've you been?"

What a loaded question. She hesitated and then said, "All right. Has Cole gone back to New York?"

"He left last night."

She handed him a mug. "You had a good visit though, huh?"

Bran nodded. "We did. We caught up about a lot of stuff. This island project of his…it's pretty cool."

"So he's going to do it?"

"Yeah, I think so." Bran's grin was genuinely wide now. "Who knew? The three of us went to school together, live within an hour or so of each other, and now have second homes here in Nova Scotia. You'd almost think we were brothers."

Her heart melted at the genuine affection in his voice. "You are, in all the ways that count. I think it's lovely."

"Thanks. Hey, got any milk or cream for this?"

She'd forgotten he liked his coffee light, and before she could move he'd gone to the fridge, making himself at home as he had the last several times he'd visited. But when he turned around, his face dropped and she realized she'd left the pregnancy test box on the counter.

He put the mug down very quietly.

"Bran, I—"

"Are you pregnant?"

The way he said those three words sent her heart straight to her feet. He made it sound as if the world were truly ending. The last time she'd heard that exact tone, Ana had taken her hand and said, "I have cancer."

Bran was so repulsed by the idea that it wasn't just undesirable. It was a world-ending scenario.

She wanted to say something, but the words wouldn't

come together in her mind, let alone out of her mouth. Bran's lips tightened and he picked up the box. "You told me you were on the pill. I bought condoms to double up. And now you're pregnant? I told you I don't want more children. I was very, very clear about that."

His voice wasn't angry. It was worse. It was surgically precise, almost emotionless. She understood he didn't want more kids. She understood that came from grief and that it was his right. He'd been honest from the start. But she also knew that it had taken two of them, and right now it certainly felt as if any blame would have fallen on her, rather than be shared, and that made her angry.

Her voice shook as she replied. "If I were pregnant, we would both bear responsibility. But I'm not, so don't worry, Branson. You're off the hook. You can start breathing again."

"Oh, thank God."

He sounded so relieved that tears stung the backs of her eyes. "Would it have been so bad?" she snapped. "Would me being pregnant be the worst thing in the world to happen?"

He stepped back at the vitriol in her voice. "No. The worst thing in the world to happen is losing a child."

Dammit. Silence fell, harsh and thick. Of course it was. She wasn't that insensitive, even though she'd lashed out. "I'm sorry, Bran. Of course you're right. I didn't mean to…" She didn't know what to say after that. "Look, I'll be honest with you. The night we stayed in Halifax… I forgot to take my pill the next day. I didn't have my period this week on schedule, so I got tests this morning just in case."

"But you're not pregnant."

"No." She lifted her chin a little. "But I think this whole thing, the idea with the ground rules, the summer fling with us going our separate ways with a smile was a little disingenuous on both our parts. I don't think this is going to work anymore."

He blinked. Opened his mouth to say something, then shut it again. Then opened it again, and hesitated. "Jess, I like being with you. You've brought me back to life, you see? I'm writing. I'm looking toward a future rather than drifting aimlessly. We don't have to break it off. We can revise the ground rules—"

"No," she said, firmer now. "No, we can't. Bran, there are two things you don't want. You don't want more children, and you don't want to fall in love. But you see, I do want children someday. And I fell in love. I know that's breaking a rule, but I also know it's a deal breaker anyway. I'm in love with you, and I can't go through the rest of the summer pretending I'm not, only to break up at the end after I get in even deeper." She tried to ignore the catch in her voice. "I don't want to be left again, so we have to do this now."

"Jess," he whispered, running a hand over his face.

"Tell me you haven't been thinking the same thing. In the beginning you couldn't wait to rush over here, to steal moments together. But after the trip to the island earlier this week, you sent one text saying you were hanging with Cole. The three of you are tight, but you guys didn't come over here, and you certainly didn't steal away for a stolen hour. You're scared. So let's be honest, okay? I can't see you anymore. It's too hard."

"Yeah, I've been thinking the same thing. So what? Listen, we don't have to have sex…"

The tears behind her eyes sprang forward and trickled down her cheeks. "Is that what it's been to you? Sex? I don't believe it. Oh, Lord, Bran, this goes so much further than sex. It's about my heart, don't you see? Just being with you, holding your hand, listening to your voice…it all does stuff to me. Intimacy isn't all about the bedroom."

"I know that. Do you think I don't know that? Don't you think that's what I miss about Jennie every day?"

It was his turn to snap, and she swallowed against the growing lump in her throat. It was always going to come down to Jennie, wasn't it? Maybe he didn't compare her to his dead wife when they were together, but he certainly wasn't over her. He didn't want to love again, couldn't love again, because he couldn't let Jennie go.

She couldn't do this anymore. "I'm going to give Tori and Jeremy my notice and go back to my loft in Chicago. My agent is clamoring to do a showing, and I have more than enough work to keep me busy. And you have a book to write."

He came around the counter and took her hand, then lifted his other hand and wiped a tear off her cheek with his thumb. The contact felt so wonderful and sad. After today she wouldn't hear the sound of his voice again, or feel the pad of his thumb, or be able to run her hands through his shaggy locks. She'd be going back to Chicago alone, to the loft she'd shared with Ana, fighting against emptiness all over again. For the briefest of moments, she wished the test had been positive just so she'd have company in that huge empty space. A baby wouldn't leave her. And Bran wasn't leaving her, either. But she was quickly learning that it didn't matter who did the leaving. It all hurt.

"I don't want us to leave things this way," he whispered. "Not angry and hurting. What we've been to each other deserves more than that."

It did, except she was having a hard time moving past the sound of his voice and the hard lines of his face when he'd seen the test box. It left a sour taste that she couldn't quite wish away.

"It does hurt. But I'll be fine. I always am, you see. And we did have a good time, we truly did. It's just time."

He nodded. "Can I kiss you one more time?"

Her heart hadn't actually broken during the whole conversation. She'd been hurt and she'd been angry, but she hadn't actually felt the moment where the ground seemed to disappear beneath her feet and left this sense of…emptiness. But now…she knew it was for the best, and yet she wanted him to tell her that she was wrong; that he had fallen in love with her too and they could work it out.

She'd always been a stupid dreamer like that.

Her lips trembled as he bent his head and touched his mouth to hers, then pressed his forehead against hers for a long moment while his hands gripped her upper arms.

"I'm sorry," he whispered. "I'm sorry I can't give you what you want."

He let her go and turned away, and without looking back went through the door, down the steps and to his car.

Every cell in her body begged her to go after him and tell him it didn't matter.

But it did matter. And it was for the best. Because she deserved someone who loved her unreservedly.

And that wasn't him, no matter how much she wanted it to be.

CHAPTER FOURTEEN

BRAN VENTURED OUT to the lighthouse to survey the latest work. It was coming along nicely, now that the restoration had begun. The foundation had been sound, but there'd been work to do at the top, including replacing the platform and making everything airtight. The door was replaced with a replica of the old one, and fresh paint would go on early next week.

The biggest change, however, was the addition of windows on the bottom level. Now when he went inside, beams of light lit the interior, making the empty space bright and cheery.

Except nothing was very cheery at all.

He ran his finger over the top of the woodstove, remembering the day Jess had been here and she'd cautioned him not to open the stove door in case there were mice. He smiled a little at the memory, but sadness made his heart heavy. He missed her. His days had gone back to the routine of one after another, little variation, too much time on his own.

The writing was there now, at least, and he'd sent off an opening and general synopsis to his agent, who'd responded with relief. Bran wasn't a lot of things, but he was still a writer, thank God. Even if the sunshine seemed to have disappeared from his life, he was back in the land of the living.

It just seemed so very bland and pointless without her.

Despondent, he went back to the house and made himself a coffee, then wandered to the den. He booted up his laptop and then, missing her more than usual, opened the browser and went to her website.

It had been updated.

She had a show opening in late October in Chicago. A recent photo showed her laughing, her face alight with happiness and her sunshiny hair gleaming. It hit him right in the gut. Of course she was happy. He was glad. But he was resentful, too. That she'd clearly moved on and he was still…here. Moping half the time and writing the other.

But this was what he'd wanted. What he'd chosen.

His attention was diverted by a car coming up the driveway—Jeremy's Jaguar. Bran closed the window and shut the laptop, preparing himself for a visit. Cole would be closing on the island property soon, and then the three of them had made a promise to spend a weekend after the possession date, a guys' weekend with some deep-sea fishing, maybe some rounds of pool in the games room, and unhealthy food like chicken wings and pizza. Bran was looking forward to it.

Anything to be able to stop thinking about her all the time.

He opened the door for Jeremy, and immediately had a moment of alarm. The man looked like he'd hardly slept. His hair stuck up on one side, and his eyes were red.

"What's happened?" Bran asked, his heart freezing.

"Rose is sick. She's in Halifax at the children's hospital right now, but I've just spent twenty-four hours there and came home to get stuff to take back. Except… I can't go in the house, Bran. I didn't know where else to go."

Bran took a deep breath. While memories threatened to overwhelm him, he pushed them aside. His best friend needed him, and Bran knew the fear and shock Jeremy was going through. "Is Tori okay?"

Jeremy nodded. "She's fine. Still at the hospital. We didn't want to leave Rose alone, and there was no way I was going to be able to tear Tori away, so…"

His voice trailed off, weak and shaky.

"It's okay. You need to pick up what, clothes? Toiletries? Maybe some food for Tori, so she keeps eating?"

Jeremy nodded, his expression one of exhaustion and misery. "Yes, all of those things."

"I'll help." He put his hand on Jeremy's shoulder. "You don't have to do this alone, okay?"

Jeremy nodded. "I'm sorry, bro. I know this is hard for you—"

"Not as much as it used to be. I'm okay. I can deal. Promise."

He realized it was true as he grabbed his wallet and keys. Three months ago—even two—he would have run in the other direction. Not now. He took Jeremy's keys from him and drove them over to the house, then waited while Jeremy gathered clothes and personal items. Bran walked over to the sofa and paused, staring down at a little yellow bunny on the cushions. He remembered that bunny. Jess had bought it during one of their trips to the market.

Things were suddenly very quiet, so Bran braced himself and made his way upstairs to check on his friend. He found Jeremy in the nursery, sitting in a rocking chair and holding a blanket in his hands. He wasn't crying, but Bran knew that meant nothing. He was hurting on the inside, and he was scared.

"Do they know what's wrong with her?" Bran finally asked, keeping his voice as calm as possible.

"Measles. Something about how she could have picked them up at her last checkup, but she's too little for the vaccine yet." His tortured gaze met Bran's. "Babies can die from measles, Bran."

"I know. But she's at the hospital and getting great care, right?"

Jeremy nodded.

"Okay. So let's put this stuff in the car and get to Halifax so you can give Tori a break. All right?"

Jeremy nodded. "Yeah. Yeah, let's go."

As Jeremy got up, Bran noticed a framed picture on the wall. It was a sketch, and one of Jess's, he was sure of it. Of Rose, in a little bonnet, bundled up and in presumably Tori's arms. A lump formed in his throat. That precious little girl, who smiled and gurgled at her father's silly faces, who looked at her mother so adoringly, who had studied him with such wide-eyed curiosity the night of the card game as he'd picked her up for the first time.

His best friend would not lose his daughter the way he'd lost Owen.

They packed the two bags in the car, and Bran offered to drive so Jeremy could rest. They had barely hit the highway when Jeremy fell asleep, and Bran was glad of it. He'd likely been awake all night, worrying about Rose and Tori. Bran remembered one time when Owen had got a cold and struggled to breathe so much. There'd been sleepless nights, but he'd also hated to see Jennie so exhausted and worried.

Bran found his way to the children's hospital and pulled into the parking garage, waking Jeremy as he rolled down the window for the parking stub. "We're here, buddy."

"I didn't mean to sleep. Sorry."

"Don't be. You needed the rest. Come on, I'll go in with

you. Is there someplace inside where we can grab you and Tori some food? Coffee?"

Jeremy nodded. "Yeah. I don't know if Tori will eat, but…"

"Tea," Bran suggested. "She drinks tea a lot, right? Get her tea and a sandwich she can pick at. It's your job to make sure she takes care of herself. And you can't do that if you don't look after yourself, too."

"I'm fine."

"Humor me."

They spent precious minutes picking up sandwiches and drinks, and then Bran carried the overnight bags in his hands as Jeremy hit the elevator button taking them to the correct floor. Bran's pulse accelerated as they headed for the isolation unit; he hated hospitals, and the memories bubbled to the surface simply from the sounds and the smell that was so peculiar to hospitals. But he carried on, knowing that for months Jeremy had been there for him, and it was his turn to repay the favor.

Poor little Rose was in isolation since she was so contagious. Once they arrived, Tori came out, shedding her mask and gown. She looked like hell. Her hair was pulled back in a ponytail, and there were dark circles under her eyes. She appeared to have slept in her clothes, but the relief on her face when she saw Jeremy lit up the room. Bran felt a strange emotion wash over him. It was like just being in the same room together made everything okay. He'd felt that not long ago, with Jess. She hadn't had to do anything but be there and smile, and the world was forever changed.

He was forever changed.

He put the bags down and went forward to give Tori a hug. "Hello, little mama," he said softly, giving her a squeeze. "How's she doing?"

"They're giving her fluids through an IV and stuff to bring down her fever. We just keep hoping there aren't complications like—" she took a breath, swallowed, got herself together again "—like encephalitis."

"She's a tough cookie. And Jeremy has food for you."

"I'm not hungry."

"Then save the sandwich for later and drink some tea. He got mint, the kind you like."

She looked up, and Jeremy was holding out the paper cup. "I got a large. You need to look after yourself too, honey. You haven't slept."

"Neither have you."

He smiled a little. "I slept in the car while Bran drove."

Bran peeked into the room and clenched his teeth. He couldn't see anything, but he imagined poor little Rose, blotchy and red, sleeping while an IV was taped to her, delivering fluids and medication. No little one should have to go through such a thing.

Tori sat down and peeled the top back on the tea. The scent of peppermint filled the air. "I don't want to be out here too long. I keep thinking she has to know that we're there. I've been singing to her."

"Of course she knows you're there." Bran sat down next to Jeremy, and reached for the bag of sandwiches. "Here, you two. Seriously, eat something. And while you're doing that, I'm going to book you a hotel room nearby. Even if you have to sleep in shifts, it'll give you a base until she's able to go home. You can get some good rest and have a hot shower."

"Bran, you don't have to do that."

He leaned forward and met Jeremy's eyes, and finally said something he should have said long ago. "When I needed you, you were there. Bullying me into eating and sleeping and showering. Sitting with me. This is a very small thing, Jer. Let me do it for you."

Jeremy nodded. "Okay."

"Do you need anything else? Is there anything I can do?"

"Not right now. Thank you, Bran."

He excused himself and went to a nearby lounge to make accommodation arrangements, giving Jeremy and Tori time alone. His thumbs hovered over the keypad, knowing he should send the message and afraid to all the same. He hadn't had contact with Jess since that day at the boathouse when they'd called it quits.

Still, she'd want to know.

Before he could reconsider, he typed rapidly.

Jess, just letting you know that Rose is in the hospital in Halifax with the measles. I'm here with Jeremy and Tori. Bran.

He sat back in the chair and replayed that morning in his mind. He'd been such an ass. Handled things all wrong just because seeing the pregnancy test box had scared him out of his wits. He'd known they had to break it off, but not like that. He'd wanted to explain that she deserved so much more. That she was wonderful and needed someone who could give her all of himself. Give her the family she wanted. And Lord, not ask her to take on so much baggage. Instead, he'd jumped down her throat and it had just been…awful.

He regretted that more than anything. That their beautiful friendship had ended with harsh words and hurt feelings. It seemed their relationship deserved a better ending.

His phone vibrated in his hand, and he looked at the screen. Jess had replied.

Oh, no! Is she okay? I'll call Tori. She must be so distressed.

There was a pause, and then another quick message.

I appreciate you telling me, Bran.

He didn't know what to say after that. Anything would either be too much or not enough. He tucked the phone back in his pocket and sat for a long time, replaying old thoughts in his head. Some made sense but others…others did not. What did that mean for his future? Could he truly go through life with a couple of friends and a laptop for company?

He'd missed her every single day.

Eventually he made his way back to the unit. Tori was leaned against Jeremy's shoulder, her eyes closed and breathing deep.

"I'll go so she can rest."

"Stay a minute. She'll sleep for a while now. The tea helped her relax."

They kept their voices low, and Jeremy adjusted a little so that the angle of Tori's neck was a little gentler. Then he looked up at Bran. "You and Jess. What happened?"

Bran swallowed. Thought about how happy he'd been just to see her impersonal text minutes earlier. "I wasn't ready. And she had a pregnancy scare."

"Oh, man. That sent you running for the hills, huh."

"Considering the current situation, I'm not sure you want to talk about Owen."

Jeremy nodded slowly, but then met Bran's eyes. "I'm a wreck, it's true. That little girl…and her mother…they changed my life. I can't imagine…no, that's not true. I can imagine, and it scares me to death. So I think I understand. Yours isn't just imagination. You've lived through it and would rather do anything than go through it again."

That Jeremy understood so completely came as a relief. "Yeah. There's just one problem, Jer."

"What's that?"

"I'm in love with her."

Jeremy let out a huge breath. "Well, doesn't that make the cheese more binding."

They both laughed a little.

"I couldn't admit it when she was here. I mean it when I say I wasn't ready. I wasn't over Jennie. I don't know if I'll ever be over Jennie. How is that fair?"

Jeremy frowned. "I'm not sure this is ever anything you are 'over.' I think it's a decision to leave it in the past, and be brave enough to embrace a future. It's a big thing."

"It's a huge thing. She wants a family, Jer. And she should have one. You've seen her with Rose. She loves that little girl. She should have babies of her own if that's what she wants. And I just don't know."

"All love carries risks."

"I know."

"And rewards. But only you can decide where that balance lies. If being without her is easier than taking the risk, then you know letting her go was the right thing."

"But if it's not?"

Jeremy shrugged. "You have to sort that out on your own. All I'm going to say is that I loved Jennie, but Jess had a way of making you smile that was just…different. There's no question in my mind that she fell in love with you."

Tori shifted and he moved with her, smoothing her hair off her face while she slept on. Bran marveled at the tenderness he saw in his friend's expression.

"Love changes a person, you know?" Jeremy looked away from his wife's face and smiled. "It made me a better man. It made me want things I didn't feel worthy of asking, but somehow…she makes it right. You found it once, Bran. If you are lucky enough to have found it a second time, think long and hard before letting it slip away."

CHAPTER FIFTEEN

JESS HAD NEVER been so glad for air-conditioning in her life.

Chicago was stifling. A late July heat wave was making things miserable, and she cringed to think of her power bill with how much her AC was running, but at least she was comfortable. Most of the time.

Living alone had never been this difficult. Ana had been the one to move into the loft with her, taking the second bedroom and bringing her boundless energy and kindness with her. After she'd gone, it had been hard to live in the apartment without hearing Ana's voice, singing in the shower, or the way she'd stay up on Saturdays watching old movies.

But this loneliness was different. Because it wasn't the loft that was quiet and lonely, it was her whole life. It was like taking one of her paintings and suddenly only seeing it in black and white. There was a vibrancy missing that she knew had one cause: Bran.

She missed him. It seemed impossible; they'd been together such a short time. But time didn't matter. What was time, anyway? Measurable in months, days, hours, minutes…and yet it moved slowly and quickly. Her time in Nova Scotia had been too short, and now her days were too long. And yet the clock ticked on at the same pace.

So she worked. She buried herself in it, putting all her

feelings and thoughts and longings and regrets on canvas. It was the neglected door and the determined daisies, the lighthouse strong and sure, and the waves and wind that battered it relentlessly. It was a long, white beach that stretched on forever, and a man standing on a bluff overlooking the ocean, lost.

Her agent had seen most of what she'd done and raved over it. Jess had come away from the meeting glad he was happy, but personally caring little about the commercial appeal of it and more concerned with the process.

The only thing she could think to do was paint him out of her heart. So far she wasn't succeeding.

Had she been wrong to leave? Should she have given him more time? Maybe. Though in her heart she knew staying would have just prolonged the inevitable.

A quick glance at the clock on the microwave showed just after one o'clock, so she decided it was as good a time as any for a break. She turned on the kettle to make coffee. She'd picked up some bagels at the market a few days ago, so she popped one in the toaster. A bagel with cream cheese would suffice for lunch.

The kettle had just boiled and she'd poured the water into the press when a knock sounded at the door.

She frowned. A courier, maybe? She certainly wasn't expecting anyone. She padded to the door in her bare feet and peeked through the hole to see who was there.

Bran.

Her paint-stained fingers flew to her mouth. What was he doing here? Her first thought was that something had happened to Rose. Oh, God, she hoped not. But would he fly all the way here to deliver that news?

The only other option was that he was here for her. And that was…unbelievable. Considering how they'd left things.

She opened the door, curiosity getting the better of her.

His gaze swept over her, top to bottom to top again, and a smile bloomed on his face. "You look wonderful," he said. His voice held a note of reverence that touched her deeply, and she bit down on her lip. And in the next moment she was in his arms, in the middle of the biggest bear hug she could ever remember.

It was a shock and confusing as heck, but she went with it, because it was so damned good to see him again and hold him close. The scent that was uniquely Bran—soap and aftershave and sea air. How could he smell like the sea after sitting on a plane?

"You feel so good," he said close to her ear, sending shivers down her body. "God, I've missed you."

He loosened his hold and she leaned back so she could see his face, trying not to be so glad to see him. "What are you doing here? Is Rose okay?" He'd cut his hair, she noticed. Not super short, but the shaggy locks were tamed and his beard was precisely trimmed. It was sexy as anything.

"That little bean is just about perfect. She's very close to rolling over."

Oh, bless him. He called Rose a little bean. Why did he have to be so…everything?

She wilted in relief. "Okay, good. Because I thought for a minute you'd come to tell me that…" She hesitated. "I'm sorry. I shouldn't bring stuff like that up."

"No, it's okay. She was really sick, but she's okay now. Full recovery. And that's not why I'm here. But maybe we could go inside and close the door? It's hot as blazes out here, and you're letting all your lovely cool air out."

He wasn't wrong, so she stepped back and once they were clear of the threshold, shut the door. It was a relief to be out of the midday heat.

"Do you want coffee? I just made some. It's likely to

be strong now. I poured the water in my press the moment you knocked."

"Coffee sounds great."

She led the way to the kitchen, which was about a quarter of the size of the one in his house and still held a small dining set. Heart pounding, fingers trembling, she got two mugs out of the cabinet and then pushed down the plunger in the press, pouring strong brew in each cup.

She looked up at him. "There's milk in the fridge."

His gaze held hers. Coffee and milk had been the catalyst on that last fateful day. But now he calmly went to the refrigerator, took out a carton of milk put it on the counter.

"I'm sorry, Jess. For all the things I said that day."

"Me, too. I mean… I knew we had to end, but that wasn't how I wanted it to happen."

"Do you think it ever would have been parting with a kiss and a fond farewell and a 'thanks for the memories'?" he asked. He came a step closer. "Because I think it was always going to be messy. I'm not sure it can be avoided when two people love each other."

She was holding out his mug for him to take when he said those words, and suddenly she couldn't move. Her hand started to shake. He reached out and took the mug and then set it down on the table.

"You heard me right. You said you loved me that day, and I did not. I didn't think I could. I thought it was impossible. But the truth is, I was already in love with you and too scared to admit it to myself. It was easier to say I'd never love anyone again. There was protection in it."

"You weren't ready. I knew that. It's why I had to go."

"I know, sweetheart. I know."

This wasn't happening. He wasn't here, in her kitchen, saying all these wonderful things. Panic threaded through her veins. She'd thought she'd known what she wanted.

But it turned out she didn't know anything. Oh, how smug she'd been.

"What changed?" she asked, trying and failing to keep the tremor out of her voice.

"Rose. And Jeremy. And me being a lonely, grumpy man whose closest relationship is with his laptop. And I wouldn't even have that if it weren't for you." He took her hand. "Come, sit. Let me explain, and then you can decide what you want to do with me."

Oh, she knew what she wanted to do with him. That hadn't changed. But this was about more than their physical compatibility. It always had been.

He held her hand as she across from him. "When Rose got sick, Jeremy came for me. He was a wreck. He's my best friend. Of course I was going to be there for him. And walking into that hospital made me face a lot of things. But it also helped me realize that I've healed a lot. Jennie and Owen—they're a part of my past that will always be in my heart. But I can't keep living there. It's not living at all, and after I met you, I discovered I actually do want to live again."

"Oh, Bran…"

"And then Jeremy gave me a bit of a talking-to. And I've been thinking for a while now about what I want my life to look like. I've come to the conclusion that I don't much care, as long as you're in it."

Tears threatened to spill over. "You really mean that."

"I do." He squeezed her fingers. "Loving again terrifies me, I'm not gonna lie. But being without you scares me more. I never thought I'd ever find this again. That there'd be someone I couldn't live without." He hesitated a moment, licked his lips and then said, "You told me once that the people that you loved had all left you. When I remembered that, I realized why you sent me away that day. You walked away first so I wouldn't, didn't you?"

The tears did spill over then. It was the secret wound she'd only ever shared with two people—him and Ana. And Ana was gone now. She nodded. "I suppose I did." She sniffled and wiped her fingers over her cheeks. "God, I'm sorry. I don't mean to cry."

"It's okay. I hurt you. We hurt each other because we were scared. I'm still scared, Jess. But I'm here. And I'm staying, if you'll have me."

Silence fell in the tiny kitchen. "What do you mean, staying?"

He reached out and cupped her cheek tenderly. "I mean, you get to decide. You have a life here. I can write anywhere. I have a place in New York and the house in Nova Scotia and wherever you want to be, that's where we'll go. All I need is an internet connection, a supply of coffee and you."

He was offering her everything. She loved this loft, but she loved a lot of things. And there was still one thing they hadn't talked about. A very big, very important thing.

"What about children?"

He met her gaze evenly. "I miss being a father. It's going to scare me to death, but, yes. Yes, to a family. I look at Jeremy and Tori, and it's something that's missing in my heart. I'll always have a spot for Owen. But I won't love our babies any less, Jess."

Now he really was giving her everything. She stood and went over to him, sitting on his knees, wrapping her arms around his shoulders as she started to cry for real. He was here. He loved her. He wanted babies. And Bran... she knew in the deepest parts of her heart and soul that he was not the kind of man to leave once he'd promised to stay. Not if he had any choice in the matter. And life didn't have guarantees, did it?

But it certainly had wishes and dreams come true.

"Do you know what I want the most?" she said, holding him close.

"What?"

"I want to go home."

EPILOGUE

THE CHICAGO AIR had lost the summer heat, and the breeze was now cool and brisk in the first week of November. Bran held Jess's hand as they entered the gallery, and then gave her a kiss as Jack rushed over and took her away to do artisty things. Bran knew the drill; he'd done the same during signings and events, and he was thrilled to see Jess enjoying so much success.

She was so beautiful tonight, in a long black dress that hugged her curves and her hair up in the topknot he'd come to love so much. Her freckles were hidden by makeup, and her lips were a pretty shade of pink. She'd told him, back in the hotel room, that she'd forbidden the esthetician from using false eyelashes. He'd laughed and kissed her, nearly ruining the careful makeup job.

There'd be time enough for that later.

Instead, he accepted a rare glass of champagne and took his time wandering through the gallery. The collection was small but beautiful; he was so stinkin' proud of what she'd accomplished. And these paintings would always be special to him. It was like a visual diary of how he'd fallen in love with Jess. Or as she was known tonight, *the* Jessica Blundon.

There were three paintings in black and white that he thought were stunning. One was of the reflectors of the lighthouse lamp, and so very different from her other works. A second one was a fishing boat, tied to a dock. And the third made him catch his breath. It was him. Standing on the bluff by the lighthouse, looking out over a rough sea. He looked so…lonely. Bereft. He understood why she'd done it in black and white.

An arm slid through his, and she pressed up against him. "Hello, handsome."

"Hello, famous artist. This one…wow, Jess."

"I took a pic of that the first day, when you kicked me off the property," she said softly. "Something about you just drew me in. I never believed you were an angry old troll."

He snorted and laughed, and looked down at her. She shared an impish smile with him that made him warm all over.

The last months had been nothing short of amazing. Jess had gone back to Nova Scotia with him, staying at his house, and he'd turned the lighthouse into a studio for her. He'd finished the draft of his book, and they were making a stop in New York on the way home so he could meet with his agent and editor. He'd sold his brownstone there that he'd shared with Jennie, and that had been hard, but Jeremy was going to hook them up with a new property that was just for them.

Life was moving forward, and he was happy.

Unlike the man in the painting. But instead of being sad, it made him realize how far he'd come, thanks to the love of the wonderful woman at his side.

"Come with me for a moment," she said, removing her arm from his and reaching for his hand instead. "There's something I want you to see."

She led him to the other side of the gallery, where a lone painting was displayed. He stopped and stared. It was the same painting—with him on the bluff—but it was in full color, rich and vibrant. The sea wasn't angry; the waves were joyous and playful, and the grass and flowers waved in bright sunlight next to a pristine white lighthouse. Before and after.

But what truly made it different was that he wasn't alone in this one. A woman was beside him. She was beside him, in a flowy dress and her hair up and…

And in between them was a small child, holding on to their hands.

"I was going to call this one *Dreams*," she said. "And then I decided it was something else."

"What?" he asked, his throat tight and his heart full.

"Future."

He stepped closer. The little silver plaque beneath it had *Future* inscribed. And there was a tag on it that said "Not for sale."

"Jess?"

"I'm not selling this one. It's our future, Bran."

He stared into her eyes. "Are you saying…"

She put her hand to her still-flat stomach, but a smile broke out on her face and he swore she lit up like a candle.

"I took the test last week. Barely, but yes, I'm pregnant."

He started to laugh. He couldn't help it. It was a joyful expression of happiness and disbelief, mostly that he could be this lucky. "It's funny?" she asked, raising an eyebrow.

"It's unbelievable," he confirmed, and pressed a quick kiss to her lips. "Look, I was going to do this whole big thing after your showing, but I think this is the right time." He reached into his suit jacket and took out a blue box. "I love you, Jess. I don't know that I believed in angels until you showed up at my lighthouse, being all sassy and beautiful. But if there are angels, you're mine. Will you marry me?"

She nodded. He put the ring on her finger, then pulled her close, amazed and awed that their baby was between them right now.

Jeremy was right after all. Not everyone got lucky a second time around. Now that he had, he was never going to let her go.

* * * * *

FOR THE TWINS' SAKE

MELISSA SENATE

For my wonderful aunt and uncle,
Rick and Arlene D'Alli, who came to visit me way up
in Maine just as I was finishing writing this novel.
XOXO

Prologue

Was that a baby crying?

Nah.

Noah Dawson turned over in bed and tried to go back to sleep, but he heard the sound again. A crying baby. Impossible on this isolated ranch in the Wyoming wilderness, but unmistakable. Yesterday, Noah had gone to Bear Ridge Groceries to stock up for the impending rainstorm that threatened flash flooding, and a woman in front of him on the long checkout line had had a baby in her shopping cart, wailing just like he was hearing now. A round of peekaboo had helped quiet the screecher. But, man, did he know a crying baby when he heard one.

Still, right now? He glanced at his phone on the bedside table—at 1:52 a.m.? He had to be hearing things. Dreaming. Imagining it.

"Waaaah!"

Noah sat up. The crying was getting louder—and coming through the window on the early April breeze.

Did he have a middle-of-the-night visitor and he'd missed the doorbell ringing or something? Did he even know anyone with a baby?

"Waaah-waaah!"

Noah bolted out of bed. That *was* a baby crying. And it was coming from just outside the window of his cabin, below which was the front porch. He grabbed his jeans from where he'd slung them over his desk chair, pulled them on and hurried downstairs.

The crying got louder. He pulled the front door open.

Then he looked down—and gasped.

A baby—a girl, guessing from the pink blanket covering most of her in an infant car seat, a white cotton cap on her head—was crying up a storm. A small black tote bag was beside the carrier.

What the hell? Who would leave a baby here? He glanced around for a car, for someone, anyone, but all he saw were the distant evergreens in the moon-light. The ranch was silent otherwise.

"Hello?" he called out, looking in every direction. No one. "Hello?" he shouted.

No response. No person. Nothing but the breeze through the trees.

How long has she been out here? he wondered as he snatched up the carrier and bag and brought them inside, his heart starting to pound, his brain trying to make some sort of sense of this. A baby. Left on his porch at two in the morning.

He set the carrier on the big wood coffee table in the living room. He carefully moved aside the blanket.

Whoa. Noah didn't know much about babies, but this tiny creature had to be a newborn. He wouldn't be surprised if the baby had been born today. That's how small she was. Her pink footie pajamas were way too big for her little body.

Call the police. Call an ambulance. Call social services. So many thoughts ran through his head at once that he had to just stop, stand still and breathe.

He glanced out the window, the rain starting. Just drizzling now, but within ten to fifteen minutes the skies would open up. That was a problem. The ranch was forty minutes from town down some winding rural roads, and the storm was forecasted to quickly create flood conditions, which would come before anyone could safely reach the place. Doc Bakerton, who ran the clinic in Bear Ridge, had emergency hours, and his home was only a ten-minute drive from here. Noah could get the baby over to Bakerton's faster and safer than an ambulance or the sheriff could get here, and he knew these country roads and where the river would rise the worst. He could get back.

Decision made: he'd take her over to Doc Bakerton's place.

But right now, the baby was crying her head off. Should he comfort her for a few seconds? Noah had no idea what the hell to do. She let out another wail, and he shifted the blanket aside, not surprised she wasn't even buckled in.

Hand under the neck, he told himself, lifting her out as carefully as he could. He held her alongside his arm, bracketed by his chest, not sure he was doing this right.

He touched a finger to her little cheek. She wasn't cold or hot, and her color seemed okay.

A hot burst of anger swelled in his gut over whoever had left a newborn to the elements in the middle of the night. What if he hadn't heard her crying at all? What if she'd been out there all night? In the middle of the Wyoming wilderness, a rainstorm about to pour down. Granted, the large front porch of his foreman's cabin was covered on three sides as a point of refuge for future guests of the ranch to wait out any bad weather, but still.

He swayed his arms a bit, and the crying stopped. When the baby's strangely colored eyes—a grayish blueish—closed, his anger dissipated some. The little face looked content, relaxed, the tiny chest rising and falling, rising and falling, the impossibly tiny bow lips giving a quirk.

Whose are you? he wondered. Why would anyone leave you *here*? The Dawson Family Guest Ranch wasn't due to open for seven more weeks, on Memorial Day weekend, so the guest cabins were empty. And none of the small staff he'd hired lived on the property.

He glanced at the carrier and tote bag on the coffee table. Maybe there was a note. Or a birth certificate. Something.

He couldn't reach the bag easily without putting the baby down, and he thought he should hold her a bit—why, exactly, he wasn't entirely sure. To keep her warm? To comfort her? Make her feel connected to someone and something? His gaze caught on something small and white poking up from underneath the blanket in the car seat. He shoved the blanket aside.

So there was a note. Half a page. Scrawled, crudely, in black pen.

She's your baby, Noah Dawson. Your responsibility. You won't hear from me again.

Every cell in his body froze.

What?

My baby? he thought, the idea not penetrating.

Forget the police. Or social services. Until he could think, figure out who the mother was.

His baby? Seriously?

He grabbed the tote bag and rooted around inside it for a birth certificate or envelope or any kind of paperwork. Nothing but a baby bottle, a small container of formula and two tiny diapers.

The infant's eyes opened just then, then drooped, opened, drooped, then closed again. There *was* something familiar about the little face, something in the expression, the eyes, that he couldn't pin down. He *knew* that face. The baby's mother, a woman he probably was with one night… Or maybe the little girl looked a bit like him?

Just get her to the doc, he told himself. *Now.*

He very gently laid her back down in the carrier, one little fist moving, the lips quirking again. He buckled the five-point harness and settled the blanket around her.

From the looks of her, all scrawny and tiny, tinier than your average baby, he was pretty sure she couldn't be more than a few hours old. So her mother didn't want to keep her and dropped her off right after giving birth? That hardly made sense. Mothers who'd just delivered a baby didn't jump in cars and drop off their babies in the middle of the night. Unless they were desperate, maybe.

All he knew was that someone had left a baby on his doorstep. No knock, no explanation. No concern for the infant's well-being.

No idea who that person could possibly be.

His baby? His brain wasn't fully firing right now from the shock, but as he lifted the carrier he managed to think back nine months. It was the second week of April now. Who had he been involved with last July?

There were a few possibilities. One of whom he'd seen in passing just last week as he'd parked in front of the coffee shop in town. She certainly hadn't been nine months pregnant.

Two or three others back then, one-night stands when his life had still been about drinking too much at bars and trying to forget his troubles with women whose last names he didn't know.

He wasn't proud of that time in his life.

He'd been a hot mess. Two years ago, the small ranch he'd managed to buy had gone under—like father, like son, he supposed. The woman he'd loved his entire life had told him she'd had enough and was moving on, unless he changed most things about himself. He hadn't known how, and she'd gotten tired of trying to help when all her advice fell on deaf ears. And so he'd driven her away and she'd married the biggest jerk he'd ever known. The downward spiral had continued.

And then five months ago he'd inherited the Dawson Family Guest Ranch with his five siblings, most of whom wanted nothing to do with the place. Suddenly, the man on the edge of the cliff had inched back to solid ground. Purpose. Determination. Heritage.

Before his father passed, before Noah had come back home to the formerly dilapidated guest ranch he'd grown up on, he'd had no idea heritage meant anything to him. But it clearly did. Because here he was. Not that he had anywhere else to go, but still. He wanted to be here.

And if this baby was his, she belonged here too. With him on the Dawson ranch. Until he figured out whose she was—aside from his—he'd keep his siblings out of it. Maybe he'd call his sister, Daisy, in Cheyenne. Maybe she'd come visit for a few days and help him out.

The tiny eyes opened, and her face scrunched.

"I'm taking you to the doc, little buddy."

It struck him that little girls probably weren't called "little buddy" the way boys were. He recalled how Sara—the one he'd driven away—hated that her father had called her princess. *I'm no princess*, she'd say. *Furthest thing from it.*

"You're no princess either," he told the infant. "You certainly did not get the royal treatment on your first day on earth."

Carrier in hand, he headed toward the door, setting it on the floor to put on his leather jacket. Then he picked her back up and headed out to the truck.

"I'm not gonna let anything happen to you," he said, latching the carrier rear-facing on the back seat, like the little diagram on the side of the carrier wisely showed. "You can count on that."

Chapter One

Seven weeks later

"I, Willem Michael Perry, in sound mind and body, hereby leave my second-rate wife, Sara Mayhew Perry, absolutely nothing."

Sara sat in her late husband's attorney's office, not surprised by anything in the will. The insults. The disinheritance. She wanted to run out of here, put this—including her marriage to Willem—behind her, and go home with her seven-week-old son. If she even had a home anymore.

The lawyer, Holton Parrington, who'd grimaced

through every word of the will as he'd read it aloud, put the document down on his desk and took off his glasses. "Sorry about all this, Sara," he said, shaking his head. "Willem wasn't exactly the nicest person, was he?"

Understatement of the year. Decade, maybe. But you make a deal with the devil… "No, he wasn't."

Her husband had died in a car accident five days ago. He hadn't been a good person, but Sara hadn't married him for his personality. She knew she wasn't perfect, but doing what needed to be done had always come naturally to her, and she'd hoped she could help Willem change, that she would rub off on him, that impending fatherhood would mean something to him, but he'd actually gotten meaner, more spiteful, more controlling.

She glanced at the stroller to her left; baby Chance slept peacefully. She kept her gaze on him for a moment longer; her son was all that truly mattered. Nothing else.

"Willem also left a letter to you and instructions that I read it aloud in the event of his death," Holton continued. "It's sealed, and I have no idea what's inside. Ready?"

Sara sighed inwardly. "For more bashing? No. But I guess this will be the end of it."

The lawyer nodded. He put his glasses back on,

then slit open the envelope and pulled out one sheet of paper, written in Willem Perry's unmistakable, perfect handwriting.

"'Sara, if you're reading this, I'm dead,'" the lawyer read, pausing as if bracing himself. He cleared his throat and continued. "'I don't know what got me in the end, but I hope it was quick and painless and that I lived till at least ninety-three like my father.'"

Willem hadn't made it to his twenty-ninth birthday. He'd been reckless with the brand-new Porsche, a gift to himself for becoming a father, and had been going more than ninety around the rain-slick curve on the winding service road into town.

"'I debated about putting what I'm about to say on paper,'" the lawyer continued reading, "'but decided I couldn't—make that shouldn't—take it to the grave with me. Oh yes, I want you to know. You deserve to know. Brace yourself, darlin'.'"

She was already doing that. Who knew what Willem was capable of? She did, actually. She wished she'd known the extent of his cruelty before she'd agreed to marry him. She'd known he was a snob, but he'd been so kind to her before their wedding, and she'd had such faith she'd turn him around. Back then, she'd thought his worst trait was talking down to waitstaff in the nice restaurants he'd taken her to.

She'd never take anything at face value again. That was for damned sure.

She sucked in a deep breath. *Whatever it is, whatever his last laugh is, I can take it*, she told herself. *I'm stronger than I know. Just keep chanting that and maybe it'll be true.*

The attorney glanced at her, and she nodded.

"'Our son's twin sister didn't die during childbirth,'" the lawyer read on a gasp, his eyes widening.

Sara gasped too. *What?* They stared at each other, his face as pale as hers must be.

The lawyer sucked in a breath and continued reading. "'The female twin was frail, much smaller than the male. But very much alive. Thank God I'd insisted on a home birth with a midwife, or I'd never have been able to do what I did.'"

She grabbed the sides of the chair. Her mind went blank, the air whooshing out of her, blackness threatening. *What did you do, Willem? What the hell did you do?*

The lawyer leaned back, took off his glasses and scrubbed a hand over his face.

"Finish the letter," Sara said, hearing the panic rise in her voice.

What happened to my baby girl?

Holton nodded, his expression grim. "'I threatened the midwife and paid her off not to call for medical intervention and to back me up when I told you the female didn't survive the birth. Don't be too hard on the poor lady. She accepted the bribe for the same reason you married me. She desperately needed the money.'"

The lawyer glanced at her then, and Sara, feeling her face flame, lifted her chin.

"'I told you the baby died,'" the lawyer continued reading, "'then while you were sleeping, I drove it out to Noah Dawson's place—'"

Sara bolted up. "Noah? Noah has my daughter?"

Her head was spinning. Her daughter was alive? And with Noah Dawson?

"Let's finish the letter," Holton said. "There's only one paragraph left."

Sara nodded, tears brimming as she dropped back on the chair.

The attorney cleared his throat. "'With my male heir healthy, I had no need for a sickly-looking daughter. To be quite honest, I don't particularly *like* girls. They grow up to become conniving users, don't they? I drove the baby out to Dawson's cabin and left her on his porch with that starter kit the midwife had on hand and a note saying it was his baby and his responsibility. For all I know, the twins *are* his. Maybe you were cheating on me with him during our entire marriage. Since I don't know whether any of that is true, it means it could be. Since it could also not be, I'll leave my son the bulk of my estate in trust for when he turns twenty-one. The rest will go to the development of a golf course named in my honor. You, as you already know, get nothing. Not a cent.'" The lawyer paused and put down the letter. "That's the extent of it. It's signed 'Willem Michael Perry.'"

My daughter didn't die. She's alive.

"For the past seven weeks, Noah Dawson has had my daughter?" she whispered, the blackness threatening again.

She tried to remember back to the moment when the midwife—a gentle woman in her early sixties who'd come highly recommended—placed Chance on her chest. Tears had been brimming in the woman's eyes over what Sara had assumed was the loss of the baby girl she'd helped deliver. Sara had felt so woozy, despite Willem's insistence she take no drugs. She must have fallen asleep hard after initially nursing Chance, because she'd woken up hours later, Willem letting her know Chance was sleeping like a champ in the nursery and that the midwife had gone home and that they'd taken care of the details for the loss of the twin.

She'd been so woozy still, her head feeling like it was stuffed with cotton, and she'd been so grateful that she hadn't lost both babies that she'd made her way to the nursery and held Chance against her. Her precious son had gotten her through the terrible truth that his sister hadn't survived. Over the next few days, Willem had resumed his usual twelve-hours-per-day work schedule, so she hadn't had to deal with him controlling her in person, though he'd left detailed emails about how to hold Chance, feed him, his nap schedule, and that no one was to visit until he'd had his shots.

Her baby girl was alive. And Sara wouldn't be the least bit surprised if Willem had slipped something into her water during labor, some kind of drug to keep her off balance and to make her sleep hard afterward.

Why would he take the baby to Noah, though? Willem had hated Noah Dawson.

"Sara, I'm afraid I have to prepare you for the possibility that the female twin didn't survive Willem's actions," the lawyer said, shaking her out of her question. "Left on a doorstep in the middle of the night? The second week of April, when it was still a bit chilly? Who knows when Mr. Dawson discovered the baby? If he was even home at the time? Didn't he very recently inherit the old Dawson guest ranch? I read that they're set for a grand opening this weekend, but I can't imagine how, given how run-down the place was."

She hadn't known Dawson's was reopening. She'd heard that Noah's widowed father had died and that he'd left the dilapidated ranch to his six children. She'd thought about going to the funeral but wasn't sure she'd be welcome. She'd been showing then and didn't want to make Noah uncomfortable, so she'd stayed home. She also would have had to get around Willem about where she was going, and she hadn't had the energy for that.

When she'd woken up about three hours after giving birth, the rain had been coming down hard. Willem had left their daughter on a ranch porch in the middle of the night during a rainstorm? The Dawson ranch in Bear Ridge was over an hour away from the Perry house in Wellington.

She swallowed back a wail building up deep inside her. "I'm going to see Noah now. My daughter is alive. I feel it."

"I hope so, Sara," Holton said. "It seems clear that Willem expected this letter to be read decades from now. There are two bombshells, really. Your daughter. And the midwife's culpability. We can discuss options for how to proceed there."

She'd deal with that later. Right now, she only wanted to see her baby girl with her own eyes. Hold her. Get her *back*.

She reached for her long cardigan and put it on,

then gripped the handle of Chance's stroller. He was fast asleep.

"Sara, again, I'm very sorry," Holton said. "I hate to bring this up right now, but I do need to tell you that you'll need to vacate the house within fourteen days. You may take your personal possessions, but everything else now belongs to the estate. If there's anything you'd like to take, do it before tomorrow, when the appraisals will begin."

She nodded again. She couldn't wait to leave that house. Where she'd move, she had no idea. But she did know where she was going now.

To see Noah Dawson. And get her baby girl.

"Should we give Bolt an apple slice?" Noah asked his baby daughter, snug in the carrier strapped to his chest.

He stood at Bolt's stall in front of the small barn beside his cabin, the mare nudging his arm for her apple. "We should? I agree." He pulled the baggie of apple slices from his pocket.

Annabel didn't respond, but according to the book on your baby's first year, she wouldn't make sounds or coo for another couple of weeks.

He'd learned quite a bit about babies in the past seven weeks. He'd been right that Annabel had only been hours old when she'd been left on his porch.

Doc Bakerton had been a grouch at being woken up at 2:20 in the morning—until he'd seen why Noah had come blazing over.

Because Bakerton was getting up there in years—nearing eighty—and had long been a rural doctor, he hadn't said anything about calling the sheriff or social services. Noah had showed him the note he'd found in the carrier, and that had been good enough. "The system doesn't need another abandoned baby when the perfectly good father is standing up," the doctor had said with a firm nod. Bakerton declared the infant healthy but small, recommended two possible pediatricians to follow up with and sent Noah on his way to beat the worst of the rain.

And so a little over twenty minutes after arriving, Noah had taken the baby home, shell-shocked but focused on the immediate here and now, not even tomorrow. The doc had given Noah some samples of formula and more diapers and wipes and had made a list of the basics Noah should buy in the morning.

Some of the shock had started to wear off while he'd been at Bakerton's, mostly because he'd realized he *could* simply leave the infant with the doctor, who'd call whoever needed to be called. The sheriff. Social services. And that would be that.

But what Bakerton had said kept echoing in his head as he'd watched him move that little stethoscope around the tiny back and chest…*when the perfectly good father is standing up.*

Noah Dawson, perfectly good father? He would have burst out laughing if the situation hadn't been so incredibly lacking in humor. Thing was, after all that he'd been through, all he'd lost, after the bad day he'd had with a sick calf, Noah had appreciated the extra show of faith in himself as a human being, and Bakerton had uttered the right words at exactly the right moment. The note said the baby was his. The perfectly good—or *able*, he figured Bakerton had meant—father was here with the infant, doing exactly what he should be doing. That was two for two on the faith scale.

He'd driven slow as his late grandmother's molasses back to the ranch in the pouring rain, and once inside he'd gone straight to his laptop, holding the tiny baby along his arm as he watched a YouTube video on how to mix formula, how to hold the bottle—how to hold a newborn, for that matter. Turns out he hadn't been doing that too wrong. He'd watched each video twice. By the time he'd closed his laptop, word had come that the river had flooded and two roads into town were impassable. He'd breathed a sigh of relief at the timing; the baby was safe and had been checked out, and Noah had what he'd needed to get through the night. The universe had been looking out for Noah lately.

They'd both survived that first night. While feeding the tiny infant, he'd realized he'd have to name her, and Annabel popped into his mind and that was that. He'd refused to let himself dwell on why.

Annabel Dawson. It wasn't official anywhere, not yet, but he'd have to deal with that too—getting Annabel a birth certificate while worrying that some bureaucrat would demand he hand his baby over.

His baby.

How Noah had gotten from where he'd been the night he'd found Annabel to *his baby* rolling off his tongue with ease was anyone's guess, but it had happened, and no one was more surprised than his sister. When the roosters had announced it was officially morning, he'd called his sister, Daisy, who lived out in Cheyenne, and boy, had she been in shock. She'd driven up by early evening and helped him so much—with Annabel and the ranch—the baby making her smile when he'd catch her looking so worried so often. Daisy had been close to five months pregnant then and wouldn't say a word about who the father was. She'd seemed relieved to have a reason to move somewhere, even to the family ranch, with its tangled roots and all.

Up until the moment he'd found Annabel, he'd

spent the four months prior rebuilding the Dawson Family Guest Ranch. That had changed him, turned him around, made him a better person and had to have *something* to do with how immediately responsible he'd felt for the baby left on his porch—his baby. Add that to a tiny finger clutching his pinkie while feeding her. Being up all hours of the night checking on her—sometimes just to make sure she was still breathing. Googling "lullabies newborns like" and then playing them, and then singing them himself while sitting in the rocker he'd gotten from the town swap shop. Changing diapers. Playing peek-aboo. Reading the pertinent pages of *Your Baby's First Year* and googling all the little things Annabel did that he wasn't sure was normal. Like burping so loud from that tiny body.

During the past seven weeks, he and Annabel had gotten even closer with all the walking around the vast property of the ranch, the baby against his chest in the Snugli and cozy footie pajamas. He'd told her all about the history of the ranch—how his grandparents had built it fifty-two years ago, how popular it had once been with tourists and locals coming to relax out in the country, to hike or ride on the vast trails in the woods and open grasslands, to learn to ride a horse, shear a sheep, spin fleece into yarn, milk cows and goats, and make butter and yogurt and his grandmother's award-winning ice cream, which she'd sold right in their own little shop in the main barn. Bess Dawson had always handed each of her grand-children a little spoon and sample cup of her new flavors to make sure the ice cream passed the kid test, and every flavor always had. Noah could still taste his favorites: chocolate-chocolate chip, strawberry, Bear Ridge Mix—pistachio ice cream with peanuts. Noah had also told Annabel how his widowed father had destroyed it all within three years of inheriting the place, drinking and gambling away profits, savings, their legacy, his six kids eventually scattering across the West to get away from him.

Noah was the youngest and had been trapped there for a good bunch of those low years. Daisy, two years older, watched over him the best she could until she'd been driven away by their dad's self-destruction when she was eighteen. Noah had also left the moment he'd become a legal adult, all his pleading to his father to get his act together going in one ear…

Ten years later, the Dawson Family Guest Ranch had been a ghost ranch, rarely mentioned anymore except for someone in town to shake their head over its demise. But with the money Noah and his siblings had invested, he and a hardworking crew had gotten the place in shape—albeit on a smaller scale

than the original—in just five months so they could
open Memorial Day weekend. The day after tomorrow, Friday, was the grand reopening. His brothers
hadn't responded to his invitation to stop by for the
big day, and Noah wouldn't be surprised when none
showed up.

"Let the place go," the Dawson siblings had all
said to Noah one way or another at their father's funeral.

Except Noah hadn't been able to—and then his
siblings had rallied around him, making a plan to
invest in rebuilding because doing so meant something to him and would mean everything to their
grandparents. Noah wouldn't ever let the ranch go.
For many reasons. So many reasons he hadn't even
told Annabel all of them yet. And he'd told her just
about everything. His confidante was a seven-week-
old, ten-pound, nine-ounce baby with chubby cheeks.
There was a first for everything.

He heard a car coming up the drive and turned
around. A silver Range Rover SUV was barreling
up the dirt road toward the foreman's cabin. Did
he know anyone who drove a Range Rover? The
eldest Dawson sibling, Ford, maybe. But Ford had
also said hell would freeze before he'd step foot on
the ranch again.

Whoever it was sure was in a hell of a hurry to get to the cabin.

One hand protectively on the back of Annabel's head in the Snugli, he watched the SUV suddenly come to a dead stop halfway up the drive. The glare from the sun made it impossible to see who was behind the wheel. Why stop there?

The Range Rover suddenly started up again and inched forward, this time at two miles an hour.

When the SUV finally got within a few feet, he could see inside.

Holy hell.

Sara.

How long had it been? Almost two years. After she'd told him she was marrying Willem Perry—he could barely even think the name in his head without wanting to vomit or hit something—he'd then heard they'd moved out to Wellington, an affluent town an hour away. He hadn't seen or heard from her since. He'd been close with Sara's only living relative, her father, but Preston Mayhew had gotten very sick a few months before she'd married Willem. He'd also heard Sara had had her dad transferred from the county hospital to the state-of-the-art one in Wellington. Noah had once called about visiting hours and was told that all visitors had to be preapproved by Willem Perry. So much for that. It was better that there was no one to talk to him about Sara or what she was up to or how great her life was with that bastard Willem; Noah wouldn't have been able to bear it.

The car door opened and she stepped out, and his heart lurched. That wasn't a surprise. The sight of Sara Mayhew had always had that effect. Not just because she was so pretty with her silky light brown hair and round, pale brown eyes; his attraction to her had always been about who she was, not how good she looked. Though she did look good.

She must have heard about the Dawson Family Guest Ranch reopening this weekend and decided to check the place out for herself. After all, she'd grown up here too.

"I can't tell you how great it is to see you, Sara," he said, surprising even himself with his honesty. But it was bursting out of him. He'd missed her so much the past couple of years that he'd done regretful things to forget her, nothing working.

She shut her car door and walked toward him, her gaze on the Snugli, then moving up to his face. "You found that baby on your porch seven weeks ago? The early-morning hours of April 9?" Her voice sounded strange. Desperate and shaky.

He stared at her, his grip a bit tighter on the baby carrier. "How did you know that?"

"Because Willem—my late husband—is the one who put her there. She's mine, Noah. My daughter."

What? Noah took a step toward Sara, then a step back. "There was a note with her. It said she's mine."

Sara shook her head. "She's not yours. Willem told me she died during the home birth. But he just didn't want her because she was a girl and frail-looking when her healthy, robust twin brother—the male heir—had been born two minutes earlier."

No. That's insanity. On what planet does that sound believable? Even the worst of the worst like Willem Perry wouldn't do something like that. To his own flesh and blood? His newborn daughter?

She stepped forward, her gaze on the baby's head before looking up at him. "He left a letter for me via his lawyer detailing how he drove her here right before the rain started to come down in the middle of the night. I had no idea. I thought she didn't survive the birth." A sob escaped her, and she put her hand over her mouth.

Oh God. Unthinkable.

So unthinkable that it wasn't quite sinking in. All he could do in the moment was look at Annabel, whom he'd taken care of for the past almost two months, whom he *loved*. She was his daughter. The note had said so. She was *his* child.

"That's my baby girl, Noah," she said, taking another step, then stopping. Maybe because of the expression on his face, which had to be something like horror.

For a second he could only stare at Sara, trying to process the craziness that had just come out of her mouth.

He thought about the first moments after bringing Annabel inside the night he'd found her. There had been something familiar about the little face, something in the expression, the eyes, that he couldn't pin down. He'd figured the baby's mother was a woman he'd been with for one night…

He and Sara had made love hundreds of times during their brief time as a couple, but the last time was right before she'd dumped him two years ago. He certainly wasn't the father of her daughter.

He glanced down at what he could see of Annabel's little profile, and yup, there it was, that slight something in the turndown of the eyes, the way the mouth curved upward. It was Sara's face. No wonder he'd felt so strangely connected to Annabel from the moment he'd brought her inside the cabin—before he'd even read the note falsely declaring the baby was his.

"I want to hold her so badly," Sara said. She reached out, and Noah felt the surrender everywhere in his body—the region of his heart most pointedly. This was Sara's baby. Not his.

Hell, he might break down crying. But he lifted Annabel out of the carrier. He handed her over with a stabbing awareness that this was it—it was over. His stint at fatherhood. He was proud of what he'd accomplished with the ranch, but he was proudest of what he'd accomplished with his daughter.

Not his daughter. He'd have to take that phrasing out of his vocabulary, out of his head. She wasn't his.

As Sara clutched the baby to her chest, tears streaming down her face, he closed his eyes, not surprised by the weight of sadness crushing his chest.

He loved Annabel. *That* was a surprise. But it was true.

"Is there somewhere I can go to spend time with her?" Sara asked, her gaze moving from the baby to Noah as she gently touched her wispy light brown curls, her cheek, her arm, her little fingers. "I just can't believe this is real."

Me either. He stared at his daughter—*her* daughter—and the jab in his chest intensified.

"You can take her into the cabin," he said. "She's eaten recently and been changed, so she's all set."

Now she stared at *him*, as if shocked he knew anything about Annabel's feeding and diaper-changing schedule.

"My son, her twin brother, is in the SUV," Sara

said. "Could you take him out for me? I can't bear to let go of my daughter."

My daughter. My daughter. My daughter.

Noah's head was swimming, and his knees were wobbly. He nodded and lurched toward the Range Rover, mostly to have something to brace his fall if his legs did give out.

He pulled open the door, and there was Annabel's honest-to-goodness twin in green-and-white-striped pajamas. They looked so much alike—the wispy light brown curls. The slate-blue eyes. The nose. The expression. It was all Sara.

He took out the car seat and brought it around to where Sara stood. He lifted up the seat to Annabel's level. The baby that had been in his arms until five minutes ago. "Annabel, you're about to meet your twin brother."

Sara's mouth dropped open. "Annabel? That's what you named her?"

He nodded. It was Sara's middle name.

Tears filled her eyes, and she blinked hard.

"This is Chance," she said. "Chance, meet Noah Dawson. I've known him a long time."

A very long time. "Very nice to meet you, Chance." He gently touched a hand to the downy little head with its soft brown wisps.

"And Chance, this is Annabel, your twin sister,"

Sara added. "You're back together where you belong."

Oh hell. He was about to break down himself.

"I want to hear everything," she said, her pale brown eyes imploring. "From the moment you realized she was outside on your porch to the moment I drove up. I need to know about her life these past seven weeks. But first I just need some time alone with her. To let this sink in." She cuddled Annabel against her, her gaze going from her daughter to Noah and back again.

All these weeks that Annabel had been right here, with him, her mother had believed that her baby girl was dead. He had to stop thinking about himself and focus on that—what Sara had been through.

And how twin babies had almost been separated forever.

"I understand," he said, the sturdy weight of the car seat in his right hand making him both happy and miserable. "I'll help you inside with the twins, and you can have the place to yourself for however long you need. Text me when you're ready and I'll come fill you in."

She let out a breath. "Thank you, Noah. You can't imagine." She shook her head, her tear-streaked face his undoing as much as the situation.

He *couldn't* imagine.

They started walking to the cabin, which had once been her home when her father had been foreman. She stopped for a moment, staring up at the newly renovated two-story log house with the hunter green covered porch and flower boxes his sister had insisted on putting everywhere. Sara didn't say anything about the place, how it had changed, but she had much bigger things on her mind than the ranch.

He opened the door, then stepped aside so she could enter with Annabel. He followed her in, wanting to rip his daughter from her arms. He had to stop walking for a second; the pain in his chest was that severe, and dammit, he was worried he'd start bawling like a little kid any second.

He led her into the living room and set Chance's carrier on the floor beside the sofa. Sara dropped down on the sofa, crying, laughing, staring at the baby girl in her arms.

"Her baby bag is on the stroller by the door if you need anything," he managed to say. "Plus, there's a big basket of baby stuff on the side of the coffee table."

She couldn't take her eyes off Annabel. She nodded as if barely able to hear him.

"Take as long as you want," he said. "Text me when you're ready for me to come back and we'll talk." He jotted his cell number down and left it on the coffee table.

She nodded, not taking her eyes off her daughter.

He wanted to grab Annabel away from her and run. Or just stay here, not letting the baby girl out of his sight.

Because no matter how many times he told himself she wasn't his daughter, he couldn't make himself believe it.

He forced himself out the door, his heart staying behind.

Chapter Two

Sara couldn't stop staring at the tiny baby nestled against her chest. Couldn't stop touching her, couldn't stop telling her she loved her, that she was so sorry she hadn't been there the past seven weeks, that nothing would ever come between them again.

On the drive over to the ranch from the lawyer's office, she'd kept thinking, *Please let my daughter be alive. Please let her be there. Please, please, please.* Her prayers answered, Sara's relief, her pure joy at being reunited with her baby girl, trounced her anger—murderous rage, really, at what had been done to the infant, done to Sara. *That monster took so much from us. He's not getting a second more of any piece of me. Not my thoughts or my emotions. Nothing. He's gone.*

"We have so much to catch up on," Sara whispered, in awe of everything about Annabel. Her ten fingers and toes. Her little nose and chin. The way her chest rose and fell in her sea-foam-green-and-white pajamas with little ducklings across the front. That she was really, truly *here*.

The baby's eyes were drooping, and Sara would be happy to sit here forever with Annabel napping in her arms. She glanced down at Chance, who was already asleep in his carrier. The siblings, twins, back together. She took in a deep, satisfying breath. Seven weeks felt like so much to miss out on, but she knew as time went on, she'd be grateful it had barely been two months.

She stood up, gently rocking Annabel, and walked over to the stone fireplace that dominated one wall of the living room, photos on the mantel. She'd lived in this house from the time she was born until she was sixteen, had sat on the sofa facing that fireplace night after night with her father after her mother passed away when she was nine. Talks, homework, reading, her dad's delicious sub sandwiches as they watched a series they could enjoy together. Her entire life was up in the air right now, but being here in this cabin made her feel safe.

"I grew up here," she whispered to Annabel. "Your grandma lived here. And your grandfather loved this cabin. He was the foreman here." Now Noah was.

She froze, biting her lip as Noah's words came back to her. *There was a note with her. It said she was mine.*

All this time, Noah had thought the baby was his. She glanced around the room, taking in the pale yellow playpen with its pastel mobile atop it by the bay window. The baby swing. The big basket of baby paraphernalia by the coffee table—she could see neatly folded burp cloths, a pack of diapers, a pink pacifier on a silver tray on the coffee table. An infant stroller was by the front door with a tote bag hanging from its handles. Lots of photos on the mantel were of Annabel, a few of Noah holding her.

She gasped as it *really* sank in that Annabel had lived here these past seven weeks, that Noah had taken her in—as his daughter.

Was he relieved that the mother had come back to take her? Upset? Noah Dawson was the bachelor of bachelors. Clearly he'd gotten his act together to reopen the guest ranch, but perhaps his siblings were all involved in that. The Noah she'd known near the end of their relationship two years ago didn't wake until noon, despite having a ranch to run. Didn't take care of business. Didn't take care of their fledgling romance, the one she'd fought and kicked so hard for. Turned out Noah Dawson had been right about himself—that he'd only break her heart in more ways than one.

She always thought she knew better, didn't she.

Her future was in her arms. In the carrier beside the sofa. Her children. Hours ago she'd had only a son. Now she had twins.

Take the blessing and let that fill you, she ordered herself. Because letting herself get caught up in anger over the past—recent and not so recent—would only hold her back. She had a family to raise, money to earn, a life to start.

She took a deep breath and glanced at the other photos on the mantel, surprised to see one of her and Noah in their caps and gowns, their high school graduation. They'd both worked at the Circle D then, a prosperous ranch a half hour away. Sara had lived there as the foreman's daughter, and Noah was a hand. But a month later, when he turned eighteen, Noah had moved there too, so upset by the conversation he'd had with his dad a half hour earlier that he'd gone off alone. Sara still didn't know what had gone on during that discussion.

The other photos were of his siblings, the six of them together when Noah was sixteen. They'd still come home to celebrate his birthday, though they'd refused to have Christmas at the ranch with their dad and had flown Noah to one of their homes instead.

There was a photo of his mom, a pretty brunette with blue eyes who'd died when he was ten, something that had brought Sara and Noah even closer. They never had to talk about how awful it felt to miss your mother, to wish she were there. They just knew and could be together, quiet, skipping stones in the river, throwing bread to the ducks, climbing trees and sitting up there for hours.

She missed the Noah he'd been three-quarters of the time—even to the very end of their relationship two years ago. She missed that guy so, so much.

And she'd missed this cabin. She turned to look around. She had so many memories here, so much history. She knew every nook and cranny, which floorboards creaked on the stairs, how many steps it was down to the creek (182), how she'd sat on her bed in her room upstairs, writing *Sara Dawson* in hearts in her journal like the lovesick teenager she'd been.

"Where's my sweet baby girl?" a woman's voice called cheerily through the front screen door, followed by a set of knocks. "I need my Annabelly time."

Sara froze. Oh God. Who was this?

Noah's wife? Girlfriend?

"Noah? You here?" the feminine voice called.

Sara bit her lip. Should she go to the door? Pretend she wasn't here?

Curiosity got the better of her, since this woman might have helped Noah take care of Annabel the past seven weeks. Maybe, in fact, she'd done all the work. That was more likely.

She went to the door, and her heart soared. It was Daisy Dawson, Noah's only sister.

"Daisy!" Sara said, hearing her voice break and not caring. Her long honey-brown hair in a braid practically to her waist, a straw cowboy hat on her head, pretty, sweet Daisy had been a good friend from childhood until Willem had isolated Sara from everyone she used to care about. Daisy was also at least six months pregnant.

"Whoa—Sara?" Daisy asked with a shocked grin, pulling open the screen door and coming inside. She glanced at Annabel in Sara's arms. "This is a huge surprise. Did you come for Dawson's grand reopening?" Before Sara could even respond, Daisy added, "That rascal Noah—he didn't even tell me you two had gotten back in touch. God, Sara, it's so good to see you. You look amazing. So healthy and glowy. Is Noah here or did he have to step out to deal with something?" Daisy touched a finger to Annabel's cheek. "I'm so glad you got to meet my beautiful niece. Isn't she precious?"

My beautiful niece. Sara's knees buckled.

Sara tightened her arms around Annabel, more out of instinct than because she was worried she'd really drop to her knees.

Her every emotion must have been showing on her face, because Daisy tilted her head and looked at her. "Sara? You okay?"

"Not really," Sara said. "Not by a long shot. I'll be okay, though."

Daisy put a hand on Sara's arm, her warm blue eyes filled with concern. "How about we go talk in the kitchen? I know I could use a cup of decaf. I actually could use a big mug of real coffee. But I'm limiting myself to one cup a day, and I had that." She patted her belly.

Sara glanced at Daisy's left hand. No ring. She wondered what the story was there as she followed Daisy into the kitchen. Daisy always used to talk about wanting to be a mom one day, but she was insistent on picking the right guy so she'd never get divorced like her parents had, let alone thrice divorced like her dad. Sara had once pointed out that you could pick the right guy, as her own mother had, and leave him a brokenhearted widow at age thirty-six. You just never knew what life was going to throw at you.

As Daisy headed for the coffee maker, reaching for two mugs in the cabinet, Sara found her attention taken by the refrigerator door, all the things hung up with magnets. There was a checklist of baby-proofing essentials. A cutout newspaper ad for a local grandmother of five who did hand embroidery personalization on baby clothing and blankets and towels. The American Academy of Pediatrics' rec-ommendations for feeding and napping schedules.

"Noah loves Annabel, doesn't he," Sara said, more a statement than a question, her voice sounding far away to her own ears as she stood in front of the fridge. "I can tell. I knew it as soon I saw him with her in the Snugli."

Daisy tilted her head. "Of course. He loves that baby girl to pieces. Did you hear the crazy story? How someone left her on his porch right before that terrible rainstorm just about two months ago? There was a note that said the baby was his. He had no rea-son to doubt it. He even insists Annabel looks like him, but I don't see it. Don't tell him I said that!" She laughed and pressed a button on the coffee maker.

Sara almost smiled at the thought of Noah think-ing Annabel looked like him. Once upon a time, when she'd still held out hope for marrying Noah

Dawson and having a family with him, she'd always pictured little Noahs, two or three, with intense blue eyes and wavy dark hair, mischievous grins and big hearts.

"Daisy, I have a crazier story," Sara said. And told her everything. Not leaving a detail out.

Daisy was an expressive woman to start with, but the range of emotions that crossed her face was something. "Oh my God, Sara."

Sara nodded.

"Can I be really happy for you and really sad for my brother at the same time?" Daisy asked. "He must be out of his mind right now knowing you're going to take Annabel away."

Take Annabel away. Sara's stomach flipped over. She'd never really thought of coming to get her daughter as taking the baby away from someone. But now she kept seeing the look on Noah's face as he'd taken Annabel out of the carrier and handed her over.

It was anguish.

Oh, Noah, she thought. *This part of the story never would have occurred to me.*

This whole time, from the moment the lawyer had read Willem's awful letter, Sara had only focused on the fact that her daughter was alive, that Willem had taken her to Noah's cabin. She'd never stopped to think about what had happened between then and now. Sara had just wanted to find her child and reunite.

But Noah had taken her in, had been raising her as his own, as he believed she was.

And that anguish on his face? Yes, he loved the baby.

Daisy poured two mugs of coffee and then opened Noah's fridge. "Ooh, half a pecan pie. I think we're gonna need a little of that too. Maybe a lot. Am I right?"

"Probably," Sara said. "I'm not sure if I can eat a bite of anything, but since when don't I stress eat?"

Daisy nodded sagely and grabbed the pie and the container of half-and-half, and Sara brought over the mugs to the table. By the time Sara sat down and took her third sip of the coffee and her second bite of pie, an idea had started forming in her mind.

An either really good idea or a really bad one. She truly wasn't sure.

Noah barely heard what his ranch hand was saying about the hay bales, but the guy was smiling, so Noah smiled back and nodded. Two days before the grand opening was no time to have his mind elsewhere, but every cell in Noah's body was focused on his cabin. And what was going on in there.

He knew, actually. Sara was reuniting with the daughter she'd never gotten to hold. Never gotten to meet, let alone know.

And soon she'd text him that she was ready for him to come back so they could talk, so he could fill her in on the last seven weeks.

So he could say goodbye to the baby girl he'd taken care of. His daughter who wasn't.

The pain gripped his chest again, and he sucked in a breath.

"You okay, boss?" Dylan asked, adjusting his cowboy hat as he peered at Noah. "You don't look so good."

"A-okay," Noah assured him. "So everything's in order in the main barn. What about the petting zoo?"

Dylan nodded, his mop of blond bangs shifting. "We're all set. I did inventory this morning. We won't need to place orders till Tuesday. Layla's feeding the farm animals now."

Noah nodded. "Thanks," he said. He'd hired several experienced hands for the land and animals and knew he could let go for a little while to deal with what was going on with Annabel.

He walked the quarter mile to his cabin and saddled up Bolt, riding her out to the gate a half mile down the gravel drive. He stopped and patted Bolt's flanks, staring at the hunter green metal that stretched across the road, Dawson Family Guest Ranch in gold letters, the silhouettes of a cowboy and a cowgirl on horses on either side. His grandparents had made belt buckles with the logo to sell in the gift shop, and one Christmas, he'd had six personalized with the grandkids' names. Noah still had his. In fact, he kept it on his desk, always had, and the past five months the buckle had served as a talisman, a lucky charm.

And for the past seven weeks, Annabel's presence had spurred him on to go even farther with making sure every detail of the ranch's reopening was perfect. This was going to be her future.

Now she wouldn't be part of it. She wouldn't be around at all.

His phone pinged with a text, and he reluctantly took it from his pocket. The sooner Sara was ready for him to return, the sooner she'd leave. With his baby.

But it was Daisy texting him.

U ok? Where R U? Heard whole story from S in the cabin.

At the gate, he texted back. No, not OK.

She texted back, Be right there.

A few minutes later, Daisy rode up on her bike.

She jumped off, one hand on her belly, and threw her arms around him.

"Sara's going to take her away," Noah said, letting his sister comfort him for a second before pulling back. He stared out at the woods beyond the road. "Just like that."

"I'm so sorry," Daisy said. "You know I love that baby girl."

"At least Annabel will be with her mother. And Sara will be with her daughter. I should focus on that. She got her daughter back. It's a friggin' miracle."

Daisy nodded. "It is."

"And I guess Annabel as a Perry and not a Dawson will have every creature comfort, certainly more than I could ever provide." He knew the Dawson Family Guest Ranch would do well; he was already booked for the weekend and had bookings stretching all the way to fall. Not every cabin was filled for every day, but word of mouth would spread, and the ranch would be a big success. He believed it. But he'd never be able to give Annabel the life Sara could as richer-than-rich Willem Perry's widow.

"You know what's crazy, Daize?" he said. "My heart's been broken before, so I know what that feels like. This feels like that."

His sister put her hand on his arm. "Look, I don't know what happened between you and Sara two years ago. But maybe you can stay in touch, visit Annabel."

He could just see it now. "Uncle" Noah coming to visit every couple of months, bringing a stuffed animal. How could he become Uncle Noah when that baby had changed his entire life and world? She'd turned him into a father, something he wouldn't have seen coming in a million years. And dammit, he'd been good at it. Another shocker.

His phone pinged with a text, and his heart sank.

Come talk?—Sara

He stood there, his head hung, unable to move.

"I'm so sorry, Noah," his sister said again. "I know how much you love Annabel."

Even *he* hadn't known just how much he loved that ten-pound little human until this moment. More than he'd ever realized.

Chapter Three

Sara was sitting in the kitchen of the foreman's cabin, thinking, thinking, thinking, when the tap came on the front door.

"It's me," Noah called out.

How was it possible that his voice still had the power to send goose bumps up her arms, make her feel such anticipation? No matter what she'd been going through as a kid, as a teenager, the sound of Noah Dawson's voice…

"Come on in," she said, standing up, then sitting down. Why had she told him to come back so soon? Maybe she wasn't quite ready after all.

It felt funny inviting him into his own home, but what about any of this didn't feel surreal?

Like the fact that Sara had spent the last fifteen minutes—with Annabel napping in her carrier beside her brother—working over the idea in her head.

Good idea? Bad idea? Her only option?

Was she really hoping to count on Noah Dawson?

She was in dire straits. Nowhere to go, very little money suddenly, and two babies to care for.

And Noah had clearly changed these past two years. Reopening the Dawson Family Guest Ranch had always been his dream. He'd made it happen. And he'd taken very good care of Annabel the past seven weeks. According to Daisy, he'd done 90 percent of that on his own. Daisy had helped out, and a couple times he'd called their old sitter, Mrs. Pickles, whose real name no one could even remember at this point, when he'd had emergencies he had to deal with on the ranch. But for the most part, Daisy said that Noah Dawson had been a full-time, hands-on father, Annabel in that Snugli as he'd directed the crew, made his phone calls, sent his emails, dealt with the invoices.

She heard the screen door open. "In the kitchen," she called out.

And then there he was. For a moment, she couldn't take her eyes off him. Earlier, when she'd first arrived, she'd barely been able to think, let alone focus on the fact that she had been reunited with Noah Dawson after two years. Now, his presence in the cabin was almost overwhelming.

This was the man she'd loved her whole life. The tall, sexy cowboy she'd never stopped thinking about. The person who'd taken care of her daughter for the past seven weeks, despite being a single rancher reopening the family business and clearly having a lot on his plate.

Noah had believed the baby was his, and he'd stepped up. Of course, Sara would take Annabel to Chance's pediatrician and have her fully examined, but her daughter looked healthy and happy and alert. Noah had done a good job.

She could hardly believe it. Noah Dawson.

Annabel started fussing, her eyes opening and fighting to close. Her little face turned red and scrunched up a bit, and Sara's heart leaped as she stood to go pick her up.

"May I?" he asked, gesturing toward Annabel.

No. She's mine.

The instinct was so strong that Sara instantly felt guilty. "She's only napped for about thirty-five minutes."

Sara wanted to go to her baby girl. *She knows her mother now and wants her mama.*

That was what Sara wanted to believe, anyway.

Noah might feel very differently. Like that Annabel sensed her daddy was back and wanted to be held by him. Noah was the only father Annabel had ever known.

Oh God. She hadn't really thought about that until this moment.

Suddenly, her idea, either good or bad, seemed like the *only* idea, the best plan for right now.

"Sure," Sara said.

Noah smiled and knelt down in front of the carrier, unbuckling the harness and taking Annabel out. She watched the way he carefully cradled Annabel against him, gently rocking her, and she knew this was not the same man she'd left two years ago.

That Noah Dawson was in there, she was sure. But a new one had emerged. The one who was about to make her cry with how loving he was being to the baby girl, how tender, the care he was showing in how he held her, cooed to her, rocked her.

"Her eyes are shutting," Noah said. "There's a baby swing she loves in the living room. Can you go grab it for me?"

She popped up, relieved to have something to do, somewhere to go other than sitting right there and staring at Noah Dawson in wonder. She went into the living room and got the swing and carried it to the kitchen. She set it beside Chance's carrier; he was still sleeping.

Noah knelt down again and laid Annabel in the swing, her eyes slightly opening. He pressed Gentle Sway, and the swing began moving lightly, the softest of lullabies playing from the side speakers. The baby's eyes closed.

He touched a finger to her cheek, then looked at Chance for a moment, smiling so sweetly at her son that her eyes almost welled up. She was insanely hormonal. Willem had never looked at Chance that way, with that kind of tenderness, awe. Her late husband had only looked at his son as the trophy heir.

Yes, her idea was a good one. Not just for her and Noah. But for the twins' sake.

Noah stood up and walked over to the coffee maker. He switched out the decaf and brewed a cup. "Can I get you anything?"

"I had coffee with Daisy. I'm fine for now."

"She told me," he said. "We were talking by the gate until you texted."

There was so much to say, but she didn't want to say any of it. She just wanted to sit here and not talk.

"They're both asleep now," he said with a nod toward the twins.

She glanced at them, then back at him. "You really seem to know what you're doing when it comes to babies. I'm very impressed, Noah."

She caught the way he glanced at her—the "when it comes to babies" hanging in the air as if he didn't know what he was doing in every other regard. Of course she didn't think that was true. Before Noah had started going a little too wild, heading down a road like his father had taken, he'd still been a good person, someone she could turn to. Steady. Trustworthy. Someone she could *always* count on. Until she gradually couldn't.

"I had to," he said. "I thought I was her father. Thank God for YouTube," he added.

She smiled. "I watched a few videos myself those first few days. Took me a while to get a good burp out of Chance. I'd been afraid to pat him too hard. Turns out I was way too gentle."

"Been there, learned that," he said with a nod, his gaze going to Chance. "Is Chance a family name?"

She shook her head. "It's a nickname I gave him the moment he was placed on my chest since I couldn't imagine calling him by his given name— Bancroft."

Noah rolled his eyes and she had to smile. "Willem's idea, I presume."

"His late mother's maiden name. I wanted to name him after my father, but he insisted that Preston wasn't stately enough." She shook her head. "If I could go back…"

"You had no choice but to marry Perry," he said. "Even I understand that. Barely, but I do. Your father was diagnosed with stage-two cancer when he had no health insurance. The bills took your savings, and then there was no way to pay for treatment when he needed to start radiation."

She felt tears well in her eyes. It meant so much that he *did* understand, that he didn't judge her. "I didn't realize how awful a person Willem was." She told him what was in the letter that Willem had written.

Noah's expression went from shock to horror to disgust. "Well, his sickening plan failed." He shook his head. "I'd like to scream every nasty thought I'm having about him from the rooftops, but I'll control myself because of these two," he added with a nod toward the twins. "I'd prefer never to hear his name again."

Exactly her thoughts since the lawyer's office. "Same here," she said.

She'd once really believed that Willem had loved her. He'd chased her all through high school, even though he was the town golden boy and she was the motherless daughter of a guest-ranch foreman who lived in the staff cabin she was in right now. Willem had truly seemed crazy about her—he listened when she spoke, told her interesting stories about his family, but she noticed the demeaning way he spoke to people, and she didn't like it. Besides, she'd *loved* Noah Dawson back then, and no one could ever compare.

Noah had been a wild child with a streak of good, and they'd been best friends since they were little. He'd always told her she was crazy for wanting him as a boyfriend and went for girls in his own circle instead, girls who skipped school and flashed boys in the hallway. Part of her always thought she'd dodged a bullet, but when they'd finally gotten together— for about six months—two years ago, when he had a small ranch of his own and was trying hard, she thought she'd help bring out the Noah Dawson who'd always been there. That was a mistake she'd made over and over, thinking people could change. They didn't, really. Maybe they could go a few degrees this way or that, but the core? That was settled. She understood that now.

So when Noah was sabotaging his fresh start on the ranch he'd wanted so bad, sabotaging their fledgling relationship, and then Willem Perry had started asking her out again, listening as she cried about Noah, about her sick father who would die without treatment, she'd let Willem take her away from her troubles. He'd promised her the moon, that he'd take care of her dad, and all he wanted in return was the woman of his dreams: her. She'd fallen for it all.

But what she'd really been was a notch. A conquest Willem had never been able to make until she'd been totally desperate. And the truth behind that made him resentful. And mean.

Just when things were so bad that she planned to leave her husband, determined to find a way to continue her dad's medical care, she found out she was pregnant—with twins. The news, for a while, turned things around; for a few weeks, Willem was kinder, until that changed too. He'd accused her of cheating with Noah, had gotten paranoid the twins weren't his. A prenatal DNA test confirmed they were Willem's, but his mind had gone twisted. He'd threatened her every time she told him she was leaving, and once, when she had left him, he sent a lawyer after her who scared the hell out of her that she'd lose custody of the babies entirely. She'd gone back home numb, not sure what she was going to do, how she'd get away from him and not lose her children. Then her father died, and she'd been too grief-stricken to even think about Willem.

All that was in the past, including her husband. The very recent past with lessons she'd not soon forget.

Noah came over to the table with a steaming mug of coffee. He sat down across from her, and again, she was overwhelmed by how close he was.

"Before I came here," she said, "I'd just heard from Willem's lawyer that you'd restored the guest ranch and are reopening this weekend. I immediately noticed the new signs on the road leading to the turn and the huge sign on the shiny gates. The landscaping, the foreman's cabin, the barn—you've done an amazing job. A lot of the place looks even better than when I lived here."

He smiled. "Thanks. Wait till you see the farmhouse, the cabins, barns, the pastures and the trails. We still have work to do, but the heavy lifting is done."

A wistfulness crept into her expression, her gaze moving around the kitchen. "It feels so good to be back here."

"That's how I felt when I first came home. My brothers, not so much. But I guess for some of us, roots have a grip, even when they're a tangled mess."

She nodded, her gaze shifting to the napping babies.

"I guess after we talk," he said, "you're getting back in that Range Rover and I'll never see any of you again."

There's your in, she thought. Good idea, bad idea,

whichever—right now it was all she had. "Actually, quite the opposite, if you're open to my idea."

"What idea is that?" he asked, his eyes intense on her.

"I need a job and a place to stay," she said. "I'll work for you for room and board and a reasonable salary so I can get on my feet. There's a lot I can do on the ranch."

He looked at her like she'd grown an extra head. "You married one of the richest men in Wyoming. Selling that Range Rover alone could set you up for a while."

"He left me with nothing," she explained. "Chance inherits the bulk of the estate when he's twenty-one. I have fourteen days to vacate my house, and anything that isn't clothing or personal jewelry stays. I don't even want to go back there, knowing now what that monster did." She squeezed her eyes shut. "My dad's gone—and I'm alone. Except for my children. *Children*," she repeated, her voice breaking. "Look at what I have now. *Both* babies. I just need some time and a way to get back on my own two feet."

The emotion that settled on his face looked a lot like relief. "Of course I'll hire you," he said. "Anything you need, Sara. Always."

That same relief now flooded her. Okay. She had a safe place to land with her infants. She had a job.

She had everything that was familiar and comforting. She'd be okay. This *had* been a good idea.

"Thank you, Noah."

He nodded and looked out the window as if regrouping. "I won't lose Annabel," he whispered, and he glanced back at her so fast she realized he hadn't meant to say it aloud. He picked up his mug and took a sip of his coffee. "I turned the spare room into her nursery," he quickly said, "so that's already all set up. You could take the guest room, and she and Chance can share the nursery. It's small, but hey, so are they."

"I'd prefer that to taking a room in the farmhouse. This cabin will always feel like home."

He glanced at her with such warmth in his eyes that she wanted to fling her arms around him and just hold him—for old times, for now. As a link to tomorrow and the next few weeks and months. But touching Noah Dawson had always gotten her in trouble in every way, and she had to rely on him enough right now—she wasn't going to mix up nostalgia, being grateful and need with anything else.

And anyway, she recalled that his grandparents had always kept two of the bedrooms of the main house available for emergencies regarding guests. Family members in arguments. Couples breaking up overnight. Plumbing issues. Right now, Daisy had a room and she'd need one for a nursery, so that left only two. It wouldn't be right to ask for one.

"I'm so used to Annabel being here," Noah said. "Honestly, I never thought she'd be going anywhere except when she graduated from high school."

She stared at him. "You really committed to being her father, huh."

He nodded. "I love that little girl. And I'll love her twin too. I want you all right here. Besides, the guest room is your old bedroom."

She did like the idea of staying in her old room. And she couldn't deny that Annabel looked happy and well cared for. *And* Noah had definitely turned the Dawson Family Guest Ranch around. But she didn't trust him—aside from knowing he'd never mean her harm. He'd taken her trust two years ago by sabotaging everything he held dear, including their relationship. Then her husband had obliterated what little faith she had left in people. She couldn't count on anyone but herself, and that was just the way it was. She'd do what she had to in order to fill a bank account with enough money to get back on her feet, then she'd figure out where she'd go from there. Maybe she'd leave Wyoming—not that could she could imagine it.

She'd go back to the house in Wellington tomorrow to collect her things, everything that was hers. Then she'd officially move to the ranch with the twins and start over. She could breathe here, make a plan here. Being a foreman's daughter meant she had ranch life in her blood and bones; she'd been assistant forewoman at the last ranch she'd worked at before she'd gotten married.

"Glad to have you at Dawson Family Guest Ranch, Sara," he said, extending his hand. "We can talk about what position you'd like once you're settled. I could use an experienced assistant, if you're interested. But there are a few open positions—from leading children's activities and workshops to being a cowgirl."

She nodded, so relieved at how this had all worked out. "I'm glad to be here."

He had no idea how glad she was. This had always been home. And now, for the time being anyway, it would be again. She'd get on her feet, figure things out and then off she'd go.

But Noah hadn't let go of her hand, and she wasn't pulling it away. Their history, their past, good and bad, lingered heavy in the air between them. There was *too* much to talk about, and right now, she just wanted to gaze at Annabel and get back the last seven weeks.

But then Annabel started fussing again, and Noah reached for her, then put up his hands and stepped back. "Old habits," he said. "I guess I don't have to jump anymore."

"It'll be an absolute treat to care for her," she said, holding the baby girl, who once again was struggling to keep her eyes open. "Something I'll never take for granted that I get to do after all."

He nodded and reached out a hand to hers, giving it a gentle squeeze. "Maybe we can put them both down in her crib, and then I can fill you in on the last seven weeks."

"Sounds good," she said, snuggling Annabel close, aware that Noah was watching her.

As he lifted Chance's carrier—the little guy was still fast asleep—she couldn't help but wonder what was going to happen, how this would all go. Could she and Noah share a cabin with all that had happened between them? Would the past flare up? Or would they both just ignore it?

She would definitely ignore it, she told herself. *No matter what he reminds you of or makes you think about, no matter how comforting it would be to be in his arms. Ignore it.*

This was her fresh start, her chance for a new life. Two precious little beings depended on her now, and she would *not* let them down.

"Oh, what a lovely room," Sara said, looking all around the nursery as they walked inside, each holding a carrier. She'd stopped in her tracks, her mouth slightly open as though she wasn't expecting this.

Noah realized that she'd probably been expecting the basics. Not a room fit for a...beloved baby daughter. "It helped that I couldn't sleep the past several weeks, between Annabel waking up every few hours and constantly worrying about something or other about the ranch or if I'd forgotten to take care of something. Made it easy to find the extra hours to turn this room into something special for her. Now them," he added, nodding at Chance.

He watched as Sara spun slowly, taking in the furnishings. The white spindle crib with the pastel monkey sheets. The stars and moon mobile that hung overhead and played lullabies. The white floor lamp that he'd stenciled matching stars and moons on. The big braided rug in yellows and pinks and blues. The yellow glider that he'd practically lived in the past seven weeks. The white dresser topped with the changing pad and basket of diapers and ointments. The bookcase he'd filled with board books and baby books and lined with stuffed animals. And the window with the yellow velvet drapes, tree branches and leaves and blue sky the view.

Every time Noah came in here, he felt so strongly that this was all meant to be—that Annabel was meant to be here. The first few days, his sister had asked if he was worried about splitting his time between fatherhood and getting the final details taken care of for the grand reopening, then less than two months away, and for reasons he couldn't quite ever figure out, the answer was more no than yes. Everything about Annabel in his life had felt so right, his bond with her so immediate, that he'd simply made it work. That was what you did.

He hadn't done it with Sara two years ago. Or with the small ranch he'd tried to keep going. That was what he'd thought about long and hard once he'd gotten his act together five months ago and became the person she'd wanted him to be then. Why had he let her go? Why?

He didn't know. And he hated thinking about it.

"Thank you for taking such good care of her," Sara whispered. "For giving her this beautiful home and nursery."

He managed a smile. He almost wished she'd stop reminding him that Annabel wasn't his. That was unfair; he knew it. But still.

This was going to be hard. However this new arrangement was going to go, what would happen. It would be hard. He had no doubt about it.

"How about if I put Chance down," she said, carefully taking her son from the carrier, "since I'm used to transferring him when he's asleep, and you put Annabel down?"

"Good idea," he said, reaching for Annabel and cuddling her close for a moment before dropping a kiss to her soft little head. *Love you, baby girl*, he said silently.

The moment she touched the soft sheets with the tiny pastel monkeys, she stopped fussing and her eyes closed.

He sighed inwardly with relief again. His baby girl wasn't leaving. He wasn't losing Annabel.

Thank you, universe.

"This is home for her," Sara whispered, her voice shaky. "Of course she likes her crib."

He eyed Sara, wishing he could take her in his arms and just hold her, comfort her. This had to be so damned hard for *her* on so many levels. "And luckily, Chance seems like a champion napper who can sleep anywhere," he said with a gentle smile.

She nodded, her face brightening a bit. "He's good that way." But her face fell a moment later. He knew her well enough to be able to tell she was suffering from regret-itis. Wishing things had been different, that she'd been with Annabel from the moment she'd been born.

"Hey. She's your daughter, Sara. And she'll be napping in your arms like she's been there from moment one in no time."

"How'd you know that was…" She trailed off and turned away.

"I've known you forever, Sara. Remember? Nothing escapes me about you."

She glanced at him, then gave a slow nod, and he wondered if he was getting too personal, if he should be more professional now, since they were going to work together. Heck, he was going to be her boss. "I guess we can leave them to nap and go talk," she said.

"I have a weird craving for a grilled cheese sandwich," he said. "Want one?"

"Actually, yes. An hour ago I couldn't imagine ever eating again. Now I'm starved."

Because your life is back on track, he thought. *You feel okay.* He hoped she did, anyway.

They headed down to the kitchen, and he told her to sit, that he had it. In minutes, she was sniffing the air appreciatively.

"Grilled cheese was always my comfort food," she said with a soft smile. "Whenever I was upset, if I couldn't sleep at midnight, my dad would make me a grilled cheese and I'd feel better. I think a lot had to do with him making it for me and sitting next to me at this very table while I took a few bites that made me feel so much better."

"Yup," he said. His closest-in-age brothers had been like that for him when there had been overlap with them staying on the ranch as he'd grown up. "And I'm not surprised Annabel conked out so easily. Meeting her mama was big stuff."

"It's only seven weeks, right?" she said, her voice shaky. "That's nothing."

She'd inadvertently thrown him a solid right hook in the stomach. Seven weeks had been more than enough for him to develop a serious bond with Annabel. Then again, he'd developed that bond within days. The weeks passing had just cemented it, his love for that baby growing every day. "A blip, Sara," he forced himself to say. "And you're together now. That's all that matters anymore."

"I'm glad she's staying here—for your sake too," she said.

"I'm not gonna lie. I'm very relieved. But I'm happiest for Annabel. I hope you know that. I love that baby. Truly love her, as if she were my own. I'd rather she had her mother and a twin brother and that she knew who she truly was than lived a lie with me for who knows how long."

And that was the truth, no matter how he felt about Annabel. If he loved that baby, he wanted what was best for her, not what was best for himself.

He thought about the letter Sara told him Willem had left for her. What if the rat bastard *hadn't* been reckless with that stupid Porsche? What if he *had* lived to ninety-three like his just-as-awful father had? Sara would never have known her daughter. He would never have known who'd left Annabel. All their stories would be very different.

"I believe that," she said. "You always had a big heart."

Again, so much of their past hung heavy in the air, regrets and good times. He'd let her down—hard. Driven her right into Willem's arms. He'd never forgive himself for that.

"Why do you think he left her here?" he asked. "With a note saying she was mine?"

"Probably to create havoc for you, mess up your carefree bachelor's life, screw up your good thing with the reopening of the ranch, if he even knew about that. Was there press about the grand reopening? He must have read it."

Noah nodded. "The *Bear Ridge Daily* did a big story on it. So did the Converse County paper."

"I think he thought he was getting the last laugh," Sara said. "He knew how I felt about you and he couldn't stand it, even when I told him that was in the past. He never believed me. He resented you and probably thought it was sweet justice that you'd think the baby he didn't want was yours."

He wondered how she felt about him now. Two years ago, after a drinking bender that had left Noah in no condition to drive her and her dad to his ap-

pointment at the county hospital since her car was
in the shop, she'd screamed that she was done with
him, then had sent him a text a few hours later: I'll
never be done with you, Noah. Even if we never see
or speak to each other again, I'll always wish you well
in my heart. But goodbye.

Two weeks later, he'd heard she'd married the rat
bastard.

He had a feeling he'd never be clear on why he'd
screwed up with Sara once he'd finally allowed himself to be in a relationship with her. He'd had everything, and he'd let it all go. Sara. His starter ranch.
He'd frittered away most of the savings account she
wouldn't take from him on really dumb track bets.
Then he had what he'd supposedly wanted, according to his sister, who'd eventually staged an intervention with his brothers: nothing.

"Well, I'm glad Willem chose me," he said. "Mine
or not, it was an honor to take care of her the past
seven weeks, Sara. Two years ago, I couldn't have
done it. Two months ago, I did. I'm a different person now, if you haven't noticed."

"I noticed." She opened her mouth as if to say
something else but apparently decided against it. He
imagined she'd been about to say: *It's a start, anyway. Let's see where you are in six months. Or a
year. Maybe you're one challenge away from mess-
ing it all up again.*

He could see in her face that she didn't trust him, and he didn't blame her. But things *were* different now—because he trusted *himself.* That was everything. He hadn't known anything about that two years ago or five years ago or ever. But when he'd taken on reopening the ranch, when his sister and brothers had told him he'd hit rock bottom and there was only one way to go from there, he'd grabbed control of his life with both hands. His siblings had believed in him when they'd had no reason to, when he himself had no reason to. By the time Annabel had been left on his porch, he truly was a changed man.

Sara leaned against the doorway frame, crossing her arms over her chest, her long brown ponytail falling against her neck. "What a mess this could have been had he left her with strangers. I could have had a custody fight on my hands for my own daughter."

"The universe was looking out for you all along," he said, lifting up an edge of the grilled cheese to see if it was golden brown. It was. He was surprised the conversation hadn't distracted him into burning down the entire kitchen.

"I think so." She nodded. "Wow, that looks good," she said, her gaze on the grilled cheese sandwiches.

"And here it comes, good old-fashioned comfort food," he said, putting the plates on the small round table by the window and grabbing two raspberry seltzers from the fridge.

"Thanks, Noah. I have a feeling I'll be saying that a lot."

"Sure beats the alternative," he said, then regretted it. She'd had some choice words for him back then. He didn't want to remind her of bad times. He wasn't that guy anymore.

But she gave him a smile and picked up half her sandwich. "I was wondering if I could borrow your pickup truck today. When the babies wake up, I can drive over to my house—my former house—and get Chance's things. Then I'll be done with that place."

He cracked open his seltzer. "I'll do you one better. I'll drive you and help you cart everything. And how about if we ask Daisy to watch the twins?"

Sara frowned. "I hate the thought of leaving Annabel for even a second when I just got her back."

"We could take the twins along if you prefer, but it would be a lot easier and faster to get the job done without having to worry about them or check on them."

She nodded. "You're right. And Daisy does seem to adore Annabel. Think she'd mind?"

"Mind? Annabel's her—" He clamped his mouth shut.

"Niece," she said solemnly. "Annabel sure had a lot of love here. I'm grateful. Your brothers too?"

He shook his head. "They know about her, but they all said they'd never step foot on the ranch again, that it was my thing and they were glad Daisy was here because it made them feel less guilty. I think a few of them were worried the baby news would trip me up about the ranch. I'm pretty sure they're all waiting to see how things shake down. No doubt Daisy fills them in."

She nodded. "Your sister can still be Aunt Daisy," she said, taking another bite of her sandwich. "He who won't be named and I were both only children. Annabel can use an aunt and four uncles."

He smiled. "And Daisy is six months pregnant and wants baby experience. She's loved her babysitting time with Annabel these past weeks. She's an old pro already. I'm sure she'd be happy to watch both."

"Okay, then. I'll take you up on the offer for help and your sister as babysitter."

He nodded and picked up his sandwich and took a bite. He'd eaten plenty of grilled cheeses here as a kid, just as Sara had had many meals in the main house. They'd been inseparable as children, the same age, when his five siblings had all been older and not so interested in the sprout tagging along. His eldest brother, Ford, was six years older, just a little more than a year separating all of them. They had three mothers among them. Daisy and Noah with the third wife. Axel, Rex and Zeke with the second, and Ford with the first Mrs. Dawson.

"Thank you again, Noah," Sara said, placing her hand on his. "For lunch. For the relief of a home and a job. For taking such good care of my daughter."

I'd do anything for you, he wanted to say, and it felt true, but when he'd needed to step up, he'd failed her. Gunk he didn't want to think about anymore but often kept him awake at night. For two years.

So he just nodded and squeezed her hand, then picked up his phone and called his sister.

A half hour later, Daisy was up in the nursery with the twins, happy to watch Annabel and Chance for however long they needed, and he and Sara were in his truck alone, heading down the drive until he realized they forgot about the Range Rover.

New plan. He'd follow her in the truck so she could return the fancy SUV to the house where it belonged, since the car, like everything else, was apparently in Perry's name.

Now he was behind her on the freeway, so aware of her in the silver SUV, never wanting to let her out of his sight again.

Chapter Four

Thanks to Noah's help, Sara got Chance's stuff and her clothing and toiletries and some personal items out of the Wellington house and into the pickup in under an hour—including the double infant stroller that Willem must have moved to a closet in the garage and then forgotten about. He'd gotten rid of the extras of everything they'd bought two of—a baby swing, a crib. The stroller was the only sign in the house that she'd been expecting twins.

Part of her wanted to leave it, but she'd picked out the stroller herself, knowing she'd be the one using it 99 percent of the time, drawn to the soft blue and white color. *It doesn't offend*, Willem had said when she'd shown him the online photo, so she'd ordered it. Ugh, that had been Willem's favorite description. *It offends*, he'd say about the most innocuous things.

She shivered as memory after memory hit her. *Just finish up and get out of here*, she told herself.

The shortest time possible spent in this house, the better. The three-story white Colonial with the black shutters and red door was classic and beautiful on the outside, and as cold and austere as a walk-in freezer on the inside. The walls were all the same cool gray, the furnishings white, black or cream. Willem had found color—and a whole host of other things—tacky. Since he'd passed away, out of Willem-ingrained habit she'd straightened the throw pillows if she'd sat on the sofa and shifted all the hand towels in the bathroom so they were perfectly aligned. More than once, Willem had called her upstairs as though something awful had happened and he'd point out that the shampoo and conditioner containers needed to face front, not one of them sideways or show evidence that they'd been squeezed with depressions in the center.

She'd lived like that for two years. And had lost her father anyway.

She'd tried, given it her all, done whatever it had taken to try to save her dad. Preston Mayhew had loved life and had been raring to go, to fight the traitorous cells with everything he had. She'd been given an extra year and a half with him. When he was first diagnosed, he'd told her he'd be fine with sticking around long enough to walk her down the aisle even with a cane, and the pure joy on his face when he'd done just that had let her know he'd go at peace, assured his only child would be okay without him in the world.

She had to get out of this house. "I think that's it," she said to Noah.

She'd sped through her bedroom, the room she'd shared with Willem, where she'd given birth, where her husband had tried very hard to take something precious from her. She'd been unable to look at the bed or the pretty chair where the midwife had sat beside her for hours during labor, so encouraging, so kind. Granted, Sara hadn't gotten to know the midwife, Katherine, all that well, but she could only assume the woman was racked with guilt and unable to live with herself, no matter how much Willem had paid her off, no matter how desperate she'd been. What she'd done was reprehensible. Sara couldn't imagine any amount of money making what she'd done even a serious consideration. She'd have to deal with the midwife soon. Very soon. What if she was planning to assist with another birth? Sara would call the lawyer tomorrow and discuss it all.

Her stomach turning over, Sara pushed all that away, focusing on the man watching her right now. She let herself drink in the sight of him, so different from Willem. Noah was over six feet by a couple inches at least, lanky and muscular with warm, deep blue eyes and a mop of shaggy dark hair that curled by his nape. Movie-star hair straight from the shower or bed. He was incredibly sexy—objectively speaking. Women had always buzzed around Noah. Willem had been attractive but not sexy, tall and stocky with pin-straight light blond hair and ice-blue eyes that neither twin had inherited. They both had her coloring. Was it awful that she was grateful she didn't see him in them? Grateful as she was to have them.

She stopped in front of the fireplace mantel, chills running up her spine, and then walked past, leaving the framed photographs there.

Noah nodded at the mantel. "Not taking any?"

There weren't many, since Willem had also thought it was tacky to have personal photographs all over the place. She'd always loved the idea of stairway walls lined with family pictures, but the stairway wall was blank, a cold gray like the rest of the house.

"I really don't want them," she said.

He plucked their wedding photo off the mantel. "The twins might one day," he said gently. He looked at the framed photograph and shook his head. "Perry's expression says you're his trophy. Is that what it was like? He finally got the girl?"

"Yup. It was more about the conquest than anything. Then he resented me for it."

"I'm sorry you went through all that, Sara. All of it. I wish I could have helped with your dad."

"Well, you tried," she said.

When she'd told him how bleak the situation was, that the hospital couldn't continue with treatment because of the lack of insurance and lack of payment on the last bill, Noah had handed her a check that she knew was the contents of his bank accounts—business and personal. It meant he'd lose his small ranch that he'd wanted so badly, and the gesture touched and unsettled her. He'd give up his dream to help her, but the amount, generous as it was, would pay only the last bill and barely begin to cover the month ahead. He'd lose his ranch and she wouldn't be able to keep up with the payments anyway. It was lose-lose, and so she'd turned it down. That was the first night they'd made love, when they'd tried to be a couple, but it was all too much for him. The intimacy, she thought. Just too much. Within a few months he clearly couldn't handle it and so he began acting out in ways it took her a while to catch onto. By then it was too late for them. She'd ended their relationship after only six months together and started dating Willem, who'd actually seemed like a breath of fresh air.

Ha. Not that it was funny in the slightest.

Her phone pinged with a text. It was from Holton, Willem's attorney.

Hope I'm not overstepping but please advise re: the female twin.

She texted back, Alive and well. We'll all be okay.

Wonderful news, Sara. Also, I checked into the midwife's license. According to the Wyoming Board of Nursing, she allowed her license of thirty-seven years to expire just this month without renewing, and local hospitals and OBs that I checked with let me know she called them to say she had officially retired. At least she's out of business.

Sara shivered.

It was something, but not enough. She'd have to deal with the midwife at some point soon. But for right now, when she walked out the door of this house, she'd close this chapter of her life. She'd never want to hear the lawyer's name or her late husband's again. There was too much to process right now, too much to adjust to or she'd storm the midwife's home with the sheriff in tow. Or maybe just knock on the woman's door and find out what the hell Willem had threatened her with or what dire straits she'd been in to agree to such a heinous act. When the time felt right, she would do just that.

Forcing those thoughts away right now, Sara took the photo out of Noah's hand and put it back on the mantel. "I plan to legally change Chance's name from Bancroft Perry to Chance Mayhew since I'll be taking back my maiden name."

"What do you think you'll rename Annabel?"

Sara held his gaze. "I can't tell you how touched I was when I found out you named her Annabel. *My* middle name. Unless that was a coincidence? You just happened to like the name?"

"Well, I do happen to, but it was no coincidence. You were always my best friend, Sara, no matter what. And I guess I wanted her to have a piece of the best woman I know. Who knew she had *all* of you?"

She smiled, the urge to hug him so strong. She forced herself to stay put. "I think Annabel is perfect for her. Annabel Mayhew, it is."

"I got a lot right with her. Don't know how, but I did. Gives me hope for the ranch."

"I believe in you, Noah. Always have."

"I know," he said, looking down, and she could tell a little of that old Noah was still there, the guy who couldn't handle too much emotional honesty without getting itchy or wanting to run.

She'd do him a solid and change the subject. "For the twins, for someday," she said, "I'll take one photo album that has an array of photos from when Willem and I first started dating to when we brought Chance home." She shivered. "But how will I explain why there are no photos of Annabel the day they were born?"

She burst into tears and covered her face with her hands, and Noah wrapped his arms around her. She'd been holding on, but it was the thing that whacked her legs out from under her. The idea of her children having questions she'd hate to answer.

"You have lots of time to figure out those details," he said, his arms tightening around her. "Right now, let's focus on what's necessary. Like getting the hell out of here."

He tightened his hold for just a second, and oh God, did that feel good. She let herself sag against him, needing this, his comfort, his strength, all their beautiful history like air right now.

But she couldn't need him this way. It was too, too much. She wiped at her eyes and pulled away, slightly embarrassed at falling apart, but then again, this was Noah Dawson, who'd seen her through just about all the rough times of her life.

And she couldn't lie to herself. Being in his arms again felt even better than she'd expected. Maybe because he had changed. Or maybe because she'd missed him so damned much. Either way, she had to be careful with how she responded to him. She had leaned on someone for the last time. Now, she'd only lean on herself.

"I almost forgot," Noah said as he drove down the freeway in his pickup, Sara's Range Rover left behind with her old life. "My dad left you something in his will."

Sara had had enough of wills and surprises. She couldn't even summon the polite words to feign interest so she just turned toward him.

"A garden plot behind the foreman's cabin," he said. "Apparently it was your mother's once?"

A spark of joy lit inside Sara, a warmth as memories rushed over her. Sara as a little girl kneeling in the grass in front of the wood-framed raised garden bed, her mother letting her drop in the seeds as she explained about vegetables you planted in the warmer weather, like tomatoes and green peppers.

"It was added to the letter he left me," Noah said.

"'Tell Sara I bequeath her the garden plot behind the foreman's cabin. Her mother built it and grew all kinds of vegetables. Sara was a nice gal, so I wanted to leave her something.'"

"I can't tell you how moved I am," she said. "That is really kind, Noah."

He nodded. "My dad had his moments, didn't he? You should have seen the letter he wrote me. I cried for a minute straight. I seriously couldn't stop."

She looked at him. "Really? What did the letter say?"

"That he was sorry for ruining our family legacy and everything his parents had built and dreamed of. That he was sorry for letting us down. He said he owned the ranch outright, and the land, never sold any part of it, and he'd always paid his property taxes, even if he let the place fall apart."

Sara had been leveled by what his father had done to the place, how he'd slowly destroyed it. The final straw for her dad as foreman had been the afternoon that Noah's dad had drunkenly smashed his truck into the barn next to their cabin—though luckily her and her dad's horses were in the pasture and not injured. Bo Dawson had refused to pay for the repairs to the barn and left it as it was. Between not paying his bills, storm damage he wouldn't take care of, and time, the old word of mouth had spread, and guests stopped coming completely. Out of respect for Noah's late grandparents, her dad had stayed on for a few weeks more, trying to do what he could and reason with Noah's father, but the man was beyond hope, and they'd left. That was twelve years ago.

"He still cared about Dawson Family Guest Ranch," Sara said. "Even if he didn't show it or have the wherewithal to do anything about it. The place itself meant something to him."

Noah nodded. "I used to think actions spoke louder than anything, and I've come to realize what people do masks all kinds of things they can't say or articulate."

She supposed that was true. Nothing was ever really black-and-white. She'd known that Noah had cared about her even when he was letting her down. People were complicated. Life was complicated. If anyone had told her five years ago that one day she'd be trapped in an emotionally abusive marriage, unsure how to get herself and Chance safely away, she never would have believed it. She would have smugly said she'd never *be* in such a marriage to begin with, let alone not be able to get out.

"My dad went on to say in the letter that he hoped I'd take charge of the place," Noah said, thankfully shaking her out of her thoughts. "That I'd reopen the Dawson Family Guest Ranch even on a small scale, that he felt awful he couldn't leave any money to make that happen. But that he knew I was the Dawson to do it. He said I had a streak of him running in my veins but more of my grandparents in me, and he was sure I'd reopen the place and have my grandparents smiling down at me and the ranch."

"Wow," she said, marveling at how people *could* surprise you. "To all of it."

He nodded. "He left us all letters. At the will reading after the funeral, I was the only one who shared my letter. My siblings wouldn't. Even Daisy, and she was never all that private, especially with me."

"What do you think he wrote in your siblings' letters?" she asked. "I mean, if he envisioned you reopening the ranch, what else was there?"

"Nothing as far as I know. He got so broke at the end that he even sold the chipped dishes and cheap silverware. I can't even imagine what he wrote in their letters. But whatever he did write had an impact, since they're all so tight-lipped about it."

"They invested in reopening the ranch," she added. "And they invested in you too. So he must have made some kind of amends."

He nodded. "They refuse to step foot on the property, though. Except Daisy. And only because she's pregnant and seems to be completely on her own."

"She's got you," Sara said. "And me."

He glanced at her. "I'm glad for that."

They were quiet for a few moments, the only sound the rush of the tires as they drove down the freeway.

"You know what's interesting?" she said. "That the last person you expected to change your life ended up doing just that. Your father."

He nodded. "I spent a lot of time thinking about exactly that as I was working on the ranch. My siblings and I had given up on him completely the last few years." He sucked in a breath. "I hate wishing I could go back. At the time, I felt justified in leaving him to his own destruction. We all did. He constantly told us to get lost and mind our own business, that it was his property and we were trespassing. So we stopped badgering him after a while. Once the drinking got really bad and he almost ran over Ford one morning, dead drunk at 10:00 a.m., we left him alone."

"I know all about wishing you could go back, Noah. I guess we just do the best we can at the time with what we know, what we believe is true and right."

He glanced at her and nodded. "I would have let you know about the garden plot, but I wasn't sure about getting in touch. I couldn't imagine you driving an hour a few times a week to tend to a twelve-foot-by-six-foot garden bed."

"To get away from Willem for a few hours?" she said. "I would have."

He reached for her hand and squeezed it. "Well, it's yours now. And time to plant."

"Being back at the ranch when it looks the way it does now, being with you, my old friend, it almost feels like the world's been righted for me."

He turned to look at her, and his expression was full of so many different emotions. He squeezed her hand and then returned his attention to the road, and she wondered if she'd said too much again, made too much of their reunion. To change the subject, she remarked on how beautiful the Wyoming wilderness was in late May when the leaves bloomed and wildflowers spread their gorgeous color across the brown and green landscape, the still-snowcapped mountain range in the far distance. He agreed, and then they were silent the rest of the way home.

As Noah drove through the gates of the Dawson Family Guest Ranch and up the dirt road past the foreman's cabin, Sara took in the manicured but rustic grounds, pastures and fields and wilderness in every direction. There were cute wooden signs posted with arrows, miles and timing to get to the main house, the foreman's cabin, the cafeteria, the lodge, Bear Ridge Creek, riding trails and the trail system in the woods that were part of the ranch. Wildflowers were everywhere, and there were hunter green wooden benches, picnic tables and wooden swings hanging from tree branches. The ranch looked so welcoming and inviting.

"Did you hire people to help besides you and Daisy?" she asked as they drove past a pretty, rectangular log cabin painted a rustic white with a sign reading Guest Cafeteria. Picnic tables were out front.

"I have a good staff. For one, my grandparents' old cook, Cowboy Joe, agreed to come back and take the job. No one makes better burgers or omelets or barbecue than him. He's nearing seventy, but I hired him two helpers. The caf will be open from seven to eight thirty, twelve to one thirty, and five to six thirty for dinner. Cowboy Joe will handle breakfast and lunch, and Daisy wanted to take the dinner shift. She's also the guest relations manager."

"Perfect," she said. "So you'll focus on the ranch and she'll focus on the guests."

"Yup. I have a great team assembled—maintenance, housekeeping, cowboys and cowgirls. It's a small staff, but we're starting small. We're having a final staff meeting before opening day on Thursday morning—you can come to that and we'll get your role squared away beforehand. Memorial Day weekend and through the rest of next week, all six cabins are booked with a retreat. Something about getting your groove back."

Sara smiled. "Really?"

He shrugged. "Some kind of female empowerment thing. It's led by a life coach. She's bringing her own protein shake mixes."

Sara laughed. "Sounds great. And are there bookings beyond opening weekend?"

"Not all the cabins all the weeks or weekends, but so far, so good."

"I'm really happy for you, Noah. Looks like the ranch will be a big success."

"I hope so. I know a lot can go wrong."

She glanced at him and saw for the first time the worry in his expression. Everything must be riding on the opening, she realized. His dreams and future. His siblings' investment. What he wanted to carry on for his grandparents—and now even for his father.

As the main house where Noah grew up came into view, Sara's jaw almost dropped. Once peeling with a rotting foundation, the white clapboard farmhouse looked pristine and gleaming as it stood in the sunshine, a white wood–fenced pasture beside it and several trails through the low and high grasslands leading into the woods about a hundred feet away. The guest cabins, which couldn't be viewed from the dirt road that ended at the house, were between the foreman's cabin and the creek, nestled privately in the woods. Given what the main house looked like, she knew the cabins had to be beautifully restored too.

"You've done wonders with the place," she said. "And it'll take off. I believe that."

"Here's hoping so," he said, parking along the side of the house.

They headed up the porch steps, and he pulled open the screen door, Daisy coming over with Chance fast asleep in her arms.

"This guy got fussy a little while ago, so I walked around with him, rocking him a bit, and he fell back asleep. I couldn't bear to put him down. He's such a love bug." She breathed in the baby shampoo scent of him. "Ahhh. I know being a mom twenty-four-seven like I'll be in three months won't be all rock-abye and baby shampoo goodness, but I don't care. I can't wait!"

Sara laughed. "Know what you're having?"

"I told the radiologist and my OB that I want to be surprised," she said. "Which was a surprise in itself, given that I've had enough of the unexpected lately for a lifetime."

Sara had a feeling Daisy was talking about the

father of her baby, and she was so curious, but until her old friend wanted to tell, she wouldn't ask.

"Where's my baby girl—" Noah said and then froze and turned to Sara. "Sorry. I mean, where's Annabel?" He smiled but looked so uncomfortable that suddenly Sara felt equally uncomfortable. How hard this must be for him, to have to step back from Annabel, to accept that she wasn't his baby after all.

His phone rang, and he seemed relieved for the interruption. He read something on the little screen. "Oh man. I've actually got to run. Hermione—one of the alpine goats—escaped her corral, and Dylan, one of our cowboys, is having a hard time getting her back."

Daisy laughed. "That Hermione is a wily one."

"See you in a few," Noah said, looking at his sister and then Sara before sprinting out.

"Annabel's napping in the kitchen," Daisy said. "I was just sitting at the table with the baby monitor on high volume making a list of all the things I'm going to need. Taking a peek inside the twins' baby bag helped me a lot. Taking care of two babies must feel like a huge change from just one."

"It is, but every time I look at Annabel, I almost can't believe she's real. That makes double the work a lot easier." She smiled. "And yup, sure is a lot of stuff," Sara said. "Of course for the past seven weeks, I didn't know I'd need two of everything after all."

Daisy shook her head. "I still can't process what happened. My ex—" She bit her lip. "He was this and that, but I don't think he'd ever do something like that. How *could* anyone?"

Sara felt her face fall. "It's the scariest thing, Daisy. That I didn't know what I was getting myself into. But it turns out I made a deal with the devil."

Daisy shook her head. "Don't do that to yourself. I remember you telling me how special Willem made you feel, how listened to, how important. Plus, he was instrumental in getting your dad the best care, Sara. He pulled the wool over your eyes with who he was, but he did help with your dad, so there's that. And there's also something else."

"The twins," Sara said, knowing what Daisy was doing. Letting her take herself off the hook. She put a hand on her friend's arm. "Thank you, Daisy."

Sara followed her friend into the kitchen, struck, as always, by how much she and her brother looked alike. Daisy had lighter hair—hers was a beautiful honey-brown—but they had the same blue eyes and gorgeous features. Though two years older, Daisy had always been warm and kind to Sara. When Sara had gotten her period for the first time, and her mother had been gone a year and half prior, it was Daisy she'd gone to, all nervous and worried and thrilled.

It was also Daisy she'd gone to about her first kiss and first crush, admitting it was on her brother Noah, which worried Daisy to no end, and under "no circumstances are you allowed to let him kiss you, let alone touch a piece of your clothing!" Sara had said she could only half promise, given that she was in love and only thirteen and driven by hormones and the brain of a teenager. She and Noah had been best friends, but he'd refused to date her, saying he didn't want to mess up the friendship, but she saw the girls he went for. C cups. High heels. Hips. She had none of those things. And then her father had told her they were moving when she was sixteen and that was that until Noah took a job as a cowboy on the new ranch her father managed and then moved there when he was eighteen. But he still wouldn't mess with their friendship.

That had gone on for years, and their romance had only lasted six months. No matter how helpful he was to her now, she'd never trust Noah Dawson with her heart again.

Sara saw Annabel's carrier on the floor by the window and rushed over, still amazed that she *did* have a daughter. The baby girl was sleeping and looked so peaceful. She'd made an appointment with a pediatrician in town for Annabel, but from what she could tell, the infant looked healthy.

"Coffee?" Daisy said, picking up the pot. "I was just about to pour myself a mug. It's decaf, though."

"I'd love some."

Daisy poured and brought two mugs to the table and sat down. "You should have seen Noah with Annabel the past seven weeks. I knew Noah was capable of surprising me, but he *shocked* me. When I called my brothers to tell them, they didn't believe it and thought I was exaggerating."

Sara added cream and sugar and took a sip. "Exaggerating what?"

"His devotion to that baby. The note said she was his, and that was all he needed to know. He loved Annabel from the minute he brought her inside, I think. You know how many times he watched a YouTube video about burping a newborn, how to position the bottle while feeding? Like twenty times. I went with him to the baby emporium in Prairie City, and he spent ten minutes picking out a wipes warmer." She chuckled. "Noah Dawson walking around the ranch holding a baby in pink footie pajamas, introducing her to all the new animals. One time she fell asleep, and he shushed the goats."

Again Sara wanted to smile and cry. "Our Noah Dawson. I wonder what happened to him."

"I think the ranch did, Sara. He was the one of us who loved this place. He was the baby of the six of us and the Dawson kid who lived here his whole life. Our half brothers were whisked away by divorce and only came to visit. I don't think it's in their blood the way it is in Noah's. And the letter our dad left him, wanting him to reopen the guest ranch? Something got fired up in him. Purpose. Legacy. A future."

Sara nodded. She understood all that. What she would never understand was why she hadn't been that for Noah when they'd been together. Maybe she was flattering herself or being whiny, but their friendship ran so deep and so long, and their attraction, which he'd denied both of them for years, had been crazy intense. But he'd let it all go.

Eh. Didn't matter anymore. She wasn't here to revisit their past or figure out the mind of Noah Dawson. She was here to get her life back, get back on her feet, be her own woman again. She'd save up and then she'd be on her way with her children, starting fresh.

"Did you and Noah figure out what your role will be on the ranch?" Daisy asked. "I'd love for you to help me out with the guests. Our first group is coming on Friday afternoon and staying the week. There are twelve of them sharing the six cabins. Each cabin can accommodate more people, but the group leader wanted each attendee to have a lot of space, mental and physical."

"Ooh, the female empowerment group. Noah mentioned them."

Daisy nodded. "The leader is a life coach. I might linger in the back of the room to eavesdrop on the sessions."

"Me too. Female empowerment is exactly what I need right now."

"Ditto," Daisy said. "Big fat ditto."

Sara took a sip of her coffee. "I just realized that Noah and I didn't talk about *any* of the details of my employment at the ranch. Childcare issues and all that. He did say we'd work out the logistics before the staff meeting on Thursday, when he'd introduce me to everyone."

"I'm sure he intends to be your childcare provider," Daisy said. "And Mrs. Pickles is available. And me too whenever I can. I really do need the experience."

"I feel really lucky," Sara said, taking a sip of her coffee. "You Dawsons were always wonderful to me."

"You're like family," Daisy said, touching Sara's hand.

"You're going to make me cry." She blinked back being such an emotional hormonal mess, but she was too touched and her eyes welled. "Did Noah tell you about your dad leaving me the garden plot my mom built behind the foreman's cabin?"

"Another thing my brothers and I couldn't believe," Daisy said. "The thoughtfulness involved in that. Just when you think someone doesn't care about a damned thing, including himself and his kids, he stuns us all with handwritten letters."

"You liked the letter he left you?" she dared probe.

Daisy seemed lost in thought for a moment. "It touched me. And I really fought it. But yeah, it touched me. I'm not really ready to talk about it, though."

Sara nodded. "Totally understand."

The screen door opened and there was Noah, and the sight of him almost had Sara blushing. He was just so intensely sexy. Without remotely trying. He had that tall, lanky, muscular physique, the low-slung dark jeans and dusty boots, the brown Stetson. And that face that she'd loved since she was so young, the star of her nightly dreams and fantasies.

The man who'd taken care of a baby girl left on his porch in the middle of the night. Who'd watched videos on burping and shushed noisy goats so she could nap while he walked her around the barn.

That old stirring ignited deep inside her, and she tried to toss some cold water on it from the bitter part of her heart, but then Noah came over and knelt down in front of the carriers, touching a finger to Annabel's cheek and then Chance's.

"How are these little rabble-rousers?" he asked, his expression so tender.

I. Cannot. Like. You. That. Way, she told herself. *Cannot.*

Heaven help her.

Chapter Five

"Wait," Sara said, putting her suitcases beside the bed in Noah's guest room, which would now be her bedroom. "This is your office."

"Not anymore." Noah took the big empty box in his hand and filled it with the contents of the desk by the window, then took the bulletin board off the wall and tucked it under his arm. The room had never felt like an office, and though he stored paperwork here, he didn't like to sit at the desk. He preferred the kitchen table with a view of the barn and Bolt's head poking out of her corral, which also afforded a view of the main drive up from the gates. He also liked to work in a corner of the living room with a view of the wilderness and a winding trail that led up to the main house. "Now it's your room."

"I don't want to displace you," she said. "We can move the bed into the nursery. The babies don't need their own room, really."

"Yes, they do. Because as you know, taking care of a baby is exhausting and you need *your* own space, a door to close."

She shot him an appreciative smile. "How'd you get anything done when it was just you and Annabel here?"

"I took her with me everywhere. In the ole Snugli. If I couldn't, Daisy or Mrs. Pickles would watch her for me. The crew I hired did the heavy lifting when it came to renovating. I directed."

She grinned. "I can just see you, telling the crew what to do with a pink-outfitted baby strapped on your chest."

"Hey, two of them were dads themselves. They high-fived me every day about it."

She bit her lip and turned away.

Uh-oh. What had he said? "Sara?"

She dropped down on the bed. "Just waiting for the other shoe to drop, maybe. This all seems too easy, Noah. Things falling into place for me—first with reuniting with Annabel and having her safe and sound. Getting just the right job and place to live. You—my new boss, by the way—being this new person."

He got it. Her trust in everything had been shattered.

"You know what you need?" he asked.

She tilted her head. "What?"

"Some time to put your feet up and relax. Come down when you're hungry."

She raised an eyebrow, and he realized he was pushing it, being too much the host when she expected very little from him.

Which hurt, he also understood. He'd show her who he was.

Or not, actually. His entire focus could now be on the ranch. For the past seven weeks, he'd had no idea how he was going to get everything done for opening weekend, the most important weekend of his life, with a baby in tow. But he had. Thanks to a solid team, thanks to Daisy, thanks to him caring about both the baby and the ranch more than he'd ever cared about anything.

Except Sara. And he couldn't let his residual feelings for her, which he'd been trying to tamp down since she'd stormed the drive in that Range Rover, get him distracted. The Dawson Family Guest Ranch wasn't just about him; his siblings had invested in the place. They'd entrusted him with their money and their faith, and he would not let them down. Or himself.

Just about two months ago, Annabel had been added to that list. But now he had to take her off— somehow. She wasn't his baby, and Sara wasn't going to stay here forever.

The real problem was that he couldn't imagine ever crossing Annabel off the list. Granted, it had been only hours since he learned the truth that he wasn't the baby's father. But inside, he was. And always would be.

A cry, slightly different than Chance's, came from the nursery across the hall of the foreman's cabin. Annabel. Sara's heart leaped, and she bolted out of bed with a glance at the clock—1:14 a.m.

Her first middle-of-the-night wake-up from the baby girl she thought she'd lost. She'd never been so happy to be pulled out of bed in her entire life.

I'm coming, sweetheart, she thought as she hurried across the hall into the nursery. *Your mommy's coming and will never let anything happen to you again. Ever.*

She stopped in her tracks in the doorway. A half-naked Noah sat in the glider by the window, Annabel nestled in his arms, the moonlight a soft glow around them. He was so focused on the story he was telling the baby that he didn't even seem to realize Sara was there.

"And then Hermione ran and ran and ran," Noah said, "and poor Dylan—he's one of our cowboys—tried every trick to get the black-and-white goat to come back. The *main* trick is to actually let the goat chase you. Yup, just start running in the direction you want Goaty to go and wham—back in her corral."

"Is that what happened?" Sara interrupted with a smile as she stepped into the room.

Noah looked up at her, his gaze lingering a beat longer than it normally might and she realized she was wearing her skimpy pajamas—a Wyoming Wildcats T-shirt and a pair of yoga pants with a heavenly stretchy waistline. No bra, and motherhood had done wonders with typically B-cup breasts.

He cleared his throat and smiled at her. "Hermione is especially strong-willed. She wanted the high grass on the far side of the field by the fence, so Dylan had to wait until she was ready to play chase." He frowned suddenly and carefully stood up, glancing down at Annabel, whose eyes were drooping. "I'm so used to rushing in at her every cry. I should have let you take care of it. Sorry."

"It's nice that two people care so much about her, Noah," she said, then instantly regretted those words. Did she want Noah to care about Annabel the way she did? Of course, she understood why he did right now, but once a little time passed and he got used to not being Annabel's parent, the bond would loosen, right? Seven weeks certainly wasn't a lifetime.

A blip, he'd called it. She realized now, based on how he was looking down at Annabel—like a loving, doting father, something her daughter had not experienced for even a second from her biological father—that Noah had been lying. Seven weeks weren't a blip to him. He'd said that for her sake— and Annabel's. Because he truly loved that little girl.

"Do you think Willem had a moment's pause?" she asked, unable to stop herself. "Did he reach into the car to get her carrier when he arrived at your cabin in the middle of the night, the rain probably having started, and look at her face and think, *this is my daughter, my baby girl, my son's twin sister.* Did he ever think that for one second?" A sob tore out of her throat, and tears threatened.

Bloody hormones.

She watched Noah gently lay Annabel in the crib beside her brother, then he walked over and pulled her into his arms and held tight. She let herself sag against him—again, his strength, the comfort he was offering everything she needed right now.

"I want to hope so, Sara. I think we should just leave it at that."

She nodded against his chest. His bare chest. Warm, hard muscle, soft skin.

Stop needing this so much, she told herself, unable to pull away. But in the difficult past weeks, the past few months, the past couple of years, allowing her husband to isolate her from friends to the point that she hadn't felt comfortable turning to anyone even after losing her baby daughter, she *did* need this embrace.

Noah didn't pull away either. "C'mere," he said, and led her by the hand out of the room and into her own.

He stopped in front of her bed and held up the pretty blue-and-white quilt, embroidered with little stars and crescent moons. Part of her frowned. The other part tingled. She could barely take her eyes off his chest, and when she did, his face was even better. The beautiful face she'd loved and dreamed about for so long, full of tenderness, his blue eyes blazing with what might even be desire.

But come on. "Um, I guess it's been the requisite six weeks doctors tell you to wait after childbirth, but it's only a week past." Why had she said that? It wasn't as if she'd let herself go there with Noah anyway.

He raised an eyebrow. "Sara. Get your mind out of the gutter," he said with a grin. "I'm putting you to bed—alone. Get your rest."

Oh. She felt her cheeks burning a little. *Embarrassing!* Maybe Noah wasn't attracted to her anymore anyway. *You are being jerked around by hormones*, she reminded herself. *Ignore yourself. Just go back to sleep like Noah suggested.*

She slid into bed, laying her head on the soft down pillow. He actually tucked her in and then leaned over and kissed her forehead. Oh God, now she might cry. Her dad used to do that. And she always felt so loved, so protected, so safe in the world.

"Sleep, Sara," he said, straightening. "If you hear a baby crying, just turn over. I've got it. I won't expect to see you until at least 9:30 a.m. That way we can talk over your role at the ranch before the ten o'clock staff meeting. It'll be a good time to introduce you to everyone."

She couldn't even speak. She was just too overwhelmed. By her thoughts, by him, by her life right now. She nodded and then tried to find her voice. "Noah," she finally said as he neared the door.

He turned around.

"Thank you for everything."

"My pleasure," he said with such sincerity in his voice that her eyes did well up.

Danged hormones.

It *was* the hormones, right?

Brilliant sunshine streamed through the woven shades on the window, and Sara had no idea what time it was. Given how well rested she felt, how ready to bounce out of bed, it had to be past eight o'clock. When was the last time she'd slept in?

She grabbed her phone from the bedside table: 8:17 a.m. Heaven. She'd woken naturally, not from a crying baby or an alarm clock, though hers would have gone off at eight thirty.

The twins hadn't woken her because Noah had obviously taken care of the early-morning waking; she had no doubt they were either napping in the nursery or that he was downstairs with them right now, chatting away with them about ranch life or telling a story about the goats or sheep. Noah had gone from being someone she'd run away from to a man she trusted with the lives of her babies, including the baby girl she'd just been reunited with.

Still, part of her, a big part, felt uneasy about that. Putting her trust in anyone was a bad idea. Noah Dawson was going to be her boss. Their relationship was something different now. Another new normal she'd have to get used to.

After a quick shower, she dressed in white leggings and a floral tunic, which she hoped would be appropriate enough for the staff meeting, dried her hair and then headed into the nursery. The twins were asleep. Heart at ease and filled, she tiptoed out. If they were taking their morning naps, Noah had also gotten up with them at around five and fed them and changed them and taken care of them. He'd been up with them last night as she had, and he had to be exhausted right now. Today was likely to be a very busy day for him—tomorrow was the grand reopening of the Dawson Family Guest Ranch.

She headed downstairs, also appreciating the smell of coffee. Noah was sitting at the round table by the window, a clipboard with what appeared to be a checklist, various folders, his phone, a mug of coffee—and a baby monitor, of course, in front of him.

He was in jeans, a dark green Henley shirt and barefoot. Sexy feet.

"Sleep well?" he asked, taking a sip of his coffee. His gorgeous blue eyes were sparkling with energy. Or maybe just adrenaline. If the man was tired, he didn't show it. She realized he was on new-parent time—used to the crazy hours of caring for a newborn. His schedule and hers had been exact the past several weeks—an hour's distance from each other. There was no way he wasn't tired, but he made it work because he had to.

"I think I actually got almost seven hours, thanks to you. A new record."

"Good. You needed it. I can't even imagine what all that shock yesterday did to your system. You needed a solid night's sleep."

Huh. She hadn't even thought about that aspect. "I appreciate that."

He nodded. "So how about we talk about your job on the ranch, then we'll have the staff meeting, and then I can take you on a tour of the place, since it's changed from when we grew up here."

"Sounds good." She poured herself a mug of coffee, added cream and sugar, and sat down beside him.

"So, I figure you can either be the assistant foreman, as you were on the Circle D with your dad, or you can take on a specific position—I could use an education manager and workshops leader to run the information sessions and classes we'll offer about ranch life and the petting zoo. Or you can be a cowgirl and lead rides and teach the basics. Or a housekeeper, though Daisy already hired two. She also hired a receptionist who'll have the welcome-slash-check-in shed as her station by the gate, but we could use another. Cowboy Joe could always use another pair of hands in the kitchen. In terms of splitting the running of Dawson's, as I mentioned, I'm land and animals and maintenance and all that falls under that, and Daisy's guests, lodging, food and all that falls under that. As assistant foreman, you'd be both our right hands. It's a big job but one in your veins. And it pays well." He told her the salary, noting all employees would also receive holiday bonuses since the staff would have to work on most holidays, taking shifts so they could still spend time with family.

"Assistant fore*woman*, it is," she said, extending her hand.

She liked the idea of taking a job she knew and understood. She'd worked alongside her father for years as a teenager at Dawson's back in the day, and she'd been the assistant foreman—forewoman, in her mind—at the Circle D for years afterward, a position she'd loved. When her dad had gotten too sick to keep working, she'd switched to part-time to take care of him.

Willem had once told her that he liked that she smelled like goat when they were dating, because it made him feel like she wasn't a gold digger. Of course, she had married him for his money and he knew it; she'd never lie to herself that she'd loved him, though she had liked and appreciated him before she'd known who he truly was. It was how she'd not seen the real Willem back then that worried her. Maybe the truth was that she'd ignored what she'd needed to because what he'd promised had been more important than his snobbery and disdain of perfectly normal things.

Maybe she was doing something of that herself now. Ignoring her past with Noah because what she needed from him was more important right now. A job with room and board in a place that she loved, that felt comforting and familiar, where she felt on solid ground when she was anything but.

Just be smart, she reminded herself. *Build your trust in yourself and your judgment. You're in the right place for yourself and the twins for the right reasons.*

"Sara?"

She blinked and realized Noah was holding up his coffee mug in the air as if to clink in celebration over the job. She was glad to be pulled out of her thoughts. She held up her mug, and they gently clinked and took sips.

"Welcome back to the Dawson Family Guest Ranch," he said. "Assistant Forewoman."

His smile lit up his handsome face, and she was pulled back into seeing the old Noah—the one she'd been so in love with she could hardly look at him sometimes. How she'd loved that face, dreamed about it.

Noah was now her boss. Not the old love of her life. Not an ex. Her boss.

She'd keep her attention on that word, and she'd be okay. She now had a great job, was living in her old home, one where her father had never been sick or weak, one where her mother had still been alive for the first nine years of Sara's life. She had her mom's garden plot to revive. By summer's end, she might even have enough saved to start her new life, though now that she thought about it, she wouldn't have two built-in sitters-slash-bosses like Noah and Daisy. Things *were* going to be good here.

Maybe too good to leave, though. Which doubly meant she'd have to keep her distance from the way Noah made her feel. Safe. Everything felt so fragile, so tentative, so new, and there was no way she could count her chickens or think anything was squared away. Things could change in a heartbeat. People could turn. You just never knew.

Just earn your money, build your bank account and take care of your children, she reminded herself. That was her purpose. To be self-sufficient and never rely on anyone again.

"You remember Mrs. Pickles, right?" he asked her.

"Of course," she said, the image of a middle-aged woman with a long red braid and bright green wellies coming to mind. "The babysitter. Daisy mentioned she's helped out a few times." What she couldn't remember was Mrs. Pickles's real name; her surname had been long, so she'd told everyone to call her Mrs. Pickles, and it had stuck as she'd watched over Noah and Sara until Daisy was considered old enough to keep an eye on them and a couple of the ranch hands' kids too back when.

"She's been a godsend. I hope you don't mind that I called her and told her we could use her services for a few hours of wake time and a few of nap time for the twins going forward, and then I realized I had to tell her a bit of the story. She said she'd love to work for us. She has twin grandchildren herself, high schoolers now, so lots of experience."

"Perfect. I noticed their nap times seem in sync. Both were still sleeping when I checked on them a little while ago."

He nodded. "Annabel always woke from her morning nap around ten, so I'm thinking one of us can be home to do wake-up, feeding, a little playing, then hand over to Mrs. Pickles. She can watch them for three hours till the next nap, then stay for that three-hour stretch, so it gives us a good six-hour workday uninterrupted. Then, either one of us will be with them or we'll take them in the ole Snugli on the job when it's appropriate."

No wonder she trusted him with the twins. He was completely on top of everything—from ranch details to their schedules.

"They should sleep right through the staff meeting if Daisy and I keep it to no more than twenty minutes," he said. "It's really for everyone to meet one another. When the twins wake up, I figure we can put each in a Snugli and I'll give you the grand tour."

She liked that he wanted to take the twins with them, not just cast them off to a sitter the whole day. He truly wanted to be with the twins and to immerse them in the ranch life, because it was his life. *Their* life.

Once again she found herself overwhelmed at how thoughtful he was, how kind. She felt very lucky and wanted to wrap her arms around him in thanks.

She really had to force herself not to.

Chapter Six

"I'm real happy for you two," Cowboy Joe said after the staff meeting as everyone headed to their respective stations to make sure everything was in place for tomorrow. He stood in front of Noah and Sara, each with a baby strapped on their chest, outside the main house. "I remember you both running around the ranch as kids, getting into mischief. Now you're a family raising the next generation of Dawsons to carry on the legacy of this beautiful place."

Noah stared at the tall, skinny man—the ranch's cook—in the brown Stetson and shaggy gray beard, wondering what on earth he was talking about. Then he realized Cowboy Joe thought he and Sara were a couple—and the parents of the twins. Some of the staff had met Annabel when they'd come for interviews if he'd been unable to secure his sister or Mrs. Pickles, and of course he'd introduced her as his daughter. So when he'd introduced Sara as Annabel and Chance's mother, those who'd met Annabel naturally figured he was the dad and that there was a twin brother who they hadn't met before.

Hey, fine with him. He'd always feel like Annabel's dad, and he was glad to put Chance in the mix too. Plus, Cowboy Joe's presumption had not only given him a second shot with Sara, but a lifetime in the family sense. He liked that too. The *idea*, actually. Because romance was the furthest thing from his mind. Romance took over, kept you up nights, and he was already up nights—bleary-eyed but *clear*. He didn't need his brain and newfound structure and vision and purpose turned upside down over what his heart was doing. He'd never let himself mess things up with Sara again, anyway. Too much was at stake for that.

And he was flattering himself if he thought she'd ever give him a second shot.

"Come by the caf later to test out my new blueberry muffin recipe," Cowboy Joe said, giving each baby a gentle tap on the nose. "I'm planning on them for the welcome baskets Daisy asked me to make up for the group coming tomorrow," he added over his shoulder as he headed down the path.

"Will do," Noah called after him.

"So everyone thinks we're a couple and that you're the twins' father?" Sara asked.

"Probably."

She was quiet for a few seconds, staring off into the distance. "I guess the real story is a little too complicated."

"Way too complicated." He upped his chin toward the path. "C'mon. I'll show you the main barn."

As they walked in the brilliant late May sunshine, a perfect seventy-three degrees, which would hold steady for the entire week as some kind of cosmic gift, he pointed out the different kinds of trees and birds to Chance in the carrier on his chest.

"See that beautiful black-and-white quarter horse, Chance?" he asked, pointing straight ahead where Bea, one of the ranch's cowgirls, was grooming the horse in front of the big red barn. "His name is Batman. He's getting all spiffy for the big day tomorrow. One day, you'll ride him, Annabel beside you on Bolt."

Sara went quiet again. Until she said, "You should know… I'm not really sure what my future holds. I don't know how long we'll be here."

Sharp right hook to the kidney. "What?" he said, also feeling like a hay bale had just fallen on his head. "You just got here. I just hired you. You haven't even had your first day of work yet. Suddenly you're leaving?"

He looked at Annabel—well, the back of her, anyway—strapped in the carrier on Sara's chest. *That's my baby girl. She's not going anywhere. She belongs here.*

Dammit, dammit, dammit. He knew the truth of who Annabel's parents were. Why wasn't it helping?

"I didn't say that, Noah. I only said I didn't know how long we'd be here. By the time these two are old enough to get on a horse? I don't know."

He stared at her for a moment, not liking the direction this conversation had taken one bit. "Well, I don't know why we're even talking about that, then."

"I just want to be honest and open," she said, a hand protectively on the side of the carrier. "I know you're attached to Annabel. So…"

Attached to Annabel. Attached? Was that all she thought it was?

"So I think we should continue with the tour," he said, a little grumblier than he probably should have.

"Fine," she said.

"Fine."

To have something to do, they both started walking over to where Bea stood with Batman.

"Hi," Bea said, putting down the grooming brush. "I finally get to meet this little charmer up close." She bent toward Chance in the carrier on Noah's chest. "Aren't you precious. Just like your twin sis. I'll name the outdoor petting zoo enclosure for you so you'll each have your own special honor."

"Special honor?" Noah repeated.

"Go see," Bea said, gesturing at the petting zoo a quarter mile up from the main barn. The gleaming yellow barn with its white trim had several enclosed pastures for the animals, the goats and sheep grazing. Their two alpacas were in their own large area, as were the six ponies. "I wanted it to be a surprise for opening day," she added with a big smile. "I checked in with Daisy a couple days ago—she said you'd love it."

Oh hell. A couple of days go, everything was very different than it was today. A couple of days ago, he was someone's father. Now he wasn't. "Well, thanks in advance," he said, knowing Bea's heart was in the right place. "That was sweet of you, whatever it is."

He glanced at Sara, who smiled at Bea, and then they headed up the path to the yellow barn. Inside, the top half doors open to bring in the light and fresh air, the floors freshly swept and the pens recently cleaned, his attention immediately fell on a large sign handwritten in colored chalk on the wall of the barn: the Annabel Dawson Petting Zoo Barn. The sign listed rules of the barn. Not to feed the animals inside the barn. Not to enter the corrals. To wash hands before leaving. That was listed three times to stress its importance.

He glanced at Sara. She was staring at the sign, her expression…tense.

Annabel Dawson.

"Bea didn't know," he said quickly. "Nor did Daisy a couple days ago when Bea checked in with her. It's just chalk. It's easy to erase Dawson and write in Mayhew. Or we can just erase the whole thing."

Since you won't be here long anyway.

She reached a hand to Annabel's head in the sea-foam-green cotton cap, her shoulders slumping. "I keep forgetting how hard this must be for you," she said, turning to face him. "She's been your daughter for almost two months. A Dawson like the sign says. Now here I come, erasing her last name on her specially named barn. Talking about leaving one day." She stared down at the ground.

Right? he wanted to say. Smugly. Honestly.

Ragingly.

Until he thought about what *she'd* been through the past two months.

His phone pinged with a text, and he was grateful for the interruption, because what the hell was there to say about all this? The truth was what it was, and Sara had been through hell. Potentially losing Annabel to her rightful parent—and distance—was nothing compared to what Sara had had to deal with, what she could have believed her whole life.

He pulled out his phone. The text was from Carly, the receptionist and gate greeter.

Four guys who look like you just drove up and are heading toward the welcome shed at the gate.

What? Four guys who looked like him sounded like his brothers, but there was no way they'd be at the gate.

Yup, I called it, Carly added. They said they're your brothers, here to see you.

Whoa.

He pocketed his phone in what felt like slow motion, his brain not quite catching up. "I can't believe I'm actually about to say this, but my brothers are here."

"Wow," Sara said, her expression brightening. "Didn't you say they all refused to step foot back here?"

He nodded. "Wonders never cease." That rolled

off his tongue, but nothing was truer in his life right now than that old adage.

"You go meet them, Noah. I'll take myself on the tour. I know my way around, even if things have changed."

Things had changed, but not the basic paths, and Sara knew those walkways and trails, including the ones that led into the woods, with her eyes closed. Plus, he had no doubt she needed a little space right now. From him.

"I'll just need to get the double stroller from the cabin."

"No need to walk back there. See that shed?" he asked, pointing out the half door. "I keep a lot of different supplies in there, including for Annabel. There's an infant stroller. I can put Chance in and you can take him on the tour with Annabel in the Snugli."

"Is there anything you don't think of?" she remarked.

He glanced at her, catching the surprise in her eyes, her tone.

"Not anymore. It's my business to think of everything."

She half smiled and they headed over to the shed, where he took out the stroller, diaper bag attached.

"You really do have this parenthood thing down," she said, staring into the diaper bag. "Pacifier, wipes, a changing mat, diapers. A bottle, bottled water and a small container of formula."

"I worked at it." *Harder than I ever worked at anything, even rebuilding the ranch.*

She held his gaze for a moment, and he couldn't read her expression, so he took Chance out of the front pack and put him in the stroller, not a peep out of him. He unstrapped the Snugli and folded it in the stroller's basket.

"If you need me," he said, "just text or call, and I'll be wherever you are in a heartbeat."

She held his gaze again, and he still couldn't read her. She nodded. "Go see your brothers. We'll be fine."

As he watched her continue up the path toward the guest cabins and the creek beyond, he couldn't move. And suddenly it didn't just feel like Annabel was moving away from him with every step, but all three of them.

His phone pinged again—Carly at the welcome shed. They said they'd meet you at the farmhouse.

He turned and headed in the other direction, forcing himself not to turn around to watch Sara and the twins get farther away.

Focus on your brothers, he told himself. Hadn't Ford said hell would freeze over before he'd come back to the ranch? Hadn't Rex said he was done with the place to the point that it bugged him to think about Noah getting it back up and running?

They were here, and that was all that mattered.

Same with Sara and the twins.

As Ford—who as oldest still declared himself in charge of the grill—put the perfectly cooked steaks on a platter, Noah glanced around at his four brothers and sister sitting around the patio table in the backyard, unable to believe the Dawson guys were really here. They'd spent the first half hour making small talk and catching up a bit, then Ford had gotten busy cooking. Apparently, the siblings had planned the surprise visit to the ranch a week ago, so they'd shopped in town for a pre–opening night celebratory dinner involving New York strips, baked potatoes, asparagus and craft beer.

Surprise didn't begin to describe how Noah felt. Shock was more like it.

But here they all really were. Ford. Axel. Rex. Zeke. And Daisy, who he was used to seeing, of course, but he certainly didn't take her being here for granted. When he'd first arrived at the farmhouse and seen his five siblings in the yard, he'd gotten all emotional and had to take a moment. Now, they were yakking like they saw each other all the time; it was always like that when they finally did get together.

Despite having three mothers among them, the siblings looked a lot like. They had varying shades of brown hair, some very dark like Axel's and some almost blondish like Daisy's, and they all had their father's clear blue eyes. The six of them were tall, including his sister, who was five foot nine. Everyone always said it was lucky she got the tall gene too because standing up to five brothers, four of whom were older, was easier when she at least reached their chins.

Ford was from their dad's first marriage, which apparently had lasted two months before his mother found Bo Dawson cheating not once or even twice but three times and finally left, then discovered she was pregnant, dropping off little Ford every other weekend for years. Axel, Rex and Zeke were from the second marriage to one of the other women who'd left hard-living Bo for the reliable, friendly mail carrier, whom Bo had tried to beat up but had been too drunk and ended up punching himself out. Axel, Rex and Zeke had all been too young and small to carry him inside, so they covered him with a few sleeping bags and put a bag of frozen peas on his purple-and-black eye and let him sleep it off.

Noah and Daisy were from Bo's third attempt at marriage, which lasted until their mother died in a car accident when Noah was nine. *He's trouble,*

but he's my trouble, their mom would say, thinking she had the smarts, sense, work ethic and financial savvy to manage both their lives and their
children's, so she could be with the man she loved,
despite his flaws. She'd been kind to the four older
kids too when they'd come for their visitation. Daisy
had once told Noah she thought their mom was romantic *and* half-crazy, that she'd never be so reckless
with herself. Anyway, after their mother's death, Bo
had gotten a vasectomy, and word among the women
who hung out in the sticky-floored bars he liked to
frequent was that he carried around a letter from his
doctor confirming he'd had the procedure so that no
one could pin a pregnancy on him. A good-looking
man, tall and lanky with an easy smile and flirta-
tious manner, he still managed to bring home lots of
women, who never stuck around long. The Dawson
name still carried weight in those days.

"I thought you said something about hell freezing
over," Noah said to Ford as they all got busy digging
into the plates and bowls on the table, thanks to Ford,
who'd nixed their offers of help with dinner. Ford had
always been the Dawson who could do anything and
everything—from cooking to wrangling troublemak-
ers—he was a police officer out in Casper.

"Well, it kind of did," Ford said. "Daisy let us
know that not only were all renovations on sched-

ule and according to plan, but that the place looked even better than it did when Gram and Gramps ran it. And that you pulled it off with a baby strapped to your chest the past two months. Tipping my hat to you, Noah."

The praise felt good. "Well, a little determination and all your help, and the Dawson Family Guest Ranch is back."

"Our help?" Axel repeated, heaping butter on his baked potato. "What did we do, Noah? You did it on your own." A search and rescue worker, Axel had always had big expectations for the word *help*. He spent his days and nights rescuing the lost and injured from area mountains. His most recent mission—involving a toddler whom he'd eventually found and reunited with his mother—had almost done him in.

"Um, he had our *financial* help," Rex pointed out with a grin. What Rex did for a living to have helped so much in that department was anyone's guess. He clearly had money and liked nice things, so he did *something*, but he'd always been cagey about it. Noah and Daisy used to joke that he was a CIA agent. For all they knew, he could be.

"And Daisy was here," Noah added, twisting the cap off his beer. "I had her help too."

Daisy raised her sparkling water. "Sometimes I

think about how if you hadn't found a baby on your porch, I might still be in Cheyenne."

"Speaking of daddies," Ford said, eyeing Daisy. "You ever going to tell us who the father is?"

She frowned just slightly, and Noah could see how conflicted she was about the guy. "The two of us are talking again. We weren't when I first found out I was pregnant. So let me see how things go, and then maybe I'll introduce him. Maybe I won't ever get the opportunity. We'll see."

"Sounds complicated," Rex said. "You need to sic your brothers on him, you say the word."

Daisy's eyed widened, then she grinned. "Why do you think he's still anonymous?"

There was some reminiscing about the times they did face down any guy who'd dared mess with their little sister. Even Noah, two years younger, but closer to Daisy than any of the Dawsons, had been protective of her.

"Well, speaking of *babies*," Zeke said, turning to Noah, "when do we get to meet our little niece? Who's watching her right now?" Zeke, second oldest, was the businessman of the bunch, a corporate cowboy who wore suits with boots and was never without a black Stetson; in fact, he wore one right now. Noah had been in touch with Zeke the most of all his siblings besides Daisy, since every month he sent Zeke his ranch ledgers, and every month Zeke sent back a satisfying: *I'm impressed. You know what you're doing on all levels, kid bro.*

Noah took a swig of his beer. "That's kind of complicated too."

"Which part?" Ford asked in his cop tone.

"After dinner, you'll hear the whole story," he said, glancing around at all of them. "And meet Annabel."

He was about to add *and her twin brother*, but that would pause forks and beer bottles and require immediate explanation. As he'd walked up to the house to meet his brothers just an hour and a half ago, he'd texted Sara to ask how she wanted to handle said explanation, and she said she'd like to come over for dessert, twins in tow, and tell the story on her own terms.

There were some raised eyebrows and shrugs and everyone resumed eating. Daisy sent him an encouraging nod. For the next fifteen minutes they talked about the guest ranch's bookings; Noah had a solid lineup of guests coming all summer and into fall, and Zeke said he had no doubt word of mouth would fill out the empty cabins along the way. All the brothers agreed the place looked great, that the more modern aesthetic—rustic-luxe spa meets dude ranch—would appeal to a wider range of people, and it had. Noah had stormed the offices of every small and big newspaper in the county—the daily and the free weeklies—with press releases Zeke had helped him write from afar and photos as soon as prime spots were camera ready, like the cabins. The Dawson Family Guest Ranch 2.0 had gotten solid press, and the phones started ringing with bookings. People remembered the place—many locals and those spread around the state had spent their family vacations at the ranch, so that had also worked in its favor.

"Well, let's eat up so we can meet Annabel and hear this complicated story," Ford said, eyeing Noah. Again, cop face. Nothing got by Ford Dawson. Noah knew his older brother had long felt responsible for his younger siblings, living with them only part-time growing up, and now at a distance of hours.

Luckily Noah had already finished his steak and a heap of the roasted asparagus in garlic butter, his favorite vegetable. Because his appetite was shot.

"Hey, is that Sara Mayhew?" Rex asked as he and Ford came out the sliding glass doors to the back patio with three kinds of pie for dessert.

Noah turned and shielded his eyes from the glare of the sun, just beginning to make its descent. Sara was coming up the path from the foreman's cabin, wheeling the double stroller. She wore a long black sundress and sandals, a straw hat on her head, her silky brown hair in a braid down one shoulder. She looked like a vision and he could barely take his eyes off her.

"Sara *Perry*, right?" Zeke corrected. "I occasionally saw photos of her and Willem Perry in the society pages of the *Converse County Gazette*. Once I ran into them at a fund-raiser and hugged Sara hello, and Willem practically grabbed her away from me. I'm surprised he didn't take a swing at me." He tilted his head. "I read he died in a car accident a couple months ago. Is Sara okay?"

Noah glanced around at the shocked expressions, barely hearing the murmurings of "how awful" and "he was so young" and "poor Sara." None of them knew Willem the way he and Sara did—Sara most of all, of course—because the three of them had been the same age, had come up in school together. "She'll *be* okay," Noah said, offering her a smile as she got closer.

As Sara arrived on the patio, the group got up to say hello and offer condolences. She handled that well with brief thank-yous and nods, accepted their hugs, and then conversation thankfully turned to oohs and ahhs about the babies.

And then, from Ford, his focus on the twins: "So

who's who? I assume one is Noah's daughter and one is yours, Sara?"

"Actually, they're both mine," Sara said, adjusting the sun shade on the stroller so the Dawsons could get a better look. "Annabel and Chance are twins."

"Wait," Axel said. "Daisy told us Noah found Annabel abandoned on his porch in the middle of the night—right before a major rainstorm." As a search-and-rescue specialist, those details would be foremost in his mind. "Since I'd have a hard time believing *you* left your daughter like that, there has to be a story here."

Four sets of blue eyes turned to Sara, then Noah. Daisy already knew the details, of course, but even she was staring at Noah.

"There is," Noah says. "And it's ugly. I'll let Sara tell it," he said, sitting down. The brothers took his solemn cue and all sat back down at the table.

"Why do I think we're going to need whiskey for this?" Rex asked, leaning back and crossing his arms over his chest.

"It's as ugly as Noah says," Sara began and then launched into the story.

The expressions on his brothers' faces said it all.

"Wish I could arrest the bastard," Ford said, shaking his head. "I've seen a lot in my time on the force, but this?" Disgust was palpable on his face. "Have you spoken to police about the midwife's actions?"

"Not yet," Sara said. "Willem's lawyer did a little digging for me after we found out what Willem—and she—had done. She officially retired the next day."

"How are you planning on handling that?" Ford asked.

"I'd like to pay the midwife a visit," Sara said. "I know there's no excuse for what she did, given her job, her responsibility to her patient and the baby she was hired to help deliver. But I also know that Willem threatened her and that he had something on her. I'll plan on seeing her in the next couple weeks. I've just got a lot to focus on right now."

"If you need help or an escort for the visit, you let me know," Ford said.

"I will. And thank you."

"You know what I can't stop thinking about?" Daisy said. "How lucky it was that Noah actually heard Annabel's cries at two in the morning outside his window. He's always been a light sleeper. A herd of buffalo couldn't wake me up."

"Oh, trust me, one tiny peep out of your little one and you'll be bolting up," Sara assured her. "Mother radar is strong stuff."

Daisy smiled. "Glad to hear that." She took a sip of her seltzer. "You know, given what your late husband did, Sara, things sure worked out all right. Noah *did* wake up. He saw the note saying she was his and took immediate responsibility—he even had her checked out by Doc Bakerton at 2:30 a.m. And then just seven weeks later, the truth is revealed in that letter. Willem's whole terrible plan was interrupted within two months. Someone up there was sure looking out for you."

"I think about how it could have been decades," Sara said, shaking her head.

"Cosmic justice," Axel said. "Sorry if I'm speaking ill of the dead, but…"

No one disagreed. That the plan had been foiled so early because Willem had been killed in an accident and had left that "last laugh" letter for Sara did seem like cosmic justice.

Noah loved Annabel with everything in him, but now that he knew the truth of her parentage and her brief history, he wasn't Team Ignorance Is Bliss. It wasn't—and never was. Annabel deserved to know her mother; Sara deserved to be with her daughter. Things had worked out for the best for the two of them. Except when it came to what Noah would have to give up when Sara—as she put it—left one day.

"The twins are beautiful, Sara," Axel said, standing up and peering in the stroller.

"And look just like you," Ford noted.

"Didn't Noah say that Annabel looked just like him?" Rex asked with a grin. He peered closer at the baby girl. "Uh, maybe the coloring—hair and eyes. But that nose, that chin, the shape of the eyes, even her expression—all Sara."

Humph. Noah really had thought Annabel looked something like him; he had from the moment he'd brought her inside. Yeah, she'd looked more familiar than like him, but *still*.

"And both twins are safe and sound," Zeke added with a nod.

They all raised their bottles to that.

"Well, hell," Axel said. "I say they're our *honorary* niece and nephew."

As everyone clinked to that, Noah noted that Sara's smile was genuine.

So what did that make him? Honorary dad?

As the group crowded around the stroller to take closer looks and photos of their honorary niece and nephew, Ford held back.

"You okay?" his brother whispered.

"Somehow," Noah said. More glumly than he meant to.

"Probably because you care more about Sara than you do about yourself," Ford whispered back. "Always have, right?"

Noah sucked in a breath. He was always surprised

at how well his siblings knew him when they didn't get together very often the past ten years. But suddenly he understood why Ford, who'd led the intervention in Noah getting his act together *and* rallying the siblings in support of Noah's determination to rebuild the Dawson Family Guest Ranch, believed in his youngest brother. Because Ford *did* know him. And that confidence in him meant the world to Noah.

Yes. He did care more about Sara than about himself. Always had, always would. Except for those months two years ago when he'd finally given in to his attraction to her, despite how bad he knew he was for her, when he'd been at rock bottom without realizing it, putting on a good show with the small ranch he'd bought until he couldn't hide who he was back then: his father's son.

As Ford joined the others in fussing over the twins, Noah couldn't take his eyes off Sara, who'd never looked more beautiful, Annabel in her arms.

Everything that meant anything to him was in this backyard, on this property right now, including the ranch itself. And the best way to take care of Sara and the twins was to make sure the ranch was a big success. Annabel and Chance would always have a home here, Noah's own grandparents' home for many years. There was family history here for them, and he wanted Dawson's to succeed for them.

He owed his siblings that too—for their investment in the ranch and in him. He couldn't fail, couldn't lose sight of the prize: steady bookings, good reviews, word of mouth. Nothing could get between him and making this ranch everything it needed to be for his family—and Sara's.

So keep your distance from her, no matter how attracted you are to her.

Not going to be easy, since they were not only sharing a cabin, but essentially a workplace. He was her boss, and he was going to have to keep things very professional between them.

And his thoughts were anything but professional as he took in how beautiful she was, how sexy, memories of their brief romance hitting him left and right.

If you care about her, you'll keep your hands and lips to yourself.

He made that silent vow, then headed over to where the group stood around Sara and the babies, his head clear, his heart guarded.

Chapter Seven

After a brief tour of the guest ranch and more hat tipping to Noah at what he'd done with the place, the Dawson brothers—except for Ford—got back in their rented truck and headed off to the Airbnb they'd booked in town. There were free rooms in the main house and a bunch of comfortable couches in the lodge, but between being honest about the place still having too many bad memories attached *and* not wanting to distract from the big day tomorrow, Axel, Rex and Zeke opted to stay elsewhere. Sara had gotten the impression that Noah understood; he still seemed to be marveling over the fact that they'd come at all. Ford had been cryptic about why he wanted to stay at the house, and Noah hadn't pushed, but Sara sure was curious. Ford was the Dawson sibling who held the worst memories of the ranch.

Now, just after 9:30 p.m., she and Noah were in the nursery, putting the twins to sleep in their crib. She stood beside Noah as he told a story about Batman, an Appaloosa, escaping his stall and running all over the ranch in search of the perfect carrot. Noah's voice was so soothing, so beautifully familiar, that even Sara almost fell asleep, but the twins were out within two minutes.

"My work here is done," he said with a smile, but it quickly faded.

"Everything okay?" She knew he had a lot going on, a lot on his mind, but she had a feeling he was still thinking about their conversation in the barn earlier that day.

"Are you planning to leave?" he asked, finally turning his head to look at her. "If you are, I want to know. I need to prepare myself so I'm not blindsided by losing Annabel."

She liked how direct this new Noah was. But then again, this wasn't a conversation she could have now. How could she possibly answer him?

"I have no idea what I'm doing, Noah. Right now,

I want to be here. I *need* to be here. That's all I know."

He crossed his arms over his chest. "So maybe you'll stay for a couple of months."

"I really don't know. I guess it depends on how things between us are. And right now, they're not good."

He stared at her. "In general or this minute?"

She felt herself relaxing. "This minute. And the minute earlier in the barn."

"I don't want to run you out of here," he said, taking her hand. "I want you to stay."

If she wasn't mistaken, he'd been about to add the word *forever* but then clamped his mouth shut.

So why did that make her feel so…prickly? Because that *want* had nothing to do with her and everything to do with his love for the baby he'd thought was his daughter?

Maybe. That should make absolute sense to her. It wasn't as if she wanted Noah Dawson to be romantically interested in her. Did she?

Oh hell. She did a little. Because she was still reeling from all that had happened and needed a pair of strong, familiar arms? Or because her residual feelings for him would never, ever fade? Noah was her first love. Her only love. Yeah, she'd been married. She'd also had some short-term relationships over the years that hadn't gone anywhere—maybe because she'd never felt about anyone the way she'd felt about Noah. Despite how wild he'd been, how she hadn't been able to tame him. He'd done that reining in himself, now that she thought about it. Maybe that was why she was even remotely thinking about him *that* way.

When she was ready to find love again—though that felt very far off—she'd look for a man who'd be a great father to her twins. Like Noah.

She'd look for a man who was responsible and reliable in ways she could plainly see. Like Noah.

She'd look for a man who sent little chills of anticipation up her spine at the thought of kissing him, of being in bed with him. Like Noah.

Oh hell. She was sunk!

She wanted to flee the room *and* fling herself into his arms. That's how much she couldn't get a handle on herself.

She needed fresh air and more open space, somewhere his tall, muscular, sexy being couldn't dominate. She gave his hand a squeeze. "Let's go enjoy the gorgeous night. We can sit outside and *not* talk."

He laughed. "Let's do that."

Downstairs, he grabbed a baby monitor from the hallway console table and they headed out to the front porch, so big and welcoming. His sister had told her she'd planted all the beautiful flower boxes that hung from the windows, and there were four white rocking chairs and a porch swing along the side porch where it wrapped around. They opted for the swing, Noah giving them a push with his foot.

She had the urge to wrap her arm around him, and whether she should or not, she was going to. Doing so earned her a smile and Noah scooting a bit closer. "How many nights did we sit here and look at the stars and not talk because there was too much to say and we both knew what the other thought anyway?"

"I feel like that's both the case and not, now, though," he said. "We do have a lot to talk about, but it's so complicated—and not—that there's really nothing to say at all." He shook his head. "Did any of that make sense? Was it actually English? Between you saying things like you're leaving and my brothers' surprise visit, I'm a little out of whack."

"What if I promise I'll stay the summer at the very least?" she said, turning to look at him.

He got up abruptly and walked to the porch railing, facing away from her, then turned around. "Great. So three more months of getting attached to Annabel and now her brother and then you'll leave? That's great, Sara."

"I thought we weren't going to talk because it's too complicated."

"I don't push things under the ole rug anymore," he said. "You talk or you fester and implode. I'd rather talk."

"I suggested the summer because you'll know we're staying put for at least that long."

"I *love* Annabel, Sara," he said, a fierce edge in his voice. "She's my daughter. There, I said it. She's my daughter," he shouted into the sky. "I know she's yours, but she's mine too."

Sara gasped. "I get it. I do."

"Marry me. Let's get married. That's the solution. Annabel stays forever. And not only that, but I get to be dad to her twin brother too. The twins grow up in the place where they have so much family history. Both Annabel and Chance will have a loving, devoted father. You'll have the security of the ranch that means home to you. And to sweeten that end of it, I'll split my share of the ranch with you fifty-fifty. You'll be an owner, with the same share as I have."

She gasped again. It was all too much to take in. The marriage proposal. The security. The ranch ownership.

The marriage proposal.

All because he felt like Annabel's father in his heart, in his blood and veins and every cell in his body.

Security—for the twins and for herself when she

was penniless with maybe $1,100 in jewelry to sell if she needed to.

Home—when the Dawson Family Guest Ranch was home and always had been.

And if the place went belly up, if Noah reverted to his old ways and ran the place into the ground?

He won't, a voice inside her knew full well. *He cares too much now. His family is involved. Annabel is involved. And now you and Chance are added to the mix.*

And you believe in him.

"I need some time to think," she said, turning away. It was all too much.

"Am I being selfish here, Sara?" he asked, stepping closer. "I know what you went through with Willem. Why you said yes. Am I asking the same thing of you?" He took a step back, regret all over his face. "You know what, forget I even brought up the word *marriage*. After everything you've been through, it's not fair to you."

She studied him—hard—and his sincerity was clear. His sincerity had never been the issue. "I don't think you're being selfish. I understand where you're coming from. You're making me an offer, Noah. What Willem did, what I accepted, was very different. Or it *feels* different, anyway. But I do need time to think."

He nodded. "Take all the time you want. I'll go

do my rounds on the animals. Need anything be-fore I go?"

A hug. A bear-hug.

She shook her head. "I'll just sit out here awhile and then probably go up to bed."

He nodded. And then she watched as the man who'd just proposed to her headed down the path toward the red barn.

Marry Noah Dawson? Once, that had been her dream. Now it might be her only option for security for herself and the twins. But more, she understood Noah's depth of love for the baby he'd rescued, had thought was his, had raised, even if it was for barely two months. How could she take Annabel from him when the baby meant so much to him that he was willing to give up his freedom for her?

Maybe that was what put a check mark in the no column. When she'd dreamed of marrying Noah Dawson, love was the biggest factor. Now, it wasn't even on their radar.

Noah moved sideways through the stables, giving each of the thirty-two horses a pat and a little pep talk for tomorrow. He was expecting twelve guests, which meant twelve horses would christen the new and improved Dawson Family Guest Ranch's trails and fields. And though Noah would do his best to match rider to horse based on the guest's level of experience or lack thereof, sometimes, they'd have to see how it went. Which meant having lots of solid, sweet, well-rested horses to choose from. "Based on the initial questionnaire the guests filled out," he said to horse twenty-seven, Blaze, "you'll definitely be paired with our most experienced rider. Do me proud tomorrow." He gave Blaze a pat.

He'd gotten up to horse number thirty, Sugar Cube, when he finally broke, when he couldn't pretend to have only the ranch at the forefront of his mind.

"I proposed, Sugar Cube," he said to the silvery-white quarter horse with the soulful brown eyes. "Proposed marriage. What if she says no? What if she says yes?"

Sugar Cube didn't respond, but she still got her pat. Noah moved to the next stall, Goldie, and told the gorgeous palomino with her gold-colored body and white mane that he had no idea what Sara's response was going to be. "Think she'll say yes? She might? Then we'll both have what we want and need. Right?"

He'd still considered Sara his best friend the past two years when they hadn't spoken or laid eyes on each other, when they'd known nothing about each other's lives. That was how strong their connection was. To him, anyway. That seemed like a solid basis for marriage. Much more so than the hot and cold of fleeting love with all its passion and arguments. Best friendship: lasting. Real. He'd let passion intrude on that friendship two and a half years ago, and what happened? He'd run Sara off into the arms of a psycho.

He'd be able to raise Annabel and Chance. They'd be his children for real. And his precious Sara, whom he cared about to the moon and back, would be beside him, sharing his life, his world.

"It wasn't impulsive," he told Bluebell in the next stall, giving her a pat. "I mean, it was. I didn't think of it until that moment, but it's probably the smartest thing that's come out of my mouth ever." He reached the end of the stalls, patted King and felt the tension leave his shoulders.

As he was leaving the stables to head back toward the main barn, he noticed his brother Ford walking about a hundred feet ahead, just around the side of the pasture fence. Ford was staring at a piece of white paper, then looking down, then around. He had something in his other hand. Looked like a narrow pitchfork.

What the hell was he doing?

"Ford?" Noah called out.

His brother jerked his head up, clearly surprised. "Just looking around."

"Sure you are," Noah said, walking over to him. He glanced at the piece of paper in his hands, which looked like some kind of crudely drawn map. "What's that?"

Ford sighed. "My legacy from Dad."

"Ah." He suddenly realized why Ford "Hell Will Freeze Over Before I Step Foot on the Ranch" Dawson had decided to stay the night at the main house.

"A map of some kind?" Noah asked.

Ford nodded. "It was folded up in the letter he left me. The letter rambled on about how one night when he was drunk and angry at my mother over an argument, he put her diary, which he'd jammed open with a knife, in a metal box and buried it somewhere near the stables. Or he thought near the stables."

"Her diary?" Noah repeated. "You sure you want to find that?"

Ford sighed hard. "Apparently my mother had a secret. That Dad knew about. He wrote that my mother flew into a rage and tore up the property looking for the diary but never found it. Then I guess she gave up on it, figuring he was too much of a drunk to ever dig it up himself and use it against her, since he'd likely never find it."

"Any idea what the secret is?" Noah asked.

He shrugged. "Who the hell knows. I'm not sure I want to know. But Dad's letter said it's something I *should* know, that he's sorry he wasn't a better father to me or any of his kids. I figured while I was here tonight, I might as well try to find it, since Dad made a point of saying it was far off any of the trails or paths. I didn't want to do anything to mess up the grounds the night before opening day. I've just been poking into the dirt, hoping to hit on something hard."

"I'll help," Noah said.

For a minute there, Noah thought lone-ranger Ford was going to say, *nah, you've got a big day tomorrow, I've got this,* but Ford replied, "I'd appreciate that."

Noah jogged over to the stables and got a sharp-ended tool, then jogged back over to where Ford was poking the ground in circles. "Let me see the map."

Ford handed it to him. "This seems to be the area," Noah said, taking in where his dad had drawn the stables with a few horse heads poking out, the tree line, the five-hundred-plus-acre pasture. There was an X on a tree trunk—a tree that seemed to stand alone. And the only tree that stood alone was close to where Ford was poking with the pitchfork.

They poked and poked and poked, walking in circles and squares, but both came up empty.

"I had a feeling I wouldn't find it," Ford said. He shrugged. "Just thought I'd give it a try."

Noah glanced around at the grass. There was just too much land to cover. "I can keep looking when I get the chance. And you can always come back."

Ford ran a hand through his hair. "I might. We'll

see. Sometimes it's better not to know." He shook his head. "I'm not sure I mean that. I don't know."

Noah got the sense his life wasn't the only complicated one.

"I'll be heading out first thing," Ford said. "Good luck tomorrow. I know this place will be a big success."

Noah extended his hand, and Ford glanced at it, then pulled his youngest sibling into an embrace.

"You did good, Noah," Ford said. "With the ranch, with Annabel. With whatever's going on with Sara and both twins, considering that they're all here."

Noah nodded, Ford's words of praise a boosting balm as he embraced his oldest brother. "I'm trying. Hard." *To the point that I* proposed.

Let her say yes when I get back to the cabin, he thought.

Sara sat in the kitchen, on her third cup of decaf, picking at the leftover peach pie that Daisy had packed up after dinner for Noah to take to the cabin. She heard the key in the lock, and her pulse leaped.

Yes, no, maybe so. She had no answer yet. Her answer was all of the above.

Noah came into the kitchen and gave her such a forced casual smile that she laughed. Sara could plainly see how tightly wound he was right now and how he was trying to fight it.

Because he'd proposed and wished he hadn't? Because he worried she'd say no?

She took a sip of her coffee. "I'll get right to the point. If we're going to put a marriage on the table, we'd better square away some important details."

She could see the relief in his eyes, the way his shoulders relaxed some.

He got himself a bottle of water, then sat down. "At least it's up for discussion."

She was about to blurt out, *Well, I did it once before with a monster, so why not with my one true love?*

Which just made her feel worse, more tied up in knots over the whole damned thing.

"Noah, marriage is supposed to be sacred. It's supposed to mean something more than a mutually beneficial partnership."

"That's what it is for everyone who gets married," he said. "A couple is madly in love. That's mutually beneficial, so they marry."

She raised an eyebrow. "You know what I mean."

"I do. And my point still stands. We've got a lot of water under the bridge, Sara. And we have some very good reasons to band together and do this. Unless you think your soul mate is out there, waiting for you to be ready. Do you?"

She stared into her coffee for a moment, his words jabbing her in her chest. "You obviously don't think either of ours is. Or you wouldn't be proposing what's basically an arranged marriage."

He took a swig of his water. "I guess different things are more important to me now. I figure to you too."

She stood up and walked to the window, looking out at the night, at the pasture, at the Wyoming wilderness beyond. "What the hell happened?" she asked.

She could see in the reflection from the window that he stood up.

"What do you mean?" he asked, concern deepening his voice.

She turned around. "This entire conversation. A marriage of convenience. How the hell did my life come to this?" She stalked over to the chair and sat down. "I'm just whining and feeling sorry for myself. I'm pissed, Noah."

He sat back down too. "You have every right to be angry. But that isn't my aim—to dredge up bad feelings. If that's what the proposal is doing to you, let's forget it. You stay here as long as you want. I just want you to be happy and feel safe."

She glanced at him, her eyes welling. *I just want you to be happy and feel safe.* A person who said that was a person who cared about her. And he was the only person saying anything like that. Her family was gone. Her friends scattered. She had no one left.

"I used to believe in soul mates," she said. *You, you big dope. You were my soul mate.* "I don't believe in that stuff anymore, Noah."

He leaned forward. "Let's be each other's family, Sara. You, me and the twins. A family, right here where it all began for both of us in so many ways. And you'll have half my ownership of the ranch."

Could this work? If she didn't believe in love and romance anymore, if her first marriage had blown everything she'd once cared about to bits, then why not accept a partnership with Noah Dawson? They'd set terms. They'd treat each other respectfully. They'd get what they needed.

"I'd never take any part of your share of the ranch, Noah. But yes," she added, standing up again. "I will marry you."

Before Noah could stop himself, he got up and held out his arms, and Sara rushed into them. He could feel her holding herself a bit stiffly, which he completely understood. This hug was about gratitude on both sides, about the friendship that would never fade, no matter what. It was their handshake on an agreement.

"I was so afraid you'd say no, Sara." He found himself holding her an extra beat too long, inhaling the balsamy scent of her hair, remembering how good having her so close against him used to feel.

She stepped back and leaned against the counter. "We should discuss logistics, of course."

He nodded and sat back down.

She did too. "Let's just go to the town hall. There's no waiting period in Wyoming. We could be married in the morning."

"My head might explode," he said. "Getting married right before the ranch reopens. How about we wait till the first group leaves? That'll give us time to decide if we're telling people about this or keeping it our secret. If we're wearing rings." He took a drink of his water.

"But there are some issues we can settle right now," she said, looking everywhere but at him.

"Like?" he asked.

"Separate bedrooms. No sex. No kissing, no touching, no hanky-panky of any kind, Noah Dawson. We're making a deal for those mutually beneficial reasons you listed. I don't want any confusion about what the marriage is."

He wasn't so sure they had to make any proclamations. Who knew how things would evolve?

Then again, sex had destroyed their relationship once and sent her away.

On one hand, he could see them returning from a

long day, a problem with a guest, a sick calf, and having the urge to take her in his arms and kiss her, hold her, this beautiful woman he'd loved for so long and who'd share so much of his life going forward. He'd always been so physically drawn to Sara, including right now. How would he tamp down these feelings?

He'd just have to. Because on that other hand, the confusion she'd mentioned had the potential power to ruin their arrangement entirely and send her away again. He couldn't risk that.

He took in one last long drink of her luscious body, her pink lips, her brown eyes and long silky brown hair. He closed his eyes for a half second, vowing that when he opened them, he'd see her as discussed: off-limits.

"Agreed," he said. "We're friends. We won't let anything get in the way of that and what we're doing."

She gave him something of a smile that didn't last very long. "Good. Then we have a deal."

The problem was that the vow he'd just made to see her as off-limits wasn't working. She was still sexy as hell. But if there was one thing Noah Dawson had developed the past few months, it was self-control.

He'd do this because he *had* to.

Chapter Eight

The next morning, at just after 11:00 a.m., Sara stood beside Noah and Daisy outside the Dawson Family Guest Ranch lodge as a silver van pulled up in the parking area. The first guests had arrived, and she could feel the Dawsons practically vibrating with excitement and nerves.

The weather couldn't have been better—blue skies, brilliant sunshine, low humidity and sweet breezes in midseventies temperatures. Sara smoothed her hunter green polo shirt with the ranch's logo on the pocket, Staff spelled out in caps on the back. Last night, Noah had knocked on her door and said he'd forgotten to give her an employee shirt; all staff would wear the green shirts and jeans during working hours.

When he'd held up the shirt in her doorway, she'd been so moved by it, by her memories, that she'd wanted to pull him into her bedroom and never let him go. She'd had a Dawson's staff T-shirt when she was a teenager. She still had it, though she was a size small back then and seven weeks after giving birth, Sara was a definite L for large. The old one was a burnt tan color, and she liked the forest green even better. The new shirt reminded her of all good things, of new beginnings. Before Noah had knocked on her door, she'd wondered how she'd sleep with questions of their pending marriage looming in her thoughts. But somehow the green shirt representing her employment, money coming in, *security*, had her falling asleep within a half hour.

The twins had woken her up twice, and a third time, very early this morning, she'd gone into the nursery to find Noah already taking care of business. He'd looked wide-awake and alert, excited about his first guests. Mrs. Pickles was with the twins now in the cabin, and Sara liked that she just might see the sitter wheeling them around the grounds in the stroller during the day.

A thirtysomething redhead stepped off the van,

shook hands with Noah and Daisy, and then Noah introduced her to Sara as Connie Freedman, the life coach running the retreat.

As the retreat participants came off the van— eleven aside from the coach—Connie introduced everyone. But Sara was surprised—and thrilled—to already know one of the women, an old friend from high school named Tabitha Corey. Since the retreat was getting underway immediately, Sara would have to wait to catch up with Tabitha until this evening.

As guest relations manager, Daisy led the group to their cabins to settle in before the tour, opening session and meet and greet of the horses Noah had chosen for each participant. But Sara couldn't help but notice most of the guests looked kind of…glum.

"Is it my imagination, or do the guests not look very excited to be here?" Noah whispered.

"Oh wait," Sara said. "The retreat is called Get Your Groove Back."

"What does that mean—exactly?" he asked, tilting his head. "I thought it was about getting some R and R."

"Well, that too, but getting your groove back generally means you've lost that spark and you want to find it. A recharge kind of thing for the heart, mind and soul."

Noah raised an eyebrow. "I just ride Bolt when I need that."

She smiled. "That's why they're here. Nature helps. Horses help. Inspiring talks help. Like-minded people who won't make you feel like you're whining or just need to man up or chin up. Hopefully they'll look very different in a week."

He nodded. "I'm pretty sure I recognized one of the guests—and her name too. Tabitha Corey. We went to high school together, right?"

Sara nodded. Tabitha looked very in need of a recharge, even if she was in full Western regalia, the kind of outfit that said she'd gone all out on new riding gear and Stetsons and Western-style shirts when plain old jeans and T-shirts would do. Sara couldn't help but be curious about why Tabitha had signed on for the retreat. She had been a golden girl, the kind you couldn't hate because she was kind and friendly to everyone, even if she was a queen bee. She'd recently gotten engaged to a tall, good-looking endodontist Willem had played squash with, but they hadn't socialized as couples. Willem would insist on showing up for fund-raisers and important events, but then he'd want to leave after fifteen min-utes, which had always been fine with Sara. She'd noticed the diamond ring on Tabitha's finger. Huge. And she looked like a million bucks, despite the lack of light in her eyes. Sara couldn't help but wonder why Tabitha was here.

As the afternoon went on, Sara helped both Daisy and Noah in various capacities, and she found herself loving the fast pace and constantly changing duties. This morning, before the guests had arrived, she'd double-checked the cabins with Daisy to make sure they were all ready with welcome baskets and fresh wildflowers and had all the necessary supplies. She'd helped Noah and Dylan in the main barn with lining up the saddles the guests would likely be using. Since the group would hit the cafeteria for lunch at twelve thirty, she'd stopped in a bit before to see if Cowboy Joe needed any help. He had everything under control with his small staff. Lunch was his specialty, chili and corn bread, and the entire caf smelled amazing.

At two, the life coach and retreat director, Connie, was giving a talk called "What Happened to My Groove, Anyway?" in the lodge. Sara had been assigned to work the concessions counter, offering coffee and tea and lemon-infused water and snacks, and she'd been riveted by Connie within a minute. The life coach was in her late thirties with pretty shoulder-length red hair and dark brown eyes, in a forest green pantsuit that managed to look woodsy and professional at the same time. Connie stood at a podium in front of the eleven seated participants, who all held little silver notebooks. Sara had never met a life coach before, but Connie's talent at public speaking and conveying her message was an immediate given.

"Feeling stuck," Connie was saying. "Knowing you're stuck and knowing there are probably steps you could take to get yourself unstuck but being too down in the dumps to do anything but mope on your sofa with a stack of tabloid magazines and the remote control and a family-size bag of sour cream and onion potato chips. And a two-liter bottle of soda. And a big bag of fun-size chocolates." She gazed at the group. "How many of you can relate?"

Sara's hand shot up in the air before she could stop herself. She pulled her hand down, but not before Connie sent her an encouraging smile. Twelve hands, including Connie's, were up. Sara wanted to stick hers back up too. Hell yeah, she could relate.

"But guess what?" Connie said. "All of you, every single one of you, has already started the process of getting yourselves unstuck, getting your groove back. Because you're here. You did something proactive. You got off the sofa, figuratively and literally." She smiled. "Round of applause, ladies." Connie clapped, and so did everyone else, including Sara, down low under the table.

Maybe she shouldn't be cheering herself on, though.

She hadn't gotten herself off the sofa—figuratively speaking. She'd been propelled off it by Willem's death. She'd learned the truth about her daughter, sped over to the ranch and here she was. In a new life entirely.

But she had to wonder just how long she would have lived under Willem Perry's thumb. Being chastised for installing the toilet paper roll the "wrong" way. Night after night, unable to dislodge the lump in her chest, in her throat.

"We all have our breaking points," Connie continued. "You're all here because you're either close or you've reached it and you're ready to break out, break free, be who you actually are."

The part about the breaking point made Sara feel better; she'd reached it—she'd briefly left during her pregnancy and had been pulled back out of fear, but she would have figured out a way to leave again. She was sure of that. And anyway, going over this was pointless. She was in a new life—with her son and daughter. What mattered was what she did with her present and how she planned for her future—their future.

She frowned as she recalled how sure she'd felt earlier about accepting Noah's proposal. But had she been operating out of fear, out of feeling like she was stuck? She had a job, a place to live, a good roof over her babies' heads. She was earning her way here. Noah had offered her half his share of the ranch to sweeten the security deal, but she didn't want that from him. She'd never take that from him.

Suddenly she was only 50 percent on the idea of marrying.

There was a solid week between now and when they'd go to the town hall to legally become husband and wife. She'd see how things felt.

"Sometimes, the hardest part can be doing just that—getting up, asking for help, making a commitment to yourself," Connie went on. "And sometimes the hardest part might be yet to come—really examining what you want and how to achieve that. Sometimes we don't feel like we deserve what we want, let alone to actually get it. I'm here to tell you, we all do deserve it. So at this retreat, let's commit to giving ourselves a chance. Baby steps, big steps, whatever you're ready for. We're all on our way!"

Yeah! Sara almost cheered as she straightened the bananas in the pretty blue bowl on the table.

Connie handed out schedules and outlined the rest of the day—next up was being matched with horses, so the group got up, a few stopping at the concession table for the lemon-infused water or a coffee or a piece of fruit. As the participants left the lodge, former golden girl Tabitha hung back, then came over to the table and made herself a cup of coffee. She looked amazing—gorgeous long blond hair, light

makeup that looked completely natural, the fancy
Western outfit and dark pink cowboy boots. But she
sure didn't look happy. Newly engaged to a young
Brad Pitt endodontist or not. And, of course, she was
here at a retreat for getting her groove back. Sara
would have never in a million years thought Tabitha
Corey had ever or would ever *lose* her groove.

*You never know what goes on in someone's private
life*, Sara thought as Tabitha stirred her coffee. *Appearances are deceiving. Yup, I know all about that.*

"So far, so good," Tabitha said, a hopeful light
suddenly in her pretty hazel eyes. "Right?" But then
the light disappeared and she seemed so conflicted.
Something was definitely bothering her.

Sara reached out a hand and covered Tabitha's.
"I'm not even a participant in the retreat and I feel
empowered." She smiled.

Tabitha nodded and seemed about to say something, then she lifted up her coffee cup as if toasting
in agreement and shuffled out, catching up with the
rest of the group.

Sara wanted to run after her, give her a hug, tell
her she was here for her if Tabitha wanted to talk, but
she could see Connie now standing next to Tabitha,
chatting away as the group headed to the barn. She
had a good feeling about Connie and what this week
would give all these women. Maybe even Sara herself.

Her phone pinged with a text. Daisy.

Have fifteen minutes to help set up the meditation room in the lodge? Second floor event room.

Meditation? Sara thought. *I might lie down and stay there myself.*

Be right there, she texted back.

Between the retreat and her job, Sara just might get her own groove back. If she watched her step with Noah Dawson. And she would.

The barn hadn't collapsed. A horse with a guest on its back hadn't gone rogue, throwing her fifty feet in the air. No one had gotten food poisoning from Cowboy Joe's chili (not that they would). These and many more were the irrational fears that had kept Noah up at night when he should be getting any chance of sleep he could, particularly with two babies in the cabin. But opening day of the Dawson Family Guest Ranch had gone off without a hitch so far—knock on every piece of wood in the vicinity.

He stood at the small barn beside his cabin and gave Bolt, whom he'd just returned to his stall, a piece of carrot. Then he lifted his face to the gorgeous late-May sunshine and breathed in the warm, breezy, fresh air. Between the weather and the total lack of problems, he could almost relax, but he'd save that for the end of the week. He'd spent the past hour with the retreat guests in the barn and pasture, first making sure they were matched to the right horses for their level and comfort and then joining in on their first ride in the huge expanse of prairie to the right of the main barn. Satisfied that the group was comfortable and set for the time being, he'd left them in the horse leader's capable hands with Dylan and Bea, the ranch hands, who'd ride alongside the group as backup.

About to walk the paths to keep a general eye on things, Noah saw Mrs. Pickles come out of his cabin with the twins in their double stroller, using the ramp he'd built. That tiny burst of joy, still so unexpected, went kaboom in his chest at the sight of the babies.

"There are my sweet twins," Noah said, walking over with a smile. He leaned over and unbuckled Chance, carefully lifting him out of his infant seat.

He froze, just for a moment, sucking in a breath. *My twins?*

Reaching for Chance as easily as he would Annabel?

The little cowboy had worked his way into Noah's heart just as his sister had. And just as fast. He couldn't really even think of Annabel without thinking of Chance; they were a pair, a package, a set. Individuals, but he loved them with equal ferocity.

Oh God. He did love them. Both. Hard.

"I was hoping to run into you, Mrs. Pickles." Sara's voice came from down the path. There was tension in that voice, if he wasn't mistaken.

He turned around, Chance cradled against his chest. Sara was coming from the direction of the lodge. As it had earlier, the sight of her in her Dawson Family Guest Ranch staff shirt shot straight to his heart, and despite his vow to keep his mind off how attracted to her he was, every cell in his body went on red alert. "Same here. And I did."

She smiled sort of vaguely, her gaze on the baby in his arms. What? Why did she seem uneasy?

She leaned over the stroller and gave Annabel a kiss on the head, then got as close to Chance as she could while keeping her body as far away from Noah as possible, and deposited a kiss on her son's head.

Hmm. She was definitely bothered by something.

"These two are such good babies," Mrs. Pickles said, grinning at her charges. "I love watching them. And what a lovely day for a walk."

"Well," Noah said, putting Chance back and running a finger down Annabel's cheek. "I won't keep you." He turned to Sara. "I was about to take a walk of my own on a grounds check. Join me?"

"Sure," she said. She leaned over the stroller. "'Bye,

sweets," she cooed to her twins. "See you later. I love you," she whispered.

Then they both watched as Mrs. Pickles wheeled the stroller toward the lodge.

"There goes my heart," Sara said, her expression wistful as she stared after the sitter and the stroller.

He stared after them too, then looked at Sara. "I know what you mean."

She frowned, took one last look at the retreating figure of Mrs. Pickles, then turned for the path toward the main barn.

So he was not mistaken that something was bugging her. And it was something *he* was doing.

"You seemed uneasy before, when you saw me holding Chance," he said, walking beside her.

She turned and looked at him. "I hate that you know me so well, Noah Dawson."

He grinned. "Actually, us knowing each other so well might make things easier. Because it makes us talk about even uncomfortable stuff."

"I also hate talking about uncomfortable stuff." She bit her lip. "I guess I'm just taking everything in, Noah. The idea of getting married. What that will mean going forward. About the twins too."

He stopped. "What do you mean?"

"You already feel like Annabel's father," she said. "You're going to feel like Chance's father too."

He was already beginning to.

She crossed her arms over her chest. "And I'll have to factor you in when I think about what's right for me and the twins. How did that happen? When did you become a vital part of my plans for my life?" She frowned and turned away.

"When—"

She whirled back around. "Rhetorical question. I know, I know. When you brought Annabel inside and took responsibility for her. When a note said she was yours."

Damned right. But he understood how strange that must be for her. And yeah, maybe even unsettling. He wasn't Annabel's father. He'd met Chance the day Sara arrived on the ranch. Noah shouldn't factor into Sara's decisions for herself.

But he also couldn't help how he felt or that circumstances had unfolded as they had. Her baby girl *had* been left on his porch. He *had* taken her in. He *had* claimed responsibility. And he *loved* Annabel. She'd always feel like his child. Chance now did too, because he was Annabel's brother, because they were living in his cabin, and the little guy had grabbed hold of his heart and wasn't letting go.

"Ah," she said with an exasperated tinge to her voice and throwing her hands up in the air. "I get your side. I get my side. But I need to get *my* groove back, Noah. Sounds cute and all on retreat flyers, but it's serious stuff and hard work, and I don't know that coming into my own means marrying you for security." She shook her head. "In fact, it doesn't."

Oh hell. He understood that too well. He'd had to fight his butt off to stand up again—and the only person he'd been fighting was himself. He'd found his way. He wasn't going to stand in Sara's while she worked out her past.

"If you're telling me you've changed your mind about getting married, I…understand," he said, holding her gaze for a moment, and then he had to look away and let the disappointment sock him in the gut. She'd leave. She'd leave and take the twins. Not immediately, not even in a few months, but a new year always meant something to Sara, stood for new beginnings and possibilities. She'd probably leave by then.

"That would kill you, wouldn't it?" she asked. "If I told you I changed my mind. I think that's what bothers me, Noah. That it would."

"Should I be honest? It would. And you know why."

"Yes, because of Annabel," she said.

"And Chance. They're a pair."

Tears welled in her eyes, and he took a mental step back. He was overwhelming her, and that wasn't fair. She knew he meant it—that he loved Chance too. And that was killing *her*.

He put his hands on her shoulders. "Look, Sara. I want to be very clear. I like the idea of getting married and what that means for me as the twins' acting father. If you change your mind, yes, it'll knock me to my knees, but I'm all about getting up again. That's who I am now."

She stared at him. Almost looking confused.

He removed his hands and stuffed them in his pockets. "But I'll tell you something else. Yes, I have my good reasons for wanting this marriage, wanting you to stay with me forever. There are reasons involved that have nothing to do with the twins."

She tilted her head. "Like what?"

"Like that you've been my best friend since I was a little kid. Separated for the last two years or not. You mean a lot to me."

She gave a slow nod. "Same," she whispered.

He let that sink in for a moment, and it gave him the courage to say what had been building inside him the past couple of days. "And because—" He shut up fast. He couldn't say *that*. He took off his Stetson and ran a hand through this hair, glad he hadn't blurted out the rest of that whopper.

"And because what?" she asked, staring at him.

He had no idea why he thought she'd let him off the hook.

Hell. Just be honest. Say what's on your mind. "And because maybe, somewhere in there, months, years from now, whatever feels right—if it does—" Man, he was rambling. "Maybe there's a possibility of a second chance."

There, he said it.

He caught the intake of breath, the shielded surprise in her eyes.

But should he have said it? If he meant it—and he did—then why not? Why not put his cards on the table, say what he meant and felt? Even if it did get him knocked to his knees. Ignorance was never bliss. Everyone knew that.

His phone buzzed with a text.

"You should take that," she said fast. "I'll go check the main barn." She walked away—even faster—before he could say anything else.

A conversation we'll finish later. Or not.

He grabbed his phone. Carly, the welcome manager.

There's a reporter here from the Converse County Gazette. He says he's interested in writing a story about the grand opening. Should I let him through?

Noah's stomach flipped. Then flopped. A reporter. Press for the ranch: good thing. Bad press: bad thing. What if the reporter didn't like the looks of the place? What if something went wrong just as the reporter happened to be there, taking pictures and notes? An accident on the trail. An unhappy guest complaining about the water pressure, which was actually just fine.

You put your heart and soul into the reopening, he reminded himself. *Hired a top-notch crew. Everything is set for today. Everything is going great. The article will be glowing.*

Maybe. Or maybe not.

Cripes.

Why the hell was everything in his life so up in the air?

By the main barn, he could just make out Sara giving a wave to Mrs. Pickles, who was over by the small barn, pointing out the goats to the twins. *I have to believe in this place—for Sara, Annabel and Chance. If I don't believe in what I've rebuilt here, no one will.*

Noah's Magic Eight Ball answer had to come from himself: *It is decidedly so.*

Sure, send him up to the lodge, Noah texted back to Carly.

This was make or break for the guest ranch. Just like Sara marrying him was make or break for his heart.

Chapter Nine

Avoiding Noah in a twelve-hundred-square-foot cabin wasn't easy. Once Sara was officially off-duty, she'd rushed back to the cabin to take over from Mrs. Pickles and was there when the twins woke up from their nap. Over the next few hours, she told them all about opening day, her surprise at finding herself wishing she could sit in on every retreat lecture, and the even bigger surprise of running into Tabitha Corey. And then she started talking about Noah, how he'd rebuilt the ranch, how proud she was of him and how she couldn't figure out what to do.

Should I marry him?

Make a pro and con list, she could hear her mother saying any time she couldn't decide what to do about something, when both sides of the issue had check marks. She'd have to make it a mental one since she certainly didn't want to accidentally leave a piece of paper around with all that info for Noah to come across.

She sat on the sofa, Annabel finishing her bottle, Chance half-asleep in the swing on the floor beside her. *Okay, here we go, guys*, she told the twins.

Pro: I've known him forever. He will always feel like family, no matter what. I don't want to trust him, but dammit, he's given me no reason not to this time around. His sincerity leaps off him. I know the twins are safe with him. I do like the idea of them having a father—a father who actually loves them and cares about them and wants what's best for them, not himself. The sight of Noah Dawson gives me goose bumps. Everywhere.

Was that also a con? It was, given that the marriage Noah had proposed was like a business arrangement of sorts. Well, as businesslike as it got when children were involved. Scratch that, there was nothing businesslike about sharing a home and raising children together. This would be very personal. And Noah had said he liked the idea of a second chance—down the road.

Perhaps another con. How could she keep her

heart out of things in that case? When Noah did give her goose bumps?

Another pro: she adored his family. Daisy was right here. The ranch would be Sara's home on a permanent basis, and she did love this place. Everywhere she turned today, memories filled her. Her mother teaching her how to ride a two-wheeler. Her dad teaching her everything he knew about horses, his great love. Noah showing her a few secret trails he'd made that led to the river, where they'd fill backpacks with chips and the occasional stolen bottles of beer from both their houses, Sara hoping against hope he'd make his move, despite what he'd said. He never did. Not once. He'd written himself off as a jerk and told her she deserved the world. He'd seemed to believe that about himself to the point that it was automatic for him not to touch her.

She hated remembering that. And she'd hated remembering that he'd turned out to be right. Not about being a jerk; he wasn't. But about being wrong for her, unable to pull himself up and out of the hole he'd fallen into.

Pro: all these memories. Con: all these memories.

She sighed, cuddling Annabel against her and peeking over at Chance, who was just lying peacefully in the swing, gently swaying, fighting sleep as his little eyes drooped.

"Noah loves you both," she said to Annabel as she tilted up the bottle. "I really see that. If he acted like only you mattered, Annabelly, I could have reason to make some sort of fuss. But of course, he adores Chance too."

Every time she felt that frisson of fear about Noah getting too involved—as if there was anything more involved than the two of them marrying—she'd think about how he truly did seem to love both babies, and she'd feel that rush of gratitude that the twins were loved by someone else in this world. Someone pretty special, at that. She had no family, and Willem, an only child, had lost both his parents during the past five years. Noah really was the closest thing to family that she had.

Just when she thought she was acting out of devotion to the twins, making decisions for their sake, she'd feel that tap on her shoulder with the flip side, the other hand, the "yeah, but."

So am I marrying him or not? she silently asked both twins. *Am I committing to life with him as my best friend and my twins' acting father? Or am I committing to myself and finding my own way without needing security from anyone else?*

She heard his key in the lock, and on cue, goose bumps ran up her spine and along her arms and the nape of her neck.

"How are the twins?" he asked as he came into the living room.

She kissed Annabel's sweet-smelling head. "Fed, burped and ready for their cribs."

"Would you like to do the honors or should I?" he asked.

"It's kind of amazing that after hours and hours of work and running around, you're up for putting them to bed." *Because he's committed to them. Because he loves them.* "How about we both do the honors?" she said, getting up.

He smiled and took Chance out of his swing. The little guy fell asleep in Noah's arms before they even hit the stairs.

With both babies in their cribs, the lullaby player on a low setting and the door ajar, they headed back downstairs to the living room. Because Noah was Noah and would probably go into the kitchen to whip them up a three-course meal when he had to be exhausted, she beat him to it.

"I'm going to make us dinner," she said. "You sit and put your feet up."

"Dying to," he said, dropping on the sofa and putting his legs up on the coffee table beside the baby monitor. "Ah, that does feel good."

"Pasta with prosciutto and peas in a creamy pink sauce and garlic bread coming right up." She still had cravings for rich comfort food and had been dreaming of that very dish all day yesterday. A quick trip to the market last night, and she had the missing ingredients.

"Hurry," he said. "Now that you said it, I want it immediately. Five minutes ago."

She grinned and got to work in the kitchen, enjoying the domesticity.

Ah, another pro, she thought as she put the water on to boil and grabbed the prosciutto from the refrigerator and a cutting board from the cabinet. She liked cooking for herself and Noah because she liked Noah. Cooking for Willem had been a chore because he'd been so picky and finicky. Once, early on in their marriage, she'd grabbed his plate away when he'd complained how his steak looked before he'd even tried it and told him to make dinner himself, then stalked off. His passive-aggressive behavior that followed for days had ended up shaping more of her behavior and response to him than she'd realized. Willem had a been a gaslighter, making her feel crazy for complaining, and in her eyes, he controlled whether her father lived or died. So she'd kept the peace. And destroyed herself in the process.

Not exactly good companion thoughts for making a nice dinner. She poured herself a glass of lemonade and drank half, letting it refresh her, then set her thoughts on her twins and the hot guy on the sofa with his feet up.

Her head set back on straight, she sautéed the prosciutto and garlic, the delicious aroma taking over and making her stomach grumble.

"Can I help with anything?" Noah called from the living room.

Another for the pro column. "I've got it, but thanks," she called back.

How many times had she stood in this very spot at the stove, beside her mother or her father, and shared cooking duties with them? Her dad's specialty was his favorite dish, chicken parmigiana with a side of very saucy spaghetti. Her mom loved making every kind of seafood and salads with vegetables from her little garden.

There were times, particularly lately, when she thought about her parents and felt so sad that she'd need to sit down and just cry. But right now, sweet memories were coming at her, making her smile. Her parents had loved each other so much.

Con: marrying a man who doesn't love you that way.

Addendum: she used to believe that Noah *did* love her that way, even when they were teenagers, and that he truly was protecting her from himself. She'd believed he loved her during their brief and disastrous relationship two years ago. It was now that she wasn't too sure about. Noah was such a different person these days, and sometimes she couldn't even read him when she'd been easily able to before. His focus was brand-new to her, and it wasn't on her or a good time or sex. He was all about the success of the ranch—and now the twins.

But with that little hint of possibility he hadn't meant to utter aloud, *Maybe a second chance for us...*

Marrying Noah Dawson would be a leap of faith. Plain and simple. Who knew what would happen?

Con: she didn't know what was going to happen.

She'd been the one to say their marriage would be strictly business—no hanky-panky, no confusion over what they were doing. So there would be no sex to muck anything up, making her feel closer to him—or farther away, depending. Her feelings for him would be based on how they operated together, how they got along, worked together, took care of the twins together.

"Smells amazing!" she heard Noah call from the living room.

She gave the sauce a stir, not even guilty that it was from a jar. Hey, infants and working and making dinner? Sauce from a jar.

Five minutes later, she had everything stirred in a big blue ceramic bowl and brought it to the table. There was no dining room in the cabin, but the kitchen was eat-in and big enough for a round table for six by the window.

"Come and get it," she called out.

He appeared in the kitchen doorway, looking at her like he intended to do just that. His blue eyes were intense on her. This wasn't about appreciation for cooking or anticipation of eating. This was desire—for the chef.

"Now that I put it out there," he said, "I can't stop thinking about it."

"About what?" she whispered, a plate of garlic bread in her hand.

"Second chances. Everything I am is about second chances right now. I screwed up things the worst with you, Sara. I'd give anything to make everything right."

She put down the garlic bread. And rushed into his arms and wrapped her legs around him like she was Rachel McAdams and he was Ryan Gosling in *The Notebook*.

Not bad for seven and a half weeks postpartum, she thought, their mouths meeting, their bodies pressed so tightly against each other that she truly felt like they were one. They kissed so fervently that her legs couldn't retain their hold and they slid down. He pressed her against the counter, kissing her harder, hotter, his hands roaming into her hair, down her back, up her back under the light cotton tank top she'd changed into.

Just go with it, she told herself. *Go with what you feel, what you want. That is how you get your groove back. Stop overthinking and just feel.*

"Uh-oh," he said, putting her hands on his shoulders, his forehead against hers. "You said this was a no-go if we get married."

"My way of taking some control of things," she said. "I don't know what I'm doing, Noah. I just know that I wanted to kiss you."

"Me too," he whispered.

"But, but, but, I don't want to get emotionally caught up in you. That's not good for me. That's what I need to avoid. And yes, sex will absolutely push me into that." She threw up her hands, then grabbed the plate of garlic bread to have something sturdy between them. "What am I doing?"

This was nuts. A minute ago, she was feeling and going with it. Now she was overthinking again and letting that do the controlling.

Why was this so damned hard?

Because she was scared, she suddenly realized. That was it. Scared of losing herself again. And getting hurt again.

"Let's eat, okay?" she said, pushing past him to the table.

"I'll try not to look at you like I want to devour you again," he said. "That wasn't a fair move."

For a woman who hasn't had sex since she conceived? So true. At least she was pretty sure that night was the last time. Willem had been obsessed with her menstrual cycle and planning, and once he'd hit on the right window, he'd ignored her.

Anyway. It had been a long time since anyone had looked at her the way Noah had just then. Kissed her like that. Made her want so much more.

She sat down and heaped some pasta on her plate, then busied herself eating. The rich, creamy pink pasta and bacon and peas were every bit as delicious and comforting as she'd expected.

"Mmm, this is so good," he said, reminding her of sex again. She paused, her fork in midair, and watched him twirl a forkful into his gorgeous mouth. He took a drink of his bottled beer, then looked at her. "I'm going to take your lead from here on in. On whether we get married, whether we continue that kiss. No pressure from me, Sara."

"I appreciate that."

"Oh, and I should qualify that comment about the second chance. I mean just having you with me. My partner. My wife. Having you back." He glanced down, then cleared this throat. "But not in a romantic sense. Just like you said. We tried that, and we both know what happened. There's way too much at stake to mess anything up between us."

She stared at him. Was he backtracking or did he mean that? Was he truly worried that he'd drive her away again? She wasn't sure.

She cleared her throat and then just nodded.

Great, she thought, pushing her pasta around on her plate. She had no idea what she wanted, what she was doing. But what he'd said helped put things in a stalling pattern, which was exactly what she and they did need.

Feeling better, she took a bite of garlic bread. She really had to get herself assigned to another of the retreat seminars. Because she felt a part of her groove burning brightly back inside her—the red-blooded woman who'd thought that piece of her was gone.

Thanks to Noah just *looking* at her, she knew it wasn't.

After dinner, Sara had excused herself to her room and tried to read a book from the living room shelves on animal husbandry, but she couldn't concentrate. What she needed was a walk, some space from Noah where he wasn't upstairs or downstairs, so aware of his presence in the cabin, despite the closed door and a gleaming gold lock on it.

That kiss just loomed a little *too* large.

Wow.

Now she'd had a taste of what it was to be an actual sexual person again, and there was an incredibly sexy man in the vicinity who made her legs feel all rubbery.

She found Noah in the kitchen, drinking a cup of coffee and going through a stack of invoices, his laptop open in front of him.

"Can I help with anything?" she asked, standing in the doorway.

He looked up at her, and for a split second she saw so much in his eyes, in his expression, but then he flipped neutral. "Nope. Just reconciling some inventory."

"I thought I'd go for a walk," she said. "Get some air. You've got the twins?"

"Absolutely. Go ahead."

What a luxury. To be a single mother of infants and to be able to do anything on her own, let alone take a refreshing walk. That was thanks to Noah.

He glanced at his watch. "The retreat group's final lecture of the evening is scheduled to go on until nine thirty, so you might want to head away from the lodge if you're looking for time alone."

Hmm. It was 9:10 now. Maybe she would actually head straight for the lodge and make sure all was well, that the lodge fridge had enough bottled waters and that the fruit bowls weren't depleted. She could catch the last of Connie's talk from just outside the doorway.

She checked on the twins, then headed back to the kitchen. "The babies are fast asleep. Thanks for letting me get some air. I appreciate it."

"Anytime," he said. "I mean that."

He did. That wasn't in doubt.

As she turned to go, she could feel his eyes on her. The pull to turn back, to just walk up to him and hug him for so many different reasons, was almost too strong. She forced herself to the door.

The moment it closed behind her, she let out a breath. Up ahead on the path toward the lodge, she saw a slim figure with long wavy hair. A retreat participant? She couldn't tell in the dim lighting offered by the light posts that dotted the paths every now and then. But when the woman turned slightly toward the sound of an owl hooting in the distance, she could see a pregnant belly. That was definitely Daisy Dawson.

"Daisy!" she called out in as hushed a voice as she could muster.

Daisy turned around, and Sara could tell she was straining to see. "Sara?"

Sara jogged over. "Taking a walk, getting some

air, a breather. Noah's watching the babies. Well, they're sleeping, but he put himself on twins duty."

Daisy grinned. "How'd he become father of the year?" she asked, then her eyes widened and she touched Sara's arm. "I'm sorry. I keep putting my foot in my mouth about that. I know he's not Annabel's dad. Or Chance's, of course. And clearly, you two have worked something out. But I need to stop thinking of my brother as Annabel's dad."

"He still thinks of himself that way. Of both babies. Talk about taking responsibility," she added with a chuckle, trying to make Daisy less uncomfortable.

"So…how does that work, exactly?" Daisy asked. "I mean, you're playing house, but you're not a couple and he's not their father."

She'd always admired Daisy's forthrightness. Her brother shared that with her. "Can I swear you to secrecy? I only want your discretion because I'm not sure I should be sharing your brother's private business, you know?"

"Promise," Daisy said, holding up two fingers.

"He proposed to me. A marriage-in-name-only kind of thing. He'd get to be the twins' father. I get the security of a home on the guest ranch I was raised on. He even offered me half his share of the place, Daisy. That's how serious he is."

Daisy stopped on the path, the moonlight filtering through the treetops and capturing her amazed expression. "Wow. I mean, I'm not surprised to hear any of it. But wow."

"Wow is right."

Daisy stared at her. "And *you* said, I ask nosily?"

"I said yes, then basically said I don't know. I *don't* know. For all the reasons you can imagine. You know my history with Noah. And after what I went through in my marriage, I want to stand on my own two feet. No one is dying. I'm not desperate. I'm not trying to save anyone's life. It'll be hard, but I can do this on my own. I have this great job now. A place to live that makes me feel safe and comforted."

"I get it," Daisy said. "It's like you want to say yes for some reasons and no for other reasons, and no side is stronger than the other."

"Exactly. So what do I do?" Sara asked on another chuckle but immediately sobered.

"Sometimes my secret dream is that someone amazing will propose to me," Daisy said, a hand on her belly. She sighed and stared up toward the moon. "I was dating the father for three months. The condom broke, and then suddenly he was scarce. When I found out I was pregnant and told him, he said he was really sorry but he wasn't serious about me and he was only in Cheyenne temporarily, and then he just disappeared."

"Oh, Daisy, I'm so sorry."

"I don't know what's in my future. Well, except being a single mother."

"I'm here for you," Sara said. "Anything you need, I'm here."

Daisy pulled her into a hug. "Thank you. A lot." She stepped back, and they resumed walking. "Is it terrible that I'm finding reasons to listen in on Connie's talks? She's so good."

Sara smiled. "I know! I'm doing the same thing. In fact, that's why I'm headed toward the lodge. To check that the fridge is stocked with enough water bottles."

"Um, that was *my* plan," Daisy said with an evil grin. "There's only about fifteen minutes left, so I don't feel too guilty."

They linked arms and kept walking, the pretty white clapboard lodge with its steeply pitched roof and wraparound porch coming into view.

"Let's go check that water," Sara said.

"And the fruit bowls and granola bar bowl," Daisy added with a nod.

They headed inside and walked over to the kitchenette in the corner. A rectangular bar table separated the kitchen from the room, and they stepped behind it, both quietly "taking inventory." Sara made a note to add more apples to the bowl for the morning.

"So let's go over the most important step to getting your groove back," Connie was saying to the participants seated before her in a semicircle. "Figuring out what you *want*."

Sara glanced at Daisy, who was riveted by Connie. Daisy pulled a small notebook and pen from her back pocket and jotted something down. Sara could just make out that it said, *What do I want?*

"Maybe you want your husband to cook two nights a week," Connie went on. "Maybe you want a more satisfying job. Or a raise. One hour to yourself every night. Or your teenaged daughter to stop talking to you disrespectfully. Maybe you want more intimacy with your husband. Or a divorce. Or to stop arguing with your mother. Maybe you want a week's vacation at a beach. Or to see Italy. Maybe you want to read more. Become a mother. Or not. Maybe you want to learn to knit or take a German class or go skydiving. Whatever it is you want, identify it. If there's more than one immediate thing, write down the top three things you want, no matter how big or how small."

"Man, she's good," Daisy whispered, jotting down the assignment and then flipping her notebook closed and returning it to her pocket.

Sara nodded, her attention on Connie's words. *What is it that I want? Really want?*

I want to feel safe in the world.

The answer came faster than Sara thought. There it was, loud as it could be in every part of her. *Safety.*

"And the next step?" Connie went on. "Making a list of what steps you can take to get what you want. For example, let's say you want more intimacy with your husband, who watches the game, then a movie, and you've barely said two words since either of you got home. Maybe you suggest *going* to a movie, even if you have to see something you're not all that interested in. Maybe you suddenly give him a neck and shoulder massage. Maybe when you get out of the car in the Home Depot parking lot, you take his hand. You can start and see where it leads. Little things can lead to results."

Huh. *Steps to feeling safe in the world. What makes me feel safe? Feeling financially secure. Being able to take care of my children. So having a good job, which I now have. A nice home, which I now have, even if it's not the most traditional living situation.*

And somehow, out of nowhere, Noah Dawson makes me feel safe.

So, I'm doing exactly what I need to in order to get what I want.

"Tomorrow, we'll talk more about what to do when those steps don't feel feasible," Connie said. "But tonight, our homework is to think about what we want and if we feel comfortable, to start making those lists of steps we can take to achieve our goal or goals." She looked around at the participants with a warm smile. "It's been a great first day, full of wonderful new experiences. This time is your own. Perhaps for an evening walk or back to your cabins to rest up for tomorrow. The lodge's fridge is stocked with beverages and snacks that are free for the taking, so help yourselves."

"We're a bit low on fruit for the morning," Daisy said. "I'll go pop by the kitchen and replenish, then I'll head home. I want to start my homework right away."

Sara grinned. "See you tomorrow, Daize."

She watched Daisy leave, feeling buoyed for both of them—and thinking she should pay Connie for eavesdropping so much on just the first day. She smiled as two women approached to grab bananas and noticed Tabitha Corey heading out of the lodge. Instead of turning right for the cabins, Tabitha went straight on the path that led to the creek.

Go talk to her. If she doesn't want company, her body language or expression will let you know and you'll give her space.

Sara grabbed two waters and two small bags of pretzels and followed her, hoping she wasn't overstepping.

She saw Tabitha sitting on one of the large rocks that faced the creek, her knees pulled up to her chest, her arms wrapped around her legs. Almost like a self-hug.

"Hi, Tabitha," Sara said gently so as not to startle her.

Tabitha turned around, eyes wide, but she seemed to relax when she saw it was Sara.

"Water and pretzels?" Sara offered, holding them out.

"Sure," Tabitha said. "I wanted to stop and take something to drink and nibble on, but I didn't want to get caught up in chatting with the group. I'm feeling pretty talked out, and I've barely said ten words all day."

"I know what you mean."

Tabitha tilted her head. "I'm sorry about your husband. I would have attended the funeral, but I didn't hear a thing about it."

Sara opened her water. "Willem was very clear about not wanting a funeral. He instructed his lawyer to spread his ashes in the Bear Ridge River at sunset."

Tabitha raised an eyebrow and looked a bit surprised.

"Our marriage was pretty awful," she admitted, and it felt good to say it aloud to someone besides Noah. The truth was the truth.

Tabitha gasped. "I thought you had this perfect life!"

"Oh, I'd say it was quite the opposite. I'm working on creating the right life for me and my twins, though."

Tabitha looked confused again, as if she'd probably thought Sara had only one child, a baby son. But Sara didn't want to get into the details.

"I've been eavesdropping on Connie's talks," Sara admitted, popping a pretzel into her mouth. "I find her so inspiring and helpful and comforting. I only caught the last five minutes, but luckily it was a wrap-up and I applied the question to my own life. What do I really want? I was surprised to have an immediate answer."

"Me too," Tabitha said. "I mean, I know what I want. How to achieve it, another story."

Sara was so curious. But she couldn't just ask Tabitha what she wanted. It was personal, and if her old friend wanted to share, that would be one thing.

"From the outside, I probably look pretty blessed," Tabitha said. "Well, if you don't look too closely at me lately." She flipped up a hank of her frizzy hair.

"You're clearly engaged," Sara prompted, gesturing at the at least two-carat diamond ring sparkling in the moonlight. She'd seen Tabitha with the endodontist with his movie star–like blond hair and easy laugh at a fund-raising barbecue once. They looked like the perfect couple. But who knew better than Sara at how deceiving appearances were?

Tabitha stared at her ring. "I opened up to my mother about how I'm not sure I even love Philip, that I'm not sure I can go through with the engagement. Want to know what she said to me this morning before I left for the retreat?" she asked, looking up at Sara. "She said, 'All this finding yourself nonsense will find you alone and miserable. Your father and I will be very disappointed if you ruin your opportunity for a good life.'"

"By marrying your fiancé?"

Tabitha nodded. "He's the son of close friends of my parents. I've known him a long time. He checks a lot of the boxes."

"Which ones?" Sara asked, hoping she wasn't going too far.

"Well, for one, my parents are often disappointed in me for this or that, and I had their absolute approval for, I think, the first time in dating Philip and 'getting yourself proposed to,' as my mother put it. She actually told me she was proud of me for accomplishing that." She shook her head and turned away.

"So you *don't* actually love him?"

"He's all right. He's a good person. He's a mansplainer and we don't agree politically, and there's not a lot of chemistry in bed, if you know what I mean." She sighed. "He has a lot of good qualities, though. And I'm twenty-nine and single, as my mom points out often. She always says, 'I don't know who you think is out there that would be better than Philip. No one you meet will be perfect. Especially a guy you fall madly in love with. He'll be the *worst.*'"

Sara thought back to the Noah Dawson of two years ago. Even overbearing mothers had a point sometimes.

"Over the years I did get my heart broken a couple times by guys I fell hard for," Tabitha added. "So I know what she means. But still. Am I really supposed to settle like this? Marry the guy who seems right but really isn't?" She burst into tears and covered her face with her hands, her ring glinting on her finger.

"I'm so glad you came here, Tabitha," Sara said. "At the very least, you have a week away from your parents and Philip to really think. And to apply Connie's questions."

"What if my mother is right? What if it's guy after guy, one who wants me, one I don't want, never two of us in love, and I end up alone? I want a husband. I want children." Her voice broke. "I met a guy in the coffee shop the other day. A cowboy. He said he was a bull rider, hoping to win big in the rodeo. The way he talked about the rodeo and his love for it, how his dad took him to rodeos every weekend as a kid, he just stole my heart. He wasn't even necessarily flirting with me. He was just talking, Sara. He probably has a serious girlfriend, because he left, no name, no number, no nothing. But he made me realize that guy *is* out there. A guy who could rivet me that way, you know?"

Sara nodded. "I know. I always felt that way about Noah Dawson. That no one would ever compare. He wasn't ready when we were actually a couple. But he's ready now."

But was Noah actually ready now? He'd told her he fully agreed their marriage should be strictly platonic. That meant he didn't really trust himself with her or with their relationship."

Still, they were working toward something. "If circumstances hadn't brought me back to him..."

Huh. She hadn't really thought of it like that until just now. Circumstances had brought her back. That was how life worked.

"So if you hadn't lost Willem," Tabitha said, "you'd still be in your awful marriage when the man of your dreams was waiting here the whole time."

Sara gasped. That was exactly it. She nodded, vaguely, trying to take it in, digest it, process it. Things with Noah weren't going to be a fairy tale, but right now, Sara needed to think of the twins.

"That means the right guy for me might be out there too. I can settle and have my parents' approval. Or I can work toward finding the right man for me. Who knows, he might be in line in front of me in a coffee shop. Or leading the advanced riding lessons at the stables I love going to every chance I get."

Sara gave Tabitha's hand a squeeze. "Sounds like you're answering a lot of your questions."

Tabitha nodded. "I need to go do my homework. Write down what I want and how to achieve it. One of the problems has always been that I do want my parents' approval. I always have. If I give Philip back his ring, they'll be not only disappointed but furious. They won't understand."

"Well, maybe it'll help to write down the steps you could take to deal with that," Sara said. "If a harmonious relationship with your parents is very important to you, then write down some ways you could keep that while doing what *you* need to do to be happy. Your parents aren't living your life. *You* are."

"I keep telling myself that, hoping it'll sink in," she said. She stood up, and so did Sara. "I'm so glad you came to talk. This has been really helpful."

"For me too," she said.

They hugged and then headed back up the trail toward the lodge. Tabitha turned left for the cabins and Sara went right for the foreman's cabin.

Ping. A text. She took out her phone. It was from Noah. Even the connection by text gave her a line of goose bumps up the nape of her neck.

Just got a text from the Converse County Gazette. The review of the ranch is running tomorrow. I have a stomachache.

The review will be glowing, she texted back. The place is amazing and the guests love it. 5 stars.

He texted back a smiley emoji and a thumbs-up.

It struck her that you could only control so much. Noah had done the hard work and should be proud and pleased and expect that glowing review. But who knew if the reporter was a jerk or prickly or didn't like the color forest green or chili or the horse Noah had chosen for his mini trail ride.

All she knew was that she wanted to get back to the cabin—to be close to him. To think about what she'd said, what Tabitha had said. The man of her dreams waiting here for her this whole time... Maybe the timing was finally right, even if they were talking about a platonic marriage. And maybe she should grasp onto how she felt and not let go. Taking a leap of faith was hardly a way to feel safe in the world.

Except Noah *did* make her feel safe.

And the exact opposite.

Chapter Ten

B-rrrrring! B-rrring!

Noah opened an eye, then aimed it toward his alarm clock—6:14 a.m. His alarm would go off at six thirty, but someone was pressing the doorbell to his cabin like it was on fire.

Ping! Ping-ping!

Now someone was texting him. He grabbed his phone. It was Daisy.

Oh my God, oh my God, oh my God, his sister texted. Open up! Hurry!

He pulled on jeans and rushed out of his bedroom, meeting Sara in her bathrobe on the stairs. "Something's wrong," he said, panic edging his voice. "The ranch or Daisy's baby?"

Sara's eyes widened. "Oh God." She practically flew down the stairs and unlocked the door.

Daisy came in, clutching her phone.

"Is the baby okay? Should I call nine-one-one?" Noah asked.

Daisy stared at him as though he had two heads. "The baby is fine! The review is up!"

Noah felt himself relax for exactly one second, then all his muscles bunched up again, and his stomach flip-flopped.

"Did you read it?" he asked. "Positive or negative?"

Daisy shook her head. "I haven't read it. I just saw the headline and hurried over."

"How's the headline?" Sara asked.

"Very neutral," Daisy said. "'Dawson Family Guest Ranch has grand reopening in Bear Ridge'"

Noah sucked in a breath. "Okay, read it."

Daisy nodded. "'The once famed and popular Dawson Family Guest Ranch, which reopened Friday after years closed, is an absolute delight.'" She jumped up and down as much as a six-months-pregnant woman could. "An absolute delight!" she repeated.

Noah's legs almost gave out in pure relief. He dropped down on the second step.

"'From the immaculate grounds to the family-friendly vibe,'" Daisy continued, "'the guest ranch is a paradise tucked away toward the woods in Bear Ridge and offers riding and lessons, retreat space, a full-service cafeteria, a lodge, a petting zoo, and bountiful, well-marked trails, including several that lead to the creek. Fishing gear is available for free rental. The cabins, like the entire ranch, manage to be rustic and modern at the same time and contain everything a guest might need. The horses are gentle, and even the sheep look happy to be living at the Dawson Family Guest Ranch.'" Daisy did a little dance, turning completely around. "Even the sheep look happy!" she repeated. "Could this be any better?"

"Congratulations, Noah," Sara said. She gave him a quick hug—too quick.

Then his sister did. "I say we celebrate with decaf and bagels and cream cheese. I have such a craving. Please tell me you have veggie cream cheese."

"I actually bought some the other night," Sara said with a grin. "Sesame bagels or plain or everything?"

"Everything, of course," Daisy said.

They headed into the kitchen, Daisy going for the coffee maker, Sara for the bagels and Noah for the fridge to get the cream cheese. When everything was ready, they all sat down and toasted with their coffee mugs.

"To the Dawson Family Guest Ranch," Sara said.

"Hear, hear," Noah added with a clink.

Noah's phone lit up. Every one of his brothers either called or texted, and Cowboy Joe texted, as did several of the staff.

I did this—and I can be the husband and father of your children that you want, he sent silently to Sara. He slugged down a gulp of coffee. Where the hell did that come from all of a sudden? Well, maybe not so all of a sudden, since he'd been lobbying for the position for days. But earning Sara's yes meant everything to him.

What are you thinking? he wanted to ask her as she sipped her coffee and read the review for herself on Daisy's phone.

A yes from Sara and his life would be complete.

A cry came from the nursery, and Sara headed upstairs. He wanted to go with her, to take care of the twins together, to be true partners. In the platonic sense of the word. At first he'd been hoping they could be more than platonic, but then he'd realized that was asking for trouble. He'd messed up terribly once with Sara and couldn't risk that again.

"Everything okay, brother dear?" Daisy asked, peering at him over the rim of her coffee mug. "You suddenly look like a guy who didn't just get a rave review from a major newspaper."

"I proposed to Sara," he whispered. "I don't think she's going to say yes."

"Well, I have one piece of advice for you," she whispered back. "And you can thank Connie Freedman and her talks for that. Find out what she wants— what she really wants—and see if that's something you can provide. Maybe she's unsure."

He stared at his sister. What Sara wanted? Didn't he know? "She wants security. After everything she's been through? The rug pulled out from under her? Lies and deceit? Being left penniless? She wants security. I can provide that on every level."

"Okay, she wants security. But I said what she *really* wants. You're going to have to dig deeper under the umbrella term, Noah."

"Umbrella term? *What?*"

"Security. What does that actually mean for Sara? To Sara? Is it about money? She has a good job. A comfortable home? She has that now. So what is it she *really* wants?"

Oh God. He was bad at this. "If you know, please tell me. Right this second."

"I don't know. But if you want to marry Sara, you need to find out. And make sure you can give it to her. Or there's no point."

What did Sara really want? Women were kind

of mysterious. Everyone knew that. Was this some deep, dark puzzle or something simple?

Sara came down the stairs, eyes shining with love for the baby in her arms—Chance. "Annabel's still asleep."

As his sister doted on Chance and Sara made a bottle for him, Noah stared at his bagel, wondering what Sara wanted and if he'd ever find out.

Over the weekend and the following days of the Get Your Groove Back retreat, Sara continued her— now sanctioned—eavesdropping on Connie's talks and did her homework. She'd let Connie know the second morning how inspiring she found the talks, and the life coach invited her to listen in on all the lectures. Daisy joined her often, writing in her note-book, and Sara thought her friend seemed more at peace about the idea of being a single mother. Sara had tried to engage Tabitha a few times, but her old friend had told her she just needed to do some deep soul searching and take long walks and rides and do her homework. On the final day of the retreat, Sara thought Tabitha looked as conflicted as she had the first day.

"I don't think my friend Tabitha got her groove back," Sara said as they straightened chairs in the lodge. "I wish I had all the answers."

"Me too. Because you could tell me if I should trust Jacob."

"Jacob?" Sara repeated.

"The dad," Daisy said, patting her belly. "He showed up on my doorstep last night and said he felt guilty about just running away. He isn't sure what he wants, though."

There was a lot of that going around.

"What did he say?" Sara asked.

"He just kept saying he felt guilty and a man shouldn't shirk his responsibilities and that maybe we could just take it day by day. What the hell is that? I'm six months pregnant. This isn't a dress rehearsal." She sighed. "Or maybe it is. Maybe we should get to know each other through this stage, knowing the baby is coming in three short months. Maybe we'll really see who we are." Daisy always looked so sure of herself, and right now, she seemed anything but. "What do you think, Sara?"

"Sounds to me like you want to try," Sara said.

"I have to, right? I feel like even though he disappointed me once, he is the baby's father, and he is asking for a chance. If I don't at least try, I might regret that."

"Do you still have feelings for him?" Sara asked.

Daisy nodded. "There's something there. I tamped all that down over the past months. I don't know if it's him or the fact that he is my baby's father and it's more that than anything. I just don't know, and I hate being so out of tune with myself."

"I know what you mean," Sara said, giving Daisy's hand a squeeze.

"Here's a photo of Jacob." Daisy held up her phone. "The face helps, and it shouldn't."

Sara stared at the picture of an extremely cute blond surfer cowboy–looking guy with twinkling green eyes and a wide smile.

"I feel like I was getting my groove back, and now here he comes, throwing everything up in the air again. I feel so off balance."

Sara nodded. "Factoring someone else in when you need to keep yourself steady isn't easy. I know that for sure. Want to know what else I know for sure?"

"What?" Daisy asked.

"Our kids are going to be besties raised together," she said.

Daisy brightened. "Instant BFFs."

Sara nodded. They both drank their waters and settled back.

"Does that mean you're going to marry Noah?" Daisy asked.

Huh. Maybe it did. "I decided that when I wake up tomorrow, the retreat over, I'll know. At least, I think I'll know."

Things between her and Noah had been a little odd the past several days. They'd kept to their routine with the twins, which worked really well, but she constantly had the feeling he was trying to figure something out about her. The way he'd listen—hard—when she spoke, narrowing his eyes as if working to figure out some hidden meaning.

"Don't keep me in suspense," Daisy said. "Promise."

She and Daisy had gotten so close. Sara didn't know what she'd do without her friendship. "Pinkie swear," she said, wrapping her little finger around Daisy's.

Daisy's phone pinged. She took it from her pocket and frowned. "Uh-oh. It's a text from Connie Freedman. Tabitha Corey seems to be missing. She didn't show up for a scheduled activity and she's not in her cabin. Connie said she did a brief search on horseback in all the usual places Tabitha seemed to like to go but couldn't find her. Connie's worried about her state of mind since she skipped the talk and dinner last night too."

Sara bolted up. "I'll let Noah know right away. You stay here so you can be a ground support for Connie and the other participants. We'll find her."

Daisy nodded but looked worried.

Sara rushed off toward the foreman's cabin, texting Noah along the way.

* * *

Sara walked the creek bank again, Noah about ten feet away doing a sweep of the area from the path through the woods. Dylan and Bea, two of the ranch hands, were also searching the grounds since they'd come to know the nooks and crannies so well. She and Noah had checked and rechecked all the usual places Tabitha might be. She hadn't left the property, per the cameras by the gates on the road leading out of the ranch. The horse she'd been assigned, Nutmeg, was in her stall in the barn. All the bikes were accounted for too. Tabitha had gone off on foot.

Where are you, Tabitha? she wondered, scouring in between trees and down the edging of the creek toward the water, praying she'd find her old friend sitting curled up. Noah had said they'd give it only another half hour, because it was possible Tabitha might be injured and unable to call for help, and he'd bring in the big guns—his brother Axel, the search-and-rescue expert, and his yellow lab, Dude, an expert tracker. They'd find Tabitha in no time.

But Sara was 99 percent sure that Tabitha was safe and just hiding herself away because it was the final day of the retreat and she wasn't ready to go home, hadn't figured out what to do about her problems.

She scoured the creek bank, straining to see in

the sunny glare. Wait—was that movement? And a glint of something purple?

Sara slowly inched forward, craning her neck. Yes! That was a hand. And a sparkly purple sneaker. Tabitha wore sparkly purple sneakers.

She took out her phone and texted Noah. I think I see her! Yes, it's her! Give me a little time. I'll text you if she's hurt and needs help. Otherwise I think we should just talk a bit.

Okay, he texted back. I'll let Daisy and Connie know she's been found.

Sara pocketed her phone, then softly called out, "Tabitha?"

Tabitha didn't turn around.

"Can I sit beside you?" Sara asked.

"'Kay," came a teary voice.

Oh God. What had happened?

Sara approached where Tabitha was wedged between two big rocks, which now explained how they'd missed her on the first sweep. There was brush cover on both sides of the area she was sitting. Sara sat a good foot away, facing the same direction as Tabitha so the woman wouldn't feel stared at or crowded or pressured.

"Why do I have the feeling you came to a decision someone didn't like?" Sara asked gently.

Tabitha's eyes were teary. She lifted her head and

leaned it back against the rock. "I called Philip about an hour ago and told him I was very sorry but that I couldn't marry him. I was honest and told him I cared about him but felt pressured into the engagement by him and my parents but that it wasn't what I wanted."

"Oh wow. How'd he take it?"

"He was upset, but in the end he said he admired my courage and wished me well. And he hung up."

"So why are you so upset?" Sara asked. Then she realized Tabitha must have called her parents next and told them her news.

"I called my mom afterward. It was so hard to make that call. But I explained that I didn't love Philip and I hated to disappoint her but I had to do what feels right to me."

"Good for you!" Sara said—despite knowing full well her mother must have come down hard on her.

"I thought so. I felt so proud that I was standing up for myself and my future. And I believed, really believed, that I'd come first with my mom, you know? That she'd care more about me and how I feel than about appearances. Well, she didn't." She dropped her head onto her arms and sobbed.

"Oh, Tabitha, I'm so sorry." Sara scooted over closer beside Tabitha and put her arm around the woman's shoulders.

Tabitha glanced up with a tear-streaked face. "My mom said marriage wasn't about dumb lust and why did I think there was a 50 percent divorce rate. She said it was about partnership and well-matched couples building a future together."

Sara swallowed. Her own marriage to Noah would be a lot like the one Mrs. Corey described.

"But how can I sacrifice my happiness like that?" Tabitha asked. "It doesn't make any sense. It's sick, is what it is. But now my parents probably won't talk to me again."

Would Sara be sacrificing her happiness if she married Noah in this platonic arrangement? She would be happy feeling settled and secure. She would be happy living on the ranch. She would be happy that her twins would have a father, someone who loved them from the get-go.

But she wouldn't have a real marriage, the one she'd always dreamed of, the one Tabitha deserved, the one everyone deserved. Marriage with someone you loved and wanted to grow old with. Not a marriage that was first and foremost a business arrangement. Noah had her feeling so unsure about what he really felt, what he really wanted.

"I love my parents," Tabitha said. "I've never been able to handle when they're upset with me. And now they probably will disown me."

No way. That was nuts. Because she didn't want to marry the guy they thought she should? Because ending the engagement would cause a potential rift with their friends? "Do you really think so? They'll cut you out of the family?"

Tabitha could barely nod.

"Well, hell, Tabitha. That's not about love either. That's about control, and it's not fair. People who love and care about you and truly want the best for you don't cut you out of their life for not marrying the guy they think is right for you." Man, she was spitting mad. Sara felt like kicking something and shot up and did kick a small rock across the ground.

Tabitha hugged her knees to her chest. "I guess I'm really on my own now. In one fell swoop, I lost my fiancé and my parents of my own free will."

"The fiancé, yes. Your parents, no. I think you should write your mother an email, Sara. Right now. Speak directly and honestly to her, tell her exactly how you feel and why and how brokenhearted you are. You started on this path of honesty and being true to yourself. Continue on it. Your mother just might come around. And one parent is all you need to push the other."

Tabitha gave the smallest of shrugs. But Sara could see a glimmer of hope in her expression. "You think that might help?"

"I do."

Tabitha stood up, as well. "I'll go write it now." She glanced around at the woods. "I know I got a bunch of texts that I ignored—a few were my parents yelling at me, so I shut off my phone. I'm sure you guys and Connie were worried about where I was. I'm sorry."

"All that matters is that you're okay," Sara said.

Tabitha leaned over and hugged her. "Can we keep in touch after I leave tomorrow morning?"

"Of course!" Sara said. "And any time you need to get away or a place to go, you come straight to the ranch."

Tabitha gave a shaky smile. "Thanks. I just might."

They headed up the path to the lodge. Connie and Noah were waiting out front, and Connie came over.

"I'd love to talk a little if you're not too tired or done for the day," Tabitha said.

Connie squeezed Tabitha's hand. "How about over iced tea and really good cookies that I saved from dessert tonight?"

Tabitha smiled, then turned to Sara. "Thank you again. For everything. I'll see you in the morning to say goodbye?"

"Definitely."

She watched as Tabitha and Connie headed toward Connie's cabin, aware that Noah was walking over to where she stood by the directional sign.

"She okay?" he asked.

"She will be. She's on her way."

"Good," he said. "Ready to go home?"

Home. God, yes. How she loved the sound of that word and that it applied to here. The ranch. Dawson's. And the foreman's cabin.

She *was* home. But would she ever be truly settled?

It was pitch-dark when shrill cries woke Sara up. She glanced at her alarm—2:57 a.m. She couldn't tell which baby it was, but someone was making a racket—and these were higher-pitched cries than normal. Something was wrong.

Sara bolted out of bed and ran into the nursery to find Noah already there, lifting Chance out of his crib.

"He's really hot," Noah said, concern in his eyes. He laid a finger to the baby's forehead. "Very, very hot."

Sara put her own finger to Chance's forehead and gasped. She ran for the thermometer in the bureau as Noah laid Chance down on the changing pad. Chance's temperature read 103.2. "That's way too high. I'm calling the pediatrician." She rushed into her room to get her phone, grateful she had the doctor in her contacts. The service answered right away, despite the fact that it was almost three in the morning. She explained about Chance's high fever and raspy breathing, and the service said the doctor on call would return her call as soon as possible. It took just a few minutes.

She flew back into the nursery, where Noah was pacing, gently bouncing Chance in his arms, which didn't affect the crying. And it usually did. "The doctor said the temperature was high enough that we should bring Chance to the ER since the fever is combined with fast breathing." Sara's eyes welled. She stood there, taking deep breaths, barely able to think.

"I've got Chance," Noah said. "Call Daisy and ask her to hurry over for emergency babysitting. It's 3:00 a.m., but that's what sisters are for."

Sara's body unlocked; a mission she understood. She called Daisy, who assured her she'd be right over. A few minutes later, Daisy had arrived in her pajamas and flip-flops.

Sara and Noah rushed out with Chance in his carrier. For the twenty minutes it took to get to the clinic, Chance was shrieking, his face ruddy and sweaty. A half hour after that, he'd been diagnosed with a common respiratory virus that had flared out of control. He'd be absolutely fine.

Sara wasn't, though. This was the first time one

of the babies had gotten very sick. The panic she'd felt had taken over, and she'd appreciated the calm, cool and collected voice of Noah, giving instructions, knowing, somehow, what to do.

Feeling safe in this world meant a lot of different things. Having her person, someone she could always lean on, count on, trust, was paramount to her, more so than she'd ever realized.

That person was Noah.

She needed to be practical, not hold out for something she'd stopped believing in.

The answer to what she really wanted was summed up in how they'd operated tonight. They had been true partners.

"I've been doing a lot of thinking this week," she told him when they shut the door behind Daisy, who'd gone back to the main house. Chance was upstairs in his crib, sleeping comfortably now that he'd had medication to bring his fever down. Annabel would be staying in the bassinet in the living room for a couple days until Chance was more on the mend. "About what I really want. And what I want is for us to get married in the partnership you proposed."

That he liked what she said was evident in his expression. "We were a pretty good team tonight," he said, shutting off the hall lights and heading for the stairs.

She walked up beside him. "Exactly. We were. I panicked and you were calm, cool and collected. I needed help, and you were there. Daisy was there. I like having support. It's vital."

"It is. And you can always count on me. Always."

"I believe that. Let's go to the town hall once Chance is well enough. Probably even tomorrow."

At the landing, he took both her hands. "This is going to be the start of something great for both of us. Try to get some sleep."

"You too," she said, walking across the hall to her room. "Good night."

He held her gaze. "Good night."

Back in bed, she pulled the quilt to her chin. In just a couple days, she'd be married. Noah Dawson would be her husband. Her life would be completely different than it had been a week ago.

She was where she should be, making plans that would benefit everyone—her, Noah and the twins. Plus, Daisy would truly get to be Aunt Daisy instead of just an honorary aunt.

She smiled and closed her eyes, but sleep eluded her. Nerves about marrying a man she had so much history with?

So many what-ifs ran through her mind. She turned over and pulled the pillow over her head.

She was marrying Noah Dawson. For her sake. For his sake. For the twins' sake.

She was marrying Noah Dawson because she *loved* him. She flipped off the quilt and got out of bed. Before she could stop herself, she walked out of her room and down the hall, and knocked on his door.

"Come on in," he said.

Please mean that. In every sense.

She opened the door and closed it behind her, which made Noah sit up in bed and stare at her.

She walked over to the bed and sat beside him. Then kissed him. Then again. And again.

Don't stop this, she sent to him telepathically. *Because if I'm marrying you, I'm marrying you right. With everything I feel.*

"You're sure about this?" he asked, his blue eyes glinting with desire.

"Very," she said and kissed him again.

"And it's safe?" he asked. "Timewise?"

"It's safe," she assured him.

He peeled off her tank top, his hands all over her breasts. She watched him take in every inch of her bare torso and could feel him hardening underneath her. She took off his T-shirt and tossed it aside, and then he flipped her over and removed her yoga pants, leaving on her none-too-sexy pink-and-green granny panties with the little bow.

"I think those are incredibly hot," he whispered, hooking a finger at the waistband.

She swallowed, her insides feeling like liquid heat. "I think you're incredibly hot."

In moments, his sweats joined her pants on the floor. He lifted up over her, bracing himself on his elbows, staring down at her, kissing her, his hands in her hair, on her breasts, her shoulders, moving down her stomach...

She writhed underneath him, needing him so badly she couldn't take it. His kisses trailed up her neck, then his mouth caught hers so passionately she heard herself moan. She was kissing his collarbone and chest as he reached into the bedside table and pulled out a condom, making quick work of putting it on.

The moment he was inside her, all thought left her head and she only *felt*. *I love you, I love you, I love you* echoing in her head.

She hadn't forgotten how amazing Noah Dawson was in bed. He easily brought her to climax and then went wild to the point she was surprised the bed didn't collapse. The Wild West every night? That was more than all right with her.

And suddenly he was lying on top of her, kissing her neck, her cheek, breathing hard. "Oh, Sara. That was something."

"Yes, it was," she said. "And I guess this means our arrangement will now need some modifying."

She felt him freeze. *Crud.*

He turned onto his side. "What do you mean?"

"Well, we just had sex, Noah. And we're getting married tomorrow or the next day."

"I thought—" He clamped his lips together.

Oh hell. "You thought *what*?"

"I thought this was about tonight," he said hesitantly. "About the culmination of a rough night. Our marriage is supposed to be—" Again the lips clamped down.

"A platonic partnership," she finished for him, the ice in her voice surprising even her.

And clearly it surprised him, because his gaze swung to hers. "Sara, being platonic was your idea and a good one. A necessary one for me to make sure the marriage is a success. We need to be on the best path forward."

The best path forward? Good God. What self-help podcasts had he been listening to? Could he really want a platonic relationship at this point? Did he really not love her enough to make it work in all regards this time around?

Maybe he didn't.

"I think I hear Annabel," she said, grabbing her top and yoga pants and quickly putting them on. She darted out of the room and into the living room, where Annabel was sleeping in her bassinet for the time being.

She dropped down on the sofa beside the bassinet and looked out at the glow of moonlight amid the darkness. Noah had never veered on what he wanted; she had to remember that. He hadn't played games. He hadn't made sexual innuendos. He'd been crystal clear. Yeah, he'd brought up a second chance but then explained what he'd meant. A second chance to do things right by her. Not *with* her. He wasn't a man in love.

He wanted the twins and his former best friend to share his life on the ranch that he'd rebuilt.

She took a deep, steadying breath, feeling much calmer.

Well, at least she'd gotten great sex before entering into a sexless marriage. Tonight had been so damned good it would hold her for quite a while.

Or make her wish they could be together every night.

Partnership, partnership, partnership, she told herself. *Feeling safe in the world. Having someone you count on without all the craziness of lust and passion getting in the mix.*

A future to count on.

She heard footsteps coming down the stairs. "Sara? Can we talk?"

She stood, trying not to notice how incredibly sexy he looked. Trying to remember every moment of the past half hour. "I'm all right," she said. "Annabel's fine." She smiled and gestured to the bassinet. "Okay, that was an excuse to run away from you. But I'm fine."

"So…we're okay?" he asked. "*You're* okay?"

"I am," she assured him.

But she wasn't all that sure.

Chapter Eleven

The next morning, there was the expected awkward sidestepping as Sara and Noah ran into each other in the cabin a couple of times. Sara always had the mornings with the twins before Mrs. Pickles came so she could go to work, and Noah did his rounds on the ranch, but they'd been in the same place at the same time twice, both not quite looking at the other.

Last night, he'd accepted her "okay" and had followed her lead when she'd gone back to her room. The moment she'd heard his bedroom door close, she'd let out a huge sigh and then stared out the window at the night for what felt like hours. One moment—a half hour—they'd been so close, as close as two people could physically get. The next, separate bedrooms.

She'd felt really alone last night, but so aware of him down the hall, as always, and the dichotomy of that made her nuts. She had no idea how she'd managed to fall asleep, between thinking about their night together and what would happen in the morning: a trip to the town hall.

Now, they stood in front of the lodge at seven fifteen, preparing to say goodbye to their first guests. She forced her thoughts away from Noah as each of the participants shook their hands and let them know how much they'd enjoyed the ranch and what their favorite aspects had been. One guest, Zoe, admitted she'd cried saying goodbye to her horse, Lolly, with whom she'd felt a special bond, and she was already planning a future stay. Sara couldn't help but notice that Tabitha was looking particularly happy—and her engagement ring was no longer on her finger.

Her old friend pulled her aside for a hug. "So I did email my mom," Tabitha said. "I was very honest and emotional and put it all out there. That I couldn't marry a man I didn't love and didn't want to grow old with, but that I also couldn't bear to lose her and Dad's love over it, and if they were ready to disown me for disappointing them, I'd rethink the marriage."

Sara was surprised at that last part.

"I was bluffing," Tabitha admitted. "And seriously praying I knew my mom as well as I thought I did. I know my parents love me and I just had this feeling that if I really explained how I felt, my mother would come through."

"And she did?" Sara asked. From Tabitha's happy expression, that much was obvious.

Tabitha nodded. "With several hours to digest the news, my mother softened and said she realized what she was doing to me—the exact thing her own mother would have done to her. She said she was horrified when she realized that. She had a long talk with my dad, and they called me this morning and said I came first, it was my life, and they wanted me to be happy."

Sara was so relieved for Tabitha that she pulled her into another hug. "I'm so glad, Tabitha. Now you can go out there and find your true happiness."

"Exactly. Thank you for helping me see that and for giving me good advice. I'll never forget that."

"Aw, that's what friends are for. We'll keep in touch?"

Tabitha nodded, and they exchanged cell numbers, and then it was time for the group to board the van.

"What was that all about?" Noah asked as they waved at the van pulling away.

"Tabitha Corey got her groove back," Sara said. *By standing up for herself. By knowing what she truly wanted beyond the obvious and finding a way to make it happen. She broke her engagement and kept her parents in her life.* Sara was very impressed.

Noah grinned. "Good. The six new groups coming today aren't part of any retreats. We have two sets of couples, a few families, and friends looking for some nature time."

"They're all set to arrive at one o'clock?" she asked.

"Yup. We'll have a group orientation. After this, the orientations won't be in big groups—it just worked out that way since they were all arriving around the same time on the same day. Some of the guests will be staying a couple days, some four, some a week. Things are going to get a lot busier around here now that we'll have constantly arriving and departing guests. It's all thanks to the great review in the *Gazette*. We're booked, every cabin, every day, throughout midfall. I even have some bookings through winter at this point."

"That's great!" she said, wishing she could hug him. But she stayed put. "And Chance's temperature has been normal for over twelve hours, so I'm confident he's on the mend. We have a few solid hours to go get ourselves married before we'll need to be back and focus on the ranch."

Thank heavens for Daisy; she'd gone to the fore-man's cabin about a half hour ago to babysit while Sara and Noah said goodbye to the guests, and she'd watch the twins until they returned from the town hall.

With gold rings on.

Noah was staring at her, clearly looking for hesi-tation, for upset, for a change of heart, but she had her neutrally pleasant face on. She wanted to do this. "Well, the staff knows what they need to do to get ready for the coming guests, so we can go anytime."

"I'd like to change, of course," she said. "I mean, I know it's not a big-deal wedding, but I don't want to get married in an employee shirt and denim shorts."

"Me either," he said with a nod.

They walked back to the cabin, both briefly chat-ted with Daisy, who was with the twins in the liv-ing room, and they went upstairs, disappearing into their separate rooms. They'd agreed to meet down-stairs at eight.

It was just past seven thirty. A half hour to decide what to wear to marry Noah Dawson. She went for a pale yellow sundress that skimmed her body but was forgiving with its drape, and her bronze sandals. She left her hair loose, dusted on a little makeup, put a small dab of perfume behind her ears and that was it. Ready to get married.

A knock at the door made her jump. Didn't Noah

know he shouldn't see the bride-to-be before the ceremony? She rolled her eyes at herself. As if it was that kind of wedding.

But it wasn't Noah at the door, it was Daisy.

"Just checking if you need any help getting ready," Daisy said, sitting down on the edge of Sara's bed. "From the looks of you, you *are* ready. You look so pretty, Sara."

"Thank you for saying that, but it's not like it matters. *Pretty* and *romantic* aren't key words for these coming nuptials."

Daisy bit her lip and twisted her long hair up and let it drop over one shoulder. "Kind of reminds me of my own love life. Or lack thereof. Every time Jacob uses the phrase I *want to try*, I want to scream," she said. "I almost feel like the two of us are only getting back together for the sake of the baby. Not because there's anything between us anymore. But maybe that should be all that matters. The baby."

"I guess people end up together for lots of different reasons," Sara said. "What really matters is what *you* want, Daisy. What's right for you. I do believe that marrying Noah is right for *me*. Yeah—for the twins too, but for *me*. For a lot of reasons."

Daisy nodded thoughtfully. "And like I said, I'm just glad we finally get to be sisters." She stood up, a hand on her belly. "You've always felt like family, and now you will be. And I get to be Aunt Daisy for real."

Sara grinned and hugged her sister-in-law-to-be. "I don't know what I'd do without you."

Daisy grinned and glanced at her watch. "You'd better get downstairs, or you'll be late for your own wedding."

The town hall opened at eight thirty. Noah wanted to be among the first so they wouldn't have to wait around. She wasn't sure she would survive that.

Downstairs, she found Noah in a suit and his black Stetson. She hadn't expected him to dress up.

"You look very handsome," she said. She could barely take her eyes off him. Memories of last night hit her, and she forced the images of a completely *undressed* Noah Dawson out of her head. There would be no more of *that* in their lives.

"And you look absolutely beautiful," he said, the reverence in his voice catching her off guard. She could feel him staring at her, taking her in, liking what he saw.

But you prefer a lifetime of platonic partnership, she wanted to scream. *Safety over—*

Huh. She'd been so focused on how *she* needed to feel safe and secure that she hadn't really focused on why he was so dead set on a passionless marriage.

She knew that he needed the safety too. It wasn't

just about keeping Annabel and Chance in his life.
It was about *her*. The thought hit Sara uneasily in
the stomach, and she wasn't sure why. It wasn't as
though she didn't know he was *avoiding* how he really felt or what was between them by insisting on
a platonic marriage.

"Ready?" he asked.

Was she?

She found herself nodding, and they headed out,
the brilliant sunshine and low seventies temperatures wasted on a quickie town hall ceremony that
would last all of ten minutes. No reception. No wedding night.

Just…security. And maybe a couple of photos to
commemorate the day. Taken by strangers, employees of the town hall who'd serve as witnesses.

She sighed as she got into his truck. She'd had the
real wedding, complete with a princess ball gown,
only white flowers—per Willem's decree—a jazz
quartet and exceptional catering. Willem had hired
a high-priced wedding planner and had apparently
directed the woman not to let Sara make any changes
to anything he'd already decided. Sara hadn't really
cared. Back then, she was all about her father trying to fight prostate cancer, and that she'd danced
with him at her wedding meant the world to her.
The look on her father's face as he'd stood up with

all the strength he could muster for that dance had been priceless.

Life was about choices, and Sara had made hers for reasons she would always stand by. She would do the same about today's wedding.

Fifteen minutes later, they arrived at the brick building in the center of Bear Ridge. Sara saw a few people she knew out and about, folks heading into the coffee shop, the diner, and waiting for the post office to open. Just people going about their lives while she was about to undertake something so big, so important. She was getting married and barely getting married at the same time.

Upstairs, they found the Weddings Performed Here sign on the second door on the right. Inside the large waiting area with benches and chairs and a lot of mirrors on the walls, another couple was already there, also clearly wanting to beat any possible rush at eight thirty on a random weekday. Sara imagined the couple was in a similar boat to her and Noah. An arrangement-type marriage. Needing to get it done before work. Even if the bride was in a strapless, above-the-knee white ball gown and white cowboy boots, and the groom was in a tux with a neon purple tie and black cowboy boots. Even if the bride held a beautiful bouquet of pink and red roses. Sara did not have a bouquet. Still, she liked to imagine the couple was getting married out of necessity instead of deep, abiding love. *Petty and small, Sara Mayhew*, she silently yelled at herself. *Don't wish a lack of love on anyone!*

She need not have worried. She watched the groom take the bride's face in his hands, staring deeply into her eyes, and say, "I'm the luckiest person on earth. To get to spend my life with you. I still can't believe it."

The bride leaned up on her toes to kiss her tall groom, wrapping her arms around his neck. "No, I'm the luckiest. I can't wait to become your wife."

Sara's shoulders slumped as pure envy socked her in the heart. She caught Noah eyeing the couple before turning away from them and fidgeting, pulling at his blue tie.

A door opened, and a middle-aged woman dressed in a powder blue suit with matching heels called the Hartley-Monkowski party. The couple made squealing sounds and hurried through the doorway after the woman, who closed it behind her.

"Guess we're next," Noah said, taking in a breath.

She nodded, biting the inside of her lower lip. A sheen of sweat broke out on the nape of her neck, despite the air-conditioning. Her sundress felt itchy. Her sandals suddenly felt too small. Her throat was dry and scratchy.

And standing next to her, looking like he might either faint or jump out the second-story window, was *her* groom-to-be. He seemed preoccupied, wasn't looking at her and did not remotely seem ready to do this.

To get married.

"Are you all right?" she asked him. *Please say no. Because this isn't feeling right.*

Why had it last night but not now?

"Just hitting me that we're actually getting married," he said. "Legally. Husband and wife. I'm about to become a married man." His expression was half wonder, half something else. Like fear.

"Strictly platonic partnership," she reminded him, peering at him closely.

"Platonic," he repeated. "But still it's legal. Official. We'll be married, and we'll both know it."

"Meaning?" she asked, staring at him. Where was he going with this?

"Meaning vows are serious stuff, Sara. We're about to vow to love, honor and cherish each other till death do us part."

And we're not going to mean it the way the first couple will, she thought. Sadly.

A small sob built deep in her throat. *Just remember why you're both here and doing this. Remember how you felt last night. Remember how scared and panicked you were. How grateful that you had Noah to count on.*

Partnership is a good thing. Not getting emotion and sex involved means things stay on an even keel. Always.

In other words, settling for certainty. Not that that word could ever be applied to anything in life. She thought about Tabitha, coming into her own, not settling for a life she didn't want. Sara might want the life Noah had offered—the husband, the family, the father for her kids, the ranch, the partnership, the team…but not the platonic part. How was she supposed to live as husband and wife with the man she loved—as essentially his *roommate*?

"Mayhew-Dawson party, we're ready for you," called a voice.

Sara glanced to the left; the woman in the powder blue suit stood in the doorway of the room where the ceremonies were performed. Beyond her, Sara could see the justice of the peace at the front of the room, standing in front of the windows.

She swallowed. Partnership. Safety in the world. Noah Dawson, her friend. The man she'd always loved.

And did love.

Oh God, she realized as she slowly turned toward the smiling woman in blue. She loved Noah too much for this.

Noah stood in front of the justice of the peace, a man he'd never met, let alone seen before, Sara beside him, looking like she might throw up. Her complexion was kind of pasty and green at the same time. Her expression at the trying-to-keep-it-together stage.

This was not how this was supposed to go. Butterflies were one thing. Nausea quite another.

He wanted this marriage. But not at the expense of Sara's happiness.

"Sara, if your heart isn't in this," he whispered, "let's just go home."

She frowned. Actually, she looked pissed as hell. "Just one moment," she said to the justice of the peace, then took Noah by the hand and led him toward the back of the room.

"My *heart* isn't supposed to be in this. It's not supposed to count at all, remember?" she muttered. She shook her head. "Tabitha almost married a man she didn't love to make her parents happy. Your sister is trying to figure out how she feels about her baby's father after he disappeared on her the past six months. I'm not sure doing the right thing should be this damned hard. And I'm not sure this is the right thing anymore. Do you want to know why, Noah? The beating-heart reason why?"

He had a feeling he was finally about to learn what it was that Sara really wanted.

"Yes," he said.

"Because I love you. Not like a friend. Not like a

partner I happen to be close to. I love you with everything I am, every part of me."

He sucked in a breath and stared at her. Of all the things she might have said, he hadn't been expecting *that*.

"I had to settle once before," she added. "And I paid dearly. I won't settle again. So unless you're in love with me too, I'd like to return to the ranch and spend my morning with my twins."

Something shuttered inside him—what thing exactly, he didn't know. A wall went up or a gate came crashing down.

He didn't want to talk about love. Or think about it. That wasn't what this marriage was supposed to be about. Teamwork and partnership and knowing where they stood and what they wanted from life and the future. A solid family.

"Sara, I—" He stopped talking, unsure what he wanted to say, what he felt.

"You know what, Noah? I don't think I'm flattering myself by saying that I think you do love me. And I mean love me in *all* the ways, every way, with every part of *you*. I think you always have, since we were teenagers. But you were scared then, and you're scared now."

He didn't like being told how he felt. At all. "Regardless," he said, that wall or gate making his voice sound so...cold. "We tried having a real relationship. Remember what happened? I drove you away."

"You're not that guy anymore. Everyone knows that. Especially me. And *you* know that."

Did he? He'd stepped up, yes. He'd changed his life. But wasn't he the same Noah Dawson he always was? Wasn't that guy who'd lost everything still inside him? Of course he was. Able to take over at any time.

"Then I guess we're going home," he said. "Wedding's off," he called to the justice of the peace and walked back through the door, two more couples in the waiting area now staring at them. Both women were looking at Sara as though she'd been cruelly left at the altar.

"She changed her mind," he snapped. "Not me." Oh God, now he was acting like a seven-year-old.

He glanced at Sara, whose cheeks were red. Oh hell. He'd screwed this up.

But he'd proposed something specific. She'd agreed. Then said no. Then said maybe. Then said yes. Then said no a few minutes ago.

Love, the kind she was talking about, the kind she wanted, was not supposed to be part of the arrangement.

And now you're going to drive her away again, he chastised himself as she stalked out the door and down the steps. She barged through the door into the parking lot. He wasn't even sure he'd find her waiting by his truck when he trailed after her.

He hurried downstairs and out the door. She was there, arms crossed over her chest, steam practically coming out of her ears.

"Sorry," he said. "Just got caught by surprise and let it get the better of me."

All that anger that had been on her face, in her body language? It turned to sadness. Defeat. "Same here, Noah. Same here."

What the hell was he going to do?

The new guests required all his attention, and he barely got to speak to Sara all afternoon. A few times they'd worked together, leading trail rides, supervising the petting zoo and going over the rules with the three sets of kids of varying ages, and pairing horses and riders. But they hadn't been in a position to talk. He'd have to wait until tonight.

And say what?

He was walking the path back toward the main barn when he saw his sister up toward the farmhouse with Jacob, her boyfriend, if he could be called that. The father of her baby. Noah had only met him a couple times, but something about the guy irked him. Jacob was polite, seemed okay enough, but there was just something that Noah couldn't put his finger on. And Daisy didn't look happy when he saw them together. He got the feeling his sister was forcing something she didn't feel.

Relationships didn't seem easy for *anyone*.

A few minutes later, he saw the boyfriend driving down the gravel road toward the gates. Daisy was heading toward him. She looked upset.

"Everything okay?" he asked her.

"You know it's not. This morning I expected to have a sister-in-law. Now I don't."

He almost smiled. "I know you love Sara, Daize. And I tried. But she wants more than I can give."

She stared at him. "You're lucky I'm not holding something. Because I'd bop you over the head with it. She wants more than you can give? Are you serious?"

He turned away, hardly interested in talking about this with his sister. "I've got a lot going on. At first, I just wanted to protect my interest in Annabel. Then her twin brother got ahold of me, and I started feeling like a father to them both. So I came up with an idea that would keep me and Sara in one place, give us both what we need."

"A roommate?" Sara asked, scrunching up her face.

"A *partner*," he corrected. "Without all the nonsense."

She snorted. "The nonsense of love? That nonsense?"

"How's Jacob?" he asked. Then regretted it. His sister was just calling him on what seemed ridiculous, and he could see how it might look that way to someone who wasn't him or Sara. They'd been through the wringer in different ways, and their needs were different. Daisy was six months pregnant and trying to make it work with her baby's father. He got that too. "Sorry," he said. "Been a long day. It's going to be a long night."

"Jacob is fine, by the way," she said. "We're trying. I don't know if it's working, but we're trying. The more time I spend with him, the less close I feel to him. How is that possible?"

"You probably just have no chemistry or much in common. Except for the baby," he added, eyeing her stomach. "I think it's great that you're both trying to make it work. But don't force something that isn't there."

"You are," Daisy said.

He stared at her, narrowing his eyes. "*I* am? How?"

"Trying to marry a woman you don't love," Daisy said. "So I'm not sure you should be giving advice on this subject."

"Who says I don't love Sara?" he asked, then froze. Of course he loved her. He knew that. But until he said the words out loud, he hadn't admitted it to himself. Or anyone else.

"Aha!" Daisy said, pointing at his chest. "I knew it. You are in love with Sara."

He scowled at her. "Doesn't matter. I'm not looking for romance. I just want a partnership marriage with certain parameters so nothing gets messed up. There's too much at stake."

"Mom once told me that no matter how bad things seemed at home between her and Dad, that marriage was a beautiful thing and I should know that I'd find my Mr. Right when I was ready and that marriage could be wonderful. I always felt bad because she didn't seem to really believe that—she just wanted to put it in my head, make up for what we were growing up with, seeing every day."

Their father had cheated on their mother a bunch of times. He and Daisy had both heard the arguments, the tears, the *I'm sorry, I'll never do it again.* Until the next time. And then his mother died, and his father was never quite the same. He still ran after women, but the loss had changed his father.

"I didn't need Mom and Dad's example to tell me relationships don't last. None of mine ever have. Including with Sara."

"You sabotaged that on purpose. Only you know why, Noah."

He rolled his eyes.

"Don't roll your eyes at me, Noah Dean Dawson.

You weren't ready then in any way, shape or form. You *got* ready and you changed your life. To the point that I came back when I swore I'd never live here again. You showed me what you can do, who you are, and I came home to be part of this. And because I was scared myself and needed a place to go where I could relax, where there was someone I could count on. You."

Oh hell. Now she was getting him all mushy. "Of course you can count on me, Daisy. I'd never let you down."

"I know you won't. And don't let *yourself* down. That's what you'll be doing if you let fear hold you back. You've got to be in it to get anything in this world. You know that."

"I'm doing that with the ranch. There's no way I'd blow the investment you all made in me. I've got enough riding on this place. I can't take more risks, Daisy. Not when it comes to Sara and the twins. I lose them, that's it."

"Well, Sara wants something very different, so you're going to lose her anyway. Kind of dopey of you not to *try*."

His phone pinged with a text. *Saved*, he thought. He pulled out the cell. His cowboy, Dylan. "Dylan needs me in the petting zoo. Runaway sheep."

"This conversation isn't over," Daisy said. "You and Sara both deserve better."

"Gotta run," he said and headed in the opposite direction.

Sisters, he thought. Good thing he had only one. His brothers liked to challenge him, but they didn't stand around talking about relationships the way Daisy did.

He headed over to the pasture beside the main barn, and between him and Dylan they got the runaway sheep back in his pen. He passed the petting zoo, stopping to watch his youngest guests, five-year-old Liam and his twin sister, Lyra, offer the little goats some pellets.

That'll be Annabel and Chance in just a few years, he thought, his heart close to bursting. He could just see them running around the ranch, playing with the farm animals, learning ranching by living here.

And because of you, they might not *be running around the ranch at all. In fact, they might be running around some other guy's ranch, someone else their father.*

If he couldn't give Sara what she wanted, she wasn't going to stay.

He couldn't live with that either.

Chapter Twelve

Sara wasn't sure why, but she couldn't stop thinking about Katherine Palmer. The midwife. She'd pushed the woman out of her head since the day after the bombshell in the lawyer's office, when Holton had assured her the midwife had retired, per calls he'd made to area hospitals and clinics and local OB practices she could be affiliated with and the Wyoming State Board of Nursing. Palmer's license had expired last month and she hadn't renewed it for the first time in thirty-seven years.

Holton had wanted to file a claim against Katherine Palmer, but until Sara had spoken to the woman herself, she didn't want him to do that. She knew what Willem had been capable of and could only guess what he'd threatened the midwife with. Once Sara had been assured the woman was retired and could never do anything remotely like what she'd done to Sara and Annabel again, she'd relaxed some and put Katherine Palmer out of her head until she was ready to confront her.

For some reason she couldn't put her finger on, the midwife had entered Sara's mind on the drive home from the town hall, along with the few lines Willem had written about her in his letter. She suddenly wanted to talk to Katherine, to understand why she'd done something so heinous. *How* she could have done it. No matter what Willem had threatened her with. A person who'd devoted her career to bringing new life into the world for almost forty years?

Sara sat on the couch in the foreman's cabin, the twins in their swings, staring at the sparkly mobiles hanging high above them, trying to figure out why it suddenly felt like time to pay the woman a visit. Maybe Sara was simply in fight mode. Maybe what had happened at the town hall, coming so close to marrying under terms she couldn't live by, had her ready to deal with everything that wasn't right.

She wasn't sure what talking to the woman would accomplish, but it had been hanging over her head since she'd learned the news back in the lawyer's office, and it felt like time to entirely put her past to rest.

When she heard Noah's key in the lock, she took a deep breath, preparing herself for anything. For him to say, *Actually, I don't love you, sorry.* Or, *Actually, I do, you're right, but sorry, I can't.* Either way, she lost. She'd confront the midwife, get that off her to-do list and figure out what she was going to do next. This new Sara Mayhew didn't leave things hanging. She might not exactly have her groove back, but she felt as if she was on her way.

"Crazy day," Noah said, coming into the living room. "Start, middle, finish and every moment in between. I wished I could have had just ten minutes to see you, talk to you."

"About what?" she asked. None too nicely.

"Just to check in, I guess."

"Thought so." Again, none too nicely. "I've made a decision," she said.

He paled, and she was struck by two things. One: that she knew him well enough to know he thought she was talking about leaving. And two: that it would truly tear him apart if she did leave.

But not enough to blast through the wall he'd erected where she was concerned. So that they could have a real relationship. Start a real future together.

He stood beside the coffee table, waiting. Looking…nervous.

"I'm going to see the midwife," she said. She expected him to relax since she wasn't talking about leaving at all, but he seemed more anxious, actually.

"Really? Why all of a sudden? Not that I don't think you should talk to her—I do. But just curious about why right now."

"Taking care of business," she said. "I need to close that chapter. And I need to hear why she did what she did. I need closure."

"I'm not sure she's the closure you're really after," he said.

She scowled. "Meaning? That I'm deflecting being upset about you? Yes, I'm upset about you. And us. But I'm done running away and seeking safety, Noah. Life is about risk. Being a parent is about risk. Love is about risk. I've avoided dealing with the midwife. But I'm going to face her."

He grimaced. "I'm coming with you whether you want me to or not."

"Good, because I do want you to," she said.

His entire body relaxed, and he sat down beside her, running a finger down each baby's cheek in their swings before turning his attention back to her. "And after you speak to her? Then what?"

"Then I move on mentally and emotionally from

what Willem attempted to do. I have my children—both of them. I close that part of my life so that I can start a new one. One in which I'm not scared or looking for anyone to take care of me."

"Sara, I—"

She was done with *Sara, I...* followed by either silence or Noah trying to explain himself. Unless he could say the words she needed to hear to marry him, any discussion of marriage was over.

"You know what?" she said, her eyes widening as something occurred to her. "I thought that feeling safe in the world was what I wanted and that I needed to give up other important values to have it for myself and the twins. But what I really want is to feel safe in the world at *my* own hands, Noah. Stand on my own two feet. I will never make another deal about my security, because I can support my children myself. It might not be easy, and as a single parent, my paycheck isn't going to stretch so far, but I've done the math, and I'll be fine if I'm careful. And I have been."

He stared at her, hard, and she knew his mind was churning, but she had no idea what he was thinking.

"You've always impressed the hell out of me," he said. "I understand. And I admire you."

That was all well and good. And if she were honest with herself, she'd admit he'd touched her deeply with that. But what she wanted, really wanted, was his *love*.

* * *

According to an online search, Katherine Palmer lived at 132-B Harris Road in Wellington, the town Sara had moved to when she'd accepted Willem's proposal. A quick map check showed Harris Road was near the center of town.

She decided to just show up, not call. If the woman wasn't home, Sara would simply wait until she turned up. It was kind of nutty, but the entire situation was insane, so there was no right way to go about it. Noah was unsettled about the whole thing but agreed that alerting Katherine that she wanted to talk to her might make the woman flee, and Sara would never get answers.

Because Wellington was an hour way, they'd decided to leave at eight this morning so they could be back by ten thirty or eleven at the latest, figuring they'd spend an hour or so with Katherine. Mrs. Pickles would babysit since Daisy needed to be on the job.

She was quiet on the way there, and she was grateful that Noah didn't try to fill the silence with conversation. He seemed to know she needed to just sit with her thoughts. She couldn't begin to explain how she felt at the moment anyway.

When Noah pulled up in front of an apartment complex, Sara could see 132 was the middle of three identical rows of garden apartments in a U shape around a green. In the driveway for apartment B, there was a small dumpster and a pod truck—as if someone was moving out.

"Maybe we got here just in time," Sara said. "Maybe she's moving." She sucked in a breath. "Let's knock."

They got out of his truck and headed to the front door. A small silver car was parked in front of the dumpster, so it looked like someone was home. Sara found herself unable to lift her arm to ring the bell. Her stomach churned, and she closed her eyes for a second. She squeezed Noah's hand, and he squeezed it back with an encouraging look at her. She was so damned grateful he was here, that he'd insisted on coming, because she wasn't sure if she would have asked him to otherwise, despite wanting him with her. Some things she could do alone. Some things she didn't want to. *This* was a didn't want to.

"Okay," she said under her breath and rang the bell.

She could hear footsteps. Sara's heart sped up. Katherine Palmer was about to open the door.

But the woman who appeared in the doorway was in her early thirties at most. The midwife was sixty-five years old. "Can I help you?" she asked.

Was this Katherine's daughter? she wondered. There was a definite resemblance. Similar auburn hair and hazel eyes, a similar fine-boned face.

"I'm looking for Katherine Palmer," Sara said. "My name is Sara. I was a patient of hers. Her last patient, actually."

"Oh," the woman said softly. "I'm sorry to tell you, but my mother passed away three days ago."

Sara turned to Noah, her throat closing up, her legs feeling like rubber. Of all the scenarios that had gone through her head the past several hours, this wasn't one of them.

"I'm sorry for your loss," Sara managed to say.

The woman gave a closemouthed smile of sorts. "You said your name is Sara. Sara *Perry*?"

Sara stared at her. "Why do you ask?" What did Palmer's daughter know? *Did* she know?

"My mom left a letter addressed to a Sara Perry," the woman explained. "I haven't had a chance to mail it or even drop it off. Between crying and trying to get the house sorted before the bank takes it…" She waved her hand by her face and then shook her head, her eyes welling. "Ignore me. Things are a mess."

She glanced at Noah. That the midwife had had financial problems wasn't a surprise. Willem had bribed her. She'd known that from the start.

"I am Sara Perry," she said. "And I am truly sorry for your loss. I lost my parents, and I know how painful it is."

The woman offered a small smile. "I'll just go

get the letter. It's on her bedside table. I think she wrote it the night before she passed. I was here the week prior, knowing how sick she was, and it wasn't there earlier."

"Was it cancer?" Sara asked.

The woman nodded. "The diagnosis came too late to do anything about it. I'll just go get the letter."

Katherine's daughter left the door ajar and walked up the stairs. Sara turned to Noah, unable to form words. He squeezed her hand.

"Another letter from beyond the grave," she finally said, shaking her head. "I don't know if I can bear it."

"Sounds like it might be a deathbed confession," he whispered.

She gnawed her lower lip. The woman returned, holding a letter, and she handed it to Sara.

"Thank you," Sara said. "And again, my condolences."

She nodded and closed the door.

Sara and Noah headed to his truck. She was done here, at least. She had a letter, which might explain things.

They got into Noah's pickup. "How about I drive a bit away from here, so you can read it in privacy. Without being right here, I mean."

"Actually, let's get out of this town entirely. Wellington is doubly ruined for me forever. Let's go back to Bear Ridge. You can park in town near the coffee shop—I'm going to need a boost of caffeine."

He nodded and started the truck, and once again she was so aware that he was right here when she needed someone who could see her through whatever the hell was in the letter. Explanation? Apology?

She held the letter in her hand as Noah drove the hour back to Bear Ridge. Finally, he parked near the coffee shop on Main Street.

"Ready?" he asked, gesturing at the letter.

"No. I wasn't ready for Willem's letter either. I almost wanted to flee the office before the lawyer could read it to me. Good thing I stayed."

Noah nodded. "I'll be right here. You can read it aloud or to yourself. Whichever you want."

"I'd rather read it aloud. So you hear what I hear." She cleared her throat and slit open the envelope. Inside were two pages, typed on white paper. It was signed with her full name—Katherine Marie Palmer—in black ink. She glanced at Noah, needing a gulp of him before she dived in. "Okay. Here goes."

Dear Sara,

Two weeks ago I was diagnosed with ovarian cancer, stage three. My doctors tell me it's inoperable. I did something terrible that I need to rectify. I can't fix it, but I can tell you the truth. It's only two months later, and though that must feel like a long time to you, I feel better knowing it's not.

Your baby daughter didn't die at birth. Your husband, Willem Perry, told me he'd make up a devastating lie about my daughter and ruin her life if I didn't comply. He also bribed me by paying off tens of thousands of dollars of debt, which my late husband accumulated through gambling. Anyway, it's true that your daughter was born frail, but she was alive. He told me to back him up that she died during the birth. I was horrified but said I would for the reasons I stated. Then he muttered something about "Dawson." I don't know what that refers to, and as I left your home that evening, hoping to make it home before the big thunderstorm, he left too—with the baby in a car seat. I don't know where he took the newborn. But she was alive when she was born. Maybe the word Dawson will mean something to you? A start for finding your daughter?

This letter will be a shock. I don't know why your husband didn't want the girl. I only know that I can't go without making this as right as I can. By telling you the truth. May God for-

give me. I won't ask your forgiveness, because I don't deserve it. And I've taken enough from you. I'm deeply ashamed. I don't know what your husband would have done to my daughter had I refused, and because your daughter did look so frail and small compared to her brother, I rationalized that she would probably not make it. That was not my decision to make. I hope I was wrong. I hope you find your daughter healthy and get her back.

Sincerely, Katherine Marie Palmer

Sara just stared at the words on the pages, unable to speak.

Noah took the letter and put it back in the envelope, then shoved it in his glove compartment. He leaned over and took her in his arms, and she let him, wrapping her own arms around him tightly as she cried.

He didn't say a word; he just held her, which was exactly what she needed.

Fifteen minutes later, she wiped under her eyes. "I'm ready to go home," she said. "I have my closure. And I never, ever want to think about her or Willem or what they did or why again."

"Want to get some coffee first?" he asked, pointing at the coffee shop two stores down.

"And a Boston cream doughnut," she said. "Maybe two."

He smiled and squeezed her hand. "Coming right up. Want to wait here or come in with me?"

"I'll wait here."

She watched him head in, her head clearing already. By the time he came out with a white bag and two coffees in a tray, she was ready to put her past behind her.

She had no idea what the present would hold, though. Or where she and her twins would be in the near future.

Noah told Sara to take the day off. He'd matched her with a horse when she'd first agreed to take the assistant forewoman's job, and he was glad when she agreed that taking Bluebell for a ride in the acres of open pasture would be therapeutic after the heavy morning. The moment she'd ridden off, though, he missed her and wished he were beside her on Bolt. He didn't want her to be alone, even though he knew it was probably best for her right now.

He checked in with his staff, glad to hear everything was running smoothly. He was going to lead a trail ride for parents and kids who were new to horses, Dylan as his backup. As he met the group of six in the barn, three parents and three kids, he couldn't help but notice how the moms and dads doted on their children, listening to them, assuring them, being excited about the horses along with them. This was what he wanted for himself with Annabel and Chance, and because there was something fundamentally wrong with him deep inside, where he couldn't commit to Sara the way she needed, he was going to lose the twins.

With the kids on the gentlest of ponies and the adults on sweet quarter horses, they entered the small pasture and did a slow trot around the perimeter. There was hooting and laughing and big smiles from the entire group, and Noah gave easy instructions as he rode alongside the middle of the pack, Dylan at the rear.

And then out of nowhere, somehow, a little girl fell off her pony. Lyra Barnett, five years old.

Her face crumpled in tears under her helmet, and she just lay on the grass, not moving. Her father, a very fit man in his early forties named Mike Barnett, was beside her on the ground in a heartbeat, as were Noah and Dylan.

"I'll text our on-call doctor," Noah said, pulling out his phone.

The man held up a hand. "Hang on a second." He

turned his attention to his daughter. "Where does it hurt?"

The girl just cried.

"Daddy, is Lyra okay?" her twin brother asked, still on his pony.

Her father touched her leg, slowly inching his hands around both feet and the entirety of her legs. The girl didn't wince.

"I'm a doctor," Mike explained. "Nothing feels broken."

Noah's heart was beating like a hundred wild horses galloping. She was okay. Thank God.

Lyra cried harder, then wiped at her eyes. "I stink at riding horses."

"You were doing good until you fell off," her brother put in.

"I really was, right, Daddy?" Lyra asked, wiping under her eyes.

Her father smiled at her. "You sure were. Accidents happen, right?"

"Right," her brother said.

Lyra scowled at him. "Right," she said louder.

Mike Barnett smiled, and Noah had to also.

"Dylan, why don't you take the group into the next pasture," Noah said. "I'll have Sara join you." He quickly texted her.

Dylan nodded and helped Lyra's brother off his

pony so he could sit beside his family, and then he instructed the group to dismount, helping each kid off, and they all led the ponies and horses into the next pasture. He could see Sara already coming up the path in the golf cart, her expression grim.

"I'll run her over to the clinic in town," Mike said. "We're locals, so we're familiar with the place." He turned to his son. "I'll call Mommy and she'll take you to the creek to see if there are beavers and badgers and porcupines hanging around."

"The porcupines are my favorite," the little boy said.

Sara rushed over, concern in her eyes. Noah explained the situation, and she texted Daisy to pick up Mrs. Barnett from the lodge, where she was taking some R&R with a book and Cowboy Joe's lemonade and peach cobbler.

"Your wife will be here in two minutes," Sara assured him. She turned to the little girl. "Hi, Lyra. I'm Sara. Was this your first time on a pony?"

The girl shook her head. "My third time. I rode a pony at our birthday party."

Sara smiled. "I've been riding horses a long time. I fell off one time. I was thinking about something, and plop, right off on the ground. Luckily I wasn't hurt."

"I don't feel hurt anywhere," Lyra said. "I'm upset

that I'm not on Cupcake anymore." She looked at the sweet brown-and-white pony.

Her dad grinned and patted Lyra's back. "Well, let's have you checked out as a just-in-case, and if nothing is broken or sprained, we'll get you right back on Cupcake, okay?"

"'Kay, Daddy," she said.

Her mom arrived, and Daisy drove off in the golf cart with the family—father and daughter to their car by the gate, and then mother and son to the creek. Noah dropped back down to the ground, leaning his head against a fence post. "That was lucky. And close. If she'd gotten hurt…"

"Little kids get hurt. It's what happens. I like her dad's point of getting right back on the pony. That's the lesson, Noah."

"I don't need a lecture right now," he said, squinting up at her in the bright sunshine. "I feel bad enough as it is."

"I understand that," she said. "But you absolutely do need a lecture," she added, pushing her straw cowboy hat farther on her head and taking off down the path.

Every minute he pushed her farther and farther away, when all he wanted was to have her beside him.

Chapter Thirteen

As Noah finished his chores and rounds and got a welcome text from Mike Barnett that Lyra was absolutely fine, no broken bones or sprains or torn anything, he let out one hell of a breath. He knew that little kids got hurt. Of course he knew that. He'd broken at least five bones over his childhood from being too rough with himself and from incidents he had no control over, like tripping over a hole in the ground that his father hadn't taken care of. Kids got hurt. And yes, the important thing was to teach them to dust themselves off, if possible, and get back up.

He wasn't afraid of Annabel and Chance falling

off ponies; of course they would. Of course they'd have illnesses and mishaps. That was life.

So why the hell could he commit so fervently to them and not to Sara? Granted, he wasn't afraid of her getting hurt. He was paralyzed at the notion of giving in to the full range of his feelings for her. Once he did, he wouldn't be in control. That he understood, because he'd thought of little else the past two days. He had to remain in control of himself or he'd drive her off, one way or another. He couldn't ruin what they had—he wouldn't. And keeping things as professional as possible between them, as friendship based as possible, was the answer.

As he closed the main barn door, he saw Daisy coming toward him, on foot this time.

"So I have news," she said, stretching out her hand.

There was a ring on her finger. A small round diamond in a silver band.

"You're engaged?" he asked, his mouth dropping open.

"Jacob proposed this morning. He said he felt ready to ask me last night, but didn't have a ring, so went off to the jewelry shop to buy one." She looked at her hand.

"You don't look particularly happy," he said, then

regretted it. This wasn't his business. Or maybe it was. Of course it was. He was her brother.

"I feel good about it," she said, her eyes still on the ring.

"You feel good about it?" he repeated.

"Noah. I'm almost seven months pregnant. My baby's father proposed. We're going to make this work so that we can be a family. It's the right thing to do."

"Except you don't love Jacob. Does he love you?"

"He cares about me. He's committed to our family and our future, and he thinks we'll get there as time goes on and we share a life with our child."

He stared at her. "Get *where*? To love?"

"Yes, to love. We'll be raising a child together. Our goal will be the same. We'll be parents, committed to our baby. That alone will help us grow as a couple."

"God, Daisy. Is that how it's supposed to be?"

Now she stared at him. "Um, hello, pot talking trash about the kettle."

He scowled at her. "My situation is different. I'm protecting my stake in those twins. In not destroying my relationship with Sara."

"*Riiight*, little brother. With the woman you're madly in love with."

He froze, realizing how true that statement was. He was deeply in love with Sara.

"How can I not try?" Daisy asked, tears welling in her eyes. "Things might work out great with Jacob. He's my baby's father." She stared at him—hard. "I personally don't know how you *cannot* try, Noah."

With that, she walked off, leaving him so unsettled he had to sit back down against the barn.

Had a hay bale fallen on his head? That was how he felt. Absolutely gobsmacked.

And not sure where the hell to go from here.

To make this as easy on the two of them as possible, Sara was packed before she told Noah that she planned to move into the main house. She'd been thinking about doing just that ever since she'd left the town hall without a wedding ring on her finger. There'd been a lot going on and she'd pushed moving out of her head, but there was no way she could continue living in the cabin with Noah. Yes, he'd lose home access to the twins, but the way she saw it, that was his own damned fault.

Stubborn gets what stubborn deserves, she thought, instantly feeling bad for him. She didn't know exactly what it was going to take to get through to him, to blast through the concrete he'd built around his heart. She just knew she had to protect herself.

She had spoken to Daisy, swearing her to secrecy until she could talk to Noah about her decision, and

Daisy had offered her a bedroom in the farmhouse across from the nursery, which the twins would have. The downside was that the living arrangement was temporary. Daisy was newly engaged to her boy-friend, Jacob—boy, had Sara been surprised to hear the news—and Jacob would move in after the wedding. He was a businessman, something to do with imports and exports. She understood why Daisy wanted to marry him, despite, despite, despite.

Daisy and Jacob had talked about a July wedding, a couple weeks before her due date so that Daisy could have the wedding she wanted—a church ceremony and a big reception at the ranch with family and friends. If they were going to do this, she wanted to really do it.

Sara understood that more than anyone. And, at least it gave her a solid month in the farmhouse with her good friend until Daisy married and her husband moved in and Sara would move out, finding a place she could afford in town.

Now, Sara stood in the kitchen of the foreman's cabin, making a pot of coffee, knowing that Noah would be home in about ten minutes.

She was on her second cup of the bracing brew when she heard his key in the lock.

Her suitcases were beside the table. She'd thought about collecting the twins' baby stuff and putting it all near the door so that they could get into his truck quickly, but she knew what the sight of the swings and stroller and mats would do to him.

Her stomach churned. She hated hurting him. But he'd left her no choice but to do exactly what she was doing. She couldn't live this way with him, this quarter of a life.

"I smell coffee," he said with a smile as he appeared in the kitchen doorway. Then his gaze moved to the suitcases, and the smile disappeared. "You're leaving?"

"Moving up to the farmhouse. The twins will take the nursery that Daisy has already begun creating. The three of us will leave right before her wedding, when Jacob will move in."

He sighed and crossed his arms over his chest, quiet for a moment as he seemed to take in what she'd said. "I don't think she should be marrying him so fast. I get that they want to get married before the baby comes, but why not see how things go before committing like that?"

"Because they're committing," Sara pointed out.

He shrugged. "I guess they are." He stared at her suitcases. "I don't want you to go."

"Feel free to stop me, Noah." She tried a smile, but tears welled and she shoved her half-drunk coffee mug away.

"Sara, I…"

Oh God, not that.

Maybe the real problem with Noah Dawson was that he didn't love her. Maybe that was what he—and she—couldn't face.

But she'd bet everything she had that he *did* love her—very much. She knew it, she felt it, she believed. But until he could admit it to himself and open up the gates inside him, they were stuck.

"Will you help me load up the twins' stuff?" she asked. "I know it'll be hard for you, but I can't do it alone."

He grimaced. "Of course." He poured himself a cup of coffee, added cream and sugar, and took a couple long sips, then put the cup in the sink. "For what it's worth, I am sorry, Sara."

Tears stung her eyes. "Well, it's not worth all that much to me. I don't want you to be sorry. I want you to love me. I want us to raise Annabel and Chance together, be a family. I want us both to be happy. And if you really think you can be happy by shutting off half of yourself…"

He couldn't. But she was done talking, done arguing, done trying to convince him. It was time to go.

The expression on his face as he picked up one of the baby swings almost broke another piece of her heart.

But they silently loaded the pickup. Once back in the cabin, all that was left were the babies themselves in their carriers. She picked up one, then the other. Heavy, but she had this.

He stared at her, and then reached forward to take both carriers himself, but she walked out the door toward the truck before he could.

She could feel him just standing there and had no doubt his own heart was breaking. But by his own hand.

Noah had done double rounds on the ranch and finally made himself go home. Then he tried to stick to his bedroom, where he wouldn't be overly reminded of Sara or the twins. But he'd made love to Sara in this room. And every time he closed his eyes, he'd see them in bed. He'd never been so aware of how much he felt for her as he had that other night, when he'd stopped thinking so much and just let himself *feel*.

That he loved her like crazy wasn't in doubt.

He thought he heard a cry and bolted up and into the nursery, but the cribs, which were still there, were empty. Daisy had enough of a setup in the nursery she'd started making for her own child that they didn't need to move the cribs and dresser and glider right away.

He stood in the room, his gaze on the letters spelling out Annabel's and Chance's names on the cribs. He'd painted their names himself. He dropped down in the glider, where he'd sat so many nights, a baby in his arms, telling a story or just marveling at the precious infant he held. He thought about hearing Annabel's cries the night he'd found her. The note saying she was his.

The terror that had gripped him.

He'd been so damned scared of screwing up, but he hadn't. Hadn't screwed up at all in the seven weeks he'd taken care of Annabel.

And now he'd lost not only her but Chance, as well.

Instead of focusing on that, he kept going back to the previous thought. That he *hadn't* screwed up. Huh. Why the hell was he so focused on destroying his relationship with Sara when there was nothing to indicate he would—well, other than a history of doing just that? He had a history of failure, but he'd given himself an A-plus when it came to rebuilding the ranch and an A-plus in raising Annabel those first seven weeks.

He could handle a newborn baby as a bachelor rebuilding his family's legacy, but he couldn't handle his own feelings for the woman he loved with every fiber of his being?

He shot off the chair. Wanting to go get her. Get his woman. His life, his future, his everything. His Sara.

He sat back down. Once he'd allowed himself to really go there, there was no turning back. He'd be cracked wide-open. And his least favorite word in the English language: *vulnerable.*

He thought about the most vulnerable he'd ever felt. The day he'd read the letter his father had left him in his will. The whoppers in there. About how his dad believed he was the one to restore the Dawson Family Guest Ranch, that Bo Dawson hoped he would. *I believe in you,* his father had written. *I'm sorry I was such a failure. I know you can make things right, Noah. I know it. And knowing it gives me peace at going.*

Noah felt his eyes well. He took out the letter and read it for the fifth time, then put it back in the envelope and under his socks in the top drawer of his dresser. Even his father had owned up to his failures and looked to fresh starts—for Noah, at least, if not himself.

And Noah was going to sit in this empty, silent cabin when the woman he loved was a quarter mile up the road with the family he'd already made his own?

No, he wasn't. He opened his dresser drawer

again, reaching under the socks until he felt a small velvet box that had been there for two years now.

Sara sat outside on the porch of the farmhouse where she'd spent so much of her childhood, running between this house and the cabin. She loved this house as much as she did the foreman's cabin, and she was grateful to have a room here. She might not have what she really wanted in a getting-her-groove-back way, but at least she wasn't settling for what she didn't want. That was a no-go.

She and Daisy had had a long talk when she'd arrived with her stuff, after a grim-faced Noah had brought everything in, making a thousand trips up and down the stairs. Then he was gone, and she'd let herself burst into tears, Daisy comforting her. They'd talked for the past two hours, Daisy assuring her she was doing the right thing, Sara assuring Daisy she was too. Trying was paramount. Now Daisy was in her bedroom, working on her wedding plans for July. She'd asked Sara to be her maid of honor, and Sara had joyfully accepted. According to Daisy, they were still honorary aunts to each other's children, even if they weren't going to be sisters-in-law.

Daisy heard a truck coming up the road, then saw the headlights. Was that Noah?

She stood up as he parked. It *was* Noah.

If he was here to try to convince her to come back, he was wasting his breath. But damn, it was good to see him, and they'd only been apart for two hours.

He came around the side of the truck and walked up the porch steps. "I've been doing a lot of thinking."

Don't get your hopes up, she told herself. *He's going to suggest some kind of compromise.*

"You're absolutely right," he said, his blue eyes intense on her. "I'm letting fear control me. It's what did my father in, I understand that now. He failed, and then instead of picking himself up, he fell deeper into the hole."

She stared at him, her heart surging. Maybe she *could* hope a tiny bit.

"I've loved you so much for so long that you're a part of everything I am," he said. "I'm you and you're me and we're separate but the same. There's no me without you, Sara."

Tears welled in her eyes. She'd let herself hope a second ago, but he was taking her to the moon and the stars.

"I love you, Sara Mayhew. I'm in love with you. I want to spend my life with you and the twins. I want to be your husband in every sense of the word. I want to be Annabel and Chance's father. I love you. Even more than you could possibly want."

She grinned. "Is that possible?"

"Anything is possible now," he said, the moon-light shining down on him as he got on one knee, opening a little black velvet box. "Do me the honor of becoming my wife. Will you marry me?"

Sara gasped and barely managed to whisper, "Yes," before jumping into his arms and wrapping her arms around him. "I love you too."

He kissed her and she kissed him back, then he looked at her, and she could see the change in his eyes, in his expression. He slid the beautiful ring on her finger, then kissed her again. So passionately her legs buckled.

"Get a room!" called a voice from an upstairs window. "At the cabin so you don't wake the twins. I've got them till the morning. Go, lovebirds," Daisy added with a grin.

Noah laughed. "Thanks, Daisy. I owe you."

"Yeah, you do," his sister called back with a smile before poking her head back in.

"Let's go get that room," he said, taking Sara's hand.

And then they got in the truck and headed home, where they both belonged.

* * * * *

MILLS & BOON

Coming next month

THE PRINCE AND THE WEDDING PLANNER
Jennifer Faye

Bianca shook her head. With him gazing into her eyes, her heart had leapt into her throat. Was that desire reflected in his eyes? The prince desired her? Her heart tumbled in her chest.

She didn't know how long they stood there staring into each other's eyes. It was like Leo had a gravitational force around him and she was being drawn in. Though she knew letting anything happen between them would be a mistake—compounding all of the other uncertainties in her life—she remained rooted to the spot in front of him.

Her heart raced as she found herself getting lost in his dark gaze. Her fingers tingled with the urge to reach out to him—

Someone cleared their throat. Loudly. Annoyingly.

And in that second, the connection dissipated. Bianca blinked and glanced away. Heat rushed to her face. She was grateful she didn't have to speak because she didn't trust her tongue to work correctly.

Leo cleared his throat. "Yes, Michael. What is it?"

"You are needed, sir. The call from Canada."

Leo sighed. "I'll be right there." Once the man moved on, Leo turned his full attention to her. "I'm sorry. I've been expecting this call all day."

"I understand. You have important business to attend to."

Reality had come crashing in on them. And none too soon. He was a royal prince. She was a wedding planner with an uncertain heritage. They did not belong together.

"About this…" As his voice trailed off, he looked at her with confusion reflected in his eyes.

He wasn't the only one to be confused. Her heart had betrayed her mind in wanting what it could not have. And now that her feet were once again planted firmly on the ground, she couldn't forget that she was here to do a job. That needed to be her focus. Not getting swept up in some fairytale.

"It's okay," she said. "You have important work to do."

"You're not upset about ending the evening so soon?"

She shook her head. "Not at all. I understand that business must come first."

As he escorted her back to the palace, he didn't offer her his arm. And she made sure to keep a reasonable distance between them. Because as much as nothing had happened between them, something most definitely had almost happened.

Continue reading
THE PRINCE AND THE WEDDING PLANNER
Jennifer Faye

Available next month
www.millsandboon.co.uk

COMING SOON!

We really hope you enjoyed reading this book. If you're looking for more romance, be sure to head to the shops when new books are available on

Thursday 6th March

To see which titles are coming soon, please visit

millsandboon.co.uk/nextmonth

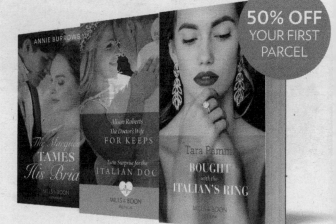

MILLS & BOON
MEDICAL
Pulse-Racing Passion

Set your pulse racing with dedicated, delectable doctors in the high-pressure world of medicine, where emotions run high and passion, comfort and love are the best medicine.

MILLS & BOON

HISTORICAL

Awaken the romance of the past

Escape with historical heroes from time gone by. Whether your passion is for wicked Regency Rakes, muscled Viking warriors or rugged Highlanders, indulge your fantasies and awaken the romance of the past.